TWICE AN
ASSASSIN

BART W. CASSIDY

ISBN 978-1-66789-557-4 eBook 978-1-66789-558-1

CHAPTER 1

EVIL

The driver adjusted the wipers as the cold rain turned into snow with the chill of the night. He was bitching about the call in midtown, while the passenger slumped back in the seat with a black cowboy hat over his face.

"Why send us to a homicide in midtown when we were all the way out in the ass end of Queens? Some other team of detectives could have handled it," he griped. "They act like we don't have our own shit to deal with—like we're just out here joyriding."

Eventually, Bart removed the hat from his face. He looked depleted; perhaps he was numb because they were going to investigate yet another homicide. He wasn't sure how many more eighty-hour weeks he had left in him. He remembered how excited he had been to receive his gold shield five years ago. After being undercover for two years, he was finally a detective. How many bodies ago was that?

As Donnie incessantly complained, Bart's mind drifted—as it often did—to what his life had become. He was only twenty-nine, but he felt much older than that most days, probably because he had experienced more in three decades than most people do in their entire lives.

He was born in Queens and lived a seemingly average life. However, danger always had an allure for him—or it seemed to find him—and he knew it would get him into precarious situations in the future if he didn't do something constructive with it, so he joined the navy while still in high school. He enjoyed the structure and experience he gained from the military, but after four long years of service, he yearned for his freedom.

After his discharge, he moved to Oklahoma and fulfilled his dream of working on a horse ranch. Although he loved the ranch and his life there, working on the ranch was a lonely life. If he was going to meet the woman of his dreams, it would likely be in New York, home to three million single females. So, he moved back to New York and put the skills he had acquired in the military to good use in the New York City Police Department. He had no idea an undercover assignment would almost immediately consume him and eliminate any semblance of a personal life, which certainly was not conducive to finding "the one." Bart's life back in New York ended up being a string of subpar dates and short-lived relationships while he aimlessly searched for his perfect match in a city that fervently tried to prevent him from doing so.

The car entered the Queens–Midtown Tunnel, immediately transforming the cold, black night into a bright cascade of lights reflecting off the wet pavement and reminding Bart of his childhood. He recalled going on vacation with his parents and driving through the Holland Tunnel. He could almost feel the wind blowing on his face through the driver's side window—which his dad always left slightly cracked—and he could nearly smell the scent of the exhaust fumes accumulating in the confined steel tube. He had always loved waving to the police officers as they drove by, but that all seemed like it was a hundred years ago.

When they exited the tunnel, Donnie turned the car south on Lexington Avenue. They were just ten blocks away from whatever was awaiting them. As they got closer, the buildings sparkled with the reflection of red lights. Tens of police cars appeared in the distance, along with a number of reporters and TV cameras. Suddenly, Bart's phone rang.

"Sullivan," he answered.

"Keep a low profile and enter from the side alleyway." Donnie could hear the muffled voice on the other end of the phone.

Donnie parked the car in the alley that led to the back of the apartment complex, and they got out. The cold rain had just started up again and battered their faces, each drop feeling heavier than the last. They walked through a small, dark passageway that led to the rear of the building. Each step was met with resistance to the unknown.

Several light bulbs were out in the hallway, but it was still light enough to notice the white paint chipping from the walls and ceiling. Some of them were barely hanging on, like deadened leaves on the trees before the first freeze of winter.

The bright yellow caution tape screamed from the apartment near the center. CRIME SCENE. DO NOT CROSS. Bart pulled it aside and pushed his way inside. Donnie followed suit. Investigators occupied every room. There were men taking samples of fluids, bagging random items, and photographing everything.

Bart and Donnie stopped upon entering to place cloth booties over their shoes and remove their damp coats. As they placed the blue covers on their boots, they assessed the dark apartment. The wood paneling covering the walls desperately needed updating, and the dirty mauve carpet obviously hadn't been shampooed in years, but besides that, everything was neat—nothing was disturbed other than what the investigators had shuffled through. It was clearly not a robbery.

Bart removed his cowboy hat that had collected rainwater around the brim. All the guys in the department gave him shit for wearing it. They constantly called him Wyatt Earp and Doc Holliday, but he didn't care because it reminded him of when he worked on the ranch—a much more peaceful time before he knew what a body devoid of life looked like.

They both put on a pair of white latex gloves and moved into the small apartment. The smell of death lingered in the air. Donnie removed a small can of VapoRub from his pocket and placed a smear of it under his nostrils, hoping to deaden the smell of decayed flesh that filled the room. He offered some to Bart, who reluctantly smeared it below his nose.

Captain Grabowski immediately snapped at them. "Took you long enough."

"We were at the ass end of Queens," Donnie irritably mumbled.

Grabowski seemed annoyed, so Bart interjected in an attempt to ease the tension. "What do we have?"

The captain motioned toward the bedroom. As they walked in, the men were stunned at what they saw. Both of them immediately understood why they were called in from Queens. A woman lay on the bed, although woman was a stretch; she couldn't have been more than twenty years old. She was positioned on her right side, completely naked, and had been hog-tied with duct tape. Her throat was cut from ear to ear, and she had a piece of cloth tied around her mouth that had been pulled between her teeth, undoubtedly from screaming. Her piercing blue eyes were still open and staring at the wall closest to the door, which was adorned with pictures of her and friends or family members.

Those harrowing blue eyes would become a permanent fixation in Bart's recurring nightmares, in which he saw the brutality and the corpses of women screaming for help and asking him why he had allowed this to happen to them. He was a policeman. He had taken an oath to protect the vulnerable. In his mind, he had failed. Hers was just another set of eyes that would forever haunt him.

The carpet was saturated with scarlet blood, which made it nearly impossible to get a close look without contaminating the scene with footprints. Bart's visceral reaction to this all-too-common homicide began kicking in. He had suffered anomalous and uncontrollable episodes since being hit by a car and suffering multiple head injuries. He could feel his heart pounding in the bottom of his throat and was sure everyone around him could hear it too. His vision was becoming blurry, and a million black and white spots littered his view of the scene before him. His hands were soaked with sweat beneath the latex gloves, and he felt nauseous, absolutely bilious. He knew what would come next—debilitating tremors, dizziness, or worse. He did everything he could to avoid drawing attention to himself. Keep it together. No one knows how you feel. Don't lose it now, you coward.

He sucked in a deep breath of air but winced at the smell. As he was slowly exhaling, the medical examiner walked in. Thank God. A distraction.

"How long has she been dead?" Bart asked, still unable to entirely recover his vision and struggling to keep his voice from quivering.

"Won't know for sure until I get her to the lab."

Bart cleared his throat. "Was she sexually assaulted?" He already knew the answer.

"Appears so, but I need to get her out of here before I can confirm anything."

Bart ordered everyone except the medical examiner to leave the room. Reluctantly, they cleared out. He carefully walked over to the body, removed the sheet covering her, and noticed the word "WHORE" written with a felt pen on her back. He inhaled the deepest breath his lungs would allow and moved the dark hair, which could have been sandy blonde or light brown but was so blood-soaked it was impossible to tell anymore, away from her neck. There it was, just as he suspected.

CHAPTER 2

BEAUTY

A black Escalade slowly veered off of Park Avenue and into the valet of the Waldorf Astoria. A doorman approached the vehicle before it came to a complete stop. He opened the door, and a long leg adorned with a crimson stiletto from Prada's latest fall collection extended from the SUV and stepped onto the sidewalk. The doorman reached inside the vehicle to assist a woman in exiting. She was wearing that season's Burberry trench coat in macchiato. It was open to reveal a striking Christian Dior pantsuit that perfectly matched her heels. The shade of red effortlessly complemented her long chestnut hair, which was delicately pulled off her face so as not to hide her large green eyes.

The doorman smiled. "Good evening, Miss Cassandra. Looking lovely as always."

She nodded and smiled warmly. "Great to see you as well, Mike."

Although Cassandra D'Angelo had money—with one glance at her, that was painfully obvious—she was as humble as anyone without a penny to their name. When she spoke, people listened. They respected her but were not intimidated by her. She had an air about her that made others feel comforted, as if they had known her their entire lives, even if it was their first encounter.

Cassandra entered the hotel. As she approached the elevator, she heard a familiar voice behind her. "Cassandra! It's so great to see you!" It was Beverly Foster, dressed in her usually quirky style. She wore an over-embellished floral dress that made her look like a walking art exhibit, with bright pink heels and far too many accessories. She smelled of lilacs and vanilla—her signature scent, which Cassandra recognized even before turning to face her.

"Bev, wonderful to see you," she said as she leaned in and hugged her.

The elevator doors opened, and they both stepped in.

As Beverly hit the button for the fourth floor, she made small talk. Unlike Cassandra, she never felt comfortable in quiet spaces, especially ones as confined as an elevator. "We really appreciate your continued support and commitment to the Women's Foundation, and please send our gratitude to your father. He has done so much over the years to help the women in this city."

"I will." Cassandra nodded. And she actually would. She was genuine in that way. "I'm honored to be involved with such a great organization. My father feels the same. He helped build this city and feels a strong obligation to help the people who live here in any way he can."

Cassandra's father, Frank D'Angelo, had come from nothing. As a young newlywed, he had dreamed of owning a construction company and building iconic skyscrapers all over Manhattan. When Cassandra's mother died, the business had just taken off, making things even more complicated than they already were. Cassandra refused to leave Frank's side for months, but he was traveling frequently. By then, he had buildings all over the world; however, success always comes with a price, and for Frank, that price was dangerously expensive.

Again, the elevator chimed, and the two women entered a lavish ballroom adorned with pink peonies delicately placed in the center of each table in crystal vases. Sets of polished silverware gleamed in front of every gold-and-white chair, with a glass charger plate separating the forks from the knives and spoons. Cassandra was immediately engulfed by a crowd of women offering their pleasantries and gratitude for her significant contribution.

Once the crowd died down and the women made their way to their seats, Cassandra was introduced and approached the podium. As usual, she was the keynote speaker of the evening. She gave her customary speech that included how honored she was and the immense happiness she felt to be able to give back to her community. It was all effortless to her; she had acquired her position with the foundation nearly seven years earlier when she was only twenty-one and had since done hundreds of events that all mimicked one another.

The D'Angelos' family foundation donated millions of dollars each year to numerous organizations, and it was Cassandra's job to be its face. Despite her philanthropic duty and the pleasure she got from her responsibilities, the monotony of it all often left her mind wandering to other potential endeavors.

As the crowd applauded, Cassandra returned to her seat to socialize with the ladies at her table. She glanced to the back of the room and noticed Anthony standing patiently near the exit, wearing a stoic grin. He was a tall man and handsome by anyone's standards, but that wasn't why she was so fond of him. Her father had hired Anthony twenty years earlier after she and her mother were almost kidnapped for a large ransom. Many of her childhood memories were lost to suppressing that event, but not Anthony. She could hardly remember when he wasn't around. He had helped raise her, had comforted her when she lost her mother, and now accompanied her to every charity event, social gathering, and convenience store run. She often wondered when he had time to spend with his own family, but she never tired of his presence.

When the event began winding down, Cassandra stood up and began saying goodbye. Anthony immediately appeared at her side to escort her to the elevator. As the doors shut, they stood quietly, facing forward.

"Another chicken dinner for the books," Anthony finally said with a wily smirk.

Although Cassandra was not looking at him, she could sense the light sarcasm in his voice and the grin occupying his perfectly symmetrical face. She let out a loud belly laugh, and he couldn't help but follow her lead. She was overwhelmed with gratitude to have him by her side to make all the tedious events enjoyable. They walked out of the elevator, through the lobby, and to the SUV the valet had pulled around to the front of the building.

Anthony opened the back door for Cassandra and offered a hand to help her inside. She let out a sigh of relief. A wave of exhaustion washed over her as if she had just completed a marathon. The car ride was silent. There was a time when Anthony attempted small talk or witty banter following these events, but he was savvy enough to know when she wanted to quietly decompress.

With the melodic hum of the engine, Cassandra's mind drifted. She thought about how much she missed her mother and how she longed to talk to her one more time, but she quickly pushed those feelings into her subconscious. Every time she considered them for too long, she felt immense guilt afterward. Evon had taken wonderful care of her since her mother had passed away, and she undeniably considered Evon like a mother—she had even long before Evon and Frank had married, when Evon was still a nanny. Cassandra cherished Evon and never wanted to imagine a life without her.

The clanking of the metal gate at the entrance of the estate brought Cassandra's attention back to the present. She hadn't even realized the car had stopped. As Anthony slowly drove up the long driveway to her home at the top of the hill, Cassandra desperately wished things were different. She hated going home to an empty house each night. As she walked up to the front door and inserted the key into the lock, she knew no one would be waiting on the other side to greet her. No husband. No children. Not even a cat or dog. She closed the door behind her and was soon standing in the dark, all alone.

CHAPTER 3

FIRE

Bart pulled up to the brick building he had seen so many times before. It was early, and the just-rising sun created an angelic halo that immersed the New York City skyscrapers. Bart's feelings about the place were anything but divine, however.

As usual, when he exited the elevator and walked through the frosted glass doors, he was the only patient in the stark white waiting room bathed in fluorescent lighting. In each corner stood a couple of modern sculptures that most likely cost more apiece than he made in a year. Dr. Lee had an extremely limited clientele that consisted mostly of the rich and famous. Bart had always considered himself very fortunate that Dr. Lee agreed to see him, especially after his most recent—and most severe—injury. He thought about that day often, and even more frequently when he had these damn appointments. He sat down, and his thoughts began to wander.

* * *

It was just two years earlier. Bart and Donnie were traveling through Brooklyn on their way back to Manhattan from interviewing an informant. This informant supposedly had information regarding the Star Killer, but, like most of their leads concerning that case, it proved to be a dead end. While they were driving up Putnam Avenue, Bart was intently looking out the passenger window.

"What are you looking at?" asked Donnie.

"The fire escapes." Bart's tone was monotonous, and his gaze never left the window. "Most burglars use them to exit apartments after a robbery."

"Yeah, I know that, but the—"

"Wait. What's that?" interrupted Bart. In the distance, a billow of smoke was coming from one of the upper windows of a building two blocks north. He pointed at the cloud. "Drive that way, Don."

Donnie turned on the lights and sirens. As they got closer, they could clearly see a fire blazing on the fourth floor of an eight-story building.

Donnie stopped the car, and Bart jumped out. "Call the fire department!"

Bart raced toward the entrance, fully aware that a fire in a building that size was risky. He would need to evacuate everyone above the fourth floor first, before the raging flames and thick smoke engulfed the stairs. Bart ran into the building and sprinted up the eight flights of stairs to the top floor. He began running down the hallway and pounding on the doors. "Fire! Fuego! Fire! Get out!"

A young Hispanic woman was the first to open the door. A gold cross hanging at the entrance could be seen as soon as the door opened.

"There is a fire. You need to leave now."

She walked back into the apartment. Bart yelled, "No! Fuego! Come back!"

She quickly returned to the doorway with two small children. All three were panicking and crying. He grabbed her shoulder and one of the children and guided them to the stairs before moving on to the next apartment. Uniformed officers had arrived, and while the young woman kept pointing back to the apartment, she was forcefully moved down the stairs with a large number of other residents. Everything seemed to be happening in slow motion, yet all at once.

After what felt like an eternity of banging on doors and herding men, women, and children toward the exits, it appeared every apartment above the fourth floor had been successfully vacated. Hundreds of people congregated outside in the middle of the street that was lit up from the flames of the blazing building; most of them were wearing their pajamas, and some were without shoes or socks in the below-freezing weather.

Bart's lungs were now polluted with smoke. He was gagging and vomiting with every breath he took. While he was keeled over, gasping for air, he noticed something in his peripheral vision. The young Hispanic woman with the two small children was frantically crying and screaming something in Spanish to a man who was trying to console her but obviously couldn't understand a word. Bart walked over and attempted to calm her down enough to find out what the problem was, but she was so hysterical he couldn't understand a word either.

Finally, Bart was able to decipher a few words between sobs. He realized she was saying her baby was still in the apartment. The haunting look in her eyes was one only a mother could have. He walked over to one of the water stations that had been set up, soaked a rag someone had given him to wipe the soot from his face, and did the only thing he could possibly do at that moment: he ran back into the burning building to find that baby.

The front entrance had been blocked with collapsed debris. Bart ran to a side door adjacent to the stairwell. Smoke was everywhere. He sprinted up the stairs with the cloth over his nose and mouth, coughing and heaving for air that no longer existed. When he finally got up to the eighth floor, each breath was grueling, and the lack of oxygen was beginning to make him disoriented. He began doubting whether he remembered which apartment was hers.

Stop. Think. Remember. The hallway was spinning, and each door looked like a carbon copy of the next, but then he remembered. The cross. He walked up to several doors, most still open, but he found no cross. Finally, he stumbled into the corner hallway apartment, and although the veil of smoke made seeing nearly impossible, he spotted the gold cross hanging adjacent to the door.

Barely able to see a foot in front of him, Bart stepped farther into the apartment and heard a faint cry. He thought he was hallucinating for a moment, but as he moved closer to the bedroom, the noise grew louder. He pushed the door open and attempted to locate the infant. He dropped to his knees and felt his way over to the bed. Nothing. He continued searching the floor, gliding his right hand over the shaggy carpet from one end of the small room to the other while holding the damp rag over his face with his left. Still nothing.

Bart crawled until his right hand hit something hard. The wall? There were handles. A dresser? He paused to listen. The crying grew louder. He moved his hand down the piece of furniture and noticed the bottom drawer had been left open. He reached inside and felt something soft. Sweaters? He rummaged around more. No, blankets. This drawer had been fashioned into a makeshift crib. He reached in and carefully picked up the infant, making sure its entire face was covered; time was now a critical factor.

Bart knew the flames below were tearing away at the building's foundation, and the upper floors must have been very unstable. He approached the stairs and began walking down as fast as he could, but he couldn't manage much more than a slow shuffle. He counted the floors as he descended, dropping his left foot first and then the right to meet it and repeating the process one stair at a time. Despite counting, he was so dazed from smoke inhalation he still couldn't distinguish where he was.

Finally, Bart got to what he believed was the first floor. It was blistering hot, and his eyes no longer functioned. The fire was consuming the building. The walls screamed as the flames engulfed them. He knew no time was left. He did the only thing he could think of. He got down on his hands and knees under the stairwell, hoping it would provide enough support to keep the building from becoming a sarcophagus forever enshrining him and the infant.

No sooner had Bart placed the baby under his body than the earth exploded. The noise was deafening, and the debris landing on his back was torturous. He knew he could not allow his body to collapse, or the baby would die. Unbearable pain shot down his spine from the weight. The dust made it impossible to breathe. He could no longer hold his eyes open.

Somehow, thanks to God or fate—whatever you call it—the firefighters who responded to the explosion found Bart and the baby in a tiny enclave created by the steel stairwell. They were able to jack up enough of the debris to slide the baby out and extract Bart. The damage to Bart's neck and back were serious, but once again, he had been given another chance at life. The police department wanted to have a ceremony and give him a medal, but he asked for a day off instead.

* * *

Bart was startled back to reality by Dr. Lee's nurse, Tonya, who was standing at the entrance of the waiting room. "Bart? Are you ready?" she said again. He promptly stood up and walked over to her.

She smiled. "Good morning. You can follow me." He walked behind her while removing his overcoat and signature cowboy hat.

Years ago, when the blackouts began and he was advised to see a neurosurgeon, Bart had gone on a few dates with Tonya, despite Dr. Lee's advice against it. She was a lovely woman whose beauty was matched by her ability to carry on an intelligent conversation, but he knew fairly early on she wasn't the one for him. She had probably known it before he did, but she enjoyed the company. Since she became a single mom of two, she welcomed any adult interaction she could get.

"How have you been?" she asked as they walked down the corridor. "We haven't seen you in a while."

"Not too bad. How are you? Are the kids doing okay?"

Bart hated formalities. Everything had ended cordially between him and Tonya, but it was always uncomfortable talking to an ex. He now understood why Dr. Lee had told him asking her out was a bad idea. She led him into room five.

"You can have a seat here. Dr. Lee will be right with you." She was still smiling—probably for no other reason than it was her job to do so—then she left and shut the door behind her.

The door had been closed for only a minute, maybe two, before Dr. Lee entered. He was petite, nearly a foot shorter than Bart, but his dark, exotic features made him exceedingly handsome. He had a chart in one hand and reached out the other to shake Bart's hand before motioning to the examination table. "Please have a seat."

Bart sat on the table and clasped his hands. A million thoughts raced through his mind.

"How are you feeling, Bart?"

"Better. Physical therapy seems to really be helping."

"Any recent blackouts?" Dr. Lee looked up from his clipboard while continuing to jot down something Bart could not make out.

"None lately. They seem to have subsided for now."

Dr. Lee continued writing. "Excellent. Do you want to continue physical therapy?"

"I can do most of the exercises at home, and when I do go to the therapist, I'm usually there for only a few minutes, so I don't really think it's worth my time."

Dr. Lee pensively examined the file for a minute and let out a muffled sigh. "I have to be honest with you, Bart. The police department is asking me whether I think you should remain on full-time duty. They are asking for X-rays, MRI scans, treatment plans—everything—and judging by the letter they sent, it seems they've already made up their minds. I hate to say it, but I'm going to have to be as honest with them as possible. I really don't think my report is going to help you keep your job.

"The multiple neck and back injuries and now the injuries to your head have put you in a precarious position. The damage from the building collapsing was bad enough, but when you were hit by the car, it catapulted things into another dimension."

Bart's stomach was in knots. He felt the color drain from his face. He knew now was not the time to lose his composure. He took a deep breath—a technique he had learned in the mandated therapy the department had assigned. It didn't help.

"I understand the position you're in, Doc, and I do think I'm close to being fully recovered, but some problems still concern me. It took me nearly three months to lift my right arm high enough to shoot. Until then, I was using my left hand, which I'm pretty proficient with, but nowhere near as close as with my right."

Dr. Lee paused for a moment. "What concerns me is another head or neck injury. You're in a very vulnerable state right now, and if you get hit in the head or take a bad fall, it could result in permanent paralysis. I realize how important your job is to you, but I think you need to put your health and future first."

Bart exited the office and decided to walk for a while to process all the information he had just received. He knew the department was pulling his medical records for review but didn't think it would happen so soon or could have been as bad as Dr. Lee made it seem. He walked down Lexington Avenue, circled around to Park Avenue in an attempt to clear his head, and then returned to the car. He began driving to the precinct, hoping work could offer a temporary distraction.

While he was driving, the burner phone his former partner, Bill Lupo, had hidden in the center console of the unmarked car, rang.

"H-Hello," he answered apprehensively.

"Hello, Bart."

CHAPTER 4

FINDING A KILLER

B art didn't recognize the voice on the other end. "Who is this?"

"I'm a friend of Lupo's. He told me I should call you if I needed to talk to someone."

"Lupo didn't have any friends, so why don't you just tell me who you really are?"

"You know who I am. Lupo and I used to talk, and he said if anything ever happened to him, I should contact you. Well, apparently, something happened to him, so here I am."

"That still doesn't answer my question, and frankly, I don't have time for this shit."

Silence. Then the person says, "That last bitch I killed, I wrote 'whore' on her back. Now, Detective Sullivan, do you know who I am?"

Bart couldn't believe what he was hearing. Is this some kind of practical joke? No one but the medical examiner, Donnie, and I knew what was written on the victim's back. It was never released to the public—not even to the family.

"I will call you another time," the voice continued. "But if you attempt to find out any personal information about me or trace my phone calls, you'll never hear from me again. If you really want to know—"

The phone went dead. Bart pulled the car close to the curb and put it in park. He grabbed the small leather-bound notepad he kept inside his pocket, removed the pen from the spiral coils at the top, and wrote down the phone number from which the call had been made. He felt ill.

Bart faintly remembered Lupo telling him he had previously talked to the Star Killer, which was the name given to the monster torturing and killing women all over the Northeast, leaving nothing behind but their naked carcasses, defiled and marked with a star strategically etched behind their earlobes and vile words written on their backs. Bart had thought it was one of Lupo's routine drunken tirades, and he sure as hell had never expected to talk to the Star Killer. Bart's chest felt heavy, and he couldn't breathe. His head was spinning. What is happening? Could it really be him? No, it couldn't be. But what if it is? What if it's real? After all, no one except me knew the Star Killer had talked to Lupo. What the hell is happening?

The thoughts were entering Bart's mind faster than he could process them. However, he was certain of one thing: if the department found out he actually had been in contact with the Star Killer, Bart wouldn't have to worry about the medical review board. They would have him committed instantly.

Once he regained a semblance of composure, Bart put the car in drive and pulled away from the curb. As he drove, he thought back to when he had met Bill Lupo. It was five years earlier, although it felt like another lifetime. Bart had just received his gold shield after working undercover for two long years. He was assigned to the major crimes unit, which investigated violent murders and, more specifically, serial killers. Unfortunately, most of the victims were female, so the investigators on the unit spent the majority of their time looking at or looking for tortured, beaten, and, often, mutilated women. It was a never-ending, sick game of cat and mouse.

These killers were strategic, intentional, and ruthless. The only evidence they left behind was what they wanted detectives to find, which was never helpful in tracking down the demented bastards. It was a physically, mentally, and emotionally exhausting job, one that could consume a person until there was nothing left of them but a shell of what once was a human being. That's what happened to Lupo.

When Bart became a detective after two years of undercover work, many veteran detectives, who had worked much longer for their gold shields, had a copious amount of animosity toward him. That's how he got assigned to Bill Lupo, the precinct drunk. The assignment was meant to be some kind of punishment for Bart, but he knew how hard he had worked and how much he had sacrificed for his shield, so he never let it bother him.

Lupo was an interesting guy—a stone-cold alcoholic, but interesting, nonetheless. After his wife left him taking their two children with her, he had nothing but a bottle of scotch and serial killer theories. He had recently become obsessed with a series of homicides throughout New York City and the Northeast conducted by a character whom Lupo, Bart, and the medical examiner knew only as the Star Killer. Lupo had uncovered much more information about that particular murderer than anyone else in the department, and on the rare occasion when Lupo wasn't absolutely obliterated, he would discuss his findings with Bart, who was undeniably intrigued by the information, although he never quite knew whether Lupo was telling the truth or fabricating details during his routine drunken stupors.

The most startling piece of information Lupo revealed was how calculated the Star Killer was. He wore a plastic jumpsuit under his clothes so no DNA could be left at his crime scenes. He shaved his entire body to eliminate the chance of a hair falling off, and if he had sex with any of his victims, the body was never found—or that's what Lupo theorized anyway. For the killer, it was not about sex; it was a game that involved domination and torture. The corpses he left for detectives to find were occasionally desecrated with derogatory terms like whore, bitch, and slut written on their backs with a felt pen.

Lupo began showing Bart the files he had accumulated on the case—files the department had no idea existed. No one knew how invested Lupo was in the case. No one understood how far he would go to catch this monster, and no one knew Lupo had been in contact with the Star Killer and had even talked to him several times over the phone.

Lupo had folders upon folders of witnesses, case information, details about the victims, and even personal information about the killer. Bart knew he was approaching dangerous territory. He now had information that could assuredly get him fired—maybe even arrested—but he knew there had to be a reason Lupo did not want to disclose the files to the department, so he agreed to keep everything between them and them only.

As the following year progressed, Bart became thoroughly educated on serial killers—how they thought and acted, why they treated their victims the way they did, and the significance of the clues they left behind, had they graciously decided to leave any. It was an entire crash course taught by someone who had dedicated—or, more accurately, sacrificed—his life to track down some of the worst criminals of all time and whose life was now ironically being destroyed by those same individuals. It was almost poetic. The murderers Lupo worked so hard to stop were slowly killing him.

Then, on a cold, rainy day in November, Bart got a phone call.

"Sullivan," he had answered.

"Bart? It's Lieutenant Marelli. I have some unfortunate news."

"What's going on, Lou?"

"It's Lupo. He was found dead in his apartment this morning. The ME believes it's a suicide. He had a gunshot wound to his head, and the bullet came from his revolver. I'm really sorry."

Suicide? Bart knew Lupo drank heavily, ate like shit, and never slept, but Lupo had never hinted at any suicidal tendencies, and Bart would know; he had spent more than eighty hours a week with the guy. It didn't add up, but he'd have to worry about that later. The first thing he needed to do was get to Lupo's apartment and grab the Star Killer files before anyone else had the chance to find them. He threw on a raincoat and walked outside to his unmarked cruiser.

When Bart arrived at the complex, everything seemed different. He had never noticed how old the building was. Some of the bricks at the entrance were so corroded it looked like an angry teenager took a sledgehammer to them. He stood for a moment absorbing the despair but quickly shook it off and ran inside, which wasn't any better. The tiles in the hallway were stained yellow from smoke or perhaps piss. It was a distinct color, so it was apparent the stairs had not always been that way. Bart envisioned the building when it was first built. It must've represented hope to a lot of people—a shiny new apartment building for a shiny new life. Now it was just another shitty complex for drunks and junkies. He continued down the hallway to the stairwell and sprinted up three flights of stairs to apartment 321, but he didn't need the number to know which door was Lupo's. The yellow tape invading the corridor could be seen from the end of the hallway.

As he approached the open door, Bart couldn't avoid the myriad of forensic investigators, cops, and paramedics swarming the apartment. How can they all even fit in there? It's the size of a shoebox—smells like one too. Right in the center of it all was Lupo's lifeless body, lying on the couch with his .38 revolver on the floor beside him and a hole in the side of his head. Bart was shaken by the thought that Lupo could have been that sick and he had never even noticed.

"You can't be in here, Sullivan. Go back to the office, and we'll talk in a few hours," barked Lieutenant Marelli from across the room.

"Yes, Sir." Bart casually surveyed the room before leaving. He didn't see any files or boxes, which meant Lupo must have moved everything back to the storage unit. Maybe he did plan on killing himself after all. Either way, it didn't matter. Even if Lupo didn't commit suicide, Bart could never suggest the department investigate his death as a possible homicide because Lupo had been casually talking to a serial killer without anyone knowing except for Bart. Yeah, that would go over really well.

He slid on his cowboy hat as he walked out of the apartment building and into the nearly frozen rain. Thoughts rattled his brain— so many that he didn't notice the rain or subzero temperature. He couldn't ignore his immense guilt over not paying closer attention to Lupo's mental state, but as he walked toward the car, a thought temporarily interrupted it. Lupo had given him a key to a storage locker but had never told him where it was. The tristate area had more than half a million storage units. Besides that, there was no way of knowing how Lupo had paid for it. If Lupo had paid by check, the department could possibly trace it.

Bart knew he should disclose everything to Marelli. He also felt obligated to continue what Lupo had started—what Lupo had died for. If the storage locker did hold the files and Bart continued hiding them, he could lose his career. If he relinquished them, he'd get reprimanded for not revealing them sooner. It was a double-edged sword, and he was conflicted.

Bart felt himself being pulled deeper and deeper into the secret investigation. Lupo had crossed the line a long time ago, but Bart wasn't sure if he was ready to. It was a decision he would never come back from. For the time being, all he knew was he had to be extremely careful. He couldn't stifle the feeling that whatever Lupo had in that locker was the key to finding the Star Killer and putting an end to the brutal murders of dozens more women.

CHAPTER 5

HOSTAGE

Bart and Donnie were driving toward Queens to interview a witness regarding the latest homicide when Bart's cell phone rang. On the other end was a frantic Maria Passenti.

Maria had been a friend and a lover during Bart's undercover time. She was a beautiful Hispanic woman who attracted attention wherever she went and had a larger-than-life personality to match. She had a young son named Juan who was her entire world, and she wanted to ensure he grew up safe—far from the drugs and crime that polluted most of the inner-city neighborhoods in New York City.

Bart could barely understand what Maria was saying. After several minutes of coaxing, he managed to calm her enough so she could speak clearly. She told him Juan and two females had been lured into a car by a couple of drug dealers. They were joyriding when the police spotted them, and a chase ensued. They crashed the vehicle, and the dealers were now holding her son and the girls hostage in an abandoned building in Jamaica, Queens.

"Please. You have to help him."

Over the two years Bart had worked undercover and was close to Maria, he got to know some very intimate details about her and her family. Juan was now ten years old and her only child. He had been diagnosed with a mental disability at the age of six and was very dependent on Maria. He was also very trusting, which made him susceptible to dangerous situations. What kind of monsters would target a disabled child? Bart was going to find out one way or another.

He got the address of the warehouse from dispatch and assured Maria he would be there within twenty minutes—a stretch considering they were still in the city and traffic was a bitch this time of the day. Before Bart could even think about how to explain this to Donnie, he began asking questions.

"Who the hell was that, Bart? Where are we going?"

"It's Maria. Her son's been taken hostage, and she needs our help." Bart turned his gaze to Donnie. "And I need yours. Head toward 163rd Street off Jamaica Avenue."

"Bart, you know I've always got your back, but this is insane. First, this is out of our jurisdiction. Second, the hostage team is going to wonder what the hell we're doing there, so you'd better come up with a damned good reason before we arrive."

"Just get there as fast as you can. I'll figure out the rest on the way."

Donnie flipped on the lights and sirens and began weaving in and out of the stagnant vehicles blocking traffic. As Donnie drove, Bart devised a plan. He knew he could not, in any way, risk exposing Maria as an informant. If anyone found out she had been working with him, she'd be dead within hours, and one more child would be in New York foster care.

Nineteen minutes later, they pulled up to a roadblock. Flashing lights came from every angle. Police vehicles, negotiation trucks, and emergency service vehicles were spread out across the street, and a large tent had been set up slightly closer to the warehouse as a temporary headquarters. Officers from the SWAT team were standing by in full body gear, holding shields.

Bart and Donnie parked about a hundred feet away from the tent.

"Here goes nothing," said Bart as he placed his cowboy hat on his head, stepped out of the vehicle, and began walking toward the barricade. "Just follow my lead."

"Well, well, well. What's the Hollywood squad doing all the way out here?" said Lieutenant Mike Wells as Bart and Donnie approached the scene.

Bart's laugh sounded hollow and forced. "Hey, Mike." They shook hands, and Bart motioned toward Donnie. "This is my partner, Donnie Ward. Donnie, this is Lieutenant Mike Wells."

Mike gave Donnie a cordial nod before repeating his original question. "So, what're you guys doing here?"

"I need a favor, Mike. I have to get in on this hostage situation. I know one of the kids in there."

"No, Bart. Hell no. I don't know how you guys handle shit in Manhattan, but we have a protocol here, and it doesn't involve you two."

Bart gestured for Mike to follow him. "A word, please?" Mike let out a large sigh and followed Bart, who walked several feet away, out of hearing range of everyone stationed at the headquarters.

"Look, Mike, I really need to get in that warehouse and get those kids out." Bart sounded desperate at this point.

"I understand this is personal to you, but even if I wanted to help, you know the rules. There's nothing I can do about it. I'm sorry, Bart."

"To hell with the rules. Those kids need help. I can get them out, and you and I both know that's the truth of it. What are you gonna do if we drive down there anyway?"

"I won't do a damn thing, but you know what you'll be risking."

Bart walked back to Donnie. "I'm going down to negotiate with these guys. Best you wait up here."

"Hell with that," said Donnie. "I'm coming with you."

Bart continued walking toward the warehouse. "It isn't safe. Just wait up here."

Donnie sped up to catch Bart and grabbed his shoulder. "No. I'm fucking tired of you always trying to protect me like I'm your kid or something. I'm not, and you're done telling me what to do."

Bart paused and looked at Donnie. He couldn't help but grin slightly. "Fine, but there's only one way we're going to get this thing done."

They had to act quickly before any more brass got on the scene and really prohibited them from getting involved. Donnie crawled in the trunk of the vehicle and placed a rag over the latch so it wouldn't lock him inside. Bart took a white handkerchief out of his pocket, hopped in the driver's side, and drove slowly toward the abandoned building. As they approached the warehouse, Bart could see a man standing in the doorway shouting something and waving his arms erratically over his head.

Bart drove cautiously alongside the building, made a U-turn at the corner of the warehouse, and slowly came back up alongside the east side of the building, strategically stopping the car so the trunk could not be seen from the entrance of the building. He stepped out of the car slowly, waving the white handkerchief to signal he meant no harm.

At the same time Bart stepped out of the car, Donnie quietly crawled out of the trunk. They closed the door and the trunk at the same time to synchronize the sounds so they sounded like a single door closing. Donnie snuck around to the back of the building as Bart walked toward the front. As Bart rounded the corner of the dilapidated orange brick building, he heard someone shouting.

"Stop right there!" It was a young Hispanic male, probably in his early twenties. He was wearing an oversized black coat and baggy blue jeans, but his thin frame was impossible to conceal despite all the layers. He couldn't have weighed more than a hundred pounds soaking wet.

Bart held the white handkerchief over his head and placed his other hand in the air. "Calm down. I just want to talk." Now that he was closer, he could clearly see the boy was holding a pistol.

"Who the hell are you?" He seemed startled; his inexperience could no longer be concealed. He had never done anything like this before. "What are you doing here?" He continued shouting as Bart moved closer.

"I'm here to try and work this out," Bart yelled.

"Do you have a gun?"

"I do," said Bart transparently.

"Throw it on the ground—now!" he howled, backing into the doorway.

"Why would I do that? You have one—throw yours on the ground."

The boy was visibly irritated. He began incessantly waving the gun again. "Do you want me to kill these fucking hostages!? Huh? Is that what you want? 'Cause I swear I'll do it!" His voice was shaking worse than his hands by now. He was obviously terrified.

"No," said Bart calmly. "I don't want to get anybody killed. I just want to try to work this out. What do you want?"

The kid scratched his head with the barrel of the pistol and then used it to push the charcoal beanie above his eyes. "I want $500,000. And a helicopter." He was still shouting to cover the distance between himself and Bart.

"Oh, is that all you want—$500,000 and a helicopter?" Bart couldn't help but grin at the childish request. He decided to humor the boy. "We can probably do that, but where the hell do you expect a helicopter to land in a neighborhood like this?"

"Who are you, anyway? I want to talk to whoever's in charge."

Bart couldn't contain the smile slowly consuming his face again. "I'm in charge. You need to talk to me. What's your name?"

"None of your goddamn business!"

"Well, okay, then. I'll just call you Johnny Boy." Bart chuckled.

Bart began slowly moving toward Johnny Boy, his hands still in the air and the white handkerchief blowing in the wind. He had tipped the brim of his hat up slightly so his entire face could be seen. He wanted to avoid further intimidation. His long black raincoat, which was sufficiently heavy most days, was no match for the blistering wind blowing through the open air surrounding the warehouse. He may as well have been wearing shorts and flip-flops.

Bart wondered how long it would take Donnie to get through the back door. They were unsure whether there was still a lock on it. That depended on how long the warehouse had been vacant. Most of the windows had been boarded up, but that didn't mean much in Queens. Fortunately, Donnie had taken an interest in picking locks when he worked in burglary. It had become a borderline obsession for a while but had since subsided. Nonetheless, he kept lock picks in his coat at all times. "You never know when you'll need one," he would always say.

"Don't come any closer! I'll kill these hostages—all of them!"

Bart realized he had unconsciously started edging closer to the building. "Okay, okay. Don't do anything you're gonna regret." He squinted to indicate he was considering the ransom again. "So, five hundred thousand and a helicopter. Suppose we get you the cash and a fast car instead. What do you think?" Bart inched closer.

The boy disappeared into the warehouse. For the first time since the negotiation began, Bart turned around and looked behind him. The number of people staked out at the provisional headquarters had at least doubled. His eyes scanned the crowd and landed on Lieutenant Wells. He was pissed and staring straight at Bart, shaking his head in disdain. What the hell, Sullivan?

He turned back around and moved a little closer to the doorway, confident that if Johnny Boy tried to shoot him, he'd be dead before he even had a chance to aim. Bart had won numerous quickdraw competitions while living in Oklahoma, although it was often much warmer during those contests. His exposed fingertips were going numb. Throbbing pain ran from his neck down the length of his arm and pulsated through his shoulder. No doubt it was from one of his many injuries over the years, but did it really have to flare up now? He wouldn't be able to hold his arm up for much longer.

Bart was in agony but tried to distract himself. He thought about where the second kidnapper might be. He thought about what other weapons they may have and if Donnie had made it inside yet. Come on, Don. Hurry up. For Christ's sake, hurry up.

"Okay." Johnny Boy was back. "We'll accept the money and the car, but the kids come with us."

Bart scoffed. "Now that doesn't make much sense, does it? I give you money and a car, and you're still going to take the hostages? I'm making a trade for the kids."

He wasn't sure exactly how much time had passed, but it felt like hours. He had no way to communicate with Donnie. He assumed if Donnie was inside, he'd hear some kind of commotion. Bart glanced to the side of the building but couldn't see anything. He tried to lean closer to the building but couldn't hear anything.

"We want something to eat, and we want some beer, man."

Bart looked back at Johnny Boy, perplexed. Are we having a pizza party now? "Yeah, okay. I'll get someone to pick up pizza and beer for you." Negotiating was officially over. The whole thing was turning into a joke.

The beanie had made its way back down over Johnny Boy's eyes, but Bart could tell he was losing his nerve. He was more than likely a kid who owed the wrong person money and was trying to take the easy road to getting it. He would've had more luck robbing a bank.

"Johnny Boy, I'm going to walk over to those guys." He motioned toward the temporary command. "And tell them to send someone for your pizza and beer."

Just as Bart turned around to walk toward the tent, he heard a loud bang echo inside the building. Donnie must have finally gotten in, but whose gun did it come from? He couldn't tell.

Johnny Boy turned quickly to look inside the warehouse. As he turned back toward Bart, he raised his gun to point it in front of him. Bart drew his revolver from his holster, and before Johnny Boy's gun was even eye level, he had a bullet hole at center mass in his chest. He fell to the ground like a bag of bricks. Bart ran as fast as he could toward the building. As he went through the door, he saw Donnie standing in the middle of the warehouse with his gun drawn. The second kidnapper was lying on the floor with a sanguine puddle surrounding his lifeless body.

Bart and Donnie cut the ropes that bound the women's wrists and feet and removed the duct tape from over their mouths. They had no coats and were trembling, either from the cold or from fear. Bart assumed both. Their blouses were torn, and their cotton skirts were ripped. One woman had a bruise on her cheek, and the other had a bloody eye.

Bart gave his coat to the woman with the black eye. She tightly wrapped her arms around his waist and sobbed into his chest. Bart looked around for Juan. He gently shifted the girl to one of the paramedics who had come running in once Donnie announced the scene was cleared. Beginning to panic, he walked from the front of the warehouse to the back along the west wall. The back door through which Donnie had entered was ajar. Bart ran out of it and shouted for Juan, looking around in all directions. There was still no sign of him.

As Bart reentered the building and paced the east wall of the warehouse, he heard a whimper that sounded like a wounded animal. He ran to the sound, but it abruptly stopped.

"Juan? Are you here?"

Again, Bart heard whining. He followed it to the corner. There on the floor, behind a stack of bricks and trash, was Juan, lying in the fetal position. His arms were clenched around his knees as tightly as his eyes were squeezed shut. He was inconsolable. His entire body convulsed with every sob he released. Bart picked him up and began walking toward the front door of the warehouse. Now, that was the easy part. Explaining to the department what he was doing in the middle of a hostage situation in another county would be much more complicated.

CHAPTER 6

WOUNDED

It had been six months since Lupo died. The department was a full-time gossip machine, and it had been working overtime. Everyone constantly hounded Bart for information concerning Lupo's unexpected suicide, but he always blew them off and gave a generic response like "Lupo's addiction finally got the best of him."

The squad had been interviewing new detectives to fill open positions in the department, and the brass was pushing for Bart to be matched with a new partner, even though he preferred working alone. Bart had established himself as a valuable member of the department and gained a great amount of respect, so now he had some input into who his new partner would be, but it was a difficult decision.

The relationship between partners is an intimate one—almost like a marriage, except partners see one another far more than spouses do—so it's fundamental to choose someone who is easy to get along with, who is like-minded, and who doesn't have too many bad habits. Besides the fact that he would have to spend eighty hours a week with his partner, Bart had to consider many other factors—most notably the never-ending decisions that must be made at the drop of a hat and sometimes meant the difference between life and death. Trust was paramount.

Lupo was a worthless partner. He was unreliable, miserable to be around, and always either drunk or hungover. If he hadn't been with the department for so long, they surely would've canned him long before his self-inflicted demise. Bart was convinced they only kept him around to punish the rookies in the same way he had punished him.

Bart thought back to the year he worked with Lupo. The first time he was injured on the job was with Lupo—unsurprisingly—despite having worked in much more dangerous situations while undercover and always making it out unscathed. They had been on the Lower East Side, looking for yet another building in which Lupo thought the Star Killer might be hiding or planning his next murder. Bart couldn't recall and may have never actually known. It seemed like they were always on one of Lupo's wild goose chases, but that time, they seemed to be in the right place at the right time for once.

As they were driving down East Houston Street, Bart noticed a man assaulting a woman. He appeared to be struggling to pry her purse from her hands, but she was putting up what looked like a hell of a fight.

Bart yelled, "Stop the car!" He already had the door open and was jumping out to run across the street toward the altercation.

It was the dead of winter, and Bart was wearing his heaviest winter coat. He considered removing it to gain speed. Surely the perp would try to run once he saw a man six foot two and in better shape than any NFL quarterback running full speed in his direction. However, sometimes the zipper got stuck, and he couldn't risk losing any time. He was right. The minute the man caught sight of him sprinting down the sidewalk, he punched the woman forcefully in the face, causing her to yell and pull her hands, clad in suede gloves, to her bleeding nose and drop her purse. Since she was undeniably preoccupied, the mugger grabbed the bag off the ground and began running down the busy sidewalk in the opposite direction of Bart.

After chasing him for a block, Bart was right on his tail. The perp disappeared into a commercial building no more than twenty feet away. Bart ran after him. The heavy metal door led to a stairwell. Bart glanced up the winding staircase to see the man climbing the flights of stairs. The mugger was beginning to tire and slow down, which gave Bart even more of an advantage; despite the weight of his jacket and the cold air saturating every cell in his lungs, he was much faster.

By the time the perp reached the top of the complex, Bart was only seconds behind him. Bart heard the door to the roof close and followed. As he pushed the door open and swiftly stepped outside, he realized he was alone. The wind was howling, and Bart tried to pull his collar up to shield his face. Where the hell is Lupo? Bart wasn't entirely surprised he hadn't caught up.

He walked to the northeast corner of the roof. Nothing. Then he turned to inspect the northwest corner. The perp was still nowhere to be seen. Did this guy disappear into thin air? Bart hadn't heard the door open or close again. When he turned to inspect the other side of the roof, the perp was standing less than a foot away with the barrel of his revolver pointed at Bart's chest. Before Bart even had time to think, he grabbed the gun and tried to pull it away from his body. He felt something turning in the palm of his hand. Click.

Click. Click. Boom. Bart's ears were ringing after the explosion, and his vision faded into darkness.

When he opened his eyes, Bart was lying on the ground, and his ears were reverberating so loudly he could feel his entire body vibrating. He reached for his gun, but it was wet. Is it raining? He lifted his hand above his face and saw it was covered in blood. The earth started spinning, and his entire body felt as if it might sink into the floor below... He passed out again. When he regained consciousness, he was still lying on his back but could see red lights reflecting off the buildings now towering over him. He realized he was moving and was now on ground level.

"Hello, Sir. You've been shot, but we're going to take good care of you. Just try to relax," said one of the paramedics pushing the stretcher toward the ambulance.

Bart tried to speak, but he was barely audible. "W-Where's the-the guy?"

"Shhh. Just try to relax," said the paramedic again.

As the ambulance doors opened, Bart heard a piercing scream. For a moment, he thought he was imagining it. Then he heard a loud thump that sounded like a flat basketball hitting the pavement at a rapid speed.

"Oh, my god," gasped one of the paramedics standing near the ambulance.

Bart's eyes rolled back into his head, and he drifted out of consciousness again. He later found out at the hospital that Lupo had called for backup—the one right thing he did—which arrived right before the revolver went off, shooting Bart in the chest. The patrol officers had the guy cornered on the roof. They said he looked at

Bart, lying lifeless on the ground below, looked at the cops, from whom he wouldn't be able to escape, and threw himself off the building. He landed on the sidewalk right next to the ambulance.

"He was dead on impact," said Lupo.

Bart couldn't help but wonder whether the mugger had really jumped off the roof, but a part of him didn't care. He had been shot in the chest, less than a centimeter from his heart, and was miraculously still alive. The doctor informed Bart that his hand must have slowed the cylinder when he grabbed the gun, preventing it from properly aligning with the barrel and slowing the bullet. That and the padding in his jacket allowed the bullet to only go a few millimeters into his chest.

"You're incredibly lucky," the doctor said.

Lucky? Lucky would've been having a partner who was worth a shit and had my back—not let me nearly be killed. Out loud, Bart replied with a simple, "Thanks for everything, Doc."

Bart was introduced to Donnie after turning down two other young detectives. There wasn't anything specific he didn't like about them; they just didn't seem like a good fit, and, after Lupo, Bart desperately needed a good fit. His first impression of Donnie was that he was very serious. Donnie probably thought the same about Bart. Donnie had just transferred from burglary and had done some time in narcotics, which made him extremely vigilant—he noticed everything going on around him all the time. Donnie also enjoyed being in the action and was not afraid of hard work. He seemed to be a perfect counterpart for Bart.

After working together for only a few months, Bart and Donnie became very close—like brothers who had been separated somewhere along the line. Donnie's wife, Jeannie, frequently made them dinner when they had time to eat something besides greasy burgers and fries in the patrol car. She was a wonderful woman who fiercely loved Donnie and their two children, and she never passed up an opportunity to set Bart up with one of her many single or recently divorced friends. He always appreciated the effort and enjoyed the company of the beautiful women—who wouldn't?—but he knew exactly what he was looking for and they just weren't it.

Donnie was a better partner in a month than Lupo had been in an entire year, but Bart was taught never to speak ill of the dead. Despite that, Lupo was gone, and Bart finally had someone he could truly trust, even with his darkest secrets.

CHAPTER 7

BUSINESS

It was a frigid January morning. Snow flurries began to fall on the extensive lawn of the D'Angelo estate. The flowers had long since died and the grass had browned, but even in the gray of winter, the property was breathtaking. Cassandra pulled on her snow boots, buttoned up her warmest winter coat, and walked across the short drive to her father's house. It was a gorgeous colonial-style home—not exactly to her taste yet still very elegant. Her father had begun building it right before her mother died. It took him nearly six years to finish, and it became a kind of homage to Cassandra's mother. It embodied everything she loved and would have been her dream home had she still been alive.

When Cassandra was twenty, she remodeled the home across the road in which she had grown up and moved back into it. It was a beautiful four-bedroom, three-bath home that was a perfect reflection of her exquisite taste and style once she completed the renovations. She and her father oversaw the remodel, and when it was finally completed, the house was unrecognizable. That suited Cassandra since she feared that if it remained too familiar, it would serve as a constant and painful reminder of her mother. She enjoyed the security of living on the estate close to her father and Evon while also maintaining her independence and privacy in her own home. It was the perfect arrangement.

"Good morning!" she yelled as she entered the foyer, which had a round red oak table in the center adorned with fresh lilies, which Evon surely had picked up at the farmer's market. The high ceilings caused her voice to echo throughout the house.

"Good morning!" shouted the personal chef, Jonathan, from the kitchen. "Would you like some breakfast?"

"No, thank you. I'll just have some coffee." She walked toward the cabinet to get a mug.

Jonathan always offered Cassandra food, although he knew she would most likely decline it. She was very disciplined with her diet and exercise regime, just like with everything else in her life. She ate a small breakfast each morning—usually fruit—and then worked out in the large gym in her father's house. Three times a week, she went for a five-mile run, usually in the morning so she could watch the sun rise.

"Good morning, Cassie," she heard her father say as he approached the kitchen from the west wing—most likely coming from his office. "I'm glad you're here early. We can talk before we meet with the attorney."

She grabbed her coffee and followed him into the den, which also served as his home office. The cream-colored walls reminded Cassandra of the sand in the Hamptons. At one end of the room was a butter-soft black leather couch, and at the other end were shelves, adorned with hundreds of books, which spanned the length of the wall. Situated in the center of the room was a large mahogany desk that perfectly matched the bookshelves.

She recalled sitting there as a child while her father worked. She would constantly ask him questions about his companies and about her mother; sometimes she would fall asleep on the couch when she didn't want to go to her own bed. It was a comfortable and safe space for Cassandra and continued to be even though she was an adult. They walked into the room and both sat down on the couch—her on one end and him on the other. She took a small sip of her coffee, which released a burst of steam from the brim as her warm breath hit the seething liquid.

"I think at this meeting we need to resolve the sale of the construction company this January and decide what our next step will be," Frank said earnestly. "Since my partner is buying me out, it should be a rather simple process. For tax purposes, the accountants want to close half the company in November and the other half in January."

Cassandra nodded. "I hope after next January you and Evon will enjoy life. You've been so busy with the company you haven't been able to travel or do what makes you happy in so long. You deserve it, and I'll be fine, so stop worrying so much about me and take care of yourselves."

"You're right, and we are going to do those things, but at the same time, I'm concerned about you having more responsibility with the foundation."

She nodded again. "I will be fine. It is important to Mom's memory that I continue with the foundation, and, besides, it's what I want. Speaking of Mom, I think we need to settle the issue with the real estate business. She started it when I was born so I would have my own company, but since her death, I really haven't been involved in it."

"Yes." Frank chortled, recalling how stubborn his late wife was. "Your mother was adamant before you were even born that you would have your own business to inherit. She invested $100,000 of her money to start it, and within just a few years, it was very successful. You don't remember, but when she was too weak to work anymore, we licensed the day-to-day operation to Michael Bandell. He's run it ever since."

"Oh, I know all about Michael Bandell."

"What do you mean?"

"I mean, I think something suspicious is going on. When I became more interested in the day-to-day finances of the real estate company, I asked our attorney, Bill, to gather the financial records so I could see what I was working with. They have reached out to Michael and his accountant a number of times but haven't received a response."

"Well, I know it's making money, but that's about all I'm sure of. Let's put it on the list of things to discuss with Bill today," said Frank.

Cassandra hesitated for a moment. "Apparently, Michael has expressed interest in purchasing the business. I find it hard, though, to let go of something my mother began specifically for me."

"Well, I wouldn't be surprised. Michael and his wife, Julie, began the company with your mom. She was an office manager and he was a salesman, which is probably why they were so willing to take it over for us. I was so blinded by grief I'm not sure I ever even looked at the contract. I certainly never expected it to last this long."

Frank looked at Cassie. "It's your decision to keep the business or sell it. I'll support you no matter what you choose."

"Thank you, Dad. I think I just need some time to think, maybe dig a little deeper into what's really going on."

"Well, like I said, we can discuss it with Bill. I also need to talk to him about his actions. He's become very liberal with his position and doesn't always act in our best interest."

Cassandra contemplated her next statement before speaking again. "I'd honestly rather work with his assistant, Claire Tran. She is bright and has been involved in every detail of all our businesses since she started. Frankly, she's done more in the past couple of years than Bill's done since he began working for us."

Frank thought working with Claire and cutting out Bill completely could actually be a great arrangement, but he didn't want to make any major decisions considering the sale of his construction business was only months away. However, he decided if they couldn't work out their relationship with Bill, then they would move to Claire. He changed the subject. He never liked to talk business for too long with Cassie. Frank tried to balance family life and business.

"How has the writing been?" he asked.

Cassandra wrote trendy articles and in-depth stories about issues that were pressing and important. She was an exceptional writer and personable, so all the magazines loved working with her. Besides, it never hurt to have her family's name on anything. In fact, it was exactly the opposite.

She subtly smiled. "It's going fine. I need to finish this article I'm working on regarding serial killers. I've been trying to get an interview with a detective who seems to be an expert on the subject, but I'm having some trouble getting a hold of him."

"That sounds interesting. Maybe I can help you reach the detective."

"Oh, that's okay. I can finish the article without him if I need to. After that, I will focus completely on the foundation."

"Once the company sells in January, I hope to have added $500 million to the trust, bringing its total to more than $1 billion. It will be a lot for you to manage. If it's not what you want, I understand."

"We are blessed to be able to help so many people, and you need to remember your hard work over the past thirty years has made it possible. There's nothing else I'd rather be doing." She leaned across the couch and gave Frank a hug.

"Okay, honey. I just want you to be happy," he said, kissing her on the cheek.

They returned to their original spots on the couch.

"Hey," said Frank. "Whatever happened to Tom the banker?" He always managed to weasel his way into her personal life.

She grabbed her coffee mug and stood up. "We're going to be late."

As they left the den, Cassandra thought back to Tom—the asshole who had gotten drunk and told her friend Denise that if it wasn't for her money, no one would ever go out with her. He was just another prick to add to the list. One more person she couldn't trust. Cassandra feared she would never find that person who would love her more than her money.

CHAPTER 8

MARIA

The sky was already dark, and the streetlights were on when Bart left his apartment. The air was crisp and smelled like spring. The leaves on the trees were fighting to grow back. They wouldn't win; winter would linger for at least a couple more months. He got in his vehicle and began driving toward Long Island. He had not seen Maria since the hostage ordeal, but he had been worried for her safety every day.

He pulled off of Northern Boulevard and into the parking lot of Vincent's Restaurant in Nassau County. They had never met there before. He was sure they wouldn't run into anyone familiar—a risk he couldn't take. Too many witnesses had been at the hostage scene, wondering why Bart was there and how he knew Maria. It was dangerous for them to be together, but he could never say no when it came to her.

Bart drove his black car to the back of the parking lot, where there was very little light, and waited for Maria to arrive. He turned the engine off and just sat there, waiting and watching. Finally, he saw her silver SUV pull into the lot. She exited the vehicle and walked inside. Bart didn't get out immediately. He waited to make sure no one had followed her.

When Bart was confident Maria hadn't been tailed, he walked inside and looked around. There were only a few other occupied tables in the restaurant and a couple of business guys sitting at the bar drinking some beers. Nothing suspicious. She was already seated at a table for two in a dimly lit corner. Perfect.

As Maria noticed Bart approaching the table, her face was overtaken with a smile. She quickly got up to give him a hug. She looked stunning in a tight black dress with a plunging neckline. Ruffles running down the length of the dress from her right shoulder to the bottom hem just above her knees accentuated her long torso and perfectly showcased her naturally tan legs. Her hair was down, allowing her beautiful dark Hispanic waves to fall delicately on her bare shoulders, and her plump lips were adorned with a bright red lipstick.

Bart noticed when he hugged her that she seemed taller than usual. She must have been wearing stilettos, but he never looked down to check. As they were locked in their embrace, he was vanquished by her scent. The perfume she is wearing should be illegal on a woman that sexy.

They sat down at the candlelit table. Maria had already ordered a glass of red wine, and the waiter arrived and asked if Bart wanted anything from the bar. Although he rarely drank, he ordered an Irish on the rocks. It was never polite to make a lady drink alone.

"How have you been?" he asked once the waiter had left. "And how is Juan?"

"We're both doing okay. He's still a little shaken. He hasn't left the house since it happened, not even to go play in the yard with the neighbor girl, Bella." Maria paused for a moment, as if hypnotized by her own thoughts. She looked back up, tears welling in her dark brown eyes. "I can't thank you enough, Bart. What you did for him—for us—" She trailed off, stifling sobs.

He placed his hand on top of hers on the table. "It's the least I could do considering how much you two mean to me."

She flashed a grateful smile at him and wiped the tear that had fallen down her cheek.

They spent the remainder of the evening talking and reminiscing until they were the last customers in the restaurant. The servers had begun sweeping the floors, the bartender was polishing the glasses, and some of the chefs had already left.

"Maria, I'd like to talk to you about one more thing. I'm worried for your and Juan's safety. The hostage situation put us in a very vulnerable spot. The department is asking how I got involved and what my relationship is to the victims. I'm worried someone might find out how we know one another."

"What should we do?"

"I think the only option is for you and Juan to move to Florida with your mom, at least for a while. I know the last time we had this conversation, you wouldn't even consider it. Now there is more urgency."

To his surprise, Maria agreed. Maybe it was the wine, or maybe she could see the desperation in his eyes, but she offered no resistance. "You're right. It isn't safe for us here. I've felt it ever since the day they took Juan, maybe even a little bit before that."

"I have some money saved from when I worked undercover. Stealing cars was lucrative, to say the least. I thought the department would ask for it, but they never did. It should be more than enough to get you on your feet."

"Thank you, Bart. You've been so good to us. I don't know how I'll ever repay you."

"You don't owe me anything, Maria. I'm the reason you're in this mess."

"You know, there was a time I thought you and I had a future. I know now you're looking for someone, and I thought—I hoped—it might be me, but it clearly isn't. I really do hope you find her, Bart. You're a good man, and you deserve to be happy."

He didn't reply. He just smiled at her and drank the last swig of his whiskey.

When they exited the restaurant, Bart walked Maria to her car. They embraced one another, and as he released her, she leaned in and passionately kissed him. She tasted of vanilla with a hint of tart cherries. Bart didn't want to let her go.

She whispered in his ear, "I saw a motel about half a mile down the road. Meet me there."

As Maria sauntered away and got in her car, she turned around and gave Bart a seductive smile before stepping in and closing the door. He was still standing in the spot where she had kissed him. He turned and slowly walked to his vehicle. He knew what he should do—go home and get some sleep—but he was weak, and the sweetness of her tongue lingered on his lips. He got in his car, turned on the ignition, and began driving.

Maria sat in her car as Bart walked into the lobby and requested a room for the night. He got a key from the desk clerk and paid him cash. No credit cards. No records. Before he could even unlock the door to the motel room, she was kissing him—hard. He pushed the door open with their lips still locked and kicked it shut behind him. He kicked his shoes off and lifted her off the floor as she wrapped her legs around his waist and caressed his neck with her lips and tongue.

He threw her on the bed and removed her lace panties from beneath her dress. The scent of her perfume continued to intoxicate him. Bart wanted nothing more in that moment than to make love to her. He unbuckled his trousers as Maria slid her dress over her head, revealing her bare breasts. While he tugged his shirt off, he could feel her hands on his waist, pulling him closer to the bed. He threw his shirt on the floor as he continued to devour her with every kiss, knowing it was the last time they would ever be intimate.

It was early in the morning before they checked out of the motel. As they stood near Maria's vehicle, she looked at Bart with longing eyes. It was difficult for him to say goodbye. They had been very close for a long time. He cared deeply for her, but she was right. He was looking for someone, and it wasn't her. He handed her an envelope with $25,000 in it.

"Promise me you'll take your son and run," Bart insisted.

"We'll be gone by tomorrow."

They kissed one last time before Bart opened her door and helped her into the SUV. Once she was in the driver's seat, he closed it behind her. He felt a loss as she drove away. A part of him didn't want to let her go, but he knew there was no other way. She had been his rock during his time undercover. Without her, he would have never survived more than two years in constant fear of being found out.

* * *

MARIA

The next morning, when Bart arrived at work, he was surprised to find out he had to report to internal affairs regarding his interference with the hostage situation. He had figured punishment for getting involved would be handled within the precinct, as it usually was, but they were being sent to police headquarters. That meant one thing—he and Donnie had better get their story straight.

CHAPTER 9

INTERNAL AFFAIRS

Bart and Donnie met at the precinct early to drive downtown together for their meeting with internal affairs. They had spent the past twenty-four hours developing their story—one that was believable but did not expose the truth about Maria. The department had too many leaks. Bart couldn't risk anyone finding out the truth. He had enough blood on his hands already.

"I had some time last night, so I went and talked to Maria about the meeting," said Bart as Donnie drove them to One Police Plaza.

Donnie grinned. "Oh, yeah? You had some time?"

"Yeah. I figured she should know what's going on. I also wanted to talk to her about getting the hell out of the city."

Donnie had a full-blown smile. "Son of a bitch. You slept with her again, didn't you?"

"No, we didn't sleep together—we just talked."

Any other time, Donnie would've given Bart shit. He was so nervous about their meeting. However, he let it go, although he couldn't help but laugh. "Okay, whatever you say."

A few minutes later, Donnie spoke up again. "What if you were followed to the restaurant or the hotel?"

"I wasn't. I made sure."

"Well, what if she talks?"

"What if a 747 crashes into us right now? Or what if my heart stops as we're walking into the meeting?" said Bart sardonically. "I wasn't followed, and she won't talk. Besides, we have bigger things to worry about right now."

They spent the rest of the drive reviewing their story. It was calculated but still weedy in certain areas. They decided to tell the internal affairs division Bart had received a call from a confidential informant—a guy he had worked with while undercover—who told him three people had been kidnapped, one of them a child. The informant allegedly told Bart the kidnapper was someone Bart had worked with while undercover, and he thought Bart could get through to him. The story was complete bullshit, but it was designed so internal affairs could not confirm any of it.

It seemed like a solid plan. The confidential informant could not be named. Since Bart's two-year stint undercover was strictly classified, no one could check the story. His work undercover was so top secret that when the FBI and the NYPD arrested the people involved, Bart was arrested alongside them. After processing and fingerprinting, he was escorted out the back door. All the Mafia members involved in the multimillion-dollar car theft ring were sent to different jails, and Bart seemed to disappear. When it was time to testify, his testimony was taken secretly, with no one allowed in the courtroom. Most of the guys arrested ended up turning on each other and cutting deals. Internal affairs could not force them to reveal these informants or dig into Bart's time undercover.

"This will work, Donnie. Trust me."

They drove the unmarked car into the parking garage under Police Plaza and through security. They got out of the vehicle and walked toward the elevator, where more security awaited them. They flashed their badges, emptied their pockets, and removed their watches to go through the metal detectors. Once they made it into the elevator, they went through their story one final time. Bart was confident the story was foolproof, but he could see Donnie was nervous.

"Just let me do the talking," said Bart. The elevator bell chimed once they reached the fourth floor, and the doors opened.

The union attorney was waiting for them. It was Frank Grillo—a bulldog who took no shit from anybody and looked every bit the part. He was a large man—nearly Bart's size—and could have come straight from The Godfather. His black hair was always neatly parted, and he carried a small comb in his pocket for his thick mustache.

Bart was a union delegate, so he knew all the rules regarding interviews and interrogations. He had asked for Grillo specifically. They all shook hands before being taken to a conference room to strategize. Frank already knew the story. He was convinced the debriefing was a formality and would be immediately handed off to the police commissioner's office to decide on discipline. Despite everything going on in the foreground, the medical review board's decision was lingering in the back of Bart's mind. Perhaps it was because they were in the same building where the fate of his career would be decided or because the twitch in his right hand had returned as soon as they had entered the parking garage. Bart was concerned the conference room might be bugged—he put nothing past those sons of bitches. So, they kept the conversation light.

"Look, Frank, if they separate us, we are both entitled to an attorney, which means they can interview only one of us at a time since you'll have to be there."

"I know, Bart, but I don't think they're going to talk to you separately."

The door opened. In walked a tall white man with a razor-sharp jawline and a full head of dark brown hair. His name tag said "Lieutenant Hanson." Behind him was a black man who was much shorter, but, through his slacks and button-up, it was obvious he was incredibly athletic. He had a charming demeanor and a bald head that reflected the lights above him. His name tag read "Sergeant Miles." They introduced themselves, but Bart sat quietly. He didn't shake their hands or acknowledge them. Donnie followed his lead. Grillo introduced himself and said he was representing both Bart and Donnie.

The three men sat down, and Hanson began the process. "We will be interviewing you separately and on the record. I will take Detective Sullivan, and Sergeant Miles will take Detective Ward."

"Recording is fine, but I get a copy by the end of the day," said Grillo, whipping a recording device out of his leather bag. "I will also be recording. You can interview only one at a time since I have to be present."

"So, it's going to be like that?" asked Hanson.

"Looks that way," responded Grillo with a smug smile.

Hanson and Miles stepped out of the room for a moment.

When they returned, Hanson said, "Okay, we'll take Detective Sullivan first."

They walked Donnie outside and down the hall to a separate conference room. Bart knew Donnie would be nervous sitting alone waiting to be interviewed, but he was optimistic Donnie would maintain his composure. He always did.

In the other room, Hanson began the interview. "Do you understand the charges brought against you?"

"No, why don't you explain them," replied Grillo before Bart had a chance to answer.

Hanson read from a document in front of him. "You disobeyed a direct order given to you by Lieutenant Mike Wells not to interfere with the hostage situation and then continued to defy him and do whatever the hell you wanted."

Grillo looked at Bart and nodded. "Tell your story."

Bart looked Hanson directly in the eye and began. "I got a call from a confidential informant telling me a guy I knew from my undercover days had kidnapped some kids. He thought I could maybe talk some sense into him."

"Who was the informant?" asked Hanson.

"Does the term confidential mean anything to you? I can't disclose that."

"You can't or you won't?"

"If I give it to you, it will be leaked to news media all over the world by lunchtime. So I can't, and I won't."

Hanson was clearly irritated and snapped. "Then who was the individual you were told was the hostage taker?"

"John Morelli," Bart replied calmly.

"Who the hell is he?"

"A low-level, dope-selling Mafia guy I worked with while undercover. A druggie."

"Can you show proof of working with him?" asked Hanson, still clearly frustrated.

Bart pointed to the stack of papers in front of Hanson. "Look in the file."

Hanson was standing now. He was pacing the room, running his hands over his forehead and through his thick brown hair. He turned to Bart and slammed his hands on the wooden table where Bart and Frank were seated.

"This is bullshit! You're telling me you get to the hostage taker, realize it's not Morelli, and yet you continue negotiating, and then both hostage takers end up dead. It doesn't add up."

"Once I realized it wasn't him, there was no going back. I was already there. Already talking to the hostage taker. Already invested."

"Alright, Sullivan. I'll check on these people, but I think it's bullshit. All lies. Something else is going on here, and I will get to the bottom of it. I have seen guys like you before, guys who think they don't have to follow the rules, who think they are better than everyone else—"

"The only way you might see someone like me is in the movies," Bart interrupted. "You are busy hiding out in this fucking office, afraid to go out on the street. Everyone knows the truth about you empty suits."

Hanson's nostrils were flaring. If they had been in a cartoon, his face would be fire-engine red, and he'd have smoke coming out of his ears. "This is going to the PC's office." He gathered the files, walked out of the room, and slammed the door behind him.

Grillo responded, "Well, that went well."

They asked Bart to leave the room and brought Donnie in. He wasn't in the room for even ten minutes before walking out with a somber look on his face, Grillo trailing behind. The three of them walked to the elevator, careful not to talk in the halls.

Once they were in the elevator, Grillo said, "Listen, guys. All they have on you is disobeying orders. There is a lot of public support for what you did, but these guys are pissed because you made them look stupid. I don't think they want this thing to blow up. They just want to make clear you overstepped your boundaries."

They shook hands outside of the building, and Bart and Donnie walked to their car. They got in the car, with Bart in the driver's seat. They sat there for a few minutes without saying anything. Finally, Donnie spoke. Bart could barely hear him over the hum of the engine and the blare of the police radio.

"I think I should call that woman who knows the commissioner and ask for her help. I have a bad feeling about this."

"If you think she can help, then call her," mumbled Bart. "Who is she again?"

"I passed information to her when I worked in narcotics. She worked for the Daily News. Her name is Cassandra D'Angelo. I think she has some juice in the PC's office. She always said to call her if I ever needed help."

Bart didn't say anything. He just looked at Donnie as if trying to recover a misplaced memory.

"Remember? She writes those articles for the hoity-toity magazines. I told you she wants to interview you for the article she's writing about serial killers. You keep blowing her off."

"You never told me about her," said Bart.

"You're un-fucking-believable, you know that? I asked you about five times to do the interview. If you'd get Maria out of your head, then maybe you could think straight, and we wouldn't be in this situation in the first place."

Bart wanted to defend Maria, but he was already exhausted, and it was barely noon. So, he simply said, "Just call her, Donnie," as he put the car in reverse and left the parking garage.

CHAPTER 10

FACE OF A KILLER

It was January in New York, and a layer of fluffy white snow covered the ground, yet to be disturbed by the bustle of people on their commutes. The air was so callous it felt like razor blades on any skin unfortunate enough to be exposed. More than four years had passed since Lupo's death, but Bart had kept in touch with his widow, Maryann, and his kids. He even gave her money—sometimes from fundraisers, other times out of his own pocket. She had called Bart and asked if he could come by their house to talk.

When Bart arrived and knocked on the door, he noticed stacks of boxes through the window. As he entered the home, he saw even more boxes. The entire house had been almost completely packed up. Maryann informed him she was moving to Florida but didn't want to leave without telling him. He understood. It couldn't be easy living in a city that constantly reminded her of her failed marriage and her dead ex-husband. She must not have wanted that for her children either.

Bart still had not found Lupo's storage unit. As far as he knew, the NYPD still knew nothing about it. The only way he could find it was if Maryann would let him see Lupo's personal checkbook or credit card statements, but it was too awkward to ask. However, before Bart left the house, Maryann mentioned that, while she was packing, she had found some papers with Bart's name on them. She had loaded them into two boxes, which Bart gathered before saying his goodbyes. They vowed to stay in touch, although it was unlikely. He was just another thing that reminded her of a life she wanted to forget.

Bart left Maryann's and went directly home. As soon as he walked into his apartment, he dumped the boxes in the center of his small living room and began scouring them for any information related to the storage locker. After he had rummaged through nearly all of the papers, he sat on the floor, leaned his back on the front of his couch, and let out an exasperated sigh of disappointment. Those boxes were his last hope for finding Lupo's years' worth of research.

As Bart scanned the mess of papers, something caught his eye. He pulled out a piece of paper from the bottom of the stack, and there it was—a receipt from a storage company in Whitestone for a locker that had been paid for in advance for five years. He immediately jumped up and threw on his coat before running out of the apartment like the place was on fire.

Bart got in his car and drove to the address on the receipt. Once he pulled onto 150th Street, he drove slowly until he saw a large sign: "Whitestone Budget Storage." Bart wore a baseball cap and sunglasses in hopes that he wouldn't be recognized by any cameras at the facility. He parked the car far enough away that any cameras would not be able to read the license plates. He walked into the office and signed Lupo's name in the log. The teenage girl sitting behind the counter never even looked up from her magazine to acknowledge him. He walked out of the office and down a row of units that resembled tens of mini-garage doors painted blue. He finally found the locker with the number that matched the one on the keychain. He pressed the key into the padlock and tried to turn it. It wouldn't budge. Shit. Is this the wrong place? The wrong locker? He double-checked the numbers. They matched. Again, he slid the key into the lock. It still wouldn't turn. Bart was tired and agitated, and he couldn't believe that after all these years, Lupo was still pissing him off. He took the key out, examined it, and put it back into the padlock. The key went in all the way this time and clicked. He turned it, and the lock released. He reached down to lift the heavy door. There it was.

* * *

Bart was put on temporary leave following the hostage incident, which wasn't good news for him—it gave him far too much time to think. He was extremely apprehensive about his future. Between the medical review board, the internal affairs hearing, and the Star Killer, his head was in a constant state of disarray. On top of it all, for the first time since they became partners, he was seriously concerned about Donnie. Bart was sick with guilt for not being honest with him; Bart's future with the department could very well come to an end sooner than later, and Donnie had no idea. He was also still completely oblivious to the files Lupo had left in the storage locker. Donnie was always so honest with Bart that it seemed wrong, but Bart wasn't quite sure Donnie could handle it all, especially since he was already having such a difficult time with their impending date with the police commissioner.

The information Bart had uncovered regarding the Star Killer was overwhelming, but with all the free time he had unwillingly acquired recently, it was on his mind more than ever. He knew once he began delving into the files, there would be no turning back. What haunted him most was personally dealing with such a monster.

Since Lupo had obtained everything illegally, there wasn't enough evidence to indict the Star Killer. Bart did, however, have a confession from that first phone call. If he played his cards right, he could gather more information and get closer to the killer. He knew what the guy was capable of. He also couldn't afford to make any wrong moves and have the department look into him for anything, especially with all the other shit he had going on.

Bart always had a plan and a backup plan, and even a backup to his backup plan. He didn't want to keep the files in his apartment because he still didn't know exactly what the department had found in Lupo's place. No one would tell him since it was an "ongoing investigation." If they found any evidence at all indicating Lupo knew the Star Killer or was somehow in contact with him, they certainly would look at Lupo's partner, Bart. They might even have the nerve to search Bart's apartment, but allowing a murderer to continue brutalizing women was not an option.

Bart had hidden some of the boxes in the apartment next door. It belonged to a man named John Wiley. He was a professor who was in London for one year teaching a seminar on Orwell, or maybe Dickens. Bart couldn't remember. He had left a key for Bart in case of an emergency, so Bart hid Lupo's boxes in Wiley's bedroom closet, safe from the department and anyone else.

Bart knew he needed to go through them while he had extra time on his hands. He had put it off as long as he could, and the clock was ticking. The professor would be gone for only four more months, and even more urgent than that, it was only a matter of time before the Star Killer chose his next victim.

The Star Killer had been quiet in the city for the past few years, which most likely meant he was murdering women in another part of the country. Bart knew what he was jeopardizing by becoming a co-conspirator, and with his pending forced retirement, it was a lot to risk. How could he turn a blind eye, though, when all of this information was within his reach?

He grabbed the key hanging on a single key ring next to his door, walked out of his apartment, and went to Wiley's. He walked straight to the bedroom where he had hidden the boxes, grabbed as many as he could carry—only two because they were nearly overflowing—and walked back to his apartment. He began rummaging through the first box. After three hours, he had developed a system: find documents he believed were pertinent, place them to the side in the pile that would go back into the box, and put the irrelevant documents on the other side in a pile that would be taken downstairs to the furnace.

It was appalling how much information the boxes contained. Lupo had videos of the guy, license plate numbers, and a dozen different addresses. It was everything an investigator would need to know about a suspect, which made it even stranger that Lupo kept it all a secret. What was he planning on doing?

Bart found documents stating the Star Killer took a souvenir from each woman he killed—a detail the department was entirely unaware of. He always took a lock of hair, but on other occasions, he took panties, car keys, pictures, or even the victim's driver's license. It was bizarre. Lupo was sure the Star Killer was keeping all the souvenirs close by. He had planned to break into his apartment and find them, but he was a fuckup and couldn't stay sober long enough to do it.

After hours of weeding through papers, Bart finally saw the information he had feared he would find. It was a picture of a man with a name and residential address scribbled on the back. Before he died, Lupo had explained to Bart that he had a picture of the Star Killer and his fingerprints. Lupo knew his real name and where he lived. Bart wasn't sure if he completely believed Lupo, but the evidence was sound and right before Bart's eyes. Something was missing, though—the smoking gun.

Bart had no verification that the person in the picture was indeed the Star Killer, but somehow he knew it was. It was his greatest fear. He could see his face and the malevolent look in his eyes. It was chilling. And now he had no more excuses. He had to decide. Murder the Star Killer or let him continue to slaughter women. There was only ever one option for Bart. He could never live with himself if he saw that face and didn't do anything about it.

Bart took several trips to the furnace downstairs and burned everything except for the picture with the address and the set of fingerprints with the name Renee Angler marked by the Chicago Police Department. When he got back upstairs to his apartment, Bart pulled the back panel off of the television in his living room. It had stopped working eight months earlier, but he never watched it, so he hadn't bothered getting a new one. He placed the photograph in the back and snapped the plastic cover back on.

The constant urge to meet Angler face-to-face was always in the back of Bart's mind. He wanted to see Angler's face one time before he assassinated him, but that was out of the question. Angler knew what Bart looked like, and if he caught so much as a glimpse of him, Angler would be gone in an instant. Bart couldn't risk that. Someone else would have to observe Angler's daily routine.

Bart put on his coat, grabbed his cowboy hat, and walked down to the parking garage. He opened the passenger side door of his car, pulled Lupo's burner phone out of his glove compartment, and did the one thing he thought he never would.

CHAPTER 11

MONEY AND POWER

Cassandra waited at the side door while Anthony pulled the black SUV around to the house; she had an appointment in Manhattan with the editor of People to discuss her serial killer article. When they arrived at the restaurant, Anthony got out and opened the door. Cassandra exited the vehicle.

"I have a three o'clock appointment only a few blocks from here, so if you want to take a break and relax, I will shop a little bit and then just walk there."

He smiled. "No, that's fine. I'll be here when you come out."

Cassandra entered the restaurant and immediately spotted Wanda Weitz's signature brown bob at a table across the room. She was always dressed exactly as you would expect the editor of one of the top magazines to dress. That day, she was wearing a tweed dress with three gold buttons extending from the collar to her waist. The hem fell just below her knees, where her fabulous black leather boots began. They had just enough of a heel to make her look established and intimidating without crossing the line and looking like a streetwalker.

Cassandra waved and headed toward the table. Wanda stood up, and they hugged before sitting down.

"How are you?" asked Wanda.

"I'm doing great. Just busy as usual."

They bantered back and forth a bit about traffic and the weather before Wanda anxiously asked how the article was coming along.

"I finished it, but I'm waiting to interview a detective who seems to be the expert on serial killers."

"That's great!" said Wanda excitedly. "Do you think you'll get the interview soon?"

"I hope to have it within the next few weeks, but if not, I can finish the story without him. I think something big is going on with serial killers in the tristate area, but I don't have any proof. However, my sources are telling me this one detective seems to show up at every homicide involving a woman in the city."

"Who is this detective?"

"If you've been watching the news, you would know that a few months ago, a detective got involved in that hostage situation."

Wanda laughed. "The Wyatt Earp–looking guy in the cowboy hat?"

"Yes, that's him." Cassandra laughed. She wasn't the only one who thought he resembled Earp. "He's been popping up all over the place. It's bizarre. And from what I hear, some shady stuff is going on. I think the department is trying to keep it a secret."

"Interesting," said Wanda. "I can try my sources at the department. Between the two of us, we'll see if we can find out what's really going on."

"I think for the moment I should just work things out on my end. I'm afraid if we start asking too many questions, he's going to get spooked. I'll never have a chance to talk to him."

"Now seems like a perfect time for us to get this article out there, and sooner would be better than later," said Wanda. "With that serial killer in Europe and everything going on in the Northeast, people are fascinated with these stories right now."

"I agree. I just need a little bit longer, I promise."

They ordered their lunch, and as they were eating, Cassandra decided it would be as good a time as any to break the news she had been dreading. She took a large sip of her water and began. "Wanda, I've been thinking a lot, and I believe this will be the last article I will write. I need to focus on the foundation. Next year, the net worth of the foundation is expected to grow considerably, and it will require much more of my attention."

"Well, I'm sorry to hear that, Cassandra, but I do understand how important your work is to the community. As a matter of fact, if you have time, I would like you to talk to friends of mine who have just begun a charity and need money."

"Not a problem. Just give them my name and phone number, and we can talk."

After a few moments, Wanda broke the silence.

"How is everything else in your life going? Have you had any time for dating?"

Cassandra grinned. "Mr. Right seems to be Mr. Wrong most of the time." She sighed. "It seems most of the men I run into are real losers." They both laughed.

Cassandra asked in return, "How is your life going, Wanda?"

"Since the wedding, my husband and I seem busier than we've ever been, but it's going very well. Marital bliss," Wanda said with a smile and a slight eye roll.

Once they finished their lunch, they politely declined dessert from the handsome waiter and got their check. Before they left, they gave each other a hug and said their goodbyes.

"I'll be in touch very soon," Cassandra said before walking out of the restaurant and onto the sidewalk.

It was bitterly cold, but Cassandra thought she could get some shopping done before her next appointment. She saw a small shop with a beautiful navy dress and blazer in the window and stepped inside. Just as she entered the door, her phone rang. She looked at the number. It was Donnie Ward.

She answered. "Well, I haven't heard from you in a long time."

"No. I'm sorry. We have been really busy," he replied.

"I know. I saw you on TV the other day. Seems like you and your partner are busy saving the world."

"About that," said Donnie. "That issue has created some problems for us. I need some advice from you if possible."

"What can I do for you?"

"I think it's best if we meet in person. I'd rather not talk about it on the phone."

"Okay. When would be a good time for us to meet?"

"Anytime. You just tell me."

"Well, I've got some free time right now. We could meet in front of the Plaza Hotel if you aren't busy," suggested Cassandra.

"I'm free. I'll head that way."

"Great. See you soon." She hung up.

It was nearly two o'clock, and Cassandra was waiting in the foyer of the Plaza. Donnie walked in, and they shook hands.

"It's been a long time since we worked in Brooklyn," said Donnie. They walked inside the lobby, where small tables nestled against the walls. They both sat down. A waiter walked over and asked if they wanted menus.

"Just a coffee for me," said Donnie.

"Sparkling water, please. No menu," said Cassandra.

Once the server was out of sight, Donnie got straight to the point.

"This hostage situation we got involved in has created some problems for us. Internal affairs is going to refer the issue to the police commissioner."

"What does that have to do with me?"

He smiled. "Well, you once told me if I ever need any help, you might be able to put in a good word."

She looked at him. "I can probably put in a good word with the right people, but it has to stay between you and I."

He nodded. "I completely understand, but I believe this is going to happen sooner than later."

She smiled. "No problem. I can make a call today, but I want something in return."

"What's that?"

"I want my interview with your partner. I contacted you and him at least five times and got no reply."

"I'm sorry. He's a stubborn bastard, and he doesn't like the press—doesn't trust them—but I'm sure he'd be willing to do the interview, especially considering what a huge favor you'd be doing for us."

"Great. So, how would we do this? Legally, I can't pay him, and if he's that reluctant, then how can I trust he will show?"

"Do it as a date. I mean, you're both single, and you might even end up enjoying each other's company. In return, he'll give you the interview. That's your best shot."

"Okay. So, what do I need to know about your partner?"

"Not too much. He's a straight shooter. When he tells you he'll do something, you can count on it. We have had issues with the press in the past, and that's why he doesn't want to talk with you. Of course, you realize any interview cannot include ongoing investigations."

"Of course," she replied.

They got up and shook hands.

"I will have him call you, but I think as far as discussing this other issue, we need to not do it over the phone," said Donnie.

Cassandra replied with a smile, "It's as good as done. You will have his favor."

"Thank you, Cassandra," said Donnie before walking away.

As Cassandra left the hotel, Anthony pulled up, got out, and opened the back door for her.

She got in. "You know where my three o'clock appointment is. I probably need to get there before I'm late."

"Don't worry. I'll have you there in time," said Anthony.

As Anthony drove to the next appointment, Cassandra took out her phone and called her father.

"I need to talk to you tonight," she said. "I'll be home at about six o'clock. I need a big favor, and it's important."

CHAPTER 12

UNDERCOVER

Bart's cell phone rang just before 6 a.m. He reached his arm across the bed to his nightstand and felt around until his hand made contact with his phone. He picked it up and answered.

"Hello?" he said wearily.

"Good morning, handsome."

He immediately recognized Maria's voice. "Good morning—it's a little early," he said, still half asleep.

"I was just thinking about you, so I thought I would call."

"You were just thinking about me?"

"Yes, I was just lying here—naked—and wishing you were here with me," she replied seductively. "I don't suppose you have some time off to fly to Miami?"

"This isn't fair. The first time I get a chance to sleep eight hours since—I can't even remember when—and now I'm wide awake and thinking about you instead."

Bart's mind wandered back five years to the first time he saw Maria. She was managing an auto body shop in Brooklyn that was a front for a car theft ring. The business was legitimate, and she had nothing to do with the illegitimate parts, but it was the perfect setup.

The Mafia used a warehouse behind the auto body shop to strip down cars and ship parts all over the world. They also had a car order business. Someone would give them a car's make and model, exterior and interior colors, and anything else they may want, and they'd find it, steal it, change the VIN, and deliver it to the new owner. The business brought in tens of millions of dollars a month and was growing by the day.

How Bart got involved with the Mafia's car theft ring was a complicated story. The FBI and the NYPD had worked on the case for a year before they met with Bart about going undercover to infiltrate the stolen car business. The FBI had arrested one of their top dealers in Las Vegas and had flipped him so he would cooperate. Now they were planning on replacing him with someone from the NYPD. It was tricky.

They had to introduce Bart as a car thief from Las Vegas—Anthony Jordan, one of the Mob's top producers in Vegas. He was rarely seen, and he was known as somewhat of a recluse. He even had all of his earnings deposited in a bank in California, so he never had to meet with anybody. He just had to steal the target vehicles, usually high-end exotic cars, and deliver them to the drop location. Since he had no actual contact with the Mob, he thought he would be immune to any charges, but that wasn't exactly the case. The FBI arrested him for money laundering and transferring money over state lines. Since he did not want to serve serious prison time, he was willing to cooperate.

Bart's handler was Jack Curry. He was an expert in car theft and had worked in the auto theft department of the police department for years. He could steal any car and knew more about them than even the most esteemed car enthusiasts. His job was to train

Bart how to steal cars, strip them down, and transfer the funds once they were sold. While he was a great source of information, his main advice to Bart was to be careful. Even in a city of eight million people, as soon as Bart went undercover, he might start running into everyone he knew.

"When this happens," Jack advised, "you have two options: either exit the area quickly before they see or talk to you or stop them before they mention your name."

On Bart's first day undercover, he showed up to find the man in charge. He walked into the body shop business by mistake and asked for Frank. That was when he met Maria. There was an undeniable attraction between the two of them. She was beautiful and charming, and her friendly demeanor won over everyone who met her.

"I think you're in the wrong building. Frank is in the building behind us," she said with a striking smile. "If you can't find him, come back. I'll be here," she added as Bart was walking out the door.

Over the next two years, Maria was the only sense of comfort Bart had. He couldn't talk to his friends or family, but Maria always felt familiar to him, and he enjoyed the time they spent together. Although there was nothing stating their relationship was forbidden and no one in the car theft ring would care, Bart kept their meetings very clandestine. He knew at some point things would blow up and everyone would be arrested. Maria would be safe from the law, but not from the Mob.

Bart went over to the next building and asked for Frank Derusso. He introduced himself as Anthony Jordan. He had grown a short beard, sideburns, and a mustache to look more like Jordan, but if anyone knew Jordan and met Bart, they would immediately know

Bart was an imposter. The FBI had assured everyone very few people knew what Jordan looked like. Bart had a valid driver's license, social security number, and birth certificate to verify his fictional identity, but not a day went by during which he didn't fear someone would find out who he really was.

Bart would sometimes make $8,000 to $10,000 a week stealing luxury cars—Maseratis, Porsches, Ferraris, and Lamborghinis—money he never reported to the police department or the IRS. Bart wasn't sure what to do with it, so he stuck it in a safe and held onto it in case someone asked about it once the operation was over, but they never did.

When Bart was interviewed for undercover work in the police academy, he never thought anything would come of it. Lieutenant Chris Rapone had interviewed Bart the first time concerning working undercover and interviewed him a second time a few weeks later. Bart had no serious no wife, no children, no serious relationship and that was a big plus in choosing him for the job. Undercover operations can often last several years, and it was difficult to find someone like Bart who was completely independent.

The undercover assignment lasted for approximately two years, and as it was just about to wind down, the Mafia associates had a meeting one morning.

"It has come to our attention that there's a rat among us," said Frank, the head of the operation.

Bart's palms were clammy. He could feel beads of sweat forming above his eyebrows. His heart sank to the floor as he prepared for what was about to happen.

"And when someone's a rat, they must be treated like a rat—handled like a rat," continued Frank.

Bart was sure it was him, and since they frisked everyone before the meetings, he had no weapon to protect himself. After all, they couldn't risk having weapons in a room full of millions of dollars. Basically, he was screwed.

After ranting and raving for a few minutes, Frank walked up to Bart. At that point, Bart had to wipe his forehead a couple of times to keep sweat from getting into his eyes. Frank, however, walked past Bart and over to a guy named Paul Watson. He reached into Watson's pocket, pulled out a .38 revolver, and struck him with it on the right side of his head. Watson stumbled and hit the ground before a couple more guys approached him. They proceeded to beat the shit out of him before dragging him out the door, throwing him in the trunk of a car, and disappearing.

Bart was conflicted. He knew he couldn't interfere and risk blowing his cover, so once the meeting was over, he drove to a phone booth a few blocks away and called 911. They never found the body of Paul Watson. No doubt he was killed and thrown in the river behind the auto body business. When Bart's handler found out what had happened, he thought it was time to shut down the operation.

The next week, they raided the whole operation and locked everyone up, including Bart. Everyone was taken to central booking, separated, and sent to Rikers Island. As soon as Bart was separated from them, he was put on another bus and taken to a different precinct, where he was debriefed for about eight hours. He then went home for the first time in two years. He shaved, and as he looked at himself in the mirror, he barely recognized the person staring back. What was he supposed to do now? When cops go undercover, they socialize by drinking or doing drugs. Bart never did drugs. Having seen what they did to others, he was very cautious. Drinking became a twenty-four-hour habit, and he knew he had to get it under control before it controlled him.

A few months later, Bart testified against everyone he had worked with in the ring, but the testimony was in closed court, with no one except the defendant's lawyers present. Most of the Mafia guys turned on each other and were sent to prison. Throughout all of it, Maria was never informed of what was happening. All she knew was that Bart, or Anthony Jordan, as she knew him, was gone.

Soon after, Bart contacted Maria and asked her to meet him at a small bar in Queens. It was an out-of-the-way place patronized mostly by locals. Bart told Maria the truth. She was devastated he had lied to her for so long, but she was also relieved he wasn't a thief and felt she could trust him more than ever before. They continued their relationship for the next three years, keeping it hidden from prying eyes.

"Hello? Are you still there?" Bart was snapped back into reality. "Are you still there?" asked Maria again.

"Yes, I'm still here."

"So, will you visit me in Miami, or am I going to have to fly to New York to see you?"

"I'll visit the first chance I get," he replied, even though deep down inside he knew he couldn't visit her. He was painfully aware he had to cut off all contact with Maria if she was going to be protected. She was safe right now, as safe as she ever would be, and he couldn't jeopardize that.

"I love you," she said.

"Take care of yourself," responded Bart before hanging up. He tried to go back to sleep, but thoughts of Maria wouldn't allow it. He remembered the previous January, when he had taken a week off with Maria and gone to the Bahamas. She brought along a yellow two-piece bikini that she wore as soon as they arrived. Bart was coming off of four years of working eighty hours a week, and after seeing her in that bikini with her tan skin and long hair, he spent the next week with Maria, enjoying delicious food and exotic drinks. They never left the room.

He returned to New York whiter than when he left, and everyone made sure to point it out. He just replied with "It was cloudy" and an uncontrollable smile, knowing he was the only one who knew the real reason he didn't get a tan.

Finally, Bart rolled out of bed to make some coffee. The following day, he would have a date with the police commissioner, and he had no idea how it would end.

CHAPTER 13

DISCIPLINE

The next morning, Bart got a call from Donnie saying he'd meet him at the precinct at eight o'clock. They would go to the police commissioner's office together. Bart was surprised at how calm he felt. In the days leading up to the meeting, he had been full of doubt and uncertainty, but when he woke up that morning, his mind was at ease. He shaved, took a shower, put on a dark suit and dress shirt, and grabbed his cowboy hat before heading to the diner on the corner to pick up breakfast. When he walked in, Lou, the diner owner, greeted him.

"Morning, Bart. The usual?"

"Hey, Lou. Yeah, that'll be good. Thanks."

Bart was in and out within ten minutes. As he exited the diner, he noticed a black sedan idling about one hundred yards away. He could vaguely make out two occupants sitting in the front. Bart noticed it was the same vehicle he had seen when he left his apartment to walk to the diner. He thought it might be internal affairs or even the Star Killer. There were several different possibilities, but he wasn't really worried about it at that moment. He had a meeting to get to.

He turned the corner and walked toward the underground garage where his vehicle was parked. As soon as he entered the garage, he stopped and hid behind a concrete stanchion, waiting for the black sedan to follow him in. It didn't. Relieved, he got in his car and began driving downtown.

When Bart arrived at the precinct, he offered Donnie some breakfast, but Donnie declined.

"No eating at a time like this," snapped Donnie. "Our lives are hanging in the balance, and you're eating a ham and egg sandwich like it's just another day."

"You need to eat and keep up your strength. You never know; you might be in a construction job by next week," replied Bart sardonically.

Donnie flipped him the bird. "Better get going."

They walked downstairs, got in the unmarked car, and drove slowly down to One Police Plaza. As anxiety permeated the car, the space between them got quieter. Most of the discipline the police commissioner meted out was interoffice. Officers were notified by mail as to the outcome. A meeting like this was very unusual, which could be positive or negative. There was no way of knowing until they were there.

Bart and Donnie entered underneath the building. Again, they emptied their pockets, removed watches, belts, and guns, and walked through security. It seemed like they had just been there for the meeting with internal affairs. Too many trips to One Police Plaza were not a good look. They walked through another security checkpoint and entered the elevator. The ride up to the fourteenth floor felt like an eternity, and Bart swore he could hear Donnie's heart pounding against his sternum. As they exited the elevator, a petite blonde woman met them, wearing a slim black skirt, a matching blazer, and a white button-up shirt underneath. She politely but seriously introduced herself as Katie Walsh and said she was the aide to the police commissioner.

"Follow me, gentlemen. I'll take you to the conference room."

They walked down the hall, around the corner, and into a large room with double doors. In the center of the room was a beautiful cherrywood table with twenty chairs methodically surrounding it.

"Please have a seat. The police commissioner is running a little bit behind this morning, but he will be with you as soon as possible." She motioned to a smaller table in the corner. "Help yourself to refreshments while you wait."

The last thing Donnie needed was to sit there and fret about worst-case scenarios. His knee was tapping up and down like a jackhammer, and he was moving around in his chair as if his pants were on fire. Bart was tempted to say something to him, but he was hoping Donnie could hold it together long enough to get through the meeting. Bart also wasn't sure whether the room had cameras or listening devices, so they remained silent for the most part. He had to clear his head. The medical review board was right below, the Star Killer wasn't far away, and Maria seemed like a refuge at this moment.

After what seemed an eternity, the door opened. Two men in suits and a woman dressed similarly to Katie Walsh walked inside; behind them was the police commissioner. Bart and Donnie stood up but didn't salute since they were in civilian clothes. They weren't sure what else to do. The entire situation was awkward.

Everyone sat down, and the commissioner motioned for Bart and Donnie to sit down also. The female handed a folder to the police commissioner. He sat there for five to ten minutes and flipped through it, studying each page judiciously. Finally, he spoke.

"Okay, so we all know why we're here. The charge internal affairs has brought against you is disobeying a direct order, and from what I can tell, that's exactly what you did."

Neither Bart nor Donnie answered. They just sat there and looked at him.

"Well, would you mind telling me why you did it?" he asked after there was no response.

"It's all in the file. We already told internal affairs what happened, and that's basically the story," said Bart.

The commissioner smiled. "After looking through your file, I find it hard to believe that's the story."

Bart looked at him. "That is the story."

The commissioner looked at his three assistants and asked them to leave the room. Reluctantly, they filed out. Once it was just the three of them in the room, the commissioner looked at Bart. "I really would like the true story just between us. There aren't any microphones in here. There are no cameras, and you have my word that whatever is said in here will stay in here. I just want the truth."

Bart took a moment to gain his composure. "Commissioner, with all due respect, if the story gets out, someone will die."

The commissioner frowned at him.

"Looking at your service record, I would have to say you're quite a hero. I don't think you would throw away your years of service without a good reason. What I'm going to do as a punishment is admonish you and warn you not to do something like this again."

And that was it. He stood up and smiled. "You have some good friends who think very highly of you, and I hope we never meet under these conditions again."

He turned and walked out of the room. Just like that, it was over. There was no real punishment, no threat to their careers, and no fuss.

Katie Walsh appeared at the door. "Right this way, please," she said as she walked them toward the elevator. Bart and Donnie got in and rode to the ground floor in silence. They walked outside, got in the car, and just looked at each other, speechless at what had just happened.

Finally, Bart spoke. "That woman you talked to—Cassandra—she must have some juice down here for us to walk out with no punishment. I'd like to thank her in person sometime."

As they drove away, Donnie glanced at Bart. "You'll get a chance to thank her. You have a meeting with her soon to do those interviews she wants. Try not to fuck it up—the way things have been going for you, it wouldn't hurt for you to have friends in high places."

CHAPTER 14

VOICE OF A KILLER

Calling the Star Killer was one of the most difficult decisions Bart ever had to make, but he knew the DA could not get an indictment with the small amount of evidence he had. Bart had no other option. Even if he tried to meet with the Star Killer to gather information, it could never be legitimized due to how he learned the killer's identity. There was no way to win. The more prominent concern was that if he took the information to the district attorney's office and they didn't act on it, he'd be unable to kill the Star Killer himself. At that point, it'd be far too obvious.

This whole operation was so far out of Bart's wheelhouse that to say it made him extremely uncomfortable was a substantial understatement. Many things could go wrong if he contacted the Star Killer. He could record their conversations or take pictures. The department could be tapping Bart's phone and hear their conversations, or even worse, tapping the Star Killer's phone and hear him talking to Bart. What else could he do? Everything about the situation screamed "stay away," but Bart knew he couldn't.

For the past few years, the Star Killer didn't appear to be very active in the New York area—at least not that anybody knew about. Since he was so meticulous, it was possible there were women whose bodies were never discovered. He was the type of murderer who, if he made even the slightest error that could compromise his anonymity, would find a way to dispose of the body so no one would ever find it.

Bart tried to push the thoughts out of his mind, but deep down he knew the only way to end the Star Killer's reign of destruction was to get rid of him once and for all. There was no other way to approach it. The only other option was to sit back and watch him continue what he was doing. As Bart stifled thoughts of murder, another point entered his mind—the dark sedan he had seen outside his apartment before the meeting with the police commissioner. It was not the usual unmarked police car—that he was sure of—but if it wasn't the police, who could it be?

Bart got Lupo's phone out of its hiding place in the back of the TV. The only time he took it out was to charge it. He walked outside and dialed the number from which the killer had previously called him. It rang five or six times. Bart began to suspect it had been a burner phone or he'd get voicemail. What would a murderer's outgoing message sound like? Then he heard a click.

"Well, it's good to finally hear from you. I had almost given up. You must be really desperate to call me," said the voice on the other end.

Bart was surprised at how calm he sounded. It was the kind of voice heard on self-help cassettes people listen to while they sleep, hoping they'll wake up and all their problems will have disappeared overnight. It was not the voice of a monster who tortures and brutally murders innocent women.

"Trust me, it's not something I'm happy about, but I want to work out a deal with you," replied Bart.

"You're not going to work anything out with me. I'm in charge, and I decide what happens. It's strange you called me at this time because I have been gone for a few years except for the bitch the other night, but I've been thinking about starting up business in New York again."

"Oh, lucky us. I don't suppose there's anything I can do to talk you out of this."

"Lupo learned you can do nothing to control me. I decide who dies and who doesn't."

"Did you ever meet with Lupo?" asked Bart.

"What do you think?"

"I wouldn't be surprised. You and Lupo had some unusual shit going on."

"Well, I want something from you, and if I don't get it, I'm going to start making my way through the city again—one dead bitch at a time."

"What could you possibly want from me?"

"I want you to go away and leave this alone. I don't need you poking around making trouble for me, even though I know you aren't smart enough to catch me."

"I know you're going to find this strange, but I really don't care what you want. Maybe Lupo did. I don't give a shit—and let's be clear about something. If I ever get the chance, I will end this thing."

"Trust me. You won't get the chance. Do yourself a favor and leave me alone."

"I know you keep souvenirs of your victims. When I put you in the ground, I will keep a souvenir for myself," threatened Bart.

"Fuck you," said the killer, and then nothing. The phone was dead.

Bart hung up, went back upstairs to the apartment, and put the phone in the back of the TV. The thought of killing the guy kept running around in his head because he knew it was the only thing he could do. It was kind of ironic. He had become a cop in order to help people and enforce the law. He was now in a position where he might have to kill someone, all because there was no way in hell he could get a conviction. Why the hell did Lupo talk to that sick fuck? What was he trying to accomplish? Why was he gone for a few years? When Bart took a step back and looked at himself, he felt like he was becoming Lupo—no wife, no kids, no friends, no one to whom he could tell what was going on. He was beginning to worry.

CHAPTER 15

ANSWERS

The following week, Cassandra decided to work from home instead of going to the foundation's headquarters. When she remodeled her house, she and her father spent a significant amount of time designing it, including a comfortable office. She wanted to recreate her father's study and the warmth and safety she felt every time she sat on his soft leather couch, discussing various topics with him—sometimes so late she would drift off and end up sleeping there. Cassandra realized she would be the face of the foundation for years to come, so comfort was important to her. As she often did, she looked around at her beautiful home and deep down inside wished she had someone to share it with, but at the moment that dream was nowhere within sight.

The meeting with Detective Sullivan was soon, and Cassandra knew nothing about him. If she was going to use him as a source in her article, she needed to find out a little bit about his background. She had a one o'clock meeting with their accountants in the city, but she kept the morning open to meet with Anthony and discuss Detective Sullivan. If anyone could dig up dirt on this guy, it was Anthony.

Right on cue, at 9 a.m., Anthony knocked on the door before walking in. He had papers in one hand and a Styrofoam cup of coffee in the other. He seemed more excited than usual for this time of day, especially before he finished his coffee.

"I've got some good information on your buddy," he blurted out almost immediately after they exchanged their morning pleasantries.

"That's great," said Cassandra with a smile, and it really was because she had had no luck finding any information.

Anthony sat down across from her desk. "Where do you want me to begin?"

"Just give me everything you have."

"Bart Sullivan was in the military for four years. He spent a few years in Oklahoma working on a horse ranch—apparently, he loves horses and the Western lifestyle, ergo the cowboy hat he's always wearing. I could only find out that as soon as he graduated from the academy, he went undercover for a couple of years. All of the work he did during this time seems fairly well hidden. I couldn't find any specifics about what he did or what he worked on, but it had something to do with a nationwide auto theft ring.

"After the undercover assignment, he became a detective. He was assigned to a 'major case squad,' which seems to be code for an operation that deals with murdered women and serial killers. He was assigned to work with Detective Lupo, the resident alcoholic. Lupo apparently was nuts. He was obsessed with serial killers—so obsessed it led him into a downward spiral of booze and conspiracies. His wife left him and took his children with her, and he ended his life because of it all."

Cassandra interrupted, "You mean he killed himself?"

"It seems that way. The big mystery here is Lupo was working on some serial killer case that no one seems to know anything about.

The killer operated mainly in the Northeast and for a long time in New York. Apparently Sullivan was smart enough to gather as much information about the serial killers from Lupo as he could, so it seems now he is the preeminent expert in serial killers. He seems to be a good guy and an extremely active policeman. He has a little trouble with the rules but is so good at his job that it doesn't matter much. He also seems very popular with the ladies."

Cassandra looked up from taking notes and looked at Anthony. One of her eyebrows was slightly elevated.

Anthony laughed. "Let me tell you a story."

"If it's about his dating conquests, you can spare me. I don't think that information is relevant to the article."

"Trust me. I think you'll want to hear this."

"Okay, then. I'm listening."

"It seems that, as a favor for some politician—probably the mayor—your detective went to the Bahamas in search of one of the mayor's constituents, a rabbi in Brooklyn searching for his daughter. His daughter and her husband disappeared while on their honeymoon. The Bahamian police were not much help, so they talked your friend into going down there and investigating. It was done strictly on his own time. I would assume they paid his airfare, but he and his partner went down there and discovered the daughter and husband had been murdered. This is the kind of guy you are dealing with—nothing is out of bounds for him, and he'll do anything he thinks is worthwhile."

Anthony paused his story to clarify. "But, Cassie, let's be clear—a lot of this information is secondhand. I mean, I had to pay people—bribe them, beg them for information. How much of it is accurate? I don't know, but it certainly paints a picture of a guy willing to go the extra mile for a good cause."

"Certainly seems so."

"Now here's the bombshell. I don't know how much of this is true because, again, it was secondhand and thirdhand information. You asked me why this guy would go out to Queens and get involved in a hostage situation without any authorization. Then he gets disciplined, and everyone is shaking their heads and wondering why. Well, I think I have the answer. Apparently, while he was undercover, he met a woman named Maria Passenti. Keep that name in mind. He actually should've gotten a medal, but instead he gets disciplined."

"Right. None of it makes sense," said Cassandra.

"Well, here's the interesting thing. Do you remember one of the hostages was a ten-year-old boy? Guess what the boy's name is. Juan Passenti. I think you have your answer as to why he did what he did."

Cassandra's green eyes widened. "Are you telling me he risked his life and his career to help some mystery woman? Who is she? What's his relationship with her?"

"That's the big question. Nobody seems to know. I hear they had an ongoing relationship, but there's no actual proof. No one's ever seen them together. I don't know what to say."

"Wow," replied Cassandra. "That's unbelievable that somebody would risk their life and career for love, especially this guy. He doesn't seem like a hopeless romantic. Almost the opposite, actually."

"I didn't say it was love. I don't know what's going on with the two of them or even if something is going on, but it's an awful coincidence that he knows this woman, her son is kidnapped, and all of a sudden, he shows up to save the day."

Cassandra thought for a minute. "I can't get beyond the fact that he put himself out there for nothing. There's got to be more to the story."

She paused again, as if waiting for Anthony to disclose more, but he was silent. "Okay, well, now let me tell you what I found out. Apparently, he and his partner respond to all female homicides that fit the MO of serial killers—one specifically. In other words, if someone is murdered by a spouse or during a robbery, they are not called. It has to be very specific homicides. I also found out he has been injured a number of times. From what I can tell, he's been shot, stabbed, and hit by a car, and he was in a building explosion while saving a baby from a fire. I mean, who is this guy, Superman or something?"

"I don't know, but I'm definitely intrigued," said Anthony.

"I am going to call his partner to see if I can pump him for info on what he likes and dislikes. Maybe if I hit topics he's interested in, he'll open up more in the interview."

"Okay, if you think you've got enough information to meet with this guy—and I think you do—I'll pick you up at noon and take you into the city. I've got errands to run anyway."

"Thank you, Anthony. As usual, you've come through for me."

Cassandra's mind wandered. She had thought the meeting with Bart would be boring and nondescript, but it seemed Bart Sullivan was anything but. She had seen him on the news when the hostage situation occurred and thought he was rather handsome—like Wanda had said, a twenty-first-century Wyatt Earp. Cassandra found him compelling, but she could have never anticipated just how interesting things would get.

CHAPTER 16

EVON

Cassandra called Detective Sullivan and left a message referencing Donnie's suggestion that they meet and discuss their arrangement. She proposed dinner at the Rainbow Room Friday night at seven and then hung up. She was not comfortable calling any man and asking him on a date, but it was not a conventional situation, and Cassandra hardly considered it a date.

She wanted someplace nice and quiet—maybe deep down she was trying to impress him, but after learning everything she had learned from Anthony and doing her own research, she thought he didn't seem like a guy who would be easily impressed. She just needed him to cooperate so the interviews would be finished and her article completed. Then she could move on to running the foundation.

Choosing the Rainbow Room made sense to Cassandra—it was familiar. Her mother and father would take her there every Sunday for brunch. They would go to church in Long Island and then drive into Manhattan afterward. She ate fluffy, buttery pancakes smothered in maple syrup, and her parents always ordered the eggs benedict, with her father getting an extra side of bacon. She remembered the incredible smells, an abundance of laughter, and never wanting those meals to end. After brunch, they would go for a walk around the city, looking in the unique shops and staring endlessly at the tall buildings that seemed to reach to the sky.

Her fond memories of many years ago may have swayed her decision to invite Detective Sullivan to the Rainbow Room, but it was also an elegant location. The dining room was adorned with intricate handmade molding, chandeliers that created the perfect ambiance, and beautiful décor. Its location on the sixty-fifth floor provided the perfect view of Manhattan, and, best of all, Cassandra's mother was there, or at least Cassandra felt her presence.

Cassandra didn't remember much about her mother, but she did remember the scent of her perfume, dancing with her on various occasions, and, most of all, how beautiful she was; she always dressed like a princess, and even though her father constantly told her she looked just like her mother, Cassandra could never see the resemblance. She wasn't beautiful in the same way.

When Cassandra lost her mother at just eight years old, she was absolutely devastated. The world as she knew it had ended; she felt alone, abandoned, and fearful that if something happened to her father, she'd be all alone in the world. It was almost unbearable to think about.

Afterward, Cassandra was glued to her father's side, which made things difficult since he had to travel constantly for business to Europe and Asia and all over the United States. She couldn't bear for him to leave. The fear of something happening to him was paralyzing, and anytime he would try to leave her with a nanny, she would throw a fit, sobbing until she made herself sick.

After the third or fourth nanny, Cassandra's father gave in and began taking her with him wherever he went. At every new location, he would try to find a nanny, which was a daunting task on top of attending business meetings and taking care of an eight-year-old. To make matters worse, Cassandra became severely depressed and even occasionally wished she would die, just for the possibility of seeing her mother one more time.

It was about that time they traveled to Italy; her father had to meet clients who wanted him to build a high-rise in Italy. It was a small project for her father, but, in retrospect, maybe he needed something less overwhelming to get his life back on track and restore a sense of normalcy. Cassandra was so consumed by her own grief she never really understood how distraught her father was over the loss of his wife, Janet. He was broken, having lost his one true love. He could hardly function most days.

While in Italy, they stayed at the home of one of the investors in Tuscany—a beautiful villa with large rooms and a veranda with a breathtaking view overlooking rolling hills of vineyards that seemed to go on forever. They had been in Italy for only a few hours when they were introduced to a woman named Evon.

Cassandra liked Evon right away. She was young, beautiful, spoke Italian and English, and was wonderful company. Her main focus was taking care of Cassandra. The second day they were there, Evon took Cassandra into town and showed her all the little shops. They stopped occasionally and looked at jewelry, makeup, and trinkets—every girl's dream. Afterward, Evon took Cassandra to a fabulous lunch at a quaint restaurant surrounded by gardens, where she ate the best pappardelle al cinghiale she had ever tasted. For a single moment, Cassandra didn't feel so sad.

They stayed in Italy for five days, and during the course of those days, Cassandra overheard that Evon, a recent college graduate, wanted to go to America. Cassandra was unaware her father had already offered Evon a job in the States as her nanny. However, it made sense. Evon was educated, pleasant, and had great affection for Cassandra—the perfect fit.

As they were getting ready to leave, Cassandra's father told her Evon would be joining them when they returned home to be there for her while he traveled. Cassandra was not happy about being away from her father under any condition, but Evon did seem like a very nice lady and was fun to be with for an eight-year-old, so she reluctantly agreed, hoping Evon could bring some happiness to her life.

Three weeks later, Cassandra and her father met Evon at the airport. They brought her back to the house, where she settled into one of the guest rooms. She immediately adapted to their family and the American way of life, and Frank was grateful for the help. There was no question he was still struggling with his own sorrow while continuing to run the company and trying to keep his daughter happy. Cassandra didn't realize how afraid he was of losing her.

Evon became a major fixture in Cassandra's life as the years went by; she was like a second mother to Cassandra, always there to provide support and advice. Cassandra had no idea her father, now thirty years old, had fallen in love with the beautifully exotic twenty-two-year-old Italian woman. He was concerned about how Cassie would take it, especially considering how attached and protective she had become of him since losing her mother.

Cassandra heard her phone ping. Upon looking at it, she realized she had somehow missed a phone call from Detective Sullivan. She immediately called him back.

"Sullivan," he answered.

His voice was like velvet, but she didn't expect anything less—a man who looked that handsome would also sound the part.

"Hello." Cassandra's voice cracked, and she cleared her throat. "This is Cassandra D'Angelo. I'm sorry I missed your call. My phone must have been on silent."

"It's okay. I was just calling to let you know I'd enjoy meeting you for dinner Friday night. I also wanted to thank you for putting in a good word on my and my partner's behalf with your friend."

"Oh, that's no problem. My father's known him for years. Would you like to meet at the restaurant Friday? Or I can send a car for you."

"I'll meet you on the sixty-fifth floor," said Detective Sullivan.

"Great. How will I find you?"

He laughed. "I'll be the one with the cowboy hat."

CHAPTER 17

CASSANDRA'S HEART

Cassandra woke up Friday morning and was almost excited to meet Detective Sullivan that evening. This arrangement was very different than usual; most of the men she met with were business partners—financiers, bankers, developers. Detective Sullivan was an anomaly, and he intrigued her. Although she was aware this was by no means a date, she thought maybe, just maybe, she would have a good time for a change.

She had a one o'clock meeting in the city with a charity that was going to do a presentation for her and had decided that since her meeting with Detective Sullivan might run late, she would stay at their condominium on Central Park South tonight. Anthony would drive her in, take her to the meeting, and then drive her to the condominium, where she would get a car to the Rainbow Room so Anthony could go home and spend time with his family.

Cassandra always enjoyed staying at the Central Park condominium her father had bought for clients to stay at while they were conducting business in New York; it was convenient to everything and was in a beautiful location overlooking Central Park from the thirty-first floor.

Before heading into the city, Cassandra walked across the street to her father's home to discuss a new charity they were thinking of funding. He questioned her a little bit about the charity but seemed more interested in her meeting that night with the detective.

"What do you know about this guy?" Frank asked her.

Cassandra quickly went over the information she and Anthony had obtained.

Frank laughed. "He certainly seems interesting."

After inquiring about the detective, Frank once again brought up security—he was concerned, especially on nights when Cassandra would be out late alone. Even though she was using a trusted car service, he would feel better if Anthony could be with her, but that was not always the case. In January, Frank and Evon would be retired and had plans for Anthony to travel with them, so they needed to find someone who could stay with Cassandra. She understood her father's concerns and agreed that they would address the situation within the next few weeks.

To ease her father's worries, Cassandra said, "How much safer could I possibly be? I'll be out with Wyatt Earp."

"Is that what you call him?" Frank laughed before disappearing into his office. Cassandra and Evon sat in the living room and talked for a few minutes.

"Are you okay?" asked Evon. She was as beautiful as she was the day Cassandra had met her, with her olive skin, dark brown hair, and petite frame. Although she had lived in America for nearly two decades, her Italian accent was still very prominent. "You don't seem yourself lately."

"I'm fine. I just have to work my way through some things," replied Cassandra.

"I know you're frustrated with men right now. Your father told me about that banker. He was a jackass, but you can't let men like that dictate your life. You're a smart, beautiful woman, and there's someone out there for you. Right this minute, someone is looking for you like you are looking for them."

She paused for a moment, but Cassandra didn't say anything. She feared that if she spoke, the tears in her eyes would fall. She hated crying in front of people, especially Evon. She hadn't cried much since she was a young girl. She thought sometimes maybe she had used up all of her tears on her mother.

"Look at your father and me," continued Evon. "You don't think he was lonely at the time I met him? You don't think I was lonely? I had my share of bad relationships, people who had hurt me for no reason, and at times I was very bitter, but when I met your father, I realized he was a kind, loving, and caring man. I had to let go of all of those bad feelings and trust him. If you find someone whose company you enjoy, don't push them away because some fool hurt you. If you find somebody who will love you and who you love, embrace them and be happy. You deserve that."

At about noon, Anthony picked Cassandra up. She brought a change of clothes for her meeting with Detective Sullivan. Since she kept clothes at the condominium, it wasn't necessary, but she couldn't decide what to wear. Again, she knew it wasn't really a date, but still, she was nervous. Bart Sullivan was a handsome, exciting, and daring detective—nothing like the men Cassandra had dated in the past. She knew he had a reputation as a bit of a Casanova, but she hadn't been out with an attractive man who wasn't in business or banking in God knows how long, so she brought a couple of outfits with her.

Anthony dropped Cassandra off at her meeting, which was actually a luncheon—rich people love any excuse to have wine while discussing "business"—and agreed to take her clothes over to the condominium. He also said that if any supplies needed to be replenished at the condominium—coffee, wine, food—he would take care of it. She called him about three o'clock and told him she was finished. He was already waiting outside.

When they arrived at Central Park South, Anthony walked her upstairs to make sure she didn't need anything else before departing. Cassandra spent some time around the condominium leisurely—she watched some TV while she worked on a few projects and had a bite to eat. She sat down in the big, gray, cozy chair located next to the window in the living room, where she had a perfect view of a cloudy Central Park, and read a book. She didn't remember falling asleep, but she must have dozed off. When she looked at the clock, it said 5:30 p.m. She hurried up out of the chair and began getting ready.

She made sure to take her time so as not to arrive too early; she didn't want to seem desperate. While she put curlers in her long brown hair and meticulously applied her foundation, mascara, and eyeliner, Evon's words of advice kept running through her head. She hadn't realized how hurt she had been by what Tom had said about her until the tears began to form earlier that day. She had kept herself so busy she didn't have time to think about it. Evon was right. She needed to move on and stop being so guarded. She did deserve to be happy.

At a quarter to seven, Cassandra took the elevator down to the street level, where the car service was waiting for her with the driver,

Dominic, whom Anthony had set up. The restaurant was about thirty blocks away, but it was raining, and traffic was worse than usual since it was a Friday night. With each block, she got more nervous about being in the Rainbow Room with this mysterious man. Her foot kept tapping on the car floor, and despite the chill in the air, her palms were clammy. It was just about five minutes after seven when the car arrived at the skyscraper where the Rainbow Room was located. The driver brought an umbrella around to her door, helped her out of the car, and walked her to the entrance. She smiled and said, "Thank you, Dominic."

"No problem, Miss Cassandra. I'll be here when you're finished. Have a great time."

She took a moment to gain her composure, hoping the rain hadn't mussed up her hair much. She whispered to herself, "Here goes nothing," as she pushed the door open, unaware of what the night had in store.

CHAPTER 18

A VISION OF BEAUTY

At about six thirty, Bart walked out of his apartment and onto the street. It was raining heavily. It was always difficult to get a cab in New York City when it was raining, so he waited for a few minutes. A car service pulled up and dropped someone off on the corner, so he walked over to the limousine and tapped on the window.

"I need a ride down to 45th Street."

"You know I can't pick people up," replied the driver.

"You aren't picking people up. You're picking me up, and if you don't tell anyone, no one will ever know. Plus, I'll pay you cash."

"Fine, get in," said the driver.

He got in, and it was slow getting down to 45th Street. During the ride, Bart realized he had no idea what Cassandra looked like. He had been so distracted by everything going on he had completely forgotten to ask Donnie. Bart's mind drifted to all the possibilities. Maybe she'd be beautiful, and the evening could lead to something more than an interview for a magazine. Maybe he would enjoy her company and want to see her again. He snapped himself out of it. He'd never even met the woman before, and already he was planning their wedding? She could be married with kids for all he knew. Get a grip.

The driver let Bart off just around the corner from Rockefeller Center, which was about half a block away from the restaurant, but it was still pouring and nearly seven o'clock. Luckily, he was wearing his long black raincoat and cowboy hat, so his suit didn't get too wet. Bart had wondered while getting dressed whether his black suit would be nice enough for such an opulent restaurant.

As he walked up to the door, he removed his soaked cowboy hat and shook it off before placing it back on his head and walking inside. He noticed a woman standing near the elevator. She had long brown hair and was wearing a dark trench coat. Bart could barely see her, but something about her caught his attention. Perhaps it was the way she carried herself—so confident and self-assured yet elegant. The elevator door dinged, and she walked inside. He ran over and managed to squeeze inside before the doors closed.

Bart looked over his shoulder at the woman standing in the corner of the elevator. She was even more beautiful up close. Her hair fell perfectly below her shoulders and was delicately curled at the ends. Bart had never seen eyes as green as hers; they were piercing. Suddenly he realized he was staring at her, and she seemed uncomfortable, so he turned his head back toward the elevator doors.

When he looked back, he touched his hat and tipped it at her. "Good evening." What were the odds of that gorgeous woman being Cassandra?

Cassandra immediately recognized Bart from the news but could tell he didn't know who she was. She decided to keep him guessing and just smiled back. It certainly worked. For sixty-five floors, Bart couldn't stop wondering if the magnificent brunette standing behind him was his date. He couldn't help but feel somewhat embarrassed. She probably thought he was a stalker.

The elevator was full of people going to the Rainbow Room: several couples, the brunette, Bart, and a busboy. A few women stood in front of Bart, making jokes and laughing loudly. Even through their raincoats, it was easy to see they were dressed to the nines—fancy cocktail dresses with sequins and glitter all over the place. They must have been partying somewhere prior to this encounter and were feeling especially uninhibited.

A redhead in the group noticed Bart. "Hi, there. How are you?"

"I'm fine," replied Bart, tipping his hat to her.

A strawberry blonde, clearly the most intoxicated of the group, also turned around. "Is the rodeo in town?"

Bart smiled. "Not that I know of."

A brunette asked, "Do you have a date? Are you having dinner with someone upstairs?"

"Yes, I do, and I am."

"Well, do you want to ditch her and come with us? We're out on the town. We'll show you a real good time," interjected the blonde, slurring her words.

"Thanks for the invite, but I think I'll stick with my plans. You ladies have a nice evening."

The elevator ride felt like it took a lifetime. Cassandra could tell Bart was very uncomfortable with the women's attention, but at the same time, he was very polite. The elevator finally reached the sixty-fifth floor, and the doors opened. Bart waited for the ladies to exit.

Everyone except for the beautiful brunette went straight to check their coats, which were all sopping wet from the rain. The brunette walked right past the coatroom. The maître d' immediately met her and said something Bart couldn't hear. He then showed her to a table at the far end of the dining room in a small, private alcove right by the windows.

Bart was still waiting in line to check his coat when the maître d' came back with the brunette's. He immediately took Bart's coat and hat from him, walked them into the coatroom, hung them up, and gave Bart a number tag.

"Please follow me, Mr. Sullivan," said the maître d' as he led Bart toward the alcove. As they walked toward the beautiful brunette Bart had seen on the elevator, he thought to himself, this can't be happening. I can't possibly be lucky enough for this to be Cassandra.

As Bart approached the table, Cassandra stood up to greet him. She was even more stunning than before. She had decided on a sleek black long-sleeved Dolce & Gabbana dress with a conservative neckline, just low enough to reveal her collarbones but fitted enough to accentuate her lean figure. The dress barely covered her knees, and her slender legs were exposed all the way down to her black Chanel stilettos, which were adorned with diamond flower brooches.

Yet again, Bart was speechless; he stood there for a moment, captivated by her presence, before he realized she had extended her hand to greet him. He got a hold of himself.

"It's nice to meet you," he said as he reciprocated her gesture.

He sat down, still staring at her and trying to act with equanimity. After what seemed like several minutes, he looked out the window and said, "Beautiful night out there," which he immediately thought was the dumbest thing he'd ever said or heard. It had been raining all day. He was never at a loss for words, especially around women. He had dated many attractive women and was always very comfortable around them, but for some reason, she threw him off his game. He wasn't even in the stadium.

Cassandra smiled at him. "It's nice to finally meet you. It seems like I've been waiting forever to get this opportunity. You aren't an easy man to track down."

Bart replied with a smirk, "Well, if I had known we were going to meet at such a fine restaurant, I probably would've moved this along a lot faster."

As they were talking, the waiter appeared with a bottle of white wine. He poured a small amount into Cassandra's glass. She swirled it around a couple of times, smelled it, and tasted it before nodding and saying, "Thank you very much." Seconds later, a waiter appeared behind the maître d' with a glass that appeared to have scotch or rye in it and set it on the table near Bart. Cassandra raised the wineglass. "Well, here's to the beginning of a great partnership."

Bart took a sip of the brown liquor in the glass. Much to his surprise, it was Jameson Irish Whiskey. He closed his eyes and smiled. "This is just what I needed on a night like this."

"Is it so stressful to meet me?" Cassandra teased.

"Oh, no. I was talking about the weather." Bart laughed. "Meeting you is a bonus."

Cassandra blushed. Bart was much more attractive than she remembered from seeing him on television, and now he was sitting in front of her, cheeky and charming. She felt drawn to him, but for some reason, Tom the banker was making a surprise appearance in the back of her mind. The walls went up.

"Well, how do you want to work out this partnership? I need your expertise, and I need a few interviews. How do you want to go about this?" said Cassandra, shifting the conversation to business. "Donnie suggested we go on a few dates, which I will be more than glad to set up and cover the cost of since I can't legally pay you for this, and then for every meeting, you will do an interview."

"There's no need for you to cover anything. I'll be more than glad to answer any questions you have for me."

Cassandra was relieved he had agreed to do the interviews and felt pleased at the thought of more dinners with him, but she couldn't stop herself from thinking he must have some kind of an angle. People didn't do favors for nothing—especially concerning her.

Bart took another sip of his drink. "This tastes exceptionally good tonight."

"I don't know anything about whiskey, but that's Jameson Irish Whiskey."

"I can't imagine how you know I like this kind of whiskey. I have a feeling you've been talking to someone."

"I've done my homework. I thought it would be necessary if I'm going to count on you for all this information."

"So, what other information has Donnie spilled his guts about? I need to have a talk with the boy," Bart said, smiling.

Cassandra placed her napkin over her mouth and laughed at him. "No. I wanted to know what you like so I could express my appreciation for your getting involved in this venture."

Bart looked out the window. For a moment, the view from the sixty-fifth floor was breathtaking despite the weather. The millions of lights below took on a whole different expression, reflecting off the small drops of rain. It looked like the stars had descended from the sky and found a home on the buildings of New York. The city looked beautiful, but Bart knew the truth. It was anything but magical. He had seen too much. Now, though, he was sitting with a beautiful woman, enjoying a great drink and even better company.

Cassandra broke the silence. "A penny for your thoughts."

"I'm sorry. I was appreciating the beautiful view, but it doesn't hold a candle to the one across from me."

Cassandra was taken aback. She had never had a man be so candid with her, but she couldn't help but wonder whether it was all a part of his game or if he was sincere.

"I'm sorry if I'm being a little forward. I realize it, and, really, I apologize. It's just not often I'm this smitten by a woman. I'll keep it professional if you'd feel more comfortable."

"You're not what I thought you would be either. You're very different, actually."

"What exactly did you think I would be?"

"I don't know. I've heard many different things about you. It's hard to know who the real person is, but I guess I expected you to be kind of cold, and that's certainly not the case."

"It would've been easier for you to just ask me," responded Bart promptly. "I'll be one hundred percent honest with you about anything. Going forward, I'd like this relationship to be as open and honest as possible."

They sat there for a moment looking at one another. Bart was trying to take in the brilliance of the evening. This was the first time in a long time he was enjoying himself, but he had to be careful. She was a special woman—he could tell—and he wanted to make sure she didn't think she was just another notch in his belt. He liked the thought of her being around for a long time.

"Tell me about yourself," said Bart. "What makes Cassandra who she is?"

Cassandra wasn't sure whether she could tell Bart the truth. She assuredly liked him. He was handsome, funny, charming, and adventurous, and she felt safe with him, but at the same time, she was afraid of him. She didn't want to be hurt—used—again. Evon's words were revolving through her head. "Someone is looking for you just like you're looking for them." Wyatt Earp was sitting right in front of her.

CHAPTER 19

LOVE AT FIRST SIGHT

"So, you want to know about me?" asked Cassandra. "Well, I'm pretty simple. I live in Long Island near my father and stepmother, and I'm the head of our family's foundation. For a few years now, I've dabbled in writing short stories for different magazines, which I enjoy. Oh, and I like to go running every morning, as often as my schedule allows. If I have any free time at all, which I rarely do, I like to curl up with a good book and a glass of wine."

"That doesn't sound simple. Running a foundation must be a lot of work. Where does your mother live?"

Cassandra paused for a moment. "She passed away when I was eight. I don't really remember too much from that time, just a lot of sadness. I felt so hopeless, like my whole world was turned upside down."

"That must've been very difficult for an eight-year-old. I'm sorry that happened to you."

"Thank you. It was. For a while, I was afraid of everything. I was afraid of losing my father, of being alone, of not knowing where my mother went when she died and why. I just didn't understand. My father did everything he could to help me get through it. I think that's why I have such a close relationship with him. It seems like it was just him and I for a long time."

For a few moments, there was silence. Cassandra was lost in her memories, and Bart didn't know what to say to comfort her.

"All right, well, I told you about me," she said, breaking the silence. "Now I want to hear everything about you. Was your childhood as depressing as mine? And how did you become a detective? I want to know all the gritty details about the infamous Detective Sullivan."

He laughed. "I don't think you want to know everything. That might ruin the evening. My parents still live in Queens, in the same house I grew up in. Every kid should have had my parents; they're amazing. As an only child, I must admit, I was a bit spoiled, but I think it all worked out."

Cassandra laughed softly, and Bart continued.

"My dad is retired from the railroad, and my mother was a stay-at-home mom. She has a heart condition now, but I'm hoping we can get it corrected very soon. Let's see. What else? I joined the military right out of high school, lived in Oklahoma for a couple of years, and then became a cop."

Bart was never comfortable talking about himself to anyone, but this felt different. He still preferred hearing Cassandra tell him about her life, but hopefully there would be plenty of time for that in the future. He didn't want to seem too eager and risk scaring her off.

"You must have been very young when you went into the military," said Cassandra.

"I was seventeen."

"And why Oklahoma of all places? The truth."

"I love horses and always wanted to work out West—to get a feel for that kind of life. I never could've done that in New York, so it seemed like the logical thing to do. I had a friend from the service whose family owned a horse ranch in Oklahoma. They gave me an opportunity to work there."

Bart paused for a moment and continued. "You keep asking me to tell the truth. I promise I'll be completely honest with you, but if you want to make things interesting, let's play a little game."

Cassandra smiled. "What kind of game?"

"The truth game."

She laughed. "What is the truth game?"

"It's very simple. While you and I are learning about each other, if we have any questions that we want a really honest answer to, we pause the conversation and ask. We both get ten questions, and no matter what is asked, the other person must tell the truth."

Cassandra laughed again. "And if we don't?"

Bart replied bluntly, "Then this relationship is sure to crash and burn." He couldn't help grinning after he said it.

Cassandra considered the proposition for a minute. She was never one to lie, but the thought of him asking her anything and having to be vulnerable was frightening. After mulling it over, she answered.

"Okay, let's play, but go easy on me."

"First question: Do you enjoy being the head of your family's foundation? Is that something you want to do or do you like writing more?"

"I do enjoy writing. It's kind of a hobby for me, but I have to focus on the foundation this year because it's going to grow considerably. I have to give it my full attention."

"You didn't really answer my question. Do you enjoy it?"

"I enjoy the fact that I can help people in need—families who have lost their homes, children who are sick—and fund research for diseases not yet cured. That's a good feeling, and it keeps my mother's ideals alive. Now I have a question for you."

"Shoot," said Bart.

"Why did you get involved in that hostage situation a few months ago? It was completely out of your jurisdiction, and it seemed like the NYPD had it handled."

Bart thought for a moment, careful not to say anything that could put Maria in danger. After all, he was technically talking to a reporter. "The best I can tell you is I owed someone a favor—someone who has been really good to me for years—and the only way I could repay them was to save those hostages. I almost didn't have a choice. I need to know you will not write about our discussions of these topics. I could get someone in a lot of trouble by divulging this information, so I need your word that you won't mention this in any articles you're writing."

"You can trust me," said Cassandra. "Anything I write about, I will let you preview. The article is about serial killers anyway, so this information isn't relevant. Still, you have my word. Does this have anything to do with Maria?"

She looked for a reaction. Although Bart was shocked Cassandra knew who Maria was, his expression never changed.

"Maria was part of what happened, but for her safety, I can't get into details," said Bart, his demeanor still calm and collected.

"You said you would be a hundred percent honest with me," said Cassandra.

"I am being a hundred percent honest with you. The information I gave you is more than I have or would ever give anybody, but I have to be careful talking about this since it involves someone's life."

"Did you love her?" she asked.

His expression was unwavering. "No, I didn't, but I do care for her."

"Did she love you?"

Bart nodded, then quickly changed the subject. "I have one more question for you."

"Okay," she said.

"Are you in a serious relationship with anybody?"

Cassandra took a sip of wine in an attempt to stall. She hadn't expected him to ask that and was a bit caught off guard. First, it was very forward, which she wasn't accustomed to. Second, why did he want to know?

Finally, she answered. "No, I'm not."

Bart looked at her and said with a big smile, "I realize this is a stupid question, but how is it possible that someone as beautiful, smart, and kind as you has not been swept off her feet by now? I'm sure there are a million guys out there who would give anything to be with a woman like you. I know I would."

If only he knew about all the losers she had had to date, he surely wouldn't be asking such an obvious question.

"I think my radar is a little bit off. Every man I date seems to be an idiot. I could ask you the same thing. You're twenty-nine years old, good-looking, and seem to be quite an exciting character, and yet you're still single."

Bart laughed. "I've been looking for the right woman for a long time. I've come pretty close but finding her seems to be a full-time job lately."

"Who is the right woman? And how will you know it's her?"

"I'll know her when I meet her. There is no question in my mind," he responded with a cheeky smile.

"Well, if you're so confident you'll know, then you must know what she looks like."

Bart looked out the window into the dark night with all the lights sparkling in the rain. "Look at that window."

"I'm not sure what I'm looking for. I see a lot of rain and lights and cars below."

He repeated himself. "Look at the window."

Cassandra sat there, staring out the window. "I'm confused."

"That's because you're looking through the window and not at it."

Again, she looked at the window and then back at him, perplexed.

"See the reflection? That's what she looks like."

Cassandra was still facing the glass and again was completely caught off guard. Bart could sense she was a little uncomfortable.

"Why do you seem unnerved every time I tell you you're beautiful?" he asked. "Surely men tell you that all the time. Is it me saying it, is that the problem?"

Cassandra couldn't speak. All she could do was think about all the questions Bart was asking her that she wasn't sure how to answer and all the things he was telling her that she didn't believe were true.

Finally, she spoke. Her voice was soft and slightly wavering. "You know how everyone has a view of themselves growing up— in middle school, high school, college, sometimes even earlier than that? Well, my view was that I was never beautiful. I wasn't a cheerleader. I wasn't blonde or popular. I didn't spend my weekends at parties or with friends. I was the smart girl. I guess I still feel like that young girl who never got asked to dances, or on dates, or anywhere, really. I just—" Cassandra abruptly stopped speaking, embarrassed at spilling her deepest insecurities to a man she had just met.

"If you're not comfortable with me telling you you're beautiful, I'll stop, but I'll be honest with you. I mean it. It's not just something I'm saying."

Cassandra sat in a daze. She had longed to hear all of the things Bart was saying to her for a long time, but she couldn't help but be skeptical. Some men would say anything to get what they wanted, and she needed a way to be sure Bart was genuine. It wasn't going to be easy.

CHAPTER 20

FINDING THE TRUTH

Cassandra had revealed more about her life to Bart in a few hours than she had told anyone in years. Perhaps it was the two glasses of wine, or maybe he was just that easy to talk to. She couldn't tell which it was, but she was having such a wonderful time that she really didn't care.

He always managed to bring the conversation back around to Cassandra; she felt like she had hardly had a chance to get to know him yet.

"I have a question for you now," she said. "Tell me about the Bahamas and how you went there to help out a friend of the mayor—a rabbi, I think it was."

Before Bart could answer, a waiter appeared with a vibrant antipasto. He placed it on the table and walked away without saying a word. Bart took one look at it and said, "Well, this certainly looks good."

"I hear it's one of your favorites."

"Like I said before, I will have to have a long talk with the boy," Bart said, unable to control his expression. He couldn't remember the last time he had smiled so much.

He offered to help Cassandra put salad on her plate, but she politely declined.

After taking a couple of bites, Bart spoke again. "I don't know what you heard about the Bahamas, but it was actually Ocho Rios in Jamaica, so you may need new sources."

She laughed. "It's hard to keep up with all of your stories. Please tell me about it."

"Well, technically, that's not a question, but since you put it so nicely." He paused in preparation, like an actor getting into character to perform the climactic scene of a film. "Well," he began. "It all started when we were asked to do a favor for these desperate people who had lost their daughter. She and her husband went to Jamaica on their honeymoon and disappeared. The police there were having very little luck, so a go-between approached us and asked if we would try to find answers.

"I can't imagine losing a daughter like that and not knowing what was going on, so we went. It wasn't easy; the police were pissed we were there, but it didn't take us long to figure out the couple had gone for a bike ride in the mountains. They had rented motor scooters and disappeared. Strange people live in the mountains—you won't believe this, but there are headhunters up there.

"No question—they were kidnapped and killed. It was difficult to tell the parents what happened. I don't think it gave them any closure since we never found the bodies. But there's no doubt in my mind they were murdered."

"Wow," Cassandra said. "That reminds me of the hostage situation. Why would you take a risk like that, especially for people you don't know?"

"As I said, I can't imagine losing a child that way and having no answers. It was something I felt I could and had to do."

"Because Maria is in love with you? How does she not end up getting hurt in all of this?" Cassandra was surprised at herself. She sounded like a jealous girlfriend. She convinced herself she wasn't jealous, just genuinely concerned for Maria, not that it made her feel any better.

"She lives far away now. It's safer for her and her son, and that's where she belongs."

For a moment, there was silence. Bart couldn't tell whether Cassandra was upset, although she had no reason to be.

"I think you can hurt people even more if you string them along and are not honest with them," he said, breaking the silence. "She's in a good place right now."

Cassandra quickly replied, "And are you in a good place right now?"

"At this moment, I'm in a great place," said Bart. "I'm here with you, having great food and drinks in this stunning place. What more could I want?"

This was the first time in a long time Bart wasn't haunted by the Star Killer or worried about the medical review board; he was just in the moment. Bart was surprised by how comfortable he was with Cassandra. She was warm, understanding, funny, and, of course, absolutely beautiful; it was a breath of fresh air compared to the chaos of the past five years.

Cassandra said, "If we're going to make this work, I need to know what you like to do so I can plan future meetings and dates and get interviews out of you. Like I said earlier, the department won't allow you to accept payment, so it's only fair I reward you with great dates."

"Well, like I said earlier, you don't have to do anything. I'd be more than happy to do the interviews and enjoy your company."

She smiled. "That's very kind, but I think we can accomplish both things—spend time together and have some fun dates while I finish the article." She looked pensively at Bart. "Okay, spill the beans. What do you like to do? What does the famous Detective Sullivan do on his time off?"

Bart laughed. "For the past five years, Donnie and I have worked eighty hours a week. Have you ever worked eighty hours a week?"

"Not that I can remember, and I think I'd remember a week like that."

"Well, when you work eighty hours a week for five years, you have no life. You work and eat and sleep whenever you get a chance—basically, you're a zombie."

"How did you manage such a colorful dating life when you could barely get anything done?"

He laughed again. "I'm warning you this is extremely embarrassing, but the last date I went on was dinner and drinks followed by a Broadway show at which I fell asleep fifteen minutes into the show."

Cassandra let out a loud belly laugh. "That must've made that woman feel great."

"I know. It's embarrassing. She was not happy, to say the least." After they had both stopped laughing, he said, "I've had this ongoing dream for years—don't laugh when I tell you this—I wake up in a very dark, cool, beautiful room with clean bedsheets, and I had slept eight full hours. Pretty sad, isn't it?"

"I'm sorry. I shouldn't be laughing. I can only imagine what it's like to work eighty hours a week for so long. It has to take a toll on you. But now you seem to have some time off. Are you still working that much?"

"No. The union sued the city, and it turned into a federal lawsuit because they weren't paying us for working as much as we were. They were only paying us for working forty hours a week, so we got some money and time back. It has to be taken quickly. That's why I now have a lot of time on my hands."

Bart felt guilty for telling Cassandra only part of the truth, but he was concerned his injuries and the case with the medical review board might scare her off. That was a risk he wasn't willing to take.

"So, now that you have some time off, tell me what you like to do," she said.

"Well, let's see. I like sports—going to baseball and football games. I like to play golf and eat great food. And when I have time, I like to travel a bit."

"What type of music do you like?"

He grinned at her. "Well, considering the cowboy hat, what do you think?"

"I would guess country and western," she said with slight sarcasm.

"Exactly. And that's about it. Now that's not a very exciting life."

"Not an exciting life? I've never met anybody whose life is half as exciting. It must be difficult to be married to a policeman. Their spouses must worry all the time. I don't know if I could ever do that."

The evening went by so quickly that the next time Bart looked at his watch, it was three in the morning. He offered to accompany Cassandra back to the condominium. While they were riding to the condominium, he told her he would like to spend as much time with her as he could. Cassandra felt the same way, but she was apprehensive. She had been hurt many times before and was afraid of it happening again. As much as she wanted to be open and vulnerable with Bart, she wasn't sure if her heart would allow it.

"I won't be available until Wednesday. I have a baby shower tomorrow, but on Sundays, I go to church and then brunch with my parents. You're more than welcome to come."

Cassandra knew this would be a safe way of postponing their next meeting. After all, no one likes awkward church days with a family they don't know.

"I'd love that. What time should I meet you and where?" said Bart without hesitation.

She couldn't believe it. Stunned, she answered, "Ten o'clock. St. Peter's in Sands Point."

As they said good night at the door of the condominium, Cassandra was a little nervous Bart would try to kiss her, but instead he held out his hand. "I enjoyed my time with you this evening."

She blushed. "So did I."

"I'll see you on Sunday." Before he let go of Cassandra, Bart pulled her hand close to his chest and placed his lips softly on her cheek.

CHAPTER 21

CHURCH

Cassandra and her family arrived ten minutes later than they had anticipated. The church parking lot was full, but people were congregating at the entrance, so it was clear the service had not yet begun. The morning had been a fiasco trying to round up Anthony, Rose, Frank, and Evon. Frank was especially difficult to pry away from work, especially on Sundays, it seemed. Cassandra had mentioned in passing that she had invited Bart to join them for the service and brunch, but she was extremely doubtful he would show. No one made a fuss of the impromptu invitation among all the rushing around and misplacement of shoes, wallets, and car keys, which further convinced her he wouldn't come.

As they got out of the vehicle, the frosty wind blew Cassandra's hair haphazardly in her face. She anxiously looked around for Bart but couldn't see much of anything. While Anthony parked the car, Cassandra told everyone to head inside and that she would wait for him, although she was fully aware of who she was actually hoping to find.

It was nearly ten o'clock, and the service was beginning. Cassandra took one last look down the sidewalk and saw a large group of last-minute attendees walking toward her. Behind them, she spotted that black cowboy hat. Bart was already tall, and with his hat on, he towered over most people and was impossible to miss.

She smiled. He definitely had some nerve, and not because he showed up for church. He was meeting her parents, and what kind of guy willingly does that on a second date? She pulled her coat tighter around her neck and waved to him so he would see her.

"Well, hello again. Sei Bellissima," he said as he approached her and kissed her hand.

Cassandra blushed. "Grazie." She hoped he would assume her rosy cheeks were caused by the wind and not due to the fact that a painstakingly gorgeous man had just complimented her in Italian. "You look great too. Let's get inside. It's freezing out here."

They stepped inside the church. Immediately, the warmth enveloped Bart. He removed his coat and hat and looked around. It was a stunning space with ornate stained-glass windows on either side. The sound of the organ vibrated throughout the church's high ceilings, which reminded him of a castle. At the front was a carved-out spherical space where the altar was located. Behind the altar were more windows with brass-accented columns that scalloped at the ceiling between each one, and above the podium was a mural of Jesus among the clouds, surrounded by angels. Bart was speechless. He couldn't remember the last time he had been in a church.

Cassandra quickly introduced him to everyone before the priest approached the altar. "Dad, Evon, Anthony, and Rose, this is Bart. Bart, this is everyone."

They scurried to the first empty pew they saw. Frank, Evon, Rose, and Anthony entered the bench, leaving Bart and Cassandra to sit on the end. They removed their coats and passed them and Bart's hat down to an empty spot next to Frank. Cassandra could see her father examining the black Stetson cowboy hat. She smiled. She was certain the last thing Frank expected was his daughter ending up with a cowboy.

The service was extremely crowded, forcing Bart and Cassandra to sit very close on a few occasions, but neither of them minded a bit. When they held hands for prayers, Cassandra noticed Bart's hand was strong and rough and held hers gently. For some reason, she felt entirely comfortable with him. It was only their second date, and she still doubted it was even that, but he was very respectful, and she was impressed nonetheless.

The service ended, and they made their way out of the crowded church. Somehow it was colder and windier than when they had entered. Cassandra told everyone she would ride with Bart and that they would meet them at the restaurant. They all went their separate ways. Bart and Cassandra made their way to his car. He was driving his usual unmarked police car, and although it was a fairly new vehicle compared to her Range Rover, it still seemed a bit plain.

Bart started the car and said, "I apologize for the department car, but since I'm on call 24/7, I have to use it."

"It isn't a problem," she replied, slightly unnerved to be sitting in a police car for the first time—even if it was in the front seat.

They made casual conversation as they headed to the restaurant. They talked about how nice the service was, how miserable the weather had been, how they both were looking forward to warmer days. As Bart parked the car in the garage, Cassandra turned to him and looked like she wanted to say something. He sat there with the car idling until she finally spoke.

"Before we go in, I want to let you know my father might ask you some, well, unusual questions. Just humor him. He's protective."

He laughed. "I'm here to spend time with you. If I have to answer a few off-the-wall questions, that's a small price to pay, and I'll do it gladly."

Cassandra was always surprised when Bart was so candid with her. He seemed genuine and honest, and she was flattered he was so interested in spending time with her. It all just seemed too good to be true.

They entered the restaurant. She could see her parents sitting with Anthony and Rose in the back. As they approached the table, Bart noticed the seating was already assigned. Frank was sitting at the head of the table, and there was an empty chair on each side of him—one for Bart and one for Cassandra. Well played.

Bart couldn't help but chuckle to himself while he removed his hat and took a seat. Everyone made polite conversation. Anthony and Rose seemed like family, but Bart couldn't figure out what their exact relationship was to Cassandra. However, he knew he would find out with time. Frank was especially interested in Bart's job, and Bart was curious to find out how Frank went from nothing to being so successful.

Cassandra was sitting across the table, but Bart realized all eyes were on him, so he only stole a quick glance at her once or twice. He didn't want to stare, but it was difficult not to. He was mesmerized by her smile, her mannerisms, and her contagious laugh.

The food arrived quickly, considering how busy the restaurant was. Bart was relieved. He had been so nervous he had skipped breakfast and was famished, but he resisted the urge to scarf down his meal and ate like a proper human. Frank continued to ask questions about the department and various cases he had recently heard about, even after the food arrived. He also asked Bart about his hobbies and even volunteered a few details about himself, specifically his beloved car collection, which piqued Bart's interest. He had loved antique cars since he was a young boy.

Cassandra excused herself and went to the ladies' room. While she was gone, Frank took advantage of the opportunity to speak candidly with Bart.

"So it seems you're interested in my daughter."

Anthony laughed. "Frank, go easy on the boy. We don't want to scare him off already."

Bart also laughed, but he knew Frank was serious. From what Cassandra had told him, he understood how close she was to her father and how protective he must be of her, so he was cautious as to how to handle Frank's protective nature.

"Well, currently, my intentions are to spend as much time as I can with her. She's a beautiful, warm, caring, and smart woman, and I enjoy her company," said Bart, unable to control the smile consuming his face.

Anthony laughed again. "Good answer."

Bart ignored Anthony and carefully examined Frank's facial expression and body language. Being a detective, he was usually good at gauging people. In his line of work, he was constantly lied to and told half-truths. He realized quickly how people respond in stressful situations and what the slightest movements could indicate.

Frank seemed satisfied with Bart's answer, but Bart was sure Frank still had his reservations about him. Just then, Cassandra returned to the table. She really is remarkable.

"It's a good thing you're back. Your boyfriend's getting the third degree," said Anthony, still snickering. Everyone at the table laughed, including Bart and Frank. For the moment, he was in the safe zone.

Before they got up to leave, Cassandra paused. "Why don't you guys go home? Bart and I are going to spend some time together."

"What will you do?" Evon asked. "It's so cold out."

"I'm not sure. Maybe we'll find a coffee shop and get some work done on the interview."

"Since Bart likes cars so much, why don't you bring him by the house and show him your father's collection?" asked Evon with a wink. She knew exactly what she was doing.

"That may be a good idea," said Cassandra, looking at Bart to assess his reaction.

"I can show him," Frank interjected.

Evon put her hand on Frank's arm. "They want to be alone, honey. They don't need any help looking at a few old cars."

Again, the table erupted with laughter. It was quite clear Frank was the head of the household, but Evon could hold her own. They got up from the table and walked toward the exit, saying their good-byes while still in the warmth of the restaurant. They rushed to the parking garage to escape the cold, and Bart opened the car door for Cassandra. He closed it once she was inside and walked around to the driver's side.

"Do you mind looking at my father's car collection?" she asked once he was in the car. "At least it will be warm."

He smiled. "That sounds great. As long as you're there, I don't care where we go."

Cassandra was again flattered; he made no bones about the fact that he was immensely interested in her. For once, she felt secure. Finally, a man was interested in her and not her money or her father's influence.

When they got to the compound, Bart was dumbstruck by the two beautiful homes that sat on what looked like at least fifty acres of land.

"Drive that way," said Cassandra, pointing toward Frank and Evon's house. "Park by the garage doors."

Cassandra took him into the large garage where Frank kept his cars. Bart froze. He had never seen anything so incredible in his life—with the exception of the woman standing next to him.

Frank had amassed a car collection worth millions. Bart walked over to a pristine white 1948 Jaguar Roadster and encircled it in admiration. Then he made his way over to a silver 1955 Porsche Spyder.

"What a beauty," he said as he ran his finger across the hood. Bart was like a kid in a candy store; he wandered from car to car with his mouth hanging open.

"I think I made a mistake bringing you here," Cassandra said, smiling. "You may be more interested in the car collection than me."

Bart smiled back. "Trust me. These ladies have nothing on you."

Off to the side of the garage was a small office. The door was open. Bart could see it was tastefully decorated and had a bar that occupied one entire wall. There was also a small desk with two phones, a fax machine, a printer, and several pictures on it. He walked inside and surveyed the small yet comfortable space that was perfect for conducting business.

Cassandra motioned to a black leather loveseat on the wall perpendicular to the bar. He walked over and sat down next to her.

"Would you like a drink?"

Bart looked at the bar and noticed a bottle of Jameson, but he politely declined. He couldn't escape the thought of falling back into his old drinking habits.

"Suit yourself," she said as she poured herself a glass of red wine.

Again, they sat and talked. Talking to Cassandra was easy; there was so much Bart wanted to know about her, but there were also a few things he didn't want her to know about him. For now, he wanted Cassandra to know only the good things. It was the first time in his life that he was concerned with whether a woman was interested in him. There was no doubt in Bart's mind Cassandra was the woman he had been searching for. He had finally found his "one," but he was also certain there was no way she felt the same, at least not yet. He needed to take things slowly—if she knew how he really felt, it would probably scare the shit out of her, and she'd be gone quicker than they got together. After all, who would ever believe that, after just two dates, he could be in love with her? He had searched for her for most of his adult life, and now she was right in front of him. All he had to do was not screw it up.

They sat on that couch and talked until late in the night. The time flew by, and although Bart wanted to keep listening to Cassandra, it was getting late, and he needed to head back into the city.

"Let me walk you home," he suggested.

"That would be wonderful. Thank you."

They locked up the garage and began walking toward Cassandra's house hand in hand.

"I'll be at the New York Children's Hospital on Wednesday, if you'd like to join me," she said, turning her entire body to look at him. The wind had finally died down a bit, but it was still well below freezing.

"I don't have much experience with kids, but I'll give it a shot."

As they approached the door, they lingered outside.

"Well, Cassandra. I've had a wonderful time with you. Thank you for inviting me to spend the day with you and your family."

She was sure he was going to kiss her, but yet again he pulled her hand to his lips and kissed it. Before letting it go, he pulled her slightly closer and placed his lips on her cheek. He whispered in her ear. "I'll see you Wednesday."

Cassandra thought about pulling him back and kissing him on the lips, but she didn't want to seem overeager. She knew Bart was interested in her; he made that very clear, but she couldn't understand why he wouldn't make a move. Was he waiting for her to? Time would tell.

CHAPTER 22

THE CHILDREN

It was finally Wednesday. Although Bart and Cassandra had talked on the phone every day, the time could not have gone by any slower. Bart had been in his head the entire time and couldn't escape the uncertainty he was feeling. He wondered if she was as interested in him as he was in her. All he knew was his feelings for Cassandra were growing deeper and deeper, and for the first time in his life, he worried maybe she didn't feel the same way about him.

At four o'clock, Bart arrived at the New York Children's Hospital. He parked his car in the garage and walked to the elevator. As soon as he reached the sixth floor and the doors opened, he was greeted by a woman sitting behind an oval front desk. He immediately noticed her bright pink blouse and multicolored skirt.

"Hello!" she said.

Bart removed his hat. "Hello. Bart Sullivan, I'm meeting Cassandra D'Angelo."

"Yes, I know. Cassandra told me she was expecting you. I'm Beth Walker, the administrator of the children's hospital," the woman warmly responded. "She called about twenty minutes ago and said they were stuck in traffic and would be a few minutes late."

Beth walked Bart into a waiting area and told him to make himself comfortable until Cassandra arrived. The entire floor was full of colorful pictures; there were rainbows, dogs, cats, and portraits of families obviously drawn by children. It made him sad to think about a bunch of innocent children stuck in a hospital all the time instead of going to school and playing outside with their friends. Within a few minutes, two girls—around the age of seven—walked up to Bart and began asking him questions.

"Are you a cowboy?" the smaller girl asked. She had blonde, curly hair and wore round pink glasses. A small brown teddy bear was tucked underneath her right arm.

"Do you have a horse?" asked the other little girl, who was slightly taller and extremely thin. She had a rainbow scarf tied around her head.

"Where do you keep your horse? There aren't any farms in the city."

Before Bart knew it, the two girls were holding his hands and walking him over to a glass partition. About ten more children were on the other side.

"Those children are susceptible to infections and have to stay behind the glass for their protection," said Beth. Bart hadn't noticed her standing beside him. The children talked through a speaker system and asked questions that never seemed to end.

"Who are you?"

"What's it like to be a cowboy?"

"Do you have any cows?"

Bart had to laugh to himself; he could barely keep up with all of them. As he looked at the children behind the glass window, he saw they were extremely sick. Some had skin that was so pale it almost looked opaque. Others had large bald patches on their tiny heads, if they weren't entirely bald. A few needed assistance moving around, but they all seemed in good spirits. The children just wanted to act like children and meet a real cowboy, of course.

Ten minutes later, Bart was still answering questions. Several of the children were repeatedly asking to see Bart's hat up close, so he asked Beth if that was possible.

"I'll have to spray it with a disinfectant first. If that is okay with you, then it's fine."

Bart nodded. Beth took the hat, sprayed it with something, and handed it through the partition so the children could hold it. While they were taking turns passing it around and asking a hundred more questions, Bart heard a noise behind him and noticed the children's attention turn from him to whoever had just walked up.

"Hmm. Is someone behind me?" Bart asked without turning around.

They all giggled and simultaneously said, "Yes."

"Is it a beautiful woman?"

Again, they laughed and confirmed.

"Does she look mad?"

They shook their heads no.

A little boy quickly piped up and yelled, "Is that your girlfriend?"

Bart smiled. "I'm not sure at the moment, but I hope she will be soon."

He turned around to see Cassandra standing right behind him. She was wearing a mauve silk blouse with black trousers and subtle gold jewelry. Her hair was pulled up off her shoulders. Bart found himself speechless. He stood up.

"I'm sorry. I was waiting for you, then the kids came and got me. They had a lot of questions about cowboys and horses. So I figured I'd talk to them while I waited for you. I wasn't—" He was rambling. Why does she always make me so damn nervous?

"That's okay," she said, stifling any further embarrassment. "They seem to be enjoying themselves."

Cassandra waved to the children. "Hello."

They all waved back and said hello, except for the little boy, who yelled again, "Is that your boyfriend?"

"What do you think, Tommy?" she asked, smiling from ear to ear.

She leaned in to give Bart a hug, and he whispered, "Ciao, Bella, Hello, beautiful," in her ear.

All the children started giggling and synchronizing "woooooo" noises and making kissy faces at one another.

Bart looked to his left and saw Frank standing back by the door. His whole body was vibrating from laughing at the encounter.

Cassandra turned to the children. "Okay, okay." She laughed. "Settle down. I brought a very special book to read to you today—if it's okay with you."

Again, they all started shouting. "Yes! Yes!"

Cassandra sat down. All eyes were fixed on her as she animatedly read the story to the children. It was about children from all over the world and the lives they led, the dreams they had, and everything they had to look forward to. Bart found it absolutely heart-wrenching. He had no idea how sick the children in that room were, but deep down, he was sure some of them had terminal illnesses and would never live long enough to pursue their dreams. For some of them, this was all they had to look forward to—Cassandra coming to visit and bringing a real-life cowboy for them to meet. He sat quietly while she finished reading and answered their questions—all of the ones they asked before she began, after she started, and in between. The children were ecstatic, applauding after she read the final page.

"Do you think I can get a hat like his?" said a tiny voice from behind Cassandra.

Cassandra leaned down so she was at eye level with the little girl, who was wearing a purple knitted hat with a daisy on it. "I'm sure you can."

Bart found Beth and asked if she had a tape measure. "Once we finish measuring their heads and get their hat sizes, they can tell us what colors they'd like, and I'll order them if that's okay."

"That would be wonderful," she said softly.

Once the children's heads had all been measured, Beth returned. "Children, it's time for you to go down to your rooms. Say 'goodbye' and 'thank you' to the nice people."

The children all applauded and began leaving. Some of them walked away, some were in wheelchairs, and some were lying in beds that had to be pushed away.

Cassandra said to Bart, "If you'll give us a few minutes, my father and I need to talk to Beth."

"I'll wait outside," Bart began saying, but Frank interrupted.

"Why don't you come with us? It's not a big secret. We have a few things to discuss with Beth, and then we'll be out of here."

They walked into an office adjacent to the area they had been seated in and sat down. Beth sat across from them and directed her comments to Cassandra since Cassandra was the head of the foundation. "Thank you so much for all you've done."

Cassandra looked at Frank. He gave her a slight nod. "I know you have requested more money next year. My father and I are in agreement that we would like to increase our pledge from $1 million to $5 million."

Beth gasped. "Oh, my goodness. I really can't thank you enough. This is going to help so many children."

"No, it's us who should thank you for all you do for these children. We are just happy to be in a position to provide some funding."

They got up and shook hands before walking out of the conference room and toward the elevator.

"Well," said Frank, "I guess I'll head home. Anthony is waiting in the car downstairs."

The elevator doors opened, and they all stepped in. Cassandra said, "Bart and I are going to have dinner. Would you like to join us?"

"No, your mother has warned me not to hang around," he replied with a wink.

They all laughed and got out on the ground level. Frank walked toward Anthony while Bart and Cassandra walked in the other direction toward his vehicle. He was silent while they walked, his eyes fixed on the ground before them.

"I knew what you did as far as your foundation goes," he said, breaking the silence, "but seeing it up close and personal like this puts it in a different light. It's really a great thing you're doing—helping those children."

"Thank you," she said modestly. "By the way, the foundation will pay for the cowboy hats."

"It's fine. I want to buy them. It's the least I can do," Bart said, opening the car door for her.

They drove to a small, quiet bar in Midtown. Their conversation focused mainly on the children at the hospital. Afterward, they had dinner at one of Bart's favorite Italian restaurants, Volare in the Village. Just like the dates before, they talked about everything in the world. Unlike those other dates, Cassandra was finally certain that's what it was. She was growing accustomed to Bart's questions. They were always different but personal, and she liked that he was trying so hard to get to know her.

"So, when you find Mr. Right, how many children do you want to have with him?" he asked as they finished their entrees.

If Bart had asked that question over appetizers, Cassandra may have been a little more caught off guard, but since he had been more forthright than usual, she simply answered.

"Three. If possible, three. But as long as they're healthy, I don't care if it's one or ten."

He was quiet for a moment before she asked, "What about you? How many children do you want?"

Bart smiled brazenly. "I think if I were married to you, it'd end up being closer to ten. As beautiful as you are, I would have a hard time keeping my hands off you, and that could get us in a lot of trouble."

"You haven't even kissed me yet. Are you sure you want to have all those kids?" she asked, laughing.

"Absolutely. No doubt in my mind."

It was nearly midnight when Bart finally drove Cassandra home. They had talked and laughed the night away.

"Do you want to come in?" she asked.

"Not tonight. I'd better get back to the city but thank you."

Again, he took her hand and kissed her on the cheek, but when he leaned in, Cassandra turned her head slightly so her lips met Bart's. She tasted of honey and red wine, and Bart immediately knew he was doomed. He put his arms around her waist to pull her closer to him. It was long, slow, and passionate, and his tongue danced on her lips, desperate for another taste of sweetness. It was the kind of kiss Bart always imagined he would have when he finally met his future wife. Slowly, their lips parted.

"If I come in, I'll never want to leave, and that's a problem," he whispered, their foreheads still touching. He kissed her again before walking to the car, but before he got in, he stopped and turned around to look at her one more time. God, she is perfect.

"I'll talk to you tomorrow," he said.

Cassandra walked inside the house and closed the door behind her. She couldn't stop thinking about how she longed to kiss him again. Why did she let him leave? Why didn't she drag him in the house and kiss every inch of his perfectly sculpted body? She never imagined she could feel such strong feelings for someone without losing her sense of independence. It was a strange yet not unwelcome sensation.

As Bart drove back to Manhattan, a million thoughts bounced around in his head. He had finally met the woman of his dreams, and their first kiss was extraordinary, but he couldn't lose sight of everything else. He needed to handle the Star Killer more than ever. But how? If I kill him, I could jeopardize losing Cassandra—losing everything—but if I don't, more innocent women are going to die. He knew what had to be done.

CHAPTER 23

FATE

O n Thursday morning, the first thing on Bart's mind upon waking was Cassandra. It seemed like that was all he did those days. He fell asleep thinking about her. He woke up thinking about her. He thought about her while showering and while driving. Hell, he even thought about her while he was thinking about her. It was the first time in his life he actually felt like he had to sell himself to a woman. All of his other relationships were much simpler. The truth was he never really cared what a woman thought about him until he met Cassandra.

Now every move he made was calculated to convince her what a great guy he was and why she should be with him. The visit to the children's hospital the day before had reinforced what a warm, loving, and caring person she was and made Bart fall even harder and faster than before. For Cassandra, donating to organizations had nothing to do with money. It was all about how she could help others and make their lives better.

Bart had an appointment with his attorney to prepare for their meeting the following day with the medical review board. Richard Rosenthal was the attorney Bart had chosen to represent him; it was widely known that Rosenthal understood how the department's rules worked and how the medical review board followed those rules. Bart was confident Richard would protect him at all costs.

The underlying problem was Bart had not been honest with Cassandra about what was going on, and he was beginning to worry. While he had casually mentioned being injured, he deliberately hadn't gone into detail, and, from the beginning, they had agreed their relationship would be based solely on honesty. Although he had not technically lied to her, he sure as hell hadn't told her the truth.

He spent most of the day being prepped by Rosenthal as to what to say and what not to say. He was clear that he wanted Bart to be truthful about everything; after all, the board already had so much information that anything but the truth would only hurt him.

After being briefed, Bart left Rosenthal's office and immediately called Cassandra. He couldn't escape the unabated guilt for having withheld such a significant piece of information from her. Her parents were scheduled to go out of town Friday, and Anthony would accompany them, so Bart was going to drive out to Long Island to spend the evening with her and tell her the truth. Would she still want to see him? The ball would be in her court.

After a restless night, Friday morning came. Bart got up, showered, and put on a nice pair of slacks and a dress shirt. It could be the last day of his career—he might as well go out looking nice. He stopped by the diner to grab breakfast before meeting Rosenthal at the police headquarters bright and early. After going through security, they took the elevator up to the third floor, where the medical review board was located. Bart felt like he had just left that place, which meant he was spending way too much time there. If what Rosenthal told him was true, however, then his time in the department may be limited.

They sat in the waiting room for a few minutes before a middle-aged woman in slacks and a cyan blouse came out to retrieve them.

"Please follow me," she said.

She led them down the hallways and to a conference room where three men in suits were seated at a large desk facing Bart and Rosenthal as they walked in. Bart and Rosenthal took their seats, and the man in the middle introduced himself as Dr. Roland. He then told them that to his left was Dr. Chang, and to his right was Dr. Patel.

Dr. Roland looked at Bart. "This proceeding will be taped. If your attorney would like a copy, we are more than willing to provide you with one."

"Detective Sullivan, I've been doing this for a number of years," began Dr. Chang. "I've never seen a file this . . . substantial." He picked it up about a foot above the table and dropped it. The papers made a loud bang as the file reconnected with the oak desk.

"After reading everything in here, it seems you're lucky to be alive, let alone still working," Dr. Chang continued impudently. "Let's go through some of these issues, shall we? First, you were stabbed, then you were shot in the chest, then you were in an apartment building that exploded and collapsed on you, and somehow, by the grace of God, you were still alive, and then you got hit by a car. Do I have that correct?"

"Well, in as few words as possible, yes, that's correct."

"Being stabbed, we understand. Being shot, well, we've gone through all those records and have a fairly decent understanding of what happened. The same with the apartment fire. But we don't have much information regarding the car accident. Would you care to explain what happened?"

Bart's mind went back to that day. He wanted to give a detailed explanation and not sloppily blow through it, so he gathered his thoughts before he began.

"Well," he said, clearing his throat, "it was a rainy day, and we had been in Queens interviewing a witness. We were headed back to Manhattan. We were on Woodhaven Boulevard, sitting on a three-lane roadway. The rain was coming down hard. As the traffic slowly moved along, I looked at the car next to me, and, to my amazement, there was John Forsetti—a guy who was wanted for murder but had disappeared about three years before.

"We had two choices at this point: try to pull him over or handle things our way. You see, if we tried to pull him over, it would have undoubtedly resulted in a car chase. Forsetti was likely armed, so it would've turned into a shoot-out with civilians around. I told my partner the best thing to do was for me to get out of the car at the next red light and make my way through the cars. I could keep the lead cars from moving and box his vehicle in. Donnie could come up behind Forsetti and attempt to get him out of the car.

"But we only had a few seconds to develop the plan. I mean, we were at a red light. So, I made my decision. At the next light, I got out quickly and walked toward the lead cars that were stopped at the red light. I flashed my shield and told the drivers not to move, but within a few seconds, Forsetti jumped out of the car and started shooting at my partner.

"As soon as the drivers near the front heard the shooting, they hit the gas and started to drive away as fast as possible. You can't blame them; they were scared shitless. Forsetti took advantage of the chaos. He jumped back in the car. I was going to take a shot at him, but civilians were all over the place. It was rush hour. People were getting off buses, going to and from train stations, walking on the sidewalk. I knew the bullet would probably hit the windshield and ricochet and then possibly hit some innocent bystander.

"In that instant, the only thing I knew was I had to get a shot from above him that would go through the windshield. He saw me and immediately started driving toward me. I thought if I could get to the parked cars that were no more than twenty yards away, I could jump up on the hood and take a shot down through the windshield at him, but, like I said, it was raining.

"I started to run toward the parked cars, keeping one eye on Forsetti and judging my distance from the cars as I got closer. I jumped up onto the hood of a parked car. He was still heading right for me, so all I had to do was turn and fire through his windshield. Things were going according to plan.

"Unfortunately, due to the rain, my foot slipped when I landed on top of the hood of the car. I fell backward into the street. At that instant, Forsetti hit me and the parked car I had jumped on. I flipped up into the air—it seemed like at least ten feet— I came down on my head and shoulder.

"I could hear Forsetti's engine revving as he tried to back away from the car he had struck. I heard more shots, but I couldn't breathe. I couldn't swallow. I was spitting up something—blood, I'm assuming—and then I passed out, thank God. I found out later one of my ribs had punctured my lung, and I was bleeding in my lungs. Fortunately for me, my partner had wounded Forsetti. Instead of killing me, he just wanted to get out of there.

"I woke up in the hospital. You have all the information right in front of you. It was long-haul physical therapy and rehab trying to get back to where I was."

Dr. Patel inspected the information before speaking. "Do you understand, Detective, that we have an obligation to the city to decide whether you're fit for duty? There are all kinds of legal ramifications, and if we deem you unfit, we can't let you go back to work."

A few months earlier, Bart would have argued, but right then, at that moment, the only thing on his mind was Cassandra. He wanted to spend the rest of his life with her, and he knew that would be difficult given his recent circumstances. Besides that, he believed the doctors had made up their minds before he ever walked in the door.

"Do you have any questions?" Dr. Patel asked Bart before adjourning the meeting.

"No."

"What about you?" he said, turning to Rosenthal.

"If you could keep me up to speed as to where you're going with your decision, that would be greatly appreciated."

Dr. Chang asked, "By the way, what happened to Forsetti?"

Bart worked his way through moments he didn't want to remember. "He was found in a car on a road near Coney Island with a small bullet wound in the back of his head." It was eerily quiet.

Bart and Rosenthal got up and walked out of the room. As they were waiting for the elevator, Bart remembered lying in the rain on the street that day, unable to breathe, and thinking he was going to die. It was a stark contrast to his current life, where all he wanted to do was live.

CHAPTER 24

HONESTY

When Bart left the police headquarters, he called Cassandra to tell her he had just gotten out of his meeting but had a few errands to run.

"Will you come to my house whenever you're finished?"

"Of course. I shouldn't be long, mia bella."

She melted every time he called her beautiful. "If the weather clears up, we can go for a run, and then I was thinking of some dinner after we get cleaned up. I'm not sure what I have in the house, so we might have to go out. Don't forget my parents and Anthony are gone for the week, so we will have the place to ourselves."

As if I could forget. "Sounds great. I'll see you soon."

Bart headed to his apartment, picked up a change of clothes, including a jogging outfit and sneakers, and threw them in a suitcase. When he stepped out of his apartment, he noticed the rain had kicked up again and didn't seem to have any intentions of stopping anytime soon. He kicked the water off of his boots, stepped into his vehicle, and headed out to Long Island. On the way, he stopped at a supermarket and picked up a few items so he could surprise Cassandra by cooking dinner for her.

The discussion Bart had with the medical review board had brought up some painfully repressed memories. Although he was usually good at disregarding them, as he stepped out of the grocery store into the dark, rainy afternoon, his mind flashed back to lying on the street, unable to move or breathe. He keeled over to catch his breath, but the pain lingered. You're okay. Deep breaths. That's it. You're okay. Finally, he was able to catch his breath and dull the throbbing in his chest enough to get in the vehicle and drive.

The sun was beginning to set as Bart pulled into the driveway of the estate. Despite having been there before, he was as mesmerized as the first time. Elms lined the entire road, and without their leaves, the twists and turns of their bare limbs resembled ballet dancers sashaying and pirouetting solely for his entertainment. Before he approached the front door, he noticed Cassandra open it. She was standing under the portico in a jogging outfit and waving. Her hair was pulled up in a ponytail, and the orange in her outfit intensified her green eyes. Bart didn't think it was possible, but she looked even more beautiful than she did the last time he saw her.

They went inside, and Cassandra noticed the grocery bags. "Are you going to cook me dinner?"

"Yes, I am."

Her face lit up with adoration. "What are you going to make?"

"It's a surprise," he said with his signature cheeky smile and leaned in and kissed her.

Cassandra swooned back at him before taking a peek out of the kitchen windows.

"It's still raining pretty hard. I don't think we're going to get a run in today."

He glanced out the window. "No, it doesn't look like it."

"Well, in that case, I have a bottle of wine chilling. Would you like a glass?"

"No, thank you," he said. "But would you like me to pour you a glass?"

"That would be amazing," she said, pulling a bottle of Jameson from the cabinet below the wet bar. She turned around with it, smiling like she had just pulled a rabbit out of a hat.

"You're full of surprises," Bart said, reaching for the bottle.

She pulled her hand back, so the bottle was out of his reach. "First, let me give you the grand tour."

Cassandra's home was beautiful and an accurate reflection of her. It was classy yet effortless. It didn't seem over the top like some lavish homes did. Bart immediately felt very comfortable. It was the kind of house he could picture himself living in one day, maybe even raising children in eventually. You're getting ahead of yourself again.

"This is the living room."

It had a gray suede sectional couch, several bookshelves, and a large television. I bet hers actually works. Then Cassandra led Bart to an enclosed lanai situated off of the living room, before the kitchen. It was a wonderful space with a gorgeous teakwood sofa, matching chairs, and a small area with counter space for food and drinks. Strings of lights hanging from the ceiling provided the perfect ambiance for a relaxing evening.

Cassandra grabbed his hand, and before heading to the opposite side of the house, she pulled him into her office. "This is where the magic happens," she said, laughing.

It was a charming space with a chestnut desk near the east wall and a navy velvet couch on the opposite side. A small bar occupied the space near the couch, which Bart suspected was more for guests than Cassandra. He had never seen her drink liquor. She had pictures throughout the room—reminders of what she was working so hard for—a couple of her parents on the desk, one of her and Anthony at a gala on the end table by the couch, and a small one of a young girl with an attractive woman who resembled Cassandra on the wall by her desk.

"Who is this?"

"Oh, that's my mother and me—a couple of years before she passed."

"She's beautiful. You look a lot like her. How did she pass, if you don't mind me asking?" he asked softly.

"The doctors said it was a brain aneurysm. It was very unexpected."

He turned to look at her. "I'm so sorry."

Cassandra grabbed Bart's hand and pulled him toward the doorway. "Come on, let's go see the rest of the house."

They briefly looked at the three guest rooms and then made their way to the master bedroom. It was a large room with a king-sized bed in the center. Near the window was a sitting space with a couple of beige wingback chairs and a glass table with a copy of A Room of One's Own lying on it with a red bookmark near the end. A master bathroom was attached with a marble countertop and two above-mount white basin sinks. The walk-in shower was covered in white tiles with black accents that matched the faucets and cabinet fixtures. Bart noted the rain showerhead that spanned the entire ceiling and pictured him and Cassandra enjoying it together. Beside the shower was a massive Jacuzzi tub. *We'll soak in the Jacuzzi first and then rinse off in the shower. A perfect evening.*

"This is incredible," said Bart.

"Thank you. I designed it myself."

"Well, you did an exceptional job."

They walked back into the kitchen, where Bart poured a glass of Bordeaux for Cassandra and Jameson for himself.

"Would you like to sit out on the lanai?" Cassandra asked.

Bart was extremely apprehensive about revealing his secret. Everything had been perfect so far. He didn't want to ruin it by making Cassandra think she couldn't trust him. As they walked into the lanai, she pushed a button on the wall, and the gas fireplace in the center came to life. They sat next to each other on the small sofa. The room was enclosed entirely in glass, but it was wet from all the rain, and it was difficult to see anything outside. Bart looked at Cassandra and enjoyed her presence for a moment, knowing what he was about to say could remove her from his life forever.

"What's wrong?" she asked. "You're awfully quiet."

He took another minute to gather his thoughts. Though he usually had everything planned, he was at a loss. He hadn't thought about how he would tell her. Part of him hoped it would just go away if he didn't think about it.

Bart turned toward Cassandra and took her hand in his. "From the beginning, I told you we would have an honest relationship. I want you to know I would never lie to you about anything, and, while I haven't lied, I have kept some of the truth from you."

Cassandra looked worried. Her brows were furrowed, and her eyes had a sadness Bart hoped he would never have to experience or especially be the cause of.

"This morning I attended a medical review board meeting for the department to determine whether I am fit to work any longer. The injuries I kind of glossed over when we first talked were, in some ways, very serious and did a lot of damage. I don't like to talk about it because it's not something I want to keep reliving, but now there are consequences. I guess I can't escape it any longer."

"Just say what you want to say, and we will deal with it. I'm not entirely innocent either."

Bart continued staring at Cassandra, completely distracted by her mesmerizing green eyes. He noticed a thin hint of light brown just around her pupils, but it could only be seen from a proximity. His attraction to her was becoming a problem—no matter what they talked about or where they were, he could not get over how gorgeous she was. Focus. She asked you a question.

"The worst of my injuries was when I was hit by a car. It caused a major concussion and a number of internal injuries. I rehabbed for almost six months to try to get back to normal. The department apparently has decided it is not in everyone's best interest for me to continue to work full-time."

"What does that mean?"

"I believe they are going to retire me. If so, it's going to happen pretty quickly."

"Pretty quickly, as in weeks? Months?"

"I believe it'll be within the next thirty days."

They sat for a moment looking at each other in silence while Cassandra tried to digest the information she had just been given. She took her free hand and placed it on the hand she was already holding. Bart placed his free hand on top of hers.

"With the money my family has given to hospitals all over the world, I know we can get you the best treatment possible. I want you to know that whatever you need, we will get it for you."

Bart was stunned. He had expected her to be angry or at least upset. Instead, she was concerned about him and wanted to help.

He looked at her. "You realize I'm in love with you. I know you probably think this is happening too fast, and I don't expect you to have the same feelings, but you're the one I have been waiting for my entire life, and I hope that in time, you'll feel the same way about me."

She smiled and kissed him on the cheek. "I already do, but I'm not as strong as you are, so instead of being happy about it, I'm terrified. I've never felt this way about anyone. I need you to help me with my insecurities. I need you to understand there will be times when I'm afraid or overwhelmed—maybe both—and you'll have to reassure me. If you can do that for me, I know we will be fine."

Bart leaned in and placed his lips on Cassandra's. It was a kiss full of unspoken words—a kiss full of love—that seemed to last for hours but was still not long enough.

They sat and talked until Bart's stomach started to growl. He had been so enchanted by Cassandra he had completely forgotten about dinner.

"If you're getting hungry, I'll go ahead and start cooking," he said.

"Now that you mention it, I am starving."

HONESTY

They moved to the kitchen, and Bart cooked Cassandra one of his favorite meals—chicken Florentine. She sat on one of the stools at the island and watched as he sliced chicken, minced garlic, and poured wine in the skillet, causing flames to rise nearly to the ceiling. She clapped with excitement. It was impressive how dexterous he was with his hands, especially considering the numerous injuries he had just divulged to her. It made her even more impressed with how delicious the food was. It was one of the best meals she had ever eaten.

After dinner, they cleaned up and then moved to the living room to talk a little more before Bart headed back to the city. Leaving Cassandra never got easier. He wanted to be with her all the time. He wanted her to be the last thing he saw before he went to sleep and the first thing he saw when he woke up, but he was trying to be methodical about their relationship. He didn't want her to feel overwhelmed or suffocated. Before they took that next step, he wanted her to be one hundred percent confident he wasn't going anywhere.

Bart promised he would come back early in the morning and pick Cassandra up to spend the day in the city, and he did. The week flew by. They visited the Met, the Museum of Natural History, and the New York Historical Society. She showed him some of her favorite works of art, which were all beautiful, but none compared to her. He was finally in love and was quickly turning into one of those "yes men" he once laughed at—the guys who would do whatever their wives wanted them to—but he didn't mind. He had never been happier.

In the evenings, Cassandra and Bart usually retreated back to her house, where he would cook while they talked, laughed, and just enjoyed time together alone. On Monday evening, Bart cooked salmon and steamed vegetables while they reminisced about the past few days.

First thing the next morning, Bart got a phone call from Donnie.

"He struck again. I'll pick you up in forty-five minutes." The phone went dead.

Bart had been so distracted eating, drinking, and enjoying Cassandra's company he had almost forgotten about the Star Killer. While he had been busy enjoying his life, someone else had been losing theirs.

CHAPTER 25

DEATH BY TWO

Bart waited outside his apartment building with a cup of coffee in each hand. He couldn't stop thinking about how such a wonderful week had turned to shit so quickly. Another dead woman. A few minutes later, Donnie sped up in the unmarked car and slammed on the brakes to let Bart into the vehicle. The rain had stopped, but it was still freezing cold, and he relished in the warmth of the heater as he entered the car. Donnie took the coffee and sped away.

"What's going on?" asked Bart.

"We're heading out to Astoria. Two women are dead, and the medical examiner asked for you."

"That's all you know?"

"That's all I know. I didn't want to talk on the phone too long with them. Never know who's listening."

The sirens howled and screeched all the way over the bridge and out toward Astoria Boulevard.

"Where have you been for the past few days?"

"I've been with Cassandra. Her family is out of town for the week."

"Must be true love," Donnie said halfheartedly.

Silence fell between the two of them, with nothing but the sound of the siren blaring until they arrived at the apartment house. Marked police cars were all over the street, and uniformed officers were standing in front of the building. Bart and Donnie got out of the car, and as they walked to the building, Bart couldn't help but feel like he had been there a hundred times before. He took a look at the crowd for anyone he might recognize, but all the faces looked the same.

One of the uniforms took them up to the second floor. As usual, they gloved up, put on booties, and removed their coats. As soon as they walked in the door, the familiar smell of death hit them like a bag of bricks. The first thing Bart noticed was an officer sitting at the small round kitchen table. *What the hell is he doing? Having a cup of tea and crumpets?*

Bart was immediately irritated by all the uniformed officers walking around the crime scene, contaminating everything. It made it harder to identify footprints, hair, and everything else they needed to collect.

"What the hell are you doing in here?" Bart barked at a cop standing in the bedroom.

The man looked startled. "N-nothing," he managed to say in a tone just above a whisper.

"Then get out! How many times do we have to have this discussion about contaminating the crime scene?"

The cop quickly scurried out the door, and Bart walked into the bedroom, where the medical examiner was looking over the body.

"Well, you're in a good mood," he said without looking up at Bart.

"Why don't you kick these guys the hell out of here instead of letting them walk around contaminating everything?"

The medical examiner shrugged. "It's not my job."

For the first time, Bart looked down at the woman. She was sprawled out on the bed, facedown. Her hands and feet were tied to the corners of the bedpost. A sheet had been haphazardly placed over her, and when Bart asked the medical examiner who put it there, he shrugged again and continued writing his report. Bart carefully pulled the sheet back to reveal a white cream smeared all over her back, between her thighs, and on her neck, which had been cut from one side to the other, saturating the pillows and sheets in blood. Sick son of a bitch.

"What is this white substance?" asked Bart.

"It's Noxzema."

"Have you ever seen that before on a body?"

"Not like that," he said, pointing his pencil at the corpse before continuing his scribbling.

"Where's the other body?"

The medical examiner motioned to a bedroom near the back of the apartment. Bart and Donnie walked through the living room and down a short hallway that led into the other room. A young woman was hog-tied on the bed. Her throat had also been cut from ear to ear, and she was lying on her right side, facing away from the door. Immediately, Bart noticed the same white cream all over her back. He walked closer and saw it was slathered between her thighs and on her breasts, similar to the other victim.

"Have you looked?" Bart asked as he motioned to her ear.

The medical examiner shook his head no.

Bart walked over to her and gently moved her blonde hair away from the side of her face. There on the back of her earlobe was that sick little hand-drawn star. He walked out of the room and returned to the first bedroom. He gently removed the brown hair from the side of the girl's face and observed a similar star on her ear. Goddamnit.

"Did we find the bottle of Noxzema?" Bart asked the lab technician.

"Not yet, but we're not finished searching."

While Donnie was looking at the crime scene, Bart walked into the bathroom. He looked down and noticed urine in the toilet. The seat was up. If the Star Killer had used it, they could collect DNA and finally put the sick bastard away. In the back of his mind, Bart knew it wasn't the Star Killer's. He would never be that careless. He walked over to the door and called out to one of the uniformed officers.

"Hey! Anybody use this bathroom?"

"I don't know," he said, "but I'll go outside and ask the rest of the unis."

Moments later, another officer walked in.

"I-I did take a piss in here earlier. I really had to go."

"Get out." As he sulked away, Bart stopped him. "Before you leave, wipe this damn bowl down, but don't flush it. We need to check the trap in the toilet before you fuck up any more evidence."

Bart walked back into the first bedroom, where the medical examiner was talking to some of the technicians about obtaining fluids.

"Why don't you go outside and get some shots of the crowd?" The tech stared at Bart blankly.

"That isn't what I take pictures of. I'm not a reporter."

"Just get out there and do it!"

Bart took a flashlight out of his pocket and looked carefully around the beds and alongside the victims.

"How does one person get control of two women like this? Tie them both to the bed and they don't fight back?" he asked the medical examiner.

The medical examiner moved toward the victim tied to the bedposts. He shifted her slightly to the left and pointed to a small red mark on her side.

Bart looked closer. "A laser mark. He could have used a Taser on them."

"Could be how he managed both of them," said the medical examiner.

Bart had never seen that on any of the Star Killer's previous victims, but of course he had also never killed two women at once before. Bart went to find another lab technician.

"If you don't find the Noxzema jar, it might be a good idea to take that toilet bowl off and see if he tried to flush it. It may be lodged in the trap or stuck in the pipes."

The technician looked puzzled. "How do we get the bowl off?"

"Get a goddamned plumber."

As Bart turned around, he noticed a uniformed lieutenant standing behind him.

"Sullivan, we need to talk."

"I've got my hands full at the moment."

He continued anyway. "I understand you've been yelling at some of the officers."

"I just don't understand how many fucking times we have to go through the subject of not contaminating crime scenes."

"You're right. They've been told a million times to secure the scene and then get out. My apologies."

"Thank you."

"Still," added the lieutenant, "take it easy on them. This shit isn't easy for any of us."

The lieutenant walked away, and Bart stepped back into the bedroom. Donnie was rifling through boxes, dresser drawers, closets, and side tables but kept stopping to look at the naked, bloodied body that barely resembled a young woman anymore. Both of them looked through the entire apartment but didn't find anything other than diaries and a computer. No information relevant to the Star Killer was found.

"Make sure you bag these items up," Bart irritably told the crime scene investigators.

As he picked through diaries in the bedside table drawer, Bart noticed his hand was slightly shaking. He hated looking through victims' personal items. It made him feel dirty. "They aren't coming back for them," Donnie would always say, but it still felt wrong. Who has the right to go through someone's private items? Those are their personal thoughts, their memories, their dreams, the futures they were robbed of. No one deserves that.

After Bart and Donnie had rummaged through the apartment for hours, one thing was clear: the two women were picked randomly.

They didn't know the killer. The only person who actually knew the killer was standing in that room.

When they finally walked out of the apartment, the bodies had been removed and taken downtown for autopsies. The apartment was sealed, and the lab technicians were finished. One of the techs was going to wait for a plumber. It was a long shot. As soon as Donnie and Bart stepped outside, a large group of reporters began shouting questions. Nothing but a bunch of vultures feeding on the dead. They had turned their phones off while they were at the scene. When Bart turned his back on, a message from Cassandra appeared on the screen, and then another, and then one more. He didn't think it was a good idea to call her back right then. He needed to clear his head.

Before leaving, Bart met with the patrol sergeant and the precinct detectives. "We need to canvas this apartment complex and the surrounding area—all the bars and restaurants around here. We need to check the cameras and try to find out where the girls had been before they died. We need to find out if they came home with anyone and, if so, who saw them. Let's get as many detectives down here as we can, and let's use these uniformed guys to do some of the canvassing."

The whole façade seemed unnecessary since Bart already knew who the killer was. At that moment, though, he thought about Cassandra and how he so desperately wanted a future with her. If he tried to deal with the Star Killer himself, it could jeopardize everything. He needed to tell Donnie what was going on. Bart had so far kept Donnie in the dark because he didn't want anyone else to carry the burden. Bart knew he had to talk to Donnie before things got completely out of control. This could not go on any longer.

CHAPTER 26

CONFESSION

Bart had been contemplating telling Donnie about the files for months. Now, nearly forty-eight hours since the double homicide, he knew he couldn't waste any more time.

They had spent hours interviewing potential witnesses, people who were in nearby bars and restaurants, and any lead they acquired had already fallen through. Apparently, the victims had been at the bar around the corner the night they were murdered, but no one remembered seeing them talk to anyone other than each other. The investigators hadn't been able to locate anyone who saw them walking home.

The crime technicians had called the plumber as Bart suggested. They pulled the toilet bowl off the floor. To everyone's amazement, a broken bottle of Noxzema was stuck in the trap. The lab techs discovered a partial fingerprint on it. When Bart was given this information, he felt a wave of relief wash over him. Could it be possible that the Star Killer had finally made a fatal mistake? Maybe everything would work out after all.

After getting a few hours' sleep, Bart asked Donnie to meet him at his parents' home, knowing they were gone for the day. Bart and Donnie's conversation would be completely private. Bart had to be extremely careful when divulging the information concerning Lupo's secret operation with the Star Killer.

Donnie arrived early in the morning. Bart had made coffee and bought bagels.

"What's going on, buddy? What's all the secrecy about? Are you and Cassie finally going to run off and get married?"

Bart let out a perfunctory laugh. "No, but I think you may need to sit down for this."

Donnie sat apprehensively at the kitchen table. He grabbed a garlic bagel and began smothering cream cheese on it.

"You're going to have to have patience with me here because this is a long and extremely involved story," Bart began.

Donnie stared at him blankly. Bart took that as his cue to continue.

"Let's start at the beginning. You remember my time with Lupo before his suicide?"

Donnie nodded, his mouth full of food.

"Well, Lupo had a file on the Star Killer. It was hidden in a warehouse in one of those small rental units. What was in there is unbelievable." Bart paused for a moment and then continued. "You have to understand I can't tell you certain things. If this thing blows up in my face, I have to be able to say you didn't know anything, and if you take a polygraph, you'll have to be able to pass it."

Donnie looked startled. "Why didn't you tell me this sooner?"

"I didn't know what to do with this information, to be honest with you. I didn't want to know it myself, but I didn't get a choice in the matter. Anyhow, Lupo's files had the name of the Star Killer in them. His actual name. They also had a residential address and pictures, videotapes, statements from witnesses Lupo had interviewed—all kinds of shit. But I have to be clear about one thing. Everything Lupo did was illegal, so there's no way we can take this evidence to the district attorney. First of all, it will be thrown out, and second, Lupo is a conspirator. I am a conspirator. We can do nothing with this information."

Donnie sat at the kitchen table, still speechless. Bart continued explaining.

"I'm thinking the Noxzema bottle they found in the toilet trap may be the only breakthrough we have to get a copy of that partial fingerprint. I will try to match it to a set of fingerprints Lupo left in the file. Even if I can do that, what do we do with it? Lupo got the fingerprints illegally. I don't know how he got them, so I have to try to figure out how to get this information out there without involving Lupo and God knows who else."

Donnie took another bite of his bagel and looked up. "This is some shit. How did you get involved in this mess, Bart?"

"I didn't know what I was getting into with Lupo. He didn't keep the files at his house. The department never saw them. He gave me a key, I finally tracked the unit down, and here we are. I burned everything except the photo, the address, and the fingerprints. The reason I wanted you to come here was to talk. I'm afraid if the department thought we had this information, they would tap our phones. I figured this would be the safest place. You have to listen to me, Don. I can't allow this to continue. This psycho will continue to kill until somebody stops him. You are not going to believe this, but Lupo actually talked to him on the phone."

"What the hell? You've got to be kidding me."

"No, it's the truth. I've even talked to him. Lupo had a phone he used to hide in the unmarked car. It rang one day, so I picked it up, and I swear to God, Donnie, it was the Star Killer. I had no idea who it was until he started to talk to me."

Donnie tried to talk but was stuttering. Finally, he managed to speak audibly. "This is un-fucking-believable." He stared at Bart, and his eyes widened. "You're not thinking of doing what I think you are."

"We can't have this discussion. Not here, not ever. But I will do what I have to do. The medical review board is going to make a decision within thirty days, and I'm pretty sure they're going to send me packing. What do I have to lose?"

"Why don't we get an attorney? If you sue the department, maybe they'll back away."

"I can't do this anymore. I can't deal with one more dead person, and I certainly can't get injured again. Doctors have warned me one blow to the head could cause permanent paralysis, and I'm not willing to risk that."

Bart took a long pause before speaking again. "I'll be honest with you, my friend. Cassandra has changed everything for me. I just want to have some kind of normal life if she'll have me. I love her. I want to marry her and have a family and hopefully put all this shit behind me if possible."

Donnie was stunned, then smug. "Married? I never thought that word would come out of your mouth. You know you can thank me for this? I fixed the two of you up after all."

Bart laughed. "You know I love you like a brother. You and Jeannie are important to me, but for once I have to do what's best for me and not for everybody else. I need you to get me a copy of that fingerprint from the Noxzema bottle. If I can match it with the prints Lupo left me, we can deal with this somehow."

The department ran the partial fingerprint from the Noxzema bottle through federal, state, and city databases for days but found no matches. Bart's grandiose plan was quickly becoming a glimmer of hope diminishing with each passing second.

CHAPTER 27

DANGER

It was early April. The weather was finally becoming tolerable; cold and windy days were few and far between, and spring was making its debut. Cassandra and Bart had spent every waking minute together for the past few months. The foundation had taken a back seat to her desire to be with him. He still hadn't heard from the medical review board, but the department refused to let him work until a decision had been made.

They were driving to Long Island from Manhattan one evening when Bart's phone rang. The screen displayed the name Jerry Morris. He pressed the accept button and put it on speaker so he could keep both hands on the wheel.

"Hey there, Jerry."

Bart had met Jerry in the police academy. They had remained close ever since, even though they didn't talk very often. Jerry was an attractive black man notorious for being an impulsive playboy who never thought about any decision for very long.

"Well, well, well." Jerry laughed. "What's this I hear about you finally finding a woman who will put up with you?"

"Yeah, I'm not sure how I managed it, but she's really something," said Bart, glancing over at Cassandra and throwing a wink. "It's been a long time since we talked. How are you?"

"It has been a while. I'm doing okay. Do you have me on speakerphone?"

"I do. We're heading back to Long Island."

"Is Cassandra with you?"

"She sure is."

"Hey, Cassandra. Jerry Morris here. I don't know what you see in this guy. I guess you are taking pity on the poor schmuck." He let out a boisterous laugh.

She laughed and looked at Bart. "Well, I have to say, he's pretty easy on the eyes."

Jerry laughed again. "It's good to finally talk to you. I hope to meet in person very soon."

"So, what's going on, buddy?" Bart interrupted.

"We need to talk."

"I'm guessing this isn't a conversation we should have over the phone."

"No. It isn't. How does tomorrow look for you?"

Bart looked at Cassandra, and she nodded.

"Tomorrow looks good. One o'clock at the usual place?"

"See you then," said Jerry before adding, "Take care, Cassandra."

"You too!"

Bart hung up the phone. Immediately, Cassandra asked him what that was about.

"Why couldn't he just talk to you on the phone?"

"People don't want to discuss certain things over the telephone. You never know who's listening."

They arrived at Cassandra's house around nine o'clock and spent the evening discussing life and their future. Bart mentioned the pending decision of the medical review board, and Cassandra spoke about her dilemma over her mother's real estate company. They were both at a crossroads and weren't sure where the next few months would lead them, but they were certain of one thing: whatever happened, they would handle it together.

Bart left Cassandra's about midnight. They had fallen into the habit of staying up until one or two every morning as they always seemed to lose track of time, but she had mentioned feeling sluggish from their continuous late nights. He was making a conscious effort to return home at a decent hour. He longed for the day when he would never have to leave her. They were still taking things slowly, although the opportunity had certainly presented itself more than a few times. He wanted to make sure there were no reservations.

The following day, Bart drove to a road leading under the Triborough Bridge to Ward's Island, where he and Jerry always met. The road leading down to the garbage dump was long and had a turnoff right in the middle that provided a clear view in all directions. It was a dead end, so they could park and see in both directions to be sure no one was following or listening to them.

Jerry was already there. Bart got out of his car and opened the passenger door of Jerry's to get in the front seat. It was filthy—candy bar wrappers, empty soda and energy drink cans, and chip bags covered the floor. Bart used his feet to push the trash to one side as he stepped inside and sat down.

He shook Jerry's hand. "Looks like a 7-Eleven exploded in here. Some things never change." The car filled with a bellow of laughter.

Jerry's demeanor shifted, and he became serious. "It's important that what I'm about to say is kept between you and me. If anybody else finds out you have this information, it won't take anyone long to figure out it came from me."

"You know you can trust me, Jer."

"You remember a couple years ago when those Albanians were going around kidnapping people for million-dollar ransoms? They would vet families with large amounts of money and devise a plan to scoop up one of the members—usually a child—if they could get away with it. They'd give the family forty-eight hours to come up with the money, and as long as they did, they would release the hostage. Then, when they returned the relative, they'd warn them that if they went to the police, they would kill them and their entire family. Most people were too scared to go to the police, but a few did, and the FBI got involved. My organized crime unit was also called in. We worked with the FBI and arrested a bunch of the kidnappers, at least the ones who didn't flee the country."

"Why are you telling me this?"

"Well, apparently, the same group of Albanians are back at it. We turned a low-level member into giving us information, and according to him, they're planning two big kidnappings: one on the West Coast and the other on the East Coast. It's a huge operation. They're looking for $25 million for each hostage. My unit is dealing with the East Coast threat, and the FBI is putting together a list of potential targets."

"And?" Bart interrupted. "You want me to help you locate these people?"

"No, that's not it. What I'm trying to get at is that I ran into Donnie a couple of weeks ago at in-service training, and he told me all about you and Cassandra. Her name sounded familiar. I went back and looked at the list the FBI put together. One of the targets is a female whose family owns a multibillion-dollar construction company called Ryan and D'Angelo."

Bart sat there, unable to speak. He could feel anger diffusing through his veins. Every cell in his body wanted those bastards dead.

"There are only about fifty people on the list. I mean, not just anyone has $25 million to spare, but as soon as Donnie mentioned Cassandra's name, it rang a bell."

Jerry pulled a piece of paper out of his pocket with a list of names on it. The seventh or eighth name down was Ryan, followed by D'Angelo with an asterisk beside it and the words "Cassandra D'Angelo—daughter."

"I thought it best you knew. I don't know if it's going to happen, but it's important you're aware."

Bart was seething at this point, but he unclenched his fist and calmed himself enough to thank Jerry. "I sure do appreciate it. You know you can count on me to keep this confidential, but if they do try to pull anything, I'll kill each and every one of them."

"I know you will."

They talked for a while before Bart thanked Jerry once again. He got out of Jerry's car, walked back down to where he had parked, and headed toward Queens.

He had promised his mother and father he would visit since it had been quite some time. He hadn't told them much about the medical review board—no need to worry them until a decision had been made—and they also knew nearly nothing about Cassandra. He was excited to tell them all about her and how happy she made him, but now the information he had just acquired was spinning around in his head. He had looked for Cassandra for years and finally found her. Now someone was trying to take her away from him. They won't get away with it. He thought it would be best to talk to Frank first about the potential threat. Then he would discuss it with Cassandra. He needed to find a way to boost security without absolutely terrifying her.

CHAPTER 28

PROTECTION

The following morning, Bart was extremely concerned about the information he had received from Jerry. He wanted to discuss it with Frank and Anthony as soon as possible before he talked to Cassie. She had an appointment at noon with a potential charity. A car had been sent to pick her up and bring her to their office, which meant Anthony would most likely be around, and maybe Bart could talk to him and Frank at the same time.

He called Frank and asked him if they could speak privately. Frank agreed and told Bart to meet him at the garage where his car collection was located. An hour later, Bart arrived and parked out front. When he walked in, Frank was in his office on the phone, so Bart wandered around admiring the cars. A few minutes later, Frank poked his head out of the office and motioned for Bart to come in.

"Hey, Bart. Good to see you. Is everything okay?"

"Not exactly. I think we've got a bit of a problem, and I wanted to discuss it with you before I talked to Cassandra."

At about that time, a car door closed outside. Anthony walked in.

Frank filled him in. "Bart wants to talk to us about something. It sounds serious. Don't worry. This office is soundproof and electronically protected, so anything you say is safe. You'll also notice no phone reception here—no electronic devices can transmit in or out."

Bart took out his phone and looked at it. Sure enough, he had no reception.

"Seems like a lot of security," he said while looking at Frank.

"Well, for the past ten years, I've been bidding on multimillion-dollar high-rise buildings, and you can never be too careful. A lot of spying goes on in an attempt to figure out how much you're going to bid so people can underbid you. It was far easier for me to secure this office than it was to do the whole house, so here we are."

"Okay, well, let's start at the beginning. I have a friend in an organized crime unit. I don't know if you're aware of it, but a few years ago, these Albanian assholes were going around kidnapping family members of wealthy people. They would give them twenty-four to forty-eight hours to come up with a large ransom. If the families complied, they'd return the hostages—usually women and kids.

"When the Albanians returned the family members, they warned the families they knew where they lived—quite obviously— and that they would come back and kill the entire family if they went to the police. Thankfully, a few of them did go to the police, and the FBI got involved. They arrested a bunch of them, but some fled the country."

"Well, it sounds like the FBI took care of it," said Frank.

"They did. The friend I mentioned just gave me information indicating the Albanians who fled are back and plan to try one last score—one sting on the West Coast and one on the East Coast. They will demand $25 million from both and get out of the country. The organized crime unit managed to flip a low-level member, but the only information my friend knows is it's going to happen in two locations; one of the potential targets is a female, and her family owns a large construction company."

Frank looked at Anthony. "Do you know anything about this?"

"Years ago, I heard some of what they were doing, but I don't know anything about this."

Frank looked pensive. "Has Cassandra told you about the attempted kidnapping of her mother?" he asked Bart.

Bart was caught off guard. He and Cassandra had spent countless hours discussing their lives, and she had never mentioned an attempted kidnapping.

"No, she hasn't."

Frank looked at Anthony again and nodded. "Tell him."

"Well, when Cassandra was five, there was an attempt to kidnap her mother. She was too young to understand what was going on, and we were never sure whether the kidnappers were planning on just taking Janet or both Janet and Cassandra."

"She never told me anything about it." Bart looked stunned.

"Well, we didn't tell her until she was a teenager. She was constantly complaining about never being able to go anywhere without security, so we finally told her," Anthony added.

"What happened to the kidnappers?"

Anthony thought for a moment and glanced at Frank before replying curtly. "They left town."

That means they are buried somewhere, never to be found.

"So, with that said," Frank interposed, "we need to be careful when we tell her this."

"I will." Bart pulled a piece of paper from his jacket pocket and handed it to Frank.

Frank looked at the list of people the FBI had compiled. Right in the middle of it were his name and his company's name. He handed it to Anthony, looked Bart directly in the eye, and said, "Do you really think this is going to happen?"

"I'm hearing it's a fifty-fifty chance, but even if it's only a one percent chance, it's not a risk I'm willing to take."

For a moment, no one spoke. After several minutes, Bart began talking.

"I want both of you to understand I'm not trying to tell anybody what to do. I don't know how things work with Anthony, and I don't want to step on anybody's toes, but it appears that in light of what we know now, Anthony is stretched a little bit thin."

"I'm a little out of my jurisdiction here. Honestly, this scares the shit out of me." Frank looked at Bart. "What do you suggest?"

"Well, I've been thinking about this." Bart paused for a moment. Frank was obviously uncomfortable, so he looked directly at him to ensure the sincerity effectively translated. "You know how much I love your daughter. I've waited for her most of my life, and I won't let anything happen to her. Let's be clear about something—if they get anywhere close to this family, I'll personally find those Albanian fuckers and kill them myself."

Anthony laughed and looked at Frank. "Looks like your daughter finally found somebody who has a lick of sense."

"The only solution is to make sure we prevent it from happening," Frank said abruptly.

"I know a woman who was a police detective," Bart said. "She retired a couple of years ago and is starting to get a little bored. She's great with a gun, she's smart, and she sees everything—nothing gets past her. I don't know how you feel about hiring her to take care of Cassandra. As long as I'm around, I'll do whatever I can, but if we look long-term, it's a different story. Frank, you're going to retire soon, and Anthony will be traveling with you because, let's be honest, Evon is also a potential target."

Frank's face was fixed in a contemplative state. "I think it's a good idea." He turned his gaze to Anthony. "What do you think?"

"I think let's do it, and let's do it now."

"I need to find a way to tell Cassie about this without scaring her too much," Bart added. "The woman I'm talking about is named Fran. Let's assume she can be with Cassandra from nine to five every day. Cassandra's usually home with me until ten or eleven at night, which means we have midnight to seven in the morning to contend with from a security point of view."

"What do you think we should do during those hours?" asked Frank.

"Anthony, the security system could use updating. Maybe we could hire a couple of people from midnight to eight until this thing settles down—if it ever does."

Anthony looked at Bart. "I agree. The system is outdated. We can update it with your help, and I think the security people are also a good idea."

Anthony looked suggestively at Frank.

"What is it? What do you want to say?"

"I think that whether you like it or not, Bart needs to stay on the property from midnight to eight. It's the only way we can be sure, without a doubt, Cassie is safe. This is serious shit."

Frank thought for a moment. He didn't like the idea of his only daughter's boyfriend staying in the same house as her, but her safety was paramount.

"Fine," he wearily agreed. "The way this compound is designed, it's impossible to know who comes and goes, so staying at Cassandra's house overnight won't raise any eyebrows except mine."

Bart disregarded Frank's passive-aggressiveness. He understood it was an inappropriate scenario, but nothing about the situation was exactly appropriate. Albanian thugs were trying to kidnap his daughter. He will get over me staying overnight.

"Cassie and I have dinner tonight, but first thing in the morning, I will tell her what's going on and convince her Fran is our best bet."

Frank snickered. "Good luck with that."

At that moment, Jonathan knocked on the door. He had a tray full of sausages, peppers, and Italian bread. He smiled and said "Good afternoon" before placing it on the table in the corner. Lunch had come and gone, so everyone was hungry.

Bart looked at it. "That smells great, but I don't know if I can eat right now."

Anthony said smugly. "Well, don't worry. I'll eat for you. If we're going to go to battle, we'd better get our strength up."

CHAPTER 29

SAFETY

Anthony had promised Evon he'd take her to an appointment in the city, so he said his goodbyes to Bart and Frank.

After he left the room, Frank asked Bart to close the door. "What do you think you are going to do after you're through with the department?" he asked.

"I'm not quite sure. There are a couple opportunities out there, but in light of what's going on, I want to make sure Cassie is safe before I do anything."

"Let's talk within the next few weeks. I have an opportunity I think you may be able to help me with, and in return, I can help you. For the moment, don't say anything to Cassandra. But if I were going to ask you to work for me, I would run it by her before we did anything," Frank added.

They left the office and started looking at the antique cars in the garage. No matter how many times he saw them, Bart never tired of admiring them. While they were walking around, they could hear a car door close. Cassandra walked inside, and both men simultaneously said, "Hello."

"How did everything go?" Frank asked.

"I think it went pretty well. We have some background work to take care of before we do anything, but it looks good overall. What are you two doing out here?"

"Just looking at these beauties," Bart answered. "But now that the star of the show has arrived, they don't stand a chance." He walked over to her and kissed her on the cheek.

Cassie giggled. "Which one is your favorite?"

"That's tough. Besides you, of course, I'd have to go with the 1953 Buick Skylark convertible. She's a looker."

Cassandra laughed again. "Well, I know what to get you for Christmas."

"I don't think she's kidding," Frank said, laughing.

Cassandra and Bart walked toward her house to get ready for their evening out. When they got inside, Cassandra said, "I think I'm going to take a bath. Would you mind grabbing me a glass of wine?"

He kissed her on the forehead. "Of course, mia bella. I'll be right in."

While he opened up the bottle of merlot, Cassandra went into her bedroom and drew a bath. When Bart walked into the bathroom, she was already lying in the water with her eyes closed, with bubbles strategically concealing her naked body. He set the wine on the ledge of the tub, and she looked up at him and smiled.

"Will you sit and talk with me for a bit?"

He could never say no to her charismatic smile and longing eyes. He picked up the step stool in the corner, placed it near the large Jacuzzi tub, and sat down. He loved these moments when it was just the two of them lounging around, enjoying each other's company. It almost made him forget about all the fucked-up shit that existed in the outside world. He was at peace. He was happy.

"If we're going to be on time, I need to take a shower and start getting ready," he said thirty minutes later.

"Five more minutes?" She looked at him with the best puppy-dog eyes she could muster, but he matched her countenance with one that was playfully stern. "Fine, you're right. I'll drain the tub. Will you hand me a towel?"

Bart grabbed a fluffy white towel hanging on the back of the door. When he turned around to hand it to her, Cassandra was standing up in the tub. He couldn't help but drink in the sight of her standing in front of him, flawlessly naked. It took everything in him not to pick her up and carry her into the bedroom.

He stretched the towel out in an attempt to stop himself from staring, and she turned her body away from him to wrap herself in its warmth. He leaned down and kissed her softly on the neck, then turned her around and kissed her vehemently on the lips.

"If we're going to meet them on time, you'd better get out of this bathroom," she said with her eyes still closed and her nose touching his.

He went into the guest bathroom on the other side of the house, took a shower, and got dressed. When he returned to Cassandra's bedroom, she was sitting in front of her vanity with curlers in her long brown hair and applying blush to her cheeks. She had a short black silk robe on that was slightly hanging off of her petite shoulders. Bart walked over and kissed her on one of her exposed shoulders.

"I don't know why you spend money on makeup you don't need," he said in her ear.

"That's very kind," she said, glancing at him in the mirror, "but I think you're blinded by love."

"I think you're just as beautiful without any, but I do also love you . . . very much." He kissed her shoulder again and sensually moved his lips and tongue up to her neck.

She closed her eyes, lost in the sensation of his tongue on her nape, but then opened them and playfully pushed him off of her. "You need to get out of here so I can finish getting dressed."

"Fine, fine. I'll be waiting on the lanai." He kissed her one last time before retreating down the hall.

Bart walked into the kitchen, poured himself a small glass of whiskey, and returned to her bedroom. He sat on the bed as she sifted through dresses wearing nothing but her undergarments.

"Enjoying the show?" she asked as she turned around and smiled at him.

"You have no idea."

"I thought you were going to wait outside."

"What can I say? I missed you."

Even after spending so much time with her, Bart still had a nagging concern about how he felt about Cassandra. He had never been so taken by a woman. She seemed to feel the same, but he still had occasional uncertainties and wondered if it'd be better to just ask her and eliminate any lingering doubts.

After rummaging through her closet and trying on three different outfits, Cassandra finally decided on a strappy black Chanel dress and a pair of two-tone pumps. She threw on a light trench coat in case the temperature dropped, and they were out the door.

At 7 p.m., they met Donnie and Jeannie at the Waterside Inn. The ladies hugged, and Donnie shook Bart's hand. When he did, he slipped Bart a piece of paper.

"Just put it in your pocket."

They were escorted to a table, where they enjoyed a few drinks before ordering a couple of appetizers. Jeannie and Cassandra seemed to hit it off immediately, but Cassie hit it off with everyone she met. Jeannie had tried for years to set Bart up. He knew she was genuinely happy he had finally met someone he truly loved who seemed to feel the same.

They had a great meal and discussed going to the Yankee game the following week since the weather was becoming more agreeable. After dinner was over and everyone had ordered a final night-cap—everyone except for Bart, who was driving—they said their good nights.

Bart drove back to Cassandra's house. It was late when they arrived, but it was Friday night, and she had cleared her schedule to spend the morning with him. As he drove up the driveway, she grabbed his hand, appreciative to have him. She remembered a time not too long ago when she was going home to an empty house every night, feeling hopelessly alone.

As soon as Bart opened the door, Cassandra began kissing him. He could taste the blackberry and vanilla on her lips from her final glass of merlot.

"Are you going to leave me tonight?" she whispered.

"No, not tonight."

Bart leaned in and placed his lips on Cassandra's. As she pressed into him harder, he kicked the door closed with his foot and leaned her up against it. She pulled away from him breathlessly, took his hand in hers, and led him to the bedroom. He was much more nervous than he had anticipated. He'd been with plenty of women, but they were different. They weren't Cassandra D'Angelo.

His heart was beating hard and fast and even seemed out of rhythm. He hoped she didn't notice the slight quiver in his hand as he spun her around and unzipped her dress. She slowly slid her dress straps over each arm and then pulled the dress below her waist, revealing a pair of black silk underwear and a corset to match. Bart had never seen anything so magnificent in his entire life.

He stepped in and kissed her again, this time cradling her head in his large hand so that he could pull her in deeper and harder. She began to unbutton his shirt before pulling one sleeve over his shoulder and down his arm, then the other. She reached down and unbuttoned his slacks before pulling them down to his ankles. He lifted one leg and then the other while she removed them from his body and threw them across the room.

Bart had never felt magnetism like he did in that moment. He could sense every cell in his body being drawn to hers, and it would be impossible to deny them from doing so. He pulled her onto the bed and tenderly touched and kissed every inch of her body. They made love until they were exhausted and fell asleep in each other's arms. When they weren't making love, they were talking about the future and all that it held for them. She was everything he'd ever wanted in a woman, and he desperately hoped she felt the same way about him.

The next morning, they were awakened by the sun pouring through the blinds. Bart rolled over and was relieved to see Cassandra asleep, looking like an angel with the sun dancing on her face. It wasn't a dream. He ran his finger softly over her naked body, and she slowly opened her eyes and smiled at him. She leaned in and kissed him, and they made love again.

"I've never loved anyone as much as I love you," Bart said to her while they were lying in bed.

He looked over to see her face and noticed tears in her eyes—not exactly the reaction he was hoping for.

"What's wrong? Are you okay?"

"Yes," she sniffled. "I just never thought I would find this kind of happiness. I had almost given up, but then I found you, and you really have no idea how in love with you I am, but I'm still afraid. The thought of being so open and vulnerable and giving someone so much power over me is terrifying."

"Trust me, I understand, but I promise I will always be here loving you, no matter what."

They drifted back to sleep, Bart holding Cassandra in his arms, and when they woke up, the sun was high in the sky. They left the bed only long enough to go out and grab some lunch.

"Can I ask you a question?" said Cassandra after they had returned home and were back under the covers.

"Shoot."

"What made you decide to finally stay over? You've always been so concerned about what my father thinks. What changed?"

"How long do you think I could keep my hands off you? I tried to warn you once before that it would be difficult for me not to always want to touch you and kiss you and hold you. I had reached my limit—probably surpassed it even."

By the time Bart got around to talking to Cassandra about the Albanians, it was late in the afternoon, but he was enjoying their time so much he didn't want to ruin it.

She was a little annoyed he had gone to her father and Anthony before telling her, but she understood her and Evon's safety had always been in their hands, and this was no different.

Bart quietly said, "I know security is something I worry about more than you do, but I have to be very honest with you. I don't think you realize how much I love you and how long it took me to find you, and the thought of anything happening to you is not something I can deal with, so there are going to be times where it might seem to you that I'm a little overprotective. When you think that way, just remember how I feel about you and how much I need you, and hopefully that will make up for my obsession with your safety."

"Well, considering everything going on, I think it would be a good idea to have some additional security."

"I'm glad you feel that way," Bart said, relieved. "Within the next week or so, I will set up a meeting so you can meet with Fran. It wouldn't be a bad idea for you two to get familiar with each other since you'll be spending a lot of time together. I'd also like you to come with me tomorrow to my parents' house."

Cassandra looked surprised. He hadn't talked much about his family and had never mentioned her going to meet them.

"If you're going to be my wife, it might be a good idea if you meet my family."

"Well, if I'm going to be your wife, you might have to ask me to marry you first."

CHAPTER 30

FAMILY

The following day, Cassandra and Bart hopped into her Range Rover and headed to Queens. From the passenger seat, she opened the sunroof.

"What a beautiful day!"

"It's perfect," he responded, gazing at her with adoration.

Bart rarely brought women home to meet his parents, so introducing Cassandra to them was a big gesture, but he felt entirely comfortable with it. He had spent the past few weeks telling them all about the incredible woman he had been spending his time with, and they were elated to meet her.

They arrived at the two-story brick home. There was a large cherry tree in the front yard with small white and soft pink blooms all over it. They walked up to the porch, and a tall gentleman met them at the door.

Bart smiled and shook his hand. "Hey, Pop. Good to see you." He motioned to Cassie. "This is Cassandra."

"Wonderful to meet you," she said, immediately going in for a hug.

"Where's Mom?"

"She's in the kitchen making sandwiches."

Bart's mother had been using an oxygen machine for several months and tired very easily, but when they walked into the kitchen, there she was with a huge smile on her face, making refreshments for them. Bart gave her a tight hug and introduced Cassandra.

"So, you're the mystery woman we've been hearing about? She's quite the beauty," she said to Bart, making Cassandra blush.

They spent the afternoon talking about work and Bart's childhood. His mother even brought out some old family photos to show Cassandra. They loved spending the afternoon with her and Bart, and his adoration for her was unmistakable. His mother immediately noticed how lovingly he looked at her whenever she spoke—and often even when she wasn't speaking. The day couldn't have gone better.

The following afternoon, Bart met Fran at a small restaurant in Queens. He wanted to talk to her alone before they met Cassandra. When he called her on the phone, she expressed interest in working for the family but was curious as to what her responsibilities would be.

It had been quite a while since they had last seen one another, so they caught up for a bit. Fran's husband ran a travel agency that specialized in European golf tours; he was an avid golfer, and it was a great business, but he traveled a lot, and now that Fran was home all the time, it left her with a void.

Bart explained the situation to Fran and told her what her duties would be.

"Not to sound rude or ungrateful, but it seems like I'm just going to be babysitting a rich girl," she politely said to Bart.

"I understand how it may seem that way, but Cassandra is the warmest, most loving, and most giving woman I've ever met, and it won't be babysitting. She's in real danger here."

Fran sat there, seemingly unconvinced.

"Until now, we've only talked about what your responsibilities would be, but I want you to understand something else—something more important. Cassandra is going to be my wife and the mother of my children one day, so her safety is my number one priority. I'm sorry if you don't feel like this position is challenging enough for your skill set, but it's very important to me, which is why I chose you for the job."

Fran sat and thought before grinning. "I can't wait to meet this woman. So, when do you want to get started?"

The next day, Fran, Cassandra, and Bart met at Cassandra's office. It was important to Bart that they liked and trusted one another. Despite how skilled Fran was, it wouldn't matter if she and Cassandra didn't get along since they would be spending most of their time together. When Fran arrived, Bart introduced them to one another. He sat with them for a few minutes but quickly made the excuse that he had errands to run so they could get to know each other one-on-one. Fran was very surprised at how unassuming and easy it was to get to know Cassandra. She was everything Bart had said she was.

"I hope you will enjoy this work and grow to feel more comfortable with us. Uncle Anthony has always been there for me for as long as I can remember."

"I'll be honest with you," Fran said. "I was a little bit on the fence about it, but when Bart told me how much he cared for you, I knew I had to at least give it a chance. I've never seen him this crazy about anyone."

Within a few weeks, Fran fit right in. She enjoyed working—especially being out of the house again—and she was great at her job. Bart felt very secure about Cassandra being with her, and in the evenings, he was there to make sure Cassandra was safe. About once a week, Fran would accompany Cassandra to see Bart's mother. They would get their hair done, take her to doctor's appointments, and sometimes just hang out and talk. Cassandra loved getting closer to Bart's family, and his mother appreciated the company.

Toward the end of the month, Cassandra announced she had a surprise for Bart. She knew how much he loved country music, but she had never told him one of the charities the foundation supported was the Boys and Girls Club, and George Strait was one of the sponsors. They flew to Texas on Thursday, but the concert wasn't until Saturday, so they had two free days to do whatever their hearts desired. They told everyone they were sightseeing, but, in reality, they never left the room.

On Saturday night, the real excitement began. They showed up at the festival and met George Strait along with several other country stars. Bart was stunned. He couldn't believe he was meeting one of his favorite country music icons, and the show was absolutely incredible. He had the time of his life.

Afterward, they returned to the hotel and spent Sunday and Monday exploring the city. On Sunday, they found a little quaint Catholic church nearby and attended mass before finding a breakfast spot around the corner from the church.

They returned to the room after breakfast and, no surprise, ended up back in bed.

"There are some things I've never told you," Cassandra said as she was lying on Bart's chest. "They are difficult for me to talk about, so I push them away. All this talk about security and hiring Fran reminds me of when I was a child. I don't remember anything about it, but apparently there was a plot to kidnap my mother. I only found out about it when I was older because they didn't want to traumatize me. I know you think I don't care about these threats, but that's not true. I'm very much afraid, but I try to be strong and not show it."

Cassandra paused for a moment. Bart didn't respond, sensing that she had more to say.

"I feel so safe and loved by you I hardly worry about those things anymore, but as I always tell you, I need your reassurance. I need you to tell me how much you love me and how much you need me. Otherwise, I'll start to doubt it, even though I know in my heart you do."

"Bella, you can tell me anything. You know I'll understand. If you need my help with something, I'll do it without hesitation, but I can't help you if I don't understand what you're worried about."

"I'm not worried about anything specific, but sometimes I have to pinch myself to believe this is real. How much we love each other is real. I'm just so grateful I have you as a partner. I know sometimes you think you love me more than I love you, but that's not true. I am so in love with you it hurts sometimes, and I can't wait for the day we can be together all the time and you don't have to ever leave me."

After a short pause, she said, "If you don't ask me to marry you pretty soon, I'm going to have to ask you, so you better hurry up and make up your mind."

Bart laughed. "I would've married you the night we met. If I had it my way, we would've gotten on a plane to Las Vegas and never looked back."

Cassandra gave him a kiss, and they spent the rest of the day in bed.

Monday morning, Bart's phone rang. It was Richard Rosenthal.

"Good morning, Bart. I have something to tell you."

Finally, the decision he had been long expecting.

CHAPTER 31

THE FUTURE

The medical review board had decided Bart was not fit for duty and, within thirty days, he would be retired. Before he met Cassandra, being forced to leave the department would've been devastating, but now he almost felt a sense of relief. He could focus more on her, and he wouldn't constantly be in precarious situations, which he knew would make her happy.

On Tuesday morning, they boarded Frank's private jet and flew back to New York. They were energized and had a restored sense of eagerness for what lay ahead. On the flight home, Cassandra discussed with Bart the real estate business her mother had left her; she expressed to him that she almost felt obligated to get involved and would like to do so if he had no reservations about it.

"Of course, whatever makes you happy," he told her. They agreed she would discuss it with her father upon their return to New York.

Before they left New York, Bart hooked Anthony up with a friend of his who owned a reliable security company and had worked on intricate security systems for the department. They had been working on securing the perimeter of the compound, especially the houses, to ensure Cassie and Evon's safety.

THE FUTURE

The next week was going to be extremely busy. Cassandra was planning to meet with her father and tell him she wanted to take over the real estate company, and Bart needed to meet with his attorney regarding his retirement—he had no idea what the process would entail, but it was a relief to finally have a decision.

The morning after they returned to New York, Bart and Cassandra met with Frank and Evon for coffee at their house. They talked about what a great time they had on their trip to Texas and discussed how updating the security system had been progressing. Frank was extremely relieved to have the new system up and running, and Fran was around during the day. They also mentioned the department's decision to retire Bart.

At noon, Bart walked outside and got in his unmarked vehicle for the last time to drive into the city for his meeting with Richard Rosenthal. Cassandra stayed at the house and discussed her thoughts on taking over the real estate company. Her father was surprised by her interest but excited to see the change in his daughter. She seemed much happier than she had been and was undeniably more excited about the future.

"It's your business. Your mother started it so you would have something of your own in the future, so long as you wanted it. It's entirely your decision whether or not to keep it. Whatever you decide, you have my unconditional support. However, I think it's important you sit with the attorneys as soon as possible and find out what's going on in the company's finances before taking on that endeavor. It's seemed to be a mystery the past few years—maybe even longer than that. There's very little contact with Michael Bandell or his family. I think you need to find out what your options are if you're serious about this, and you also need to know the potential investment, the properties owned, the process for you to take over, and your liabilities as CEO."

"I know. I've made an appointment to meet with Bill and Claire Friday morning," replied Cassandra.

Frank's phone rang. He stood up and began walking out to answer it. Before he got to his office, he turned briefly. "Cassie, would you mind if Bart helped with some company work?"

"No," she said, a little surprised. "Why don't you talk it over with him?"

While Frank was taking his phone call, Evon and Cassandra sat at the kitchen table and drank coffee.

"You don't know how happy it makes me that you finally met someone you really care about," said Evon in her usual genuine manner. "And someone who so obviously cares about you," she added.

"It's a bit scary, especially how quickly everything happened. I had almost given up on meeting someone, and I never thought I'd meet someone like Bart."

"Well, you found each other," said Evon.

"Remember that conversation we had right before my first date with him? About how someone was looking for me just like I was looking for them? Well, I think it was destiny I met him that same night. God knew how much we needed each other and helped make it happen."

"Well, I don't think it could have worked out any better—your father seems to like him, and I think he's a true gentleman, so maybe it's destiny, maybe something else, but whatever it is, it's wonderful."

* * *

As Bart drove into Queens, he realized he was still carrying around the slip of paper Donnie had passed to him at the Waterside Inn. He parked the car and pulled it out of his pocket. It was a copy of the partial fingerprint off the Noxzema bottle found in the toilet bowl.

"Holy shit," he said aloud.

Bart faced a dilemma. He needed someone to look at this fingerprint to see if the partial was a match to the fingerprints Lupo had in the file, but whoever he asked couldn't know where they came from. It would have to be somebody outside the department. Fortunately, he knew a fingerprint expert from years back, but locating him wouldn't be easy. He was a bit squirrelly—he always flew under the radar since he was known for doing things off the record—so he was difficult to find.

Bart stuffed the paper back in his pocket and exited the vehicle. He walked into Rosenthal's office and was immediately ushered into the conference room, where Richard was sitting. He stood up, and they shook hands.

"Well, it's over. The department finally decided it's not safe for you to work. I have to tell you, Bart, I think they made the right decision. I mean, when you look at all the evidence the surgeons, neurosurgeons, and orthopedic doctors submitted, it's obvious they had no choice. We have thirty days to sign all the necessary documents, and then it's over. I'll need you to review them—they give you medical protection on all of your injuries, so if any future complications arise, the city will cover the cost. Right now, at your age, you probably don't care much about this, but as you get older, these injuries more than likely will become a problem, so it's important to protect you now."

"What do I do? Turn in my shield and my guns and everything in thirty days?"

"I have filed for a carry permit for you. Since you'll be a retired police officer, I think we can get it done pretty easily, especially if it ends up in the police commissioner's hands. Oh, and one last thing. The department wants you to turn in that unmarked car."

Bart knew it was coming, but for some reason it still stung. He had spent hundreds—maybe even thousands—of hours in that car over the past few years, and just like that, they were taking it away.

"Fine. I'll do it tomorrow and arrange for someone to pick me up."

"I suppose our business here is done. I'll be in touch with those papers," said Rosenthal as he stood up and shook Bart's hand again.

"Thank you, Richard. I really appreciate your help through all of this."

When Bart walked out onto the street, he felt a wave of relief wash over him. The department's decision had been made, and there was nothing left for him to do concerning it. Now he could focus on tying up the loose ends concerning the Star Killer, which he needed to get serious about if he wanted to ask Cassandra to marry him. As long as the Star Killer was active, Bart couldn't risk dragging Cassandra into anything or risking her safety. She had enough danger looming as it was.

Bart was torn. His love for Cassandra was so strong he sometimes considered forgetting about the Star Killer altogether and letting the department handle it. Then he and Cassandra could truly begin their life together. It was never in Bart's nature to be aware of pure evil and disregard it. He knew deep down he had to stop the killing, and he was the only one who could. Everything he had found so far in Lupo's file was solid evidence. Now all Bart needed to be absolutely sure of the Star Killer's true identity was a fingerprint match.

While he was driving back to Long Island, he called fingerprint expert Mike Wells one more time. He didn't answer the first two times. Where the hell is he? Did he change his number? Bart decided to call one more time. He was just about to hang up when Mike nonchalantly answered. "Hello?"

"Hey, Mike, it's Bart Sullivan. Would you look at a set of fingerprints for me?"

"Sure. You know the deal—as long as they weren't obtained illegally."

"No, just a case I've been doing a little extra research on," Bart lied.

"Alright. Come by tomorrow morning. Ten. You know where I am. Bring cash."

When Bart returned to Cassandra's house, she was in the office doing some work for the foundation, so he made a quick copy of both sets of fingerprints and removed the names from the top so Mike wouldn't know whose they were. The partial set of fingerprints taken from the Noxzema bottle were kept hidden from the public since the department was concerned they weren't getting a match on them. Apparently, from what Donnie had said, the person wasn't in the system, and the department didn't want to take any more heat for having two more victims and not making any headway.

Bart didn't have to leave her at night anymore. It was almost as if they were already married. Cassandra told him that she had a meeting with the attorneys Friday morning regarding the real estate company and that she wanted him to go with her.

"After all, everything that's mine will soon be yours," she said and kissed him. "We're partners, and I think it's important we make the big decisions together."

They sat on the couch, and Cassandra lay in Bart's arms. "I want to talk to you about one more thing."

Bart looked intently into her eyes, curious as to what she was about to say.

"I'm not sure if it's too early to talk about this, but it's important to me, and I want to let you know where I stand."

He continued to give her his undivided attention. What could she be referring to?

"When we have children, I'd like to stay home with them. I'll have a nursery at the office for when I absolutely have to go in, but I want to be with them at all times. It's important to me they never feel alone or afraid, and as their mother, it's my job to make sure they never do."

"I think that's a great idea, and because of you, we're going to have the most beautiful children in the world." He gave her an affectionate kiss and held her close. He couldn't imagine a time when he felt more complete. Could all these dreams come true, or would the evil that was lurking change everything?

CHAPTER 32

TRUTH

The next day, Bart woke up early to meet with Mike Wells. Although Mike had never been one to follow the rules, it was crucial for Bart to ensure the identity of the prints remained confidential. He couldn't risk having any witnesses.

The partial fingerprints from the Noxzema bottle had not been released to the public, and the fingerprints in Lupo's file had the name Renee Angler on them, but they were from the Chicago Police Department. Bart was concerned that if the fingerprints were real and if, by some miraculous coincidence, they matched the fingerprints on the Noxzema bottle, the unknown was whether they matched Renee Angler.

Mike Wells had a small storage unit in Queens. Bart met him there. It took Mike all of ten seconds to confirm the prints were a match.

"What are you up to here?"

"Nothing really. Just want to make sure my thoughts on this are the same as yours," Bart lackadaisically answered.

Mike didn't seem entirely convinced, but he figured the less he knew, the better. They made small talk for a few minutes before

Bart paid him and left the unit. He finally had confirmation that the prints in Lupo's file belonged to the Star Killer. I guess Lupo wasn't so crazy after all. Now he needed to find out whether the name Renee Angler was real. The million-dollar question now was whether the prints in the file and from the Noxzema jar matched the man identified as Angler.

After meeting with Mike, Bart had to go to Midtown to return his department vehicle. He had arranged for Cassie to pick him up from the precinct. He had already taken Lupo's phone out of the car and put it in the back of his TV, but, just to be safe, he opened the glove compartment one last time and made sure it was empty.

He arrived at the precinct, walked inside, handed the keys to the lieutenant in charge, and walked out of the building without even going up to the detective's office to say goodbye to everyone. Before he met Cassandra, this entire process would have resonated with Bart entirely differently, but now she was his first priority. That's not to say he didn't have any emotions about leaving the department. He had spent a decade of his life trying to make the streets of New York safer, and he hoped he had made an impact, but it was time to move on to the next chapter.

When he walked outside the precinct, Cassandra was sitting in the rear seat of the Range Rover with Fran driving. He opened the back door and got inside without saying much more than a hello.

"Are you okay?" Cassandra asked him after a few minutes of silence.

"As long as I have you, I'm good," he said.

They had an appointment with Cassandra's attorney, Bill Wright, to discuss her position in the real estate business. On the way to his office, Cassandra gave Bart a copy of the licensing agreement between Michael Bandell and her father, which was more than twenty years old. Bart had read through it the night before. It was a fairly simple licensing agreement that granted the Bandell family full discretion in running the business but gave them no actual ownership of the company. It was an agreement that rolled over every five years unless either party wanted to amend it, which they never did. They arrived at the attorney's office about 11 a.m. The receptionist showed them to the conference room, where Bill Wright and Claire Tran were waiting. They stood up as soon as Cassandra and Bart entered the room.

Cassandra said hello and introduced Bart as her fiancé.

"Oh, wow," replied Bill. "I hadn't heard anything about this."

"I didn't think I had to tell you about my personal life," Cassandra said curtly.

They all sat down at the large conference table. Cassandra said to Bill, "I've made a decision to take the real estate company back. It's what my mother intended and something I should've done years ago. Now, with that said, let's talk business. I don't understand why, since we are being paid a fifty percent revenue share, we have not received any tax forms from these people in more than four years."

Bill quickly interjected, "I've sent them three letters. They never reply."

"Bill, if you sent them one letter and they didn't reply, it would seem wise to take further action. According to this licensing agreement, they have to give us dollar figures every year so we understand how the profit sharing is going."

ɹn't think you were interested, Cassandra, so I didn't force
e."

Cassandra looked at Bill and Claire. "Okay, we are where we
e right now. How do I take the company back? What legal steps do
we have to take?"

Claire very rarely answered questions directly. Bill was an over-
powering figure, and he always had to get his answer in immediately.

Cassandra looked at Claire. "What do you think we should do?"

"According to the agreement, we have to send them notice that
we are about to take the company back; we own the stock, we own
the buildings—basically everything—and we need to do it within a
certain reasonable amount of time."

"What do you mean by 'reasonable'?" Cassandra asked.

Bill interjected. "I think we have to give them at least three
months to get out of the business in order to do this in an efficient
manner. We can't rush if we want to come out on top."

Cassandra looked at Bart. "What do you think?"

He thought for a moment and sternly replied, "I'm concerned
about why they're not replying to these income requests. They must
have something to hide, or they would've sent the dollar figures to
you." Bart looked at Bill. "What can you legally do to force them to
supply income numbers?"

"I can go to court, but that might wind up in a lawsuit. If we
want to take the company back without any legal issues, we may
want to think twice about involving the court."

While they were talking, Bart's phone was continuously vibrating inside his pocket. He glanced at it, trying not to be disrespectful, but it was becoming difficult to ignore. It was Jerry Morris.

"I'm sorry," he said, "but I really need to take this."

"Go ahead," Cassandra told him.

"I apologize," he said, holding up his phone. "I'll be back in a moment."

As soon as Bart was out the door, Bill looked at Cassandra. "You really should've told me your relationship with him was serious. We'll need to get a prenup together before this goes any further."

Cassandra was obviously irritated. "Bill, have I asked you to do a prenup?"

"Well, no, but—"

"Okay, then I don't want to hear any more about it from anybody, and if you keep treating me like I'm a stupid woman, we are going to have a serious problem."

Bart walked back into the room and immediately noticed Cassandra's demeanor had changed. She was visibly upset.

"Is everything okay?"

"Yes, fine," she quickly responded.

Cassandra looked at Bill and then over to Claire. "By the middle of next week, the company should be in the process of being transferred over to me. I want the best ideas you can come up with that don't end up with us in court, and I also want to know if there's some way we can get the income flow from these people before we make any moves."

Bill quickly replied, "Your father was paid for the past twenty years. They supplied proof of income up until the past few years, but your family has been paid every year. We just don't have numbers on the exact gross or net income."

Bart focused on Claire. "Help me with the details. Cassandra owns the building, true?"

"Yes," Claire said, nodding.

"And Cassandra owns the stock?"

"Correct."

"So, in other words, she owns the computers, phone systems, and everything else in the offices?"

Bill and Claire looked at each other, confused. Bill asked, "What does that have to do with anything?"

"I'm just making sure I understand how this all works and making sure you do too."

Cassandra stood up and looked at Bill, her piercing green eyes narrowing. "I want an answer to this by the middle of next week. We'll meet next Wednesday at eleven o'clock."

Bill looked at the calendar in his folder. "I can't be here at eleven o'clock. I've got an appointment."

"Are you available?" Cassandra asked Claire.

"I am."

"Fine. We'll meet with Claire, and she can present whatever resolutions you two come up with."

Cassandra stood up and turned to walk out of the room. Bart followed. He grabbed her hand and squeezed it, attempting to relieve some of her tension. Fran was sitting in the lobby, reading a book.

As soon as she spotted them, she got up and pulled the car around to the front of the building. Bart opened the door, and the two of them walked outside and got in the vehicle.

After driving about a block, Cassandra looked at Bart. "I just don't understand what's going on. This is a million-dollar operation, and we have no idea how much money it generates each year. I don't understand how Bill has allowed this to happen, and, as far as I'm concerned, this is the final nail in his coffin."

Bart could hear her voice quiver with emotion. She was upset, confused, and angry. He took her hand, kissed it, and said, "We will be fine. We will figure this out together."

Cassandra smiled and said exhaustedly, "I'm starving. Fran, can we go to the Landmark Diner, please?"

"Of course," Fran said, smiling at her in the rearview mirror.

As Fran pulled up to the restaurant, Cassandra asked if she'd like to join them. She cheerfully accepted and pulled into a nearby parking area. While they were walking through the parking lot, Bart noticed Donnie's car parked nearby. Upon entering the restaurant, he spotted Jeannie and the kids sitting near the back of the dining room.

Bart did not mention the call from Jerry to Cassandra. She was upset enough. He did want to talk to Fran about the call, though. Jerry was hearing the FBI had photos of some of the Albanian troublemakers sneaking back into the country.

CHAPTER 33

PLAY BALL

It appeared winter was finally over. The ice had disappeared, freezing temperatures were obsolete, and the trees were bustling with new life. It was a perfect day for a ball game. Donnie and Jeannie were going to meet Bart and Cassandra at her home around eleven o'clock and were going ahead to Yankee Stadium to enjoy an early game. Before they arrived, Bart informed Cassie that Jerry's call the other day was another heads-up regarding the Albanians. She assured Bart she felt one hundred percent confident with Fran.

Cassandra and Jeannie were becoming great friends. They had gone to lunch several times and on shopping trips. Cassandra had even spent time with Jeannie and Donnie's kids. When they arrived at Cassandra's house, she gave Jeannie a tour of her home while Bart and Donnie went to look at Frank's car collection. They needed to talk away from the women.

"So what's going on with our friend?" asked Donnie as he looked at a baby blue 1957 Chevy Bel Air.

Bart walked over to him, looked around, and whispered, "The partial prints on the Noxzema bottle matched the prints in Lupo's file."

"Holy shit," Donnie said, his voice barely above a whisper. He stood for a moment, trying to gather his thoughts, then turned and looked Bart right in the eye. "What are you going to do?"

"I don't know yet. I mean, how do I know those prints in the file with Renee Angler's name on them are his? It's not like I can ask Lupo, and I sure as hell can't ask the Chicago Police Department or risk going into CODIS and looking around. If something happens to him and the police department finds out he's the Star Killer, anybody who made inquiries about him will be a suspect." He paused for a second before continuing in a whisper. "I know a guy who has hacked the NYPD fingerprint system, and I will follow this Angler character around and get his fingerprints off something—a beer glass, a car door, anything."

"I don't think that's a great idea," Donnie said immediately. "If this guy is who we think he is, he's watching for people following him. You can't tail him. We have to assume he knows what you look like."

Cassandra and Jeannie walked in, startling Bart and Donnie.

"We'd better get going," Cassandra said loudly from the other side of the garage.

When they arrived at Yankee Stadium, they parked the car and took their tickets to the front gate. Frank's company had a box right behind the dugout, no more than eight rows up. They had arrived early. The team was still having batting practice. Donnie and Jeannie walked down behind the dugout to get a better look at the hitters, while Bart and Cassandra sat holding hands and chatting.

"Hey, Cassandra!" Donnie yelled from near the field. "Someone wants to say hello!"

She looked at the player standing near Donnie. Derek Jeter waved at Cassandra, and she waved back.

"How are you?" she asked.

"Great," he responded. "It's good to see you." Then he disappeared into the dugout.

Donnie came running up the stairs frantically. "Cassie, you know Derek Jeter?"

Cassandra couldn't help but laugh. Donnie was beaming like a small child on Christmas morning, and he had sweat running down his forehead from sprinting up the stairs.

"Our foundation gives money to Derek's Turn 2 Foundation. It does a lot of great work with kids."

Donnie looked at Bart. "I guess you have some stiff competition." They all laughed, but for some reason, Bart felt a ping of jealousy. Cassandra knew almost everyone in town, and sometimes he wondered why, out of all the rich and handsome men she knew, she chose him. The truth of the matter was he chose her; he was the one who had pursued her, after all, but he still found himself wavering at times.

Donnie suggested they grab beers and hot dogs before the game, but Cassandra told him to stay put. She raised her hand, and a young girl appeared seemingly out of nowhere.

"Good afternoon, Miss D'Angelo. It's good to see you again," said the young girl.

"It's great to see you again, Barbara. How's everything going?"

"My last year of law school—thank God," she said with a sigh. "If it weren't for the summer job and your help, I'd never have been able to finish."

Cassandra smiled. "That is wonderful. Keep up the great work."

They ordered a few things, and the girl vanished. Donnie felt like a king, being waited on all day in a private box with a perfect view of the park. The sun was out, and the temperature was in the seventies. It almost didn't matter that the Yankees lost. It was a dream.

Once the game was over, they sat in the box, finishing their beers and waiting for the crowd to dissipate. Then they slowly strolled back to the car. Cassandra had asked Bart and Donnie to bring sports jackets with them, but no one thought twice about it. She always had something up her sleeve.

"Let's head toward 114th Street and 1st Avenue," Cassie said as Bart drove.

Bart asked, "Why are we going over there?"

She smiled. "What's at 114th Street and 1st Avenue?"

Donnie immediately shouted out, "Rao's! You must be kidding! I know people who have been waiting to get into Rao's for years."

"One of the benefits of your father growing up with people from the old neighborhood."

They parked near Rao's and walked toward the front door. Before they even had a chance to get inside the restaurant, a well-dressed man with a thick black mustache and a balding head walked up to the door and greeted Cassandra with a hug. "Cassandra, my god, I remember when you were a small child. How are you, my dear?"

"Mr. Pellegrino, it's great to see you. This is my fiancé, Bart Sullivan, and our best friends, Donnie and Jeannie."

"It's nice to meet you all. Please, please, follow me. I'll get you a table." He took them to a booth near the bar. People were everywhere, eating, drinking, and laughing. Bart heard Mr. Pellegrino whisper to the waiter, "Mike, take very good care of these people."

Donnie sat at the table with his mouth hanging open, looking around and trying unsuccessfully to buffer his excitement.

"Close your mouth before flies get in," Bart said. "And don't look like such a damn tourist."

"So, your fiancé?" Jeannie said to Cassandra after they ordered drinks and the waiter left.

"Well, it's not official yet. I can tell he's trying to work up the courage." She looked at Bart and winked. Everyone laughed.

"Whoa, I thought I was whipped, but you're much worse." Donnie nudged Bart in the arm.

The waiter brought two bottles of wine and menus and asked if they wanted appetizers. They took their time soaking up the ambience and watching all the famous people walk around, half of whom walked over to Cassandra and said hello. They drank, they laughed, and they enjoyed some of the best meals they had ever had, including Bart's favorite, rigatoni Bolognese.

The drive back to Long Island was quiet. Everyone had had a bit too much to drink and was exhausted from the excitement of the day. As usual, Bart drove since he had stopped drinking after the game. Cassandra held his hand, occasionally kissing it, while Donnie was in the back with Jeannie—both half asleep. When they arrived at the estate, Cassandra suggested that Donnie and Jeannie sleep in the guest room, but Donnie assured her he was fine to drive home.

After they left, Cassandra and Bart went inside the house and instantly attacked each other—kissing one another, touching one another, and tearing off each other's clothes.

"Today was great, but this is what I've been waiting for since this morning," Bart said as he pulled Cassandra's blouse over her head.

She laughed. "I wonder if you'll still feel the same years from now."

"I won't," he said. "It will be worse."

Bart picked her up and carried her into the bedroom, leaving her clothes on the tile floor.

CHAPTER 34

REVELATION

Cassandra and Evon had planned to spend the day in the city shopping, which left Frank the time he needed for a long and serious conversation with Bart. They met in Frank's office shortly after the ladies had left for Manhattan. Once Bart found out about the top-tier security of that office, he felt comfortable discussing nearly anything with Frank in that location.

As usual, Frank was alone when Bart walked in, but Jonathan had obviously been there. A breakfast spread was laid out for them: eggs, fresh fruit, French toast, and coffee. It looked and smelled heavenly. Bart was too anxious to eat anything, however. He walked inside and closed the door behind him, not knowing what to expect from the conversation. Frank turned to say hello. His expression was stark.

"Have a seat," Frank said to Bart, motioning to the leather couch.

Bart sat down. He was trying to distinguish Frank's tone, but it was impossible.

"Thank you for coming by," Frank said impassively.

"No problem."

"I wanted to talk to you because I think life presents different opportunities to us all, and we have to be aware of those opportunities and use them to our advantage. Your relationship with Cassandra is one of those opportunities. She has found in you someone she trusts entirely, and I think your involvement in our family offers a potential partnership for the both of us."

Bart looked at Frank quizzically. "I'm not sure I understand."

"To get to the point of the story, I'll have to start at the beginning. You see, when I met Cassandra's mother, Janet, I immediately fell in love with her, but her family had no use for me. They had a little money and thought I would never amount to anything. They forbade her from seeing me. Obviously, she didn't listen. We were young and in love. No one could tell us a damn thing. This went on for years. It was very difficult for Janet because she was in the middle of it all. She defied her parents and married me. I think the main reason I did succeed in life is that I was driven to show everyone Janet had not made a mistake in marrying me.

"I started out building small homes, which led to larger homes, then to duplexes and small, one-story office buildings. After years of sacrifice, I got the opportunity to build a twelve-story building in Manhattan. I bid on the project and got the job. As soon as I signed the contract, all the subs involved in the building came to me and told me they needed a ten percent pay increase due to the cost of concrete, plumbing, steel, electric—everything. I was working on about a fifteen percent profit margin, but that ten percent was in the contract. I had to honor it. I could do nothing about it, but it nearly bankrupted me. Do you understand the Mafia has its hands in the construction business? I have tried for thirty years to get along, but sometimes it's difficult.

"Shortly after that, I met a friend who had been in the construction business longer than I had. He said to me, 'The only way you can control these subcontractors and keep the Mafia at bay is by owning those supply companies.' At first, I thought it was the stupidest idea I had ever heard, but the more I thought about it, the more I realized not only could I control my expenses, but I could also make a profit from owning those companies."

Bart looked at Frank and remained silent. Why is Frank telling me about his business ventures? Maybe he's trying to develop a relationship, or perhaps it has something to do with the job he mentioned.

"All my money was tied up in the construction of the highrises I was working on at the time. I had no extra cash and was too far in debt for the banks to lend me money. I was desperate. What I'm about to tell you, no one else but Anthony knows, and I don't want Cassandra or Evon to ever find out. If this information gets out, it will destroy my reputation, the foundation—everything. Do you understand?"

Bart nodded.

"I trust you to never speak about this to anyone."

"You have my word."

"I had a friend in the loan business, for lack of a better term. He dealt with numbers, prostitution, extortion—anything that could make him money. He made legitimate investments, but, unbeknownst to me, he also invested money for the Mafia. He was thinking long term for his family. He lent me $4 million, enough for a down payment on four companies, concrete, steel, plumbing and electric, giving me the opportunity to own them. I knew the money had come from strange places, but I never thought he was laundering money for the Mob.

"The agreement for that loan was that Sal would receive twenty percent of the net revenue every year and thirty percent of the profits from the sale of the four companies when I decided to sell. Obviously, we didn't have a written contract. We shook hands, and that was that. I really don't regret doing it. I never would have been able to achieve the level of success I have without that money, but if people find out about it, it'll be construed as me making deals with a crime family or something similar, which is what I want to avoid. I want to be clear about something. This has nothing to do with my main company, Ryan & D'Angelo. When the main company sells at the end of the year, the four small companies will not be part of that deal.

"I'm sure you're wondering what this has to do with you. Well, the man I borrowed the money from, Sal Alessi, has two sons—John and Vito. Unfortunately, Sal has dementia, so I deal with John and Vito for the most part. John is fairly reasonable, but Vito is a loose cannon. When I talked to him about the return on his money, he said he wanted thirty percent of the net yearly and forty percent of the sale. You got everything so far?"

"Yes, it sounds pretty simple. Vito is clearly trying to take advantage of his father's deteriorating health and get more than he's entitled to."

"That's exactly my problem. I need someone to sit down with the two of them and negotiate some kind of deal. I was about ready to hire a third party when you entered the picture. I need someone like you who understands how these people think and who can negotiate without having this thing blow up in my face. Remember Sal has dementia. I don't know who else is aware of how I got the money."

Bart looked perplexed. "What about Anthony? Can he talk with them?"

"From their point of view, Anthony is hired help. He doesn't have any clout. You being my daughter's future husband—someone who could take over the family business—provides a different incentive for them."

Frank looked Bart right in the eye. "Now that I spilled my guts to you, I think maybe it's time you tell me the truth about you and Cassie. You're in love with her, but you won't ask her to marry you. It doesn't make any sense. What is going on? Are you hiding something?"

Bart wasn't expecting Frank to ask him about marrying Cassandra, or better yet not marrying her. He knew the reason he hadn't asked her, but he wasn't prepared to tell anyone. He struggled but finally mustered a passable answer. "Something is going on in my life that has to be dealt with before I marry your daughter. I can't risk dragging her into it. It's too serious."

"I just told you something that could destroy my entire life and my family members' lives. I need you to be honest with me. This doesn't have to do with another woman or an illegitimate child or something like that, right?"

Bart quickly interposed. "No, no, absolutely not."

"You need to level with me. Is it something I can help you with?"

There was a long pause. Bart finally sighed and began speaking. "What I'm going to tell you, only a few people know about." He cleared his throat. "For the past five years, I've been hunting down a serial killer; he's killed maybe thirty women and is a sick bastard who has to be stopped. I think I know who and where he is, but I can't prove it legally, so in order to stop him, I'll have to do the unthinkable."

Frank stared at him speechless. That was clearly not the information he was expecting Bart to divulge. "There's got to be something else that can be done. There must be some way to work this out without you doing that."

"Let's deal with your issue first and then worry about mine. What's our next step with these guys?"

"Well, there are two separate issues. One, you're going to have to negotiate with the brothers so we can pay them off and get them out of our lives, and two, we need to go ahead and sell all four businesses so we can be finished with them for good. However, I don't want attorneys involved. If they start poking around, things could get complicated. So, I want to prep you on the businesses. We have concrete, plumbing, electric, and steel companies. I want to sell all of them to the employees. I need someone like you to negotiate a sale with the unions—not handle the legal issues. Let Claire handle those. Any questions?"

Bart worked through the details in his mind before responding. "Nope. I'm in, but we better get to work soon."

They shook hands, and Frank thanked Bart again for his help.

As Bart opened the door and began walking out, he heard Frank say one more thing. He paused to listen.

"About that other problem—you might want to talk to Anthony. Over the years, he's solved a number of sensitive issues for me."

CHAPTER 35

ENGAGED

Over the next few weeks, Frank educated Bart on the four companies he was planning on selling. In order for Bart to convince the employees to buy them, he would have to be well versed in each one. Frank had compiled a dossier of information about the four businesses. In addition to supplying Bart with every fact he possibly could, Frank spent a number of hours explaining the concrete industry, which was the biggest moneymaker. The only action remaining was for Bart to meet with Claire and acquire a brief understanding of the legalities of selling a company to its employees, which was very different from selling to the public.

The object was not to turn Bart into an attorney but to provide him with an overview of how the sales would go. Claire would be present for all negotiations, and any legal issues would be her responsibility. Frank needed Bart to concentrate on the unions and employees, and since Bart had experience as a union delegate, Frank had complete confidence in his capabilities. Selling the businesses to employees would not only be a simpler process, but it would also limit scrutiny from outsiders concerning any allegations of Mob ties.

Cassandra was elated that Bart and her father were getting along so well, and Bart seemed extremely interested in the business.

One day, while he was visiting one of the companies, Cassandra sat down with her father to talk about something they had not discussed in years. Before Janet had passed, she had given her engagement ring to Frank and told him if Cassandra wanted it someday, it was hers. It was a difficult conversation to have, one that brought many memories and pain for both of them, but Cassandra was determined to have her mother's ring. She remembered looking at it when she was younger—admiring how big and shiny it was on her mother's slender finger and how the light would sometimes reflect off of it and project rainbows around the room.

"Would you mind getting it out of the safe for me?" Cassandra asked her father as they sat in his office. "I may make some alterations to it so it is personalized to me, but I'd be honored to use it as my engagement ring, if that's okay."

"It's more than okay!" Frank was ecstatic Cassie remembered the ring, and she was thrilled to wear something on her hand that reminded her of her mother every single day.

"One more thing," said Cassandra. "I'm going to ask Bart to marry me. I'll ask his parents soon since that's the right thing to do."

Frank looked slightly puzzled; it was very untraditional, but Cassandra had never been a traditional woman. She was strong, independent, and had a mind of her own. She had found the man she wanted to spend her life with and wasn't going to wait on him.

Evon had walked into the room mid-conversation and was beaming from ear to ear.

Frank walked upstairs to retrieve the ring from the safe in his closet, and Evon immediately told Cassie how thrilled she was and that she loved the idea of her proposing to Bart. Coming from Italy,

Evon was an old-world woman—that was probably why she and Frank got along so swimmingly—but when it came to Cassandra, Evon supported everything she did. She had been the voice of reason in Cassandra's life for the past twenty years.

"What do you think people will say if I propose to him?" Cassandra asked.

Evon paused for a minute before answering in her rich Italian accent. "It's not important what people say or think. All that is important is that you two are happy. You love each other, and there's no doubt about that. Enjoy this time, your love, and your future, and don't worry about anything else."

Cassandra gave Evon a big hug. Right when she let her go, Frank returned with the ring. It was just as she remembered—an oval-cut diamond with a halo of smaller diamonds surrounding it and even more delicately set in the band. Now that she was older, she could tell the center stone was about three karats and the smaller diamonds were about half a karat each. They all admired how beautiful it was.

"I love this so much," Cassandra said, still examining it. She looked up at her father. "But I do want to make it my own. I'd like to redesign it using the stones."

For a long time, Frank thought that moment might never come. He was elated his daughter was so happy and excited to have found a man who loved her unconditionally. However, he was concerned about Bart's problem, and his number one priority was protecting his daughter.

The following day, Fran drove Cassandra to Bart's parents' home. She had called them earlier that morning and asked if she could stop by for a cup of coffee. She found herself much more nervous than she had anticipated. She didn't want Bart's parents to think she was being forward by asking their son to marry her.

When she arrived, she gave both of Bart's parents an inviting hug, and they told her to come inside. They bantered a bit while she worked up the nerve to tell them why she had stopped by. "I have something important I want to ask you," she finally said during a break in the conversation. They looked at her intently, wondering what she could be talking about.

"I'd like to ask Bart to marry me, but I wanted to get your blessing first."

Mary immediately smiled and began clapping her hands. She stood up and hugged Cassie as if she were her own daughter. "Nothing would make us happier. My son couldn't ask for anyone kinder than you. You go ahead and propose. If he's taking his time for some reason, then he'll just have to miss his chance to be the one to propose. I will tell you one thing for sure. He will certainly say yes. He is absolutely and completely in love with you."

Bart's father was also very excited. He and Mary had been waiting for Bart to get married since they met Cassandra, probably even before that. The truth was, they weren't sure if he would ever find a wife.

Cassandra promised to let them know as soon as she decided when and where and that she and Bart would call as soon as she had proposed. She hugged them both again and left. Cassandra mentioned to Bart's mother that she wanted a December wedding. If they could put it together that quickly, they would do it that year.

Cassandra hadn't thought about where she would pop the question, and she didn't care much. She knew she wanted to do it soon. She and Bart had made plans to go to dinner the following night at a small restaurant in Sands Point called La Piccolo. He had been spending time with Claire between being educated on the concrete business and trying to understand the legalities of selling the four businesses.

In the midst of helping Frank, Bart had also begun having casual conversations with Anthony about his predicament concerning the Star Killer. Anthony was easy to talk to, and he saw things the way Bart did—always thinking about what would happen down the road and not running around making impetuous decisions. Bart felt if he could trust anyone to help him resolve things, it would be Anthony. After all, he knew all the family secrets.

That all said, Bart was extremely busy—there was no doubt about it—but when Cassandra asked him to dinner, he immediately said yes. He couldn't help but spoil her—whatever she wanted, she got. Although he was a strong man both physically and emotionally, he was also extraordinarily kind and respectful, and he always let Cassie know she was the most important thing in his life. Cassandra knew once she asked Bart to marry her, an engagement party would follow. She had already asked Evon if she would help her throw it, and she enthusiastically agreed.

The following evening, Cassandra anxiously got ready. She took a shower and put her hair in curlers while she did her makeup. Bart was showered, shaved, and dressed before her—as usual—and was in the kitchen on the phone. She walked into her closet and chose a strappy, high-neck brown Ralph Lauren dress that hugged each and every curve of her body. It was one of her favorite dresses—comfortable yet sexy. She removed the curlers and slipped on a pair of black Steve Madden sandals with a slight heel. As soon as she walked into the kitchen, Bart's eyes widened and his face lit up as he admired her.

"I'll talk to you later," he said, hanging up the phone and walking over to Cassie.

"You look absolutely stunning, Bella," he said, sweeping her into his arms and kissing her on the lips.

She blushed. "Thank you. We better get going."

They drove to the restaurant and got a small private table in the back corner of the dining room. Cassandra had made a reservation, and although they were already booked, the owners knew Cassie and her family and were willing to accommodate whatever she needed. Once they sat down, the waiter brought over a bottle of Dom Pérignon Cassandra had pre ordered.

"Wow, what are we celebrating?" Bart asked.

She took his hand in hers and peered into his eyes from across the candlelit table.

"Bart Sullivan, I've been looking everywhere for you for such a long time. I had begun to think I was never going to find you. From the moment I saw you walk into the Rainbow Room, I knew I wanted to see you every day after. You're my favorite person in the entire world, and before I met you, I felt like a piece of me was missing. I never want to feel that way again."

Cassandra stood up, still holding Bart's hand, and dropped down to one knee. From beside the wine chiller, she pulled out a small black box.

"In this box is an engagement ring, and, if you'll have me, I would love nothing more than to be your wife."

Bart, who was very rarely surprised, stared at her, stunned. He was unable to move yet could feel his eyes becoming moist. She had joked around about proposing to him if he took too long, but he never would have believed she'd actually do it.

"I want nothing more in this entire world than to marry you," he said softly, quickly wiping his eyes before leaning down and pulling her off the floor and into his arms. He kissed her, and the guests at the surrounding tables all applauded spiritedly. "I wish you wouldn't have bought your own ring, though," Bart said, laughing and hugging her.

She leaned away to see his face and said, with tears in her eyes, "It belonged to my mother." He pulled her back in and hugged her tightly, wishing he never had to let her go.

CHAPTER 36

PRELUDE

To say both families were overjoyed by the engagement would have been a vast understatement. The excitement of the pending wedding had taken over everyone's lives. Evon, Cassandra, and Bart's mother, Mary, were knee-deep in wedding plans. Cassandra had always wanted a December wedding, and considering it was almost June, it'd be a stretch for the average person—but Cassandra D'Angelo was no average woman. She had already spoken to someone about reserving a wedding venue and hiring caterers, photographers, and an officiant. It certainly helped that she knew half the people in the city or had donated money to charities they were associated with.

Fortunately for Bart, Frank, and Anthony, the women were preoccupied with dresses, floral arrangements, and all the minuscule details of a wedding that make it unique to the couple. It gave them time to focus on the business at hand. Bart had disclosed to Cassie what Jerry had told him when he had called during the meeting with the attorneys, but surprisingly, she seemed impassive about the information. She had Fran now and felt entirely safe with her. Fran quickly became an integral part of the family and was even involved in one of the charities Frank was most invested in.

It was a foundation that supported single mothers. Frank had bought a small apartment building in Queens, remodeled it to make fifteen one-bedroom apartments, and built a fully staffed childcare center that was free of charge to the mothers. The women could live there and utilize the childcare facility while they looked for jobs and got back on their feet. Many of them had been victims of domestic violence and were seeking refuge for themselves and their children. The foundation also supplied educational opportunities for them to receive their GED or go to college.

Fran was so impressed with the operation that she began mentoring mothers during her off time. She found the entire experience enlightening and rewarding and got a much better view of who Cassandra really was. Her initial impression of Cassandra had been that she was a spoiled rich girl who had no regard for anything other than shopping, but she quickly realized how generous and caring Cassandra was and was pointedly impressed with her. This new-found notion of Cassandra and how much she and Bart cared for one another heightened her protectiveness toward Cassandra.

Frank and Bart had been meeting as often as possible to discuss the pending sale of the companies, and everything appeared to be on track. Bart also occasionally met with Claire to gain an understanding of the legalities of selling a business to its employees. He felt comfortable with Claire; she was highly intelligent and had an outstanding way of explaining every tiny detail in a way he could easily understand. She was also very transparent, unlike Bill Wright, who always seemed to be hiding something.

Bart and Anthony arranged to meet in Frank's secure office one afternoon. They had been so busy it seemed like they would never have a chance to sit down and talk. Bart had mentioned the situation to him a few days earlier in passing, but it was time for them to devise a plan. If Anthony was going to help Bart discover whether Renee Angler was indeed the Star Killer, it was going to take serious detective work from the both of them. Bart needed to explain the story in its entirety to Anthony. It would be the only way to ensure Anthony felt comfortable executing a job so risky.

They sat in the office for more than an hour while Bart went through all the facts he believed were important. Anthony was absolutely disgusted that Angler may have killed as many as thirty women in the Northeast and as many as five in the New York area alone. It was apparent that Angler knew who Bart was and what he looked like, so it was not an option for Bart to trail him. Bart needed someone skillful and anonymous—someone exactly like Anthony— to confirm Angler's identity. He explained to Anthony that following someone is much harder than it may seem, especially a serial killer. Angler would be paranoid and constantly watching his back.

That evening, the two of them went to Angler's address and looked at pictures of him, his car and license plate, and the outside of his apartment. They also discussed his daily routine; he was a stock- broker, which meant he went to Wall Street every day and possi- bly frequented other spots in the city. Anthony's initial task was to acquire something with Angler's fingerprints on it so they could be matched to the existing prints Bart had from the Noxzema bottle.

In order for Anthony to obtain a decent set of prints, he would have to get them from somewhere Angler had been firmly gripping a glass or the handle of a door in a car or building. Unfortunately, they couldn't allow anyone to see them getting these prints, so walk- ing around in the middle of Manhattan powdering random door handles was not an option. If any members of law enforcement or a good citizen with a camera saw them, they would immediately inquire about who they worked for and what they were up to—causing more problems than Bart was willing to deal with. Not to mention if Angler thought for one moment he was being followed, he might disappear, and they might never see him again. This was the Star Killer. Any mistake by Anthony would be a disaster.

"It's a dangerous situation," Bart said to Anthony as they were discussing the details. "I may be asking too much of you. If that's the case, just let me know, and I'll find another way to deal with this prick."

Anthony assuredly looked at Bart. "Cassandra is like a daughter to me. I've been with her since she was five years old. I've seen her during the good times and the worst times. I've seen her deal with being hurt over and over again by schmucks who don't give a rat's ass about her. With that said, I have never seen her this happy, and I'm willing to do anything to make sure nothing gets in the way of that happiness—but you need to understand the road you're going down. Killing this guy may be the right thing to do, but you're putting your future with Cassandra at risk."

"I understand that" Bart said. "More than you'll ever know."

* * *

The upcoming meeting with the Alessi brothers needed to be scheduled. Frank was anxious to call and make the arrangements, and he felt it might be better if Bart handled things instead so they understood who was running the show. Bart's concern was not so much that they would come armed—he had dealt with that more times than he could remember—it was that they may be wired. It was not uncommon for the FBI or other law enforcement agencies to flip those types of criminals and bribe them with some kind of deal.

Frank had not technically committed a crime since the payments to Sal regarding the companies were made from one Swiss bank to another, but if their partnership went public, it would certainly damage the foundation's reputation and possibly open the door for the IRS to conjure up charges.

Weeks went by. Anthony spent every second of his free time following Renee Angler and looking for an opportunity to lift his prints from something. He followed him to work in the mornings and back to his apartment in the afternoons, but he rarely went anywhere else except occasionally to the bar or the nearby strip joint. When he did, he never ordered drinks. He would walk around peering at women. Anthony was sure Angler was his guy—the way he stared at potential victims like they were prey to be hauled off and butchered—but he knew Bart wouldn't allow any action without definite evidence. Anthony also knew he couldn't watch that creep stalk innocent women for much longer. He was determined to get the prints so he and Bart could make sure the Star Killer would never take another life again.

CHAPTER 37

THE MEETING

Frank was walking from the house toward the car museum when Anthony pulled up in a black SUV. He asked Anthony if they needed any extra equipment—slang for weapons. Anthony opened the back of the vehicle to reveal a large black canvas bag.

"I think we got everything we need here," he confidently stated. "And with your future son-in-law, I don't think we have anything to worry about," he added with a crooked grin.

They both walked into the office. Bart was already there, fumbling around with a small metal box about half the size of a cigarette pack. He was reading from a piece of paper that looked like instructions.

"What do you have there?" Frank asked.

"This is a jammer," Bart responded, unplugging a wire from the side and inserting another one. "You place it on the table or hide it in a room, and it will disable any electronic signals from coming in or going out, including from any wires someone may be wearing."

Frank looked at him with one eyebrow raised. "I don't think the Alessi brothers are going to like this."

"Well, if we don't tell them, then they'll have no choice but to like it."

Frank turned to Anthony. "Did you find any information on them we may need to know?"

"I met with a disgruntled ex-employee," Anthony said. "So, you'll have to take the information with a grain of salt since they screwed him over. But, according to him, Alessi's are having money trouble. That may work in our favor. If they're strapped for cash, maybe we can settle this fairly quickly. Cash is a good motivator when you have none."

"I don't want to discuss money at this meeting," said Frank. "I think the best thing for us to do is to have Bart and one of the brothers sit down at a later date and negotiate some kind of deal once they're better acquainted."

"So, you're okay with them trying to screw you out of money?" Bart asked abruptly.

"No, I'm not okay with it, but I don't want this thing to blow up. I want it to go away."

"What are you willing to do then?" inquired Bart again. "If we're going to negotiate, you have to tell me what you're willing to give up."

Frank looked at Bart, his expression unyielding. "Just get it done. I trust you."

"Where are we meeting them anyway?" he asked Bart.

"I made a reservation at Seasons 52 in Garden City. I told them to get on the Meadowbrook Parkway about eleven o'clock and that I would text him directions."

Frank laughed. "That must've really pissed them off."

"Well, you can never be too careful," Bart said with a straight face. "If they don't know where the meeting is, then they can't get there beforehand and do anything we wouldn't want them to. You can introduce me to them. I can set up the next meeting to negotiate."

Frank shook his head and reminded Bart, "Remember, Cassandra and Evon can never know about this."

They piled in the car and began driving toward the restaurant. Bart texted the address to the Alessi brothers as planned, ensuring they wouldn't arrive before he and Frank did. The car ride was quiet, almost tense. Bart could tell Frank was nervous, and he decided it was best not to try to comfort him with small talk. For him, it was just another day; he had lost count of the number of times he had met with drug dealers and criminals, but his success always came from planning ahead. Today wasn't any different.

It was nearly noon when they turned into the parking lot of Seasons 52. Bart scoured the parking lot for anyone sitting in a car or looking dodgy. It was second nature for him to do so, but today he was especially aware. Everything looked normal, so they continued into the restaurant.

A young girl was standing at the entrance. She jauntily welcomed them.

"I have a reservation under Casey for six in the chef's room," Bart said as he approached the hostess.

"Certainly, Mr. Casey. Right this way."

Anthony turned to Frank and whispered, "Mr. Casey?" He laughed.

Their room was to the left of the entrance. It was near the front of the restaurant and had a door that provided privacy. However, the wall facing the outside was glass and open, so if someone sat outside, they'd be able to hear the conversation. Fortunately, it was a cloudy morning. Bart hoped the weather would deter outdoor patrons.

When they walked into the room, John and Vito Alessi were already seated at the table with another man Frank had never seen before.

Bart thought, Damn it. How did they beat us here? I gave them the address only forty minutes ago.

Frank walked toward them. The brothers both gave him a hug.

"It's good to see you," said John with a prominent Bronx accent. "This is Milton Graff, our attorney."

Frank shook the man's hand. "This is Bart Sullivan, and you all know Anthony."

They all shook hands with one another and sat down at the table. Bart quickly sized them up, taking notice of their attire, posture, body language, and facial expressions. John seemed friendly enough, and the attorney was okay, but Vito was clearly a jackass and made no attempt to hide it. He was dressed like a pimp in a blue suit, an unbuttoned dress shirt with no tie, and copious amounts of gold jewelry around his neck, tugging on his chest hair with every move he made. He even had a small gold hoop in his left ear.

"I wish your father could be here," Frank said, beginning the conversation. "I miss him, and he was always a good friend to me."

John raised his glass of water. "Salud to my father!"

They all clinked glasses, and there was a moment of silence while they took a sip.

Frank turned toward John. "No need to beat around the bush. Let's talk. I hear we have an issue with the business deal your father and I arranged. The only people involved in that arrangement were your father and me. I wish he were here to clarify what I have told you and Vito."

"My father told me exactly what you are referring to a long time ago, and I know what my brother and I are entitled to," Vito said defensively.

Frank didn't acknowledge his comment. He wanted to make clear he had no regard for Vito's childish outburst or his opinion on the subject. "I wanted us to get together so you could meet my future son-in-law," he said once he felt he had made his point. "He will be working with you on this business deal, and he will be the one to resolve it. I propose that Bart and John have a meeting following this one and come to some resolution."

"I think that's a good idea," interrupted Vito, "but I'll be the one to meet with Bart, and we will come to an agreement."

John didn't say anything. Vito obviously ran the show. As soon as they had sat down, Bart had placed the silver jamming device at the end of the table. Vito, distracted by his own narcissism, had not noticed it until now. "What's in there?" he asked, gesturing toward the box.

"It's a jamming device," Bart said frankly.

"What's it for?"

"It distorts signals and makes it impossible for anyone to listen in on this meeting or record anything."

"Oh, so you don't trust us?"

"I don't trust anybody."

John interrupted for the first time. "That's a good idea. We don't need any problems."

"Maybe we should do a contract of some type," said Alessis' attorney meekly. Bart had forgotten he was there.

"No. No contract. Nothing in writing. You and I will settle this," Bart said to Vito.

The attorney looked down at the table and never made eye contact after that.

After the initial discussion, the conversation became much lighter while everyone scarfed down lunch and made small talk. The contract and the agreement were never brought up again.

As Frank examined the table, he realized that involving Bart had been a good decision; he was smart and fearless and asserted his dominance as soon as he entered the room. He didn't need to make threats because everyone saw he was in charge and was going to get things done his way, whether people liked it or not.

As they walked to the parking lot after lunch, Anthony went ahead to get the car. Bart again unconsciously surveyed the lot. Once he felt nothing was out of the ordinary, he placed his hand on Vito's arm and ushered him out of hearing range from everyone else. "I'll be in contact within the next week or so, and you and I will plan a meeting to settle this," he said quietly.

Vito quickly challenged him. "What's all the secrecy about?"

"It's no one's business but ours what we're discussing."

Bart put his hand out, and Vito reciprocated the gesture.

"I'll be in touch."

Before Bart walked away, Vito stopped him. "I have to ask. Are you going to sell all of the companies?"

"Yes. I'll keep you informed. That way, you'll know up front what you're entitled to."

Anthony pulled up with the SUV, and Frank got in the back. Bart shook hands with John and the attorney and entered the car.

Frank let out a huge sigh of relief. "That went about as well as it could have, but one thing's for certain—from now on, I don't want to be around for any more of these meetings."

"No problem," said Bart. "I will handle it."

Frank was quiet for the duration of the ride home, lost in his thoughts. For his entire life, he had wished he had a son. His love for Cassandra was endless, but he would never put her in this dangerous situation. The meeting with the Alessi brothers made him realize what an asset Bart was going to be in his life, and he couldn't have been more grateful.

Bart was cool, calm, and collected. For him, it was just another situation he had dealt with a hundred times before. All of the men Cassandra dated before him would have pissed themselves if put in that position, but Bart thrived under pressure.

"I didn't think to ask you," Anthony said, glancing over at Bart. "Are you armed?"

"What do you think?" he asked with a grin.

As they pulled up to the main gate of the estate, Anthony spoke again. "You realize that was easy compared to the next few weeks, right?"

THE MEETING

Bart knew he was right. The upcoming weeks would be jam-packed with an engagement party and planning a wedding and honeymoon. Compared to what was to come, the meeting they had just attended was, ironically, a piece of cake.

CHAPTER 38

PRENUPTIALS

Bart headed toward the attorney's office for his final meeting with Claire before they approached the management and unions of all four companies. A parking spot was available on the street in front of the office, so he pulled the Range Rover into it and walked inside the building. The receptionist immediately recognized him.

"Good afternoon, Mr. Sullivan," said the blonde, smiling. "It's good to see you." She stood up from behind the desk. "Miss Tran hasn't arrived yet, but you can follow me."

She showed him into a conference room, and ten minutes later, Claire arrived. "Hi," she said frantically. "I'm sorry I'm late. It's been a crazy day already."

She had a briefcase slung over her right shoulder, and her arms were cradling a bunch of folders with papers desperately trying to escape from every angle.

"Let me help you with that," Bart said, standing up and grabbing some of the documents from her.

"Thank you," she said as she let out an exasperated sigh and sat down at the table. She took a moment to somewhat sort the folders, strategically placing some on the left and others on the right. She took a deep breath and clasped her hands in front of her on the desk as if she was about to deliver a long-awaited verdict to a client on death row.

"So, I think we are finally ready to meet with management and the unions," she began.

Bart agreed. "I can make a call and set up the appointments starting next week."

At that moment, the door opened, and Bill walked in the room. "Can I have a moment with Bart alone?"

Claire walked past him without making eye contact. He closed the door behind her. Bill pulled out a large stack of papers from the manila envelope he was holding and placed them on the conference table. "I want to give you this prenup so you can review and sign it."

Prenup? Cassie never mentioned a prenup. "I haven't heard anything about this," Bart responded aloud.

"Cassandra's had a change of heart and asked me to draw them up for her."

Bart slid the papers closer to him and arbitrarily flipped through them. "I'm going to need some time to read through this and have a lawyer review it."

"No problem. Take it with you and return it to me once it's signed."

Bart sat there for a moment, looking at the agreement, not sure what to make of it. He was sure of two things: one, if Cassandra wanted him to sign a prenup, she would have told him, and two, Bill Wright was a snake.

Bill left the room, and Claire returned. She instantly noticed Bart looked unsettled. "Is everything okay?"

"I'm not sure. Bill just gave me this." Bart handed the papers to Claire. "I'm going to have to get an attorney to look at it, but I don't think it can be you."

Claire quickly reviewed the document, and a disconcerted look came to her face. Claire had been in the room when Bill brought up a prenup, and Cassandra had specifically told him she didn't want one and to never bring it up again, but she feared that if she told Bart the truth, she would lose her job, so she said nothing.

* * *

Bart also had a meeting that day with the owner of the security company that monitored the real estate business. It was in a two-story office building that had accountants on one side and attorneys on the other. He had discovered the person who owned the security company was a former policeman, and he wanted to talk with him. According to Claire, Cassandra owned the building in its entirety and paid the monthly security bill, which made her the client.

He arranged to meet in a shopping center parking lot with the owner of the security business and explained to him that he wanted to get in the office one night and that it wasn't exactly trespassing because his fiancée owned the building. It needed to be done discreetly, however. He believed someone had been stealing from her, and since she paid the private security company, she was entitled to access.

The man seemed apprehensive. After all, they were discussing something potentially illegal in the middle of a strip mall parking lot, and he wasn't sure if he wanted to get involved. Bart assured him that he needed only fifteen minutes and they'd be out of there.

Bart's plan was to hack into the computer system with the help of an IT guy he knew, download the records of the company's previous ten years of income, and give them to his accountant. This was the only way to find out how much was being stolen from the real estate company. The owner of the security company was still undecided, so Bart mentioned the names of mutual friends he knew they had.

"Why don't you talk to them and then let me know?" said Bart. "I know they will vouch for me. It's also guaranteed to be a good payday for you," he added.

The owner of the security business agreed to talk to some of the people Bart mentioned and be in touch. The two men shook hands and went their separate ways.

After getting back into his vehicle, Bart realized he had turned off his phone when he went into the meeting with Claire and had forgotten to turn it back on. He had several missed calls from Cassandra. Apparently, Claire had called her and told her what Bill had done, and she was livid. Cassandra was in tears when she called Bart. When he didn't answer the phone, she assumed he was upset with her.

Cassandra had planned a Western barbecue for that night; she had hired a company that furnished cooks and a Western band, and she had invited nearly thirty guests. Bart drove through the gate, parked by her house, and said a quick hello to everyone, but Cassandra was nowhere to be found. Finally, he found Anthony, who disclosed that Cassandra was upset about something and had gone in the house before anyone arrived. Bart hurried inside and found her in the master bathroom, her face muddled with tears. As soon as he entered the room, she ran to him and jumped into his arms, sobbing uncontrollably.

"What's wrong?" he asked tenderly. "What happened?"

"I thought you were mad at me over the prenup. You wouldn't answer my calls. I swear I had nothing to do with it. It was that bastard, Bill Wright."

He caressed her tear-soaked cheek. "Cassandra, you should know by now you're the only thing that matters to me. Even if you wanted a prenup, I'd never be angry with you."

Cassandra was so upset over what Bill Wright had done she wanted to call the attorneys and have him fired immediately, but Bart managed to calm her down.

"Let's enjoy this evening and deal with Bill on Monday," he suggested. Cassandra reluctantly agreed.

"Will you go outside and mingle with everyone? I feel awful; I've been locked in here all evening wallowing. I just need a few minutes to fix my makeup, and I'll be out."

"Don't worry about these things. They aren't important, Bella." He kissed her gently on the forehead. "I'll be out there waiting for you."

When Bart walked out the door, Frank went over to him. "What's going on with Cassandra? Where is she?"

"That goddamned Bill Wright has caused some shit, and she's upset over it, but we've decided to enjoy this wonderful evening. She's cleaning herself up and will be right out. She'll fill you in tomorrow."

A few minutes later, Cassandra appeared. She walked straight to Bart and grabbed his hand.

"I'm so sorry about all of this," she whispered to him.

"I don't care, Cass. I promise. I knew he was lying. He's nothing but a rat."

After dinner, Cassandra found her father and pulled him aside to tell him what Bill had done and how disgusted she was with him. "Monday morning I'm going in there and firing him effective immediately. Claire will take over. I will not put up with this anymore, and if anyone has a problem with it, I'll find a new law firm."

Despite the mishaps, Bart managed to enjoy the evening. Cassandra had truly outdone herself—she always did. The music was wonderful and the food even better, but he couldn't shake the conversation with the security guy. He needed to get into that real estate office and obtain those records to figure out exactly how much money the Bandell family had stolen over the years. For him, it was not about revenge. It was about justice.

CHAPTER 39

WOMAN SCORNED

Nothing is more frightening than the wrath of a woman scorned, and the law firm was about to get a lesson in the consequences of treating a woman like Cassandra D'Angelo poorly. Frank had arranged a meeting with the partners of the law firm, which wouldn't even exist if it weren't for the D'Angelos. Cassandra was Frank's partner in business—everyone knew that—and for Bill Wright to treat her how he had was unforgivable.

At ten o'clock sharp Tuesday morning, Frank and Cassandra walked into the high-rise in Midtown. Cassie was wearing a black Dolce & Gabbana double-breasted pantsuit with subtle white pinstripes. Her jacket was left unbuttoned to reveal a classic white Ralph Lauren button-up shirt. She paired her outfit with black Christian Louboutin stilettos. She had calmed down, but she was ready to school the attorneys in the art of business, and she certainly looked the part.

They entered the lobby. Cassandra's heels echoed throughout the office's as they intently hit the marble floor—the sound of a woman on a mission. Frank didn't say a word in the elevator; he liked the energy Cassandra was emitting and had no intention of shifting it in any direction. The doors opened, and they were escorted into the boardroom, where ten attorneys were already seated. Frank and Cassandra acknowledged everyone, and then Frank took a seat while his daughter took care of business.

"Good morning, gentlemen. I'm going to make this quick. I have personally been disrespected by one of your lawyers. It is absolutely unacceptable, and things are going to change, starting now. I am ready to remove my family's businesses from this firm in its entirety. I've already contacted another firm that is more than willing to do anything we'd like. I do not care about the inner workings of this law firm, but if we're going to continue to keep our business here, this is what has to happen: Bill Wright is no longer our attorney. He will have nothing to do with our business or have access to it ever again.

"Claire Tran has worked with us for the past five years. I'd like her to take over our family business. This is not open for negotiation. This will be taken care of by the end of day, or we will walk. Any questions?" She looked around the table. No one said a word. "Thank you very much for your time." She picked her purse off the table and walked out of the room.

Frank stood up, smiled, and followed her lead. "Have a great day." That was his daughter, and at that moment, he could not have been prouder.

The managing partner ran out after them. "Miss D'Angelo!" Cassandra momentarily paused and halfway turned to look at him. "I have to apologize for any offense directed toward you," he said, catching his breath, "and I assure you we will deal with this, but in order for Claire to take over your accounts, she has to be a partner, and at this point, she's not."

Cassandra took a step closer to him. "That's either because she's a woman or because she's been bullied by Bill Wright. I don't care which. Claire needs to be made a partner today." Without another word, she turned around and continued to the elevator.

Before he followed Cassandra, Frank looked at the man, who was still standing there dumbstruck. "If I were you, I would handle this immediately. I don't want to have to say this again: Cassandra is a partner in everything I do, and if you don't believe she will move all our business tomorrow, you have no idea what kind of woman she really is."

* * *

Bart wished he could have been with Cassie at the meeting, but he understood it was something she needed to handle on her own. Although they had a loving and caring relationship, he realized that as a businesswoman, she could be a barracuda when necessary. He laughed to himself thinking about it. I'd hate to be on her bad side.

While Cassandra and Frank were in Midtown, Bart was getting ready for his meeting with the employees of the concrete business. Despite meeting with Claire frequently over the past few weeks, it was still an odd situation for him. After all, he was asking for a meeting with the management and the union of a company his future father-in-law owned—it wasn't like they could turn him down. Nonetheless, he felt entirely prepared, and it was a great opportunity; he couldn't think of a single thing that could possibly go wrong.

Right before Bart was about to leave, he received a call from Anthony.

"Meet me in the garage office."

He decided to walk to Frank's. It was a beautiful day, and he had plenty of time before the meeting, so he wasn't in any rush to get inside. When he got there, Anthony was nowhere to be seen. Nearly twenty minutes later, Anthony pulled up and got out of the car with a brown bag in his hand. He walked into the office, and Bart followed, closing the door behind him.

"We finally got what we needed," said Anthony.

He turned the bag upside down and slowly pulled it up, revealing a rocks glass. He was especially careful not to touch it.

"Our friend finally messed up. He must've had a rough day yesterday—he had a drink at that bar near his apartment. I snagged this before the cocktail waitress got a hold of it."

Bart thought, I can't fucking believe it. Am I actually going to find out whether Angler is the Star Killer? He and Anthony began to discuss logistics. Where was the best place to try to kill this guy? Where in the city were there no cameras or witnesses? Could they lure him outside of the city? For the first time in his life, Bart felt fearful, but it wasn't the fear of killing someone. It was the fear of losing someone. What would Cassie say if she knew what I'm going to do?

Time was of the essence. Anthony believed the best move would be to wait for Angler to leave one of the strip clubs he frequented—strip clubs didn't have many cameras around. He suggested Bart ride a motorcycle and wear a helmet and dark clothes in order to make it difficult for Angler to identify him. Bart would also need a rock-solid alibi; no doubt the powers that be would look at him as a suspect.

Just as they finished their conversation, Vito Alessi called to set up a meeting with Bart, talking business with Vito in an unsecure place was not the best situation. They agreed on a location and time, but, before hanging up, Vito laughed and said smugly, "Don't forget your little box, Bart." Prick.

"Who was that?" asked Anthony.

"Vito. He wants to meet and sort out the deal with Frank."

"You know, Sal Alessi and the Bandell family were pretty friendly when they took over the real estate business. I'm not sure what exactly their relationship was, but I'm positive Sal never mentioned his business dealings with Frank to them. Michael Bandell probably has no idea Alessi has worked with the D'Angelos all these years."

Bart cocked his head to the side and raised his dark brown eyebrow. "Interesting."

"When you meet with Vito, you should try to find out exactly how friendly they are with Michael Bandell. Maybe it'll help resolve this real estate fiasco."

Bart wasn't very concerned with recovering the books from the past ten years, but if the Bandell family were stealing—which he was sure they were—his main priority would be recovering the stolen assets. He was grateful for how much Anthony knew about the family business, considering Anthony had been with Frank during nearly every deal he had made for the past twenty-five years.

After they finished discussing business, Anthony briefly mentioned the engagement party. Bart knew Cassie, Evon, and his family were all excited, but he wished he and Cassandra were married already. His life had drastically changed in the past year. He was no longer a policeman. He had found the love of his life, and he was being introduced into a multimillion-dollar business deal. The skills he had acquired as a detective would be invaluable in navigating this minefield of strange business relations.

CHAPTER 40

THE SALE

It was early in the morning, and a thin layer of fog was dancing above the ground. Claire had agreed to meet Bart at the estate, where they would board a helicopter and head to the concrete company in New Jersey. Frank had a helicopter pad off to the right side of the property that he had used over the years; it was a much more convenient method of transportation than driving.

Bart had been meeting with the employees of the four companies Frank wished to sell. The entire process was proceeding at a quick pace. Frank had reduced the price of the companies and was willing to hold a mortgage to make it easier for the transaction to work, and Claire was constantly available to offer legal advice and consult with the employees' attorneys. The unions had balked just enough to give the impression that they had the power, but, overall, Bart had gotten along very well with everyone. He felt he had his foot far enough in the door to sway things in the right direction. The final meeting was with the concrete company, which was the largest company of the four. Although Bart had spoken to the company's representatives several times on the phone, it was time to meet in person.

Bart and Claire sat in the car, waiting for the helicopter to arrive. She had never flown in one before and was inordinately nervous.

She continuously fidgeted with her purse handles and examined her nails—even biting them a couple of times—and her left leg never stopped shaking. Bart tried to assure her it was barely a thirty-minute flight and everything would be fine, but it didn't seem to ease her fears at all.

They finally heard the faint hum of a helicopter in the background. As it got closer, the noise grew louder, and the wind began to violently circulate around them. It landed a couple hundred feet away from them, and the propellers began to slow. They scurried toward the aircraft, where the pilot was already opening the door for them. They quickly boarded, and within minutes, the engine was roaring again, and they were in the air.

Bart tried to comfort Claire by making small talk, but it was far too noisy. Within twenty-five minutes, they were back on the ground in an area outside of the concrete factory. Claire unclenched her fists and opened her eyes. Had she been praying not to die the whole time they were in the air?

A waiting car took them to the main office. When they arrived at the front building of the enormous factory, they were ushered into a room that resembled a cafeteria. The company's CEO, John Richards, with whom Bart had been corresponding over the telephone, greeted them. With him were the plant manager and a union delegates, whom John briefly introduced as Joe Gaudi and Mark Loida.

"I apologize for the room," said John. "It's the only one we have that's large enough to fit everyone. We have all of our management, management from other plants, union delegates, shop stewards—basically everyone."

"It's no problem," replied Bart as John opened the door, and they followed him inside. About seventy-five chairs were placed in a U-shape, and in the center stood a table with two chairs—one for Bart and the other for Claire.

John introduced Bart as the representative of the D'Angelo family and Claire as Bart's attorney. Until that point, only John knew what the meeting was about, but everyone had assumed that either the company was in financial trouble—which seemed to be the most prevalent rumor—or it was being sold. All of the employees had name tags with their first names only, and upon arrival, Bart and Claire were also given one.

"Hello, everyone, I'm Bart Sullivan," he said loudly. "Thank you all for coming today. I'm sure you're curious as to why you were asked to be here. I want to assure you this is a positive meeting, and in the long run, everyone will benefit. Frank D'Angelo has owned this business for twenty-five years, and it is near and dear to his heart, but he and his family have come to the point in their lives where they are ready to separate themselves and focus on other endeavors."

Many of the individuals looked concerned. Surely they were worried about what would happen to their jobs. Bart quickly reassured them they would not be laid off.

"Mr. D'Angelo is adamant the company is to be sold to the employees. He is prepared to assist in that sale. In other words, we would like for all of you to purchase this business," he said, signaling to everyone in the room. "It will be your job as employee representatives to take this offer to your fellow employees. It's a great opportunity, but also challenging. I am here today to begin discussing this process with all of you. We have a packet for you to take that will outline the price of the business. I personally guarantee all of the dollar figures cited there came straight from the company books. Your attorneys and accountants are present, and Claire is here to keep me from putting my foot in my mouth."

A few people laughed, but most of them remained impassively apprehensive.

"I'm not a lawyer," Bart continued. "So, if any legal questions come up, Claire and your attorneys will handle them. I see a lot of startled faces, but I would appreciate it if you would look at this as an opportunity for you and your families to take ownership of this company. It is a lucrative business that has grown from a six percent profit margin to twenty percent over the past twenty five years and has infinite room for growth. If anyone understands the ins and outs of this business and can facilitate success, it is you."

Bart perused the room and could tell who was interested and who had absolutely no intention of getting involved. One man in particular looked especially irritated. Bart could barely make out the name tag on his jacket, but it looked like it said "Ralph."

"Are there any questions?"

Ralph's hand immediately shot up.

Bart got out of his chair and walked closer to him to confirm his name. "What's on your mind, Ralph?"

"This is a big deal, and some guy we've never seen before comes waltzing in here acting like it's just another day. Maybe for you, this won't change anything, but we could lose our livelihoods. I mean, this is a lot of money. How can any of us afford to buy a multimillion-dollar company?"

"You're right. You don't know me. This is a lot of money, and any reasonable person would have to take a step back and think about it. It's a huge decision, but it comes down to whether you, as employees, would rather own this business and remain in control or take your chances seeing it sold to a stranger. Selling to an outside buyer may not be a bad thing—they might grow it and everyone will keep their jobs, and that's all good, but there is also the potential that it will not go that way."

Bart paused to let them ruminate over what he had said before continuing. "I'll be very honest with you. Frank D'Angelo started in the construction business with nothing; he understands what it is to struggle and to try to build something from the ground up. His philosophy is if a good opportunity presents itself, why not take advantage of it? We don't expect one of you to buy this entire company, but there is power in numbers. If you work together, it is possible."

Following that statement, Bart responded to a number of other questions. The final one came from a middle-aged woman seated to the left; her name tag read "Gina."

"If you were one of us, would you try to buy it, honestly?"

"There's no question in my mind," he said without hesitation. "Like most of you, I came from a blue-collar family. This type of opportunity never came around. Now it's right in front of you. So, as soon as your emotions settle down, look at the numbers, talk amongst yourselves and with management, and make a sound decision." He paused before adding, "To be honest, if I were you, I would not walk; I would run toward this opportunity."

Bart closed with one final bit of information. "Last but not least, when you look at the dollar figures in your pamphlets, you'll notice Mr. D'Angelo has given employees a ten percent reduction in the price in hopes that will provide an incentive for you. He also agreed to hold a mortgage. If you decide not to buy the company, it will be put on the market at its original price. If you do want to proceed with the purchase, your attorneys and accountants will supply you with a purchase plan, and I will do everything I can to help. Again, thank you for your time."

Most of the attendees stood up and applauded, while others began exiting the room. John walked up to the front and asked Bart and Claire to follow him to his office. They sat for a few minutes and talked.

"You know," said John. "I was surprised to hear the D'Angelo family was selling. Frank had never even mentioned that he had been considering it."

"Well, he didn't want to until he was sure. Even now, he'd like to keep it quiet until the offers are accepted and we're on the tail end of things."

"I completely understand. Not a word."

They thanked John for organizing everything, and before Bart could process anything, he and Claire were back in the helicopter.

While they were waiting for liftoff, Claire quietly said, "I can see why Frank wanted you to head the sale of these companies. You're great with people. You made everyone in that room feel like you genuinely cared about them, and that's a gift."

"I don't know if it's a gift," he said. "I just hope they understand an opportunity like this doesn't come around every day; sometimes it never does. I also hope there's no one with an agenda that keeps it from happening."

Claire wondered who he could be referring to. Bill Wright was out of the picture, so it couldn't be him. As the engine started, she said, "I don't know how to thank you and Cassandra for the opportunities you have given me. I am truly grateful, and I'll never be able to thank you enough for that."

"You don't know how much I want to thank you for not having to meet with Bill Wright ever again," Bart said, smiling. "It's a pleasure working with you."

They returned early enough for Bart to accompany Cassandra to celebrate the anniversary of an animal shelter the foundation had funded. He had been looking on the shelter's website and saw a small brown dog named Bear that was up for adoption. It was a vizsla and Lab mix—a perfect combination he was sure would steal Cassandra's heart. When they arrived at the shelter, Cassandra was asked to take pictures with the managers and staff. While she was occupied, Bart took the opportunity to find the dog.

The staff had several dogs in small fenced-in areas. The official event had not yet begun, so Bart was able to sneak a quick visit with the dog. He sat on the ground near Bear and noticed a scar on her face and another on the side of her body. It enraged him that someone could abuse an animal that way, but Bart knew better than most just how evil people were capable of being.

Bart observed the dogs for a few moments. Finally, Bear slowly walked over to him. She began sniffing his clothes while he sat quietly, trying not to frighten her. Once she started licking his hand, he knew she had warmed up to him, so he gave her a friendly pat on the head and back. She rolled over, and her tongue fell to the right side of her mouth. He knew she was offering an invitation to scratch her fuzzy brown belly and happily obliged. Bear climbed into Bart's lap and closed her eyes. He had a new love in his life.

Cassandra noticed Bart had disappeared. She looked around the facility and saw him sitting in one of the pens. As she approached, she spotted a small brown dog sound asleep in his lap. She snapped a picture and quietly walked closer. "Have we found a new family member?" she whispered.

Bart smiled and whispered back, "If that's okay with you."

She kissed him on the cheek. "Whatever you want, my love."

Everyone thought Bart spoiled Cassandra, but the truth of the matter was she would give him anything he wanted. Saying no to him was not something she could or wanted to do, and she was perfectly content with it. It was time for her to give herself to someone she truly loved and cared about. It was time for her to enjoy the love she had with him without limitations or fears.

CHAPTER 41

MOMENT OF TRUTH

When it came to clandestine meetings, Bart's philosophy was simple: keep a low profile and always go armed. However, it was summer in New York, and hiding a gun was more difficult without large winter jackets. Bart's favorite was a Sig P238 with an additional mag. It provided him with fourteen rounds, thirteen more than he'd ever need. It was also small enough not to draw attention.

Bart arrived at Mike Wells' storage unit in an old SUV Anthony kept for moving junk around the compound. Mike Wells always seemed like a nervous wreck. He was constantly looking over his shoulder and panicking. Bart had no idea why. Most likely, it was because he was always doing illegal shit that could land him in jail for a very long time.

Bart parked two blocks away from the unit. In one hand, he held the paper bag containing the rocks glass. In the other, he had two sets of fingerprints—one from the Chicago Police Department and one from the Noxzema bottle. Like the last time he visited the unit, he had removed all labels from both sets of prints so Mike couldn't identify where they came from.

When he entered the small metal room, Mike was working on another set of prints; he had a computer page open that he hastily closed. Bart knew Mike had figured out a way to hack into state and federal fingerprint programs but never directly confronted him about it. He didn't want to risk losing his connection.

Bart placed the brown bag and manila envelope on the desk in front of Mike. He meticulously pulled the glass out of the brown bag and dusted it before he pulled the prints off and transferred them to a piece of plastic. He then placed them under a microscope, and within minutes, he had the results.

"Yep," he said, spinning around in his chair to face Bart. "These three sets of prints belong to the same person." Angler was the star killer.

"What exactly are we looking at here?" asked Mike nonchalantly.

"Just a hunch I have."

Mike shrugged and returned the glass and prints to Bart, who placed everything in the brown bag. He thanked Mike, paid him in cash—as usual—and walked back to the SUV.

Bart was not as excited as he thought he would be. Deep down, he had known the prints would be a match. His heart raced as he thought about what he had to do next and about everything he would be risking. Killing Angler was the easy part. Risking his relationship with Cassandra was a different story.

He drove to a vacant construction site he had spotted on the way to Mike's. He put the three sets of prints in the glass and set them on fire. Once they were reduced to ashes, he put the glass back in the brown bag and stomped it into the ground, shattering the glass beneath his boot.

He got back into the vehicle and sat for a few minutes, thinking about everything that had led to that point—the suspicions, the leads, the investigations, and the women who had lost their lives. Lupo had started this, and it was up to Bart to finish it. He put the Star Killer out of his head for the time being and slowly drove into Brooklyn to meet Vito. He was going to have to answer a lot of questions. He had to also be sure he could get Vito's help.

Vito had suggested meeting at Monsignor McGolrick Park in Green Point. Naturally, Bart arrived early to familiarize himself with the location and look around for anybody who appeared to be up to no good. He drove around the perimeter of the park twice, stopped for a cup of coffee, and then drove it two more times. Everything seemed to check out. There was an older couple walking hand in hand, a young woman jogging, a man walking his dog, and another couple pushing an infant in a stroller.

Bart noticed a dark four-door Cadillac. A young guy sat behind the wheel, reading a newspaper. It wasn't unusual enough to worry Bart. He assumed it was Vito's driver, even though Bart had asked him to come alone. He left the SUV at the end of the block and walked into the park. It was small—no more than ten acres—and had a few nineteenth-century statues and a pavilion with a couple of picnic tables. Several benches were situated along the bike path that circled the perimeter, making it a perfect spot to meet. Bark sat on one in the middle of the park.

He noticed Vito walking over, wearing a royal blue jogging suit straight out of Goodfellas. Bart couldn't stop himself from laughing. What an ass. He stood up as Vito approached and shook his hand.

Bart motioned to a spot. "Let's take a walk over this way."

Although they weren't talking about anything illegal and Bart wasn't concerned about anyone listening, he wanted Vito to understand he would be the one directing the conversation. They strolled toward the edge of the park.

"So, do you have any news for me?" Vito eagerly asked.

"I do, actually. Contracts are being drawn up for all four businesses. They're being sold to the employees. Frank has agreed to hold mortgages, so I don't see any reason why they won't close. The good news is that your end of the deal at thirty percent will be somewhere around $30 million."

Vito stopped walking and looked at Bart. "That's a pretty good paycheck."

"It's a great paycheck," Bart corrected him. "Frank is very grateful for the help your father gave him years ago, and this settlement reflects that."

They continued walking before Bart spoke up again. "I thought we agreed to come alone." He pointed at the driver sitting in the Cadillac.

"I know, but I have eye problems that prevent me from driving. I'm sorry. I thought if I told you, you wouldn't agree to come."

They sat on a bench where Bart could keep an eye on the Cadillac, just in case Vito was bullshitting about not being able to drive.

"When do you think I'll get my money?" Vito impatiently asked.

He's definitely desperate. "It will take about three months to settle everything. Frank has agreed to give you your money up front even though he is going to hold mortgages on all four companies."

"Would it be possible for me to get $1 million up front while we're waiting for things to close?" Anthony was right. They needed money.

"I don't see that being a problem."

"You have the juice to give me a million bucks?"

Bart grinned. "I think we can work it out, but I need you to do me a favor."

"A million-dollar favor? I'll do what I can," Vito said blithely.

"Do you know Michael Bandell?"

Vito scrunched up his face as if he had just seen someone for the first time in a decade and couldn't quite tell if it was the same person or a stranger with a significant resemblance. "Yeah, I know him. He did business with my father years ago."

"What kind of business?"

Vito scratched his head while he thought about the details. "The only thing I can remember is he asked my father for an accounting firm that could cook the books on some business he owned." His eyes widened. "Oh, shit. Didn't he take over Frank's real estate business after Frank's wife died?"

"Yes, he did."

"Does this have something to do with that?"

"It might." Bart paused. He wasn't sure how much he could trust Vito, but $30 million was on the line, so he figured it was as good a time as any to take a risk.

"I need you to find out who his accountant was. Bandell has misplaced a significant amount of money, and I need to figure out what happened to it."

"How much are we talking about?"

"Upward of $20 million."

"Damn, that's a lot of money."

"Yeah, it is." Bart turned to face Vito. "If you can find it, thirty percent is yours."

"I'll do what I can to help. God knows I could use the money."

As they shook hands before going their separate ways, Vito added, "It must be nice marrying into the D'Angelo family. You get the daughter and the money. You'll be set for life."

"Take care of yourself," said Bart before walking away. It was time to focus on killing Angler.

CHAPTER 42

FEAR

Fran picked Cassandra up around 9 a.m. for a meeting with the magazine editor. Cassandra had submitted a final draft of an article and wanted to discuss it with the editor. During the ride into Manhattan, Cassandra received a phone call from the manager of the Swan Club confirming the venue's availability for their wedding date. Cassandra was excited about having the wedding at that facility; it was a beautiful location on Long Island Sound, and she had called in a few favors in order to book that specific date. The engagement party was coming up, and now the wedding was set for the first week in December. Everything was going as planned.

Bart had a meeting with Frank to discuss his rendezvous with Vito. Frank was anxious to find out whether Vito had accepted the conditions Bart had offered. Bart explained it was no problem. He also mentioned Vito's request for an advance and told Frank he had agreed to it as an act of good faith.

"However, I think you're giving Vito way too much money here. Thirty percent of the sale of the businesses and thirty percent of any money recovered from the Bandell family seems like more than he deserves, but I understand you want this finished as quickly and painlessly as possible. If you're okay moving $1 million from your Swiss account to his, I will let him know when it's done."

"Yes, no problem," Frank agreed.

"I think Anthony was right. They need money. I did ask him if he knew anything about Michael Bandell. He said his father and Michael discussed finding an accountant who would cook the books on some business deal he had twenty-five years ago."

"You don't think it's the real estate business?" Frank asked immediately.

"I guarantee it is. I asked Vito if he could find out from this accountant where the Bandell family is hiding this money. If I can get into the computers from the real estate company and get the numbers from the past ten years, that will give us an idea of how much they have stolen. Getting our hands on that money is a different story, though."

"Remember, I can't have anything come to light that could jeopardize the foundation. I've spent all these years trying to help people. I don't want it destroyed."

"No problem," said Bart. "I'll be cautious. I'm hoping there's a legal way we can recoup this money; after all, he did steal it from you."

"Does Cassie know anything about this?" Frank asked.

"No. She knows I've been talking to Vito, but she believes it's concerning the theft from the real estate company."

"Don't get into the habit of lying to her. She's a smart girl, and she'll figure it out quickly."

"I'm not lying to her. It's the truth. Vito is a vessel for us to get the money back from the real estate company."

"And your other issue? How is that coming along?" Frank was referring to the Star Killer.

"I'm working on it, but it will all work out. I'm sure of it," said Bart.

Frank nodded. "Don't forget the governor's fundraiser is coming up. I want you to meet him and his staff. It won't hurt for you to get familiar with them."

Bart laughed. "Your daughter is much better at that than I am. Maybe it's best to let her handle those people."

"She has a lot on her plate with the engagement party and wedding. It'll be a quick and easy trip. Trust me," replied Frank.

Bart got up to leave but stopped before walking out the door. "Explain this Swiss bank account thing to me. Can the feds get involved in transfers between these accounts?"

"No. I'm going to transfer it to Sal. Vito is already on his father's account, so there's no connection to the sale of the businesses or anything related. The feds have no ability to get into these accounts, so we're safe. His father, Sal, and I opened these accounts twenty-five years ago precisely for this purpose—so his yearly payments from the business could be transferred to those accounts and would draw no attention from the IRS."

"Sounds secure enough," Bart replied.

Bart left to meet Anthony. They got in the old SUV and made one last run over the route Renee Angler took every Thursday night on his strip club crawl. They had chosen the best location to shoot him and the optimal escape route. Anthony would provide a stolen motorcycle, and Bart had a stolen revolver. Anthony had originally suggested an automatic gun, but Bart wanted to eliminate any chance of the gun jamming. The only thing Bart had to do was shoot Angler and get away. They had decided to drive the motorcycle into the river. Bart would throw the revolver off the bridge and then burn his clothes. Anthony would then pick him up at their predetermined location.

Their plan was to put a set of stolen license plates on the SUV in case a camera picked up the vehicle leaving the area. It had no outstanding decals or anything that made it easily identifiable; it was just an old, dark SUV. Bart's idea was to place a Boston Red Sox decal on the back window and take it off before they returned to Long Island. Police would spend a lot of time looking for the dark SUV with a newly placed Red Sox sticker on the back window.

Cassandra had her meeting with the editor. On the way back to the compound, she and Fran stopped for lunch. Cassie couldn't escape thoughts of a recurring dream she had been having about her future children. They were screaming and being pulled away from their mother by some unknown person. She couldn't shake it but felt she was just being foolish. All this talk about security and what had happened to her mother was taking a toll on her and resurrecting old fears.

Bart returned home later that afternoon, and he and Cassie went for a three-mile run. It was a beautiful day, and they enjoyed the much-needed exercise. She seemed more tense than usual. Bart could sense it, so after the run, he suggested she take a bath while he showered. He walked in the bathroom just as she was getting out of the tub and offered to dry her off. He slowly ran the towel over her naked body. He kissed her on her neck and continued pressing his lips to her bare skin, over her collarbones, and down to her breasts. Bart gently scooped Cassie up into his arms and carried her into the bedroom, where they made love. Afterward, while they cuddled under the sheets, Bart turned his head to kiss Cassie's lips and noticed tears coming from her eyes but didn't know why. He thought maybe he had done something and wasn't sure what it was.

"Are you okay?" he asked, wiping the tears from her face, but the crying got worse. Bart held her tight and waited until she stopped crying enough to speak.

"Remember I told you there will be times when you have to help me with my fears?"

Bart nodded.

"Well, this is one of them." Cassandra wiped the tear away from her right cheek. "I've been having terrible dreams. You and I have beautiful children, but somebody's trying to rip them away from us. The children are crying and screaming, and I can't do anything to help them. I guess I didn't realize how much all of this talk about security and the Albanians and what happened to my mother has been affecting me."

"We can work these things out. I promise I will keep you and our family safe always."

"How can you promise that when we're trapped in this insanity?"

Bart held her close. "This is all about money and living in New York. We can separate you from the money—remove your face from this billion-dollar foundation. We can move out of New York if that's what you want. We can leave all this craziness."

"It would be best not to mention this to my father. Not yet, at least," Cassie said.

Bart pulled her to his chest and held her until her sobs softened and she dozed off.

CHAPTER 43

PREPARATION

The engagement party was coming up, a trip to Albany was the week after that, and somewhere in between, Bart was going with Cassandra to the Swan Club to discuss the wedding. Each day was so busy Bart hardly had time to breathe. On top of it all, the Star Killer was weighing heavily on his mind. Although he and Anthony had spent countless hours devising a plan and collecting the necessary resources, things could always go sideways.

Bart would normally never consider Anthony as a co-conspirator. The only way to get away with murder was to do it alone. It was one of the main reasons Angler had gone so long without being detected. But Bart knew he could trust Anthony. Anthony had handled Frank's affairs for years. He knew where all the bodies were buried, i.e., he knew about all the deals Frank had done. As far as Bart could tell, Anthony never said a word.

Before Bart left, he and Cassie had a long talk; she was much more composed than the night before but still had a million questions about his thoughts on moving forward and possibly leaving New York. It was certainly doable—there was no question about that—but sacrifices would have to be made, and Bart was apprehensive about how Frank would react. Frank had spent his whole life building that foundation to help others. Bart wasn't so sure he would be willing to walk away from it all.

The owner of the security company, Amir Irfan, called Bart and asked to meet. Bart suggested the parking lot of a nearby supermarket around noon. As usual, he arrived early. Amir pulled up in a white van. Bart walked away from the van, and Amir followed his lead.

"Is everything okay?" Bart asked Amir.

"I've spoken to mutual friends, and they had only good things to say. With that said, I think we can accomplish what you mentioned."

"And the security system—what happens if you shut it off during the night?"

"If we go in for a routine check of the property and shut the system down with a password, the cameras will be off for about thirty minutes and automatically come back on after that. We can shut them off again for another thirty minutes, but for the few seconds in between, the cameras will capture images, so we'll need to deal with that."

"And is it normal for you to go into a facility like that and check the property?"

"If we see anything suspicious, it wouldn't be out of the ordinary for us to look around."

"So, you're saying we can shut the cameras off for half an hour when we turn the alarm off? Then they'll automatically come back on, and we'll have to hit the same code to shut them off for another thirty minutes?"

Amir nodded his head. "Yes. That's the only way this will work."

"And when I input the code to shut the alarm off, none of your people or the county police department will respond to the location?"

"Our best bet is for me to go with you. I'll call in a routine check so nobody else responds. Can I ask you a question out of pure curiosity?"

Bart nodded. "Go ahead."

"Since you own the property, wouldn't it be easier for you to do it during the day?"

"That would be easier. But if we try something like that, they're going to get suspicious and most likely destroy all the digital records. We will never get the information we need."

"I understand," Amir said.

Bart told Amir he would be in touch as soon as they figured out the best date to carry out the plan. Bart needed to secure the help of a friend who was a software genius. There was no question he could get into the files and recover the income records for as long as they were kept on the software program. The only issue would be getting through the passcode. Bart was not sure how difficult that was.

Once Bart was back in his vehicle and Amir's van was out of sight, he pulled his phone out of his pocket and called his computer man, Dietrich.

"Hey, there. It's Bart Sullivan. Quick question for you. How much time do you think you would need to break through the passcode of a normal office computer without any firewalls?"

His friend said he could do it in fifteen minutes, maybe even less. Then he would need no more than ten minutes to download the information onto a drive, but if anything went wrong, it could take up to an hour.

PREPARATION

Bart was thinking of a date after Albany, the engagement party, and the Star Killer were taken care of. His concern was Vito asking questions. Talking to the Florida accountants might spook Bandell into destroying the evidence Bart needed. Moving the break-in up might be a necessity.

The plan was simple: break in and disarm the security system, download the income information to a drive, and send it to a good friend of Bart's who was an accountant—really smart, someone the department had used over the years when trying to build white-collar cases.

Vito called Bart. He had located the accountant who had worked with the Bandell family. Vito explained he had retired to Florida and Vito would have to fly there to ask him questions in person. Bart gave Vito the go-ahead and assured him he would cover the expenses. Money seemed to be a major motivator for Vito.

Bart couldn't help being concerned about Cassie. He had seen her upset before, but not nearly as much as she had been the night before. He worried she'd found out about one of the dilemmas he had been dealing with, but hoped he was wrong. Even the thought of losing her made him sick to his stomach. Fate was a strange thing—he had spent years looking for Cassandra, and, when he finally found her, it was at the worst possible time. Life is strange that way.

It was late in the afternoon as Bart approached the gate of the estate. He saw Bear running from their house to Frank's and couldn't help but laugh. He couldn't tell who opened Frank's front door, but Bear ran right in like she owned the place—just as she had done since the day they brought her home.

PREPARATION

When he walked into the house, Cassandra was on the phone in her office. He quietly went in and kissed her on the neck. Eventually, he heard her say, "I will get those papers to you and talk to you soon." She hung up, stood, put her arms around Bart's neck, and held him as tight as she could.

"I'm so sorry about last night," she said with her face still buried in his chest. "I don't know what's wrong with me. I need to get a hold of myself."

"Everything will be fine. I promise, we will work it out."

"I just don't understand how we can up and leave New York. My father would never agree to it, and I wouldn't leave without him," she responded.

"Let's use common sense here," he said calmly. "All this crap that's going on is due to us being in New York. We know that, but if we're going to leave, we can't look like we're running away because we're afraid. It has to be a strategic move that appears to be entirely our decision—maybe even a business decision."

Cassie looked puzzled. "What do you mean a business decision?"

He took her hands in his. "One option could be to say I want to go into the horse breeding business. We can't do that in New York. We would need at least five hundred acres, so we would have to relocate. That's a logical explanation for us moving."

She looked at him sideways. "That's actually a great idea. Not only would it look like it's our decision, but it's been your dream."

"Right. It'd look as if we're making a business and personal decision to leave New York. Second—and you're not going to like this—you are the face of that billion-dollar foundation. People on the outside think you have a billion dollars. They don't understand it is not entirely your money, but it makes you very vulnerable. We have to change that perception and have someone else's face on that billion dollars. You can still run the foundation behind the scenes."

"Who? We can't just grab somebody and put them in charge."

He leaned over and kissed her on the lips very gently. "We can work the details out in due time. Let's focus on the bigger picture right now—how your father will feel about this."

"You know the most important thing to me is my family. The most important thing to me is you. You are my family now. I want us to have children, and I want them to be safe. I will do whatever I have to do to accomplish that. Do you think my father would want his grandchildren in harm's way?"

"I know he wouldn't, but, again, Bella, it is imperative that it doesn't look like I'm trying to rip you away from New York, from the foundation, or from your father." If Frank thought I was trying to separate Cassie from him, he would be furious—and rightfully so.

CHAPTER 44

THE BURGLARY

The day before the engagement party, Frank's house was being transformed into a fabulous venue to celebrate Cassandra and Bart. Tables were being set, food was being delivered, and people were scurrying around like ants. Bart had decided a few days before that the best time to break into the real estate office would be the night before the party. Vito and the attorneys were beginning to ask questions about the income and the books, and the accountants were also a liability if they talked.

It was only a matter of time until Michael Bandell found out Bart was poking around, and as soon as he did, he would certainly destroy any documentation that exposed his crimes. While looking through the corporate papers, Bart had discovered Bandell's daughter was not only a fifty percent shareholder of his business. She was also the accountant. Bart could threaten legal action and jail time for her if things blew up in his face, but first, they needed to break into the office.

The break-in was scheduled for around midnight. Bart had to tell Cassie something else so she couldn't be implicated in the burglary. He told her he had to meet Vito to give him information regarding the real estate business and the theft of money. She was not happy about the explanation. She didn't want Bart involved in something that would cause him trouble. He reassured her everything would be okay, and he wouldn't be gone long.

Anthony picked Bart up in the old SUV. They drove to a nearby Walmart parking lot where Amir, the owner of the alarm company, and Dietrich, Bart's software guy, were waiting. They agreed Amir would enter the real estate office building and quickly turn off the alarm, which would automatically shut off the cameras inside and outside of the building. At that point, Anthony would drive Bart and Dietrich around to the back door, drop them off, and leave.

When they entered the building, only a few lights were on. They proceeded to the second floor. They found Bandell's daughter's office, and Dietrich immediately began working on her computer. It took him less than five minutes to hack through the passwords and access the existing business information. Within another five minutes, he had located the files with the income and expense records from the past ten years. Dietrich quickly plugged a USB drive into the computer and began copying the files to his drive. If all went well, they would be out of there in thirty minutes as planned.

Amir was standing on the second floor, looking out the big glass windows to ensure there were no surprises. Right after Dietrich began downloading the files, Amir ran into the office.

"A police car is pulling up out front. We had better hurry up," he said, breathing heavily.

"Shit," said Bart. "What do you think they want?"

He glanced at the computer. The small gray box on the monitor displayed a percentage: "24% complete."

"I'm not sure," replied Amir. "Maybe they noticed the security truck outside and want to make sure everything's okay."

"Well, we're going to need about ten more minutes," said Dietrich. "Think you can buy us some time?"

"I'll see what I can do," said Amir, hurrying out of the office.

He ran downstairs, took a deep breath, and opened the door. A police officer was standing out front, flashing his light through one of the windows. As Amir pushed the door open, the cop shifted the beam of light from the window to Amir's face.

"Good evening, officer," Amir said, squinting from the bright light in his eyes.

"I noticed the lights were on. Is everything okay?" the officer asked, pushing his way inside.

"Everything is fine," Amir answered, but he was so nervous his voice slightly cracked. He cleared his throat and continued. "We've been having a computer problem with the alarms. I was just checking to see if it had been fixed."

As soon as they heard the cop's voice inside the building, Dietrich crawled under the desk, and Bart ran into the office next door and hid under that desk. Dietrich put the screen saver on the monitor so the files would continue to download.

"May I use the restroom?" Bart heard the officer ask.

"I believe it's that way," said Amir.

Bart continued hiding until he heard a toilet flush and what he assumed was the police officer leaving the bathroom.

"Well, if everything is fine here, I'll be on my way," the officer said to Amir.

"Yep. All good," responded Amir.

As soon as the officer drove away, Dietrich and Bart came out of hiding.

"About five more minutes for the download to be completed," Dietrich told Bart.

It had been twenty-five minutes. At thirty minutes, the alarm would have to be reset, and the cameras would come back on. Bart thought it would be too risky to have Anthony come back and have the security camera pick up the SUV, even if it was for just a second. He decided the best option was for Amir to reset the security system so as to buy thirty more minutes. When the cameras flashed back on, he and Dietrich would hide in their blind spots.

Exactly thirty minutes after they had entered the building, the download was completed. Dietrich hid under the desk again, and Bart hid against a wall where there were no cameras. The system began to beep loudly, but Amir quickly reset it.

Bart called Anthony, who drove behind the building and picked up Bart and Dietrich. Amir agreed that if anyone noticed, he would tell them exactly what he had told the police officer. He saw what he thought were lights on in the building and went in to see if anyone was there, which explained why the alarm was shut off. Then he had trouble resetting it, which is why it went off again and had to be disarmed twice. Only employees of the security company would have access to that information, so Bart was not overly concerned it would raise any eyebrows.

Bart arrived back at home around two in the morning. Cassie was tossing and turning. When he walked into the bedroom, she lifted her head and looked solemnly at him. He reassured her everything was okay, and she had nothing to worry about. She pulled him into bed next to her, and he kissed her gently. She fell asleep in his arms, and a wave of relief washed over him. Slowly but surely, everything was coming together.

The following morning was Saturday, and preparations for the engagement party were going full bore. It was an exciting day for everyone. Cassie and Evon had a list of things to do despite the event planner being there, but everyone was in great spirits. Bart decided it would be best for him to stay out of their way. They were in full party mode, and he'd do more harm than good by being under their feet all day. Cassandra had more style and class than any woman Bart had ever known, and he was confident their engagement party would reflect that.

At around 11 a.m., Bart left to meet with the accountant, Chuck Price. It was meant to be a quick meeting. Bart handed Chuck the drive. Chuck plugged it into his computer, and there it was—all the finances for the past ten years. Chuck quickly browsed through them but told Bart it would take a while for him to go through everything and try to figure out where money was missing. Bart had figured as much and told Chuck to be in touch when he'd found some incriminating information, which he was certain would happen.

When Bart arrived back at the compound, Frank's house was beginning to look like something out of a fairy tale. The caterers had begun cooking prime rib, filling the air with intoxicating smells. In the front corridor, lights cascaded down from the ceiling, and white roses and lilies were in vases all over the place. The candles had not been lit yet. The kitchen was tastefully decorated with more candles and flowers, and the dining room table had become a lavish spread of treats, including a massive and colorful charcuterie board, pastries, cookies, and a two-tier white cake in the center. Out on the veranda, a bar offered fine wines and liquors. Everything was reminiscent of Cassie, who had undoubtedly hijacked most of the party planner's tasks.

Cassandra arrived back at the house at around 5 p.m. She was going to take a bath and get dressed. She had waited for this day for a long time and could not have been happier. She had gotten the ring back from the jeweler and was excited to show it off. Although her mother's ring was beautiful, it was a bit too traditional for Cassie. She had had the jeweler shave the three-karat oval diamond from her mother's ring into a solitaire teardrop-shaped stone and set it on a gold band. It was simple but absolutely stunning. She had the smaller diamonds set in a gold band that would serve as her wedding ring.

At 6:30, Bart and Cassandra walked over to Frank and Evon's house, where guests had already begun arriving. Cassandra immediately began introducing Bart to relatives and business partners. The next few hours were a whirlwind. Bart spent most of his time meeting people and sneaking looks at Cassandra every chance he got. She wore a white one-shoulder silk Valentino gown. She was beaming and in her element—meeting people and making them feel welcome. That was her gift. Bart, on the other hand, was friendly and got along with everyone, but he didn't possess that warmth.

It was nearly midnight when Bart and Cassandra sat down with Frank and Evon and discussed the party. They all agreed everyone had had a great time. Cassandra had shown off her engagement ring, and Bart and Cassandra were hand in hand the entire evening. Most of Bart's family and friends were able to make it, which made the night especially enjoyable for him, and Donnie and Jeannie were the last guests to leave. It was a perfect, drama-free evening filled with love, laughter, and celebration.

Although they had been in Cassie and Bart's lives for years, Vito and Jerry weren't in attendance. Jerry told everyone he wasn't invited because he was black—his idea of humor—but the reality was that the last thing in the world anyone needed was to have Vito and Jerry in the same house with everything that had been going on. If anyone saw Bart and Jerry together, people would figure out who was feeding Bart information. The situation wasn't very different with Vito.

Bart and Cassandra left and walked back to their house, where Bear was waiting at the front door to greet them with her tail wagging from side to side. Bart let her out, and she ran around the fenced-in enclosure, barking at squirrels and rabbits.

Cassandra was sitting in front of the mirror and taking off her makeup when Bart walked back inside. As usual, he sat on the side of the bathtub, looking at her and feeling utterly fortunate to be marrying such a beautiful woman.

"Is everything okay?" she asked, noticing him staring.

"I just love you and am so grateful to have you," he said, smiling.

"Don't you ever forget it," she said and laughed. She stood up after smothering her face in moisturizer and said she was going to get in bed.

"Let me get the dog, and I'll join you," he said to her and kissed her on the head.

"I'll be waiting."

Bear had acreage to run around, so it usually took several minutes to find her. While he waited, Bart stood outside looking at the stars. They looked like a million twinkling lights and reminded him of the party decorations. The moon was almost full and bathed the property in a soft glow. Although he was at peace in that moment, Bart wondered if there would ever be a day when he wasn't worried about something—the Star Killer, the real estate business, the Albanians. Would he ever have a life where he could relax and wasn't always solving some fiasco?

Cassandra was already asleep when he walked back into the bedroom. Bart sat in the chair taking in her beauty; he sometimes wondered if he deserved her and was trying to do everything to prove to her that he did. He wouldn't disappoint her. He couldn't.

CHAPTER 45

PREMONITION

A heavy layer of smog lay on the roadway. The sounds of horns blowing and sirens screeching could be heard from all directions—just another day in New York City. Traffic was barely moving. Fran had been sitting in the same spot for nearly fifteen minutes, and she wasn't the only one frustrated. Several drivers had cut her off while simultaneously yelling profanities, even though they knew she wasn't the one causing all the congestion.

Cassandra was attending the yearly foundation board meeting in Manhattan. The board met annually and reviewed all the money the foundation had given to various charities. While the board was basically a rubber stamp, a meeting had to be held yearly to conform with foundation rules. She was in the back seat of the Range Rover, talking to the wedding planner on the phone and making endless decisions about the big day. Cassandra normally didn't spend much time on the phone, but she figured she should make use of the extra time they had sitting in the car for an hour.

Despite being agitated by erratic drivers and stagnant traffic, Fran maintained her composure. However, she had an uneasy feeling that she couldn't shake. She felt like they were being followed and was extremely conscious of vehicles on all sides of her, just as she had been trained, but she couldn't pinpoint any specific vehicles that appeared to be following them.

Anthony had a camera installed on the rear of the SUV that ran anytime the vehicle was running. It allowed Fran, when she had the time, to review video of vehicles that were behind the car. She had looked at the video from the past few days at every opportunity and didn't see anything unusual, but she still felt disconcerted. Her premonition was so strong she began to carry extra ammunition. She carried a 1911 Super 38 with ten rounds and began carrying another magazine with ten more rounds. Being as proficient with a gun as she was, that was more than enough ammo.

Fran had known Cassandra for only a few months, but she had spent a significant amount of time with her, and she could tell how happy she was planning her wedding. Fran was even slightly jealous at times. Bart and Cassandra spent every waking moment they could together, and she wished her marriage was that way. Her husband's business forced him to travel, and that was the life they both knew they'd have when they married. Still, she had always hoped things would change. So Fran was fulfilled by the job with Cassandra's family, and her recent involvement in the foundation brought her great joy.

After Cassandra entered the office building, Fran took out her laptop and again reviewed the footage for the past two days. She watched cars, trucks, and thousands of cabs, but nothing stood out. She called Anthony and expressed her concerns. Anthony assured her he would follow Fran and Cassandra the first chance he got and try to see if her fears were warranted.

Meanwhile, Bart and Anthony were having their last meeting in Frank's office—the final run-through of Bart's plan to shoot the Star Killer. Everything had to go off perfectly in order for Bart to escape detection. Anthony had procured the motorcycle. Bart decided on a pistol he had taken from a suspect a few years prior. He had taken the gun apart and tested it with used ammunition he had also recovered years before. He was positive the gun and ammunition were not traceable, and he used latex gloves to work on the gun and handle the ammo.

They had run through the plan numerous times, but Bart felt it could be reviewed more. It had to be flawlessly executed; there were too many cameras in the city for anything to go awry. Otherwise, they'd surely be caught. Bart and Anthony got in the old SUV and drove into Queens. They started at the strip club, where Angler was every Thursday. Bart would shoot him while he was leaving the strip club since there weren't any cameras outside. After that, Bart would drive over the 59th Street Bridge, slowing down enough to toss the gun into the river below. He would drive south along the East River to the West Side Highway, then drive the motorcycle off a ramp off the West Side Highway and into the Hudson River. Since there would undoubtedly be gunshot residue on his gloves and jacket, Anthony would have a fire waiting in a big metal drum, where Bart would destroy the clothes he was wearing.

Bart and Anthony drove the route one last time, ensuring they had located all cameras. They were confident every camera—whether on businesses or the highway—would lose sight of Bart at some point. They timed the trip exactly—going from the strip club over the bridge to the West Side Highway. At that time of night, the whole operation should take no more than one hour. The only thing Bart had not figured out was what he was going to tell Cassandra about where he was going to be all night. He really didn't want to lie to her, but he had no other choice.

Bart and Anthony returned to the compound and found Frank in his office.

"Are you ready for our trip to Albany for the governor's fundraiser?" Frank asked Bart.

Bart honestly had not thought about their trip to Albany, even though he understood it was a highly exclusive event and was important to Frank and Cassandra. He had been preoccupied with the whole planning-to-murder-someone thing, but he played it cool.

"Yep, no problem," he responded.

"What have you two been up to?" Frank asked.

"Just taking care of some business," Anthony replied.

Frank looked at Bart. "Whatever you two got going on, you need to be careful. Under no conditions can my daughter be involved in any of it."

"You know I would never do that. She is my number one concern," Bart replied.

Bart walked over to the house. He sat on the porch while Bear ran around playing. He took a deep breath, but his heart was racing, and his brain was going a hundred miles an hour trying to figure out another way—another solution—but the sight of the countless dead women kept flashing in his head. He had no choice; that monster had to be stopped.

CHAPTER 46

THE FUNDRAISER

The Gulfstream jet sat on the runway with its engines idling. Frank and Evon were seated on one side of the aisle, and Bart and Cassandra sat on the other. The trip to Albany from Long Island would be short—no more than an hour and a half.

"Enjoy this plane while we've still got it because in November, when the business sells, it goes to the new owners," Frank joked.

Cassandra would've rather flown commercial. She had had a fear of flying since she was a child but had never told anyone other than Bart. Flying in larger planes always felt less like being in the air, especially during bad weather.

As the plane taxied to the runway for takeoff, Cassandra grabbed Bart's hand and squeezed it tightly. She closed her eyes, and within a matter of minutes, the plane was hovering above the ground and ascending into the clouds. It would be a quick trip—attend the governor's fundraiser that evening and be back home the following day—but Cassie didn't care how long it was; she just enjoyed spending quality time with her family.

Bart, on the other hand, was extremely conflicted. He wanted Cassandra to think he was enjoying himself, but on the flip side, as soon as they returned home, he would have to murder the Star

Killer. The thought made him sick to his stomach. It wasn't fear; it was apprehension. It was doing something that he knew was right but also had the potential to cause him to lose the love of his life.

Anthony had planned to travel with them but had come down with a cold and decided to stay home. The dinner that evening was private. It was obvious they were trying to keep it under the radar as no press had been notified. The dinner cost $25,000 per plate. Frank had purchased the table for $100,000.

The truth of the matter was that Frank didn't care for the governor, but he had known him for years and felt obligated to attend. Frank was selling the business but wasn't foolish enough to damage his reputation in New York State, where the new owners would still have to do business, so he would continue the usual handshakes and smiling.

When they arrived in Albany, a car picked them up from the airport and took them to the hotel, where they checked in and took their bags up to their rooms. Fortunately, Frank and Evon were on a separate floor from Bart and Cassandra. Despite being engaged, Bart was still a little uneasy about Frank knowing he was sleeping with his daughter and wasn't sure he'd ever get comfortable with the thought.

The couples agreed on a time to meet downstairs and went to their separate rooms. As soon as Bart and Cassandra unpacked, he began to kiss her gently on the lips and neck, and the next thing they knew, they were in bed. It was a chance for them just to lie in each other's arms for a few hours before they had to get dressed.

They met downstairs at the agreed time, and the car took them to the small, private restaurant. It was not a black-tie affair since they were trying not to attract unwanted attention, so it was casual attire. As soon as they arrived, Bart noticed state troopers in civilian clothes waiting by the front door. Frank presented the invitations to the gentleman at the door, and they proceeded to the back room, where there were no more than fifty people socializing.

As soon as the governor noticed Frank, he immediately stopped what he was doing and walked over. He gave Frank a firm handshake followed by a big hug and then hugged Evon and Cassandra.

"This is my fiancé, Bart Sullivan," said Cassandra, introducing Bart to the governor.

The governor looked at Bart and quietly said, "I hope you realize what a great family you are marrying into."

"I certainly do," Bart said, smiling and shaking the governor's hand.

Frank began making his rounds, introducing Bart to everyone he knew. Frank finally introduced him to a gentleman who was the attorney general. Bart was very interested in meeting him in case the real estate issue with Michael Bandell turned into a legal issue, and he wasn't sure whether the local district attorney or the state's attorney would handle the prosecution. Either way, it would never hurt to personally know the attorney general.

The evening progressed very quickly. Bart saw Frank as a master politician; he knew exactly how to handle everyone, and it seemed people liked him, but he was still not as charming as Cassandra. She was skilled at meeting people and carrying on meaningful conversations. She was so genuine and warm that people were drawn to her.

Politics was not something Bart thought he would ever be good at; he was polite and charming, but he had little desire to be in a room full of people whose world revolves around money. It wasn't very late when people began dispersing. The car returned them to the hotel, and all four of them went to the bar and had a nightcap.

"So, what did you think?" Frank asked Bart, who was sitting next to him.

"You and Cassie and Evon are great with people. I'm not sure I'll ever possess that skill. I believe you should always do what you are good at, so I think I'll leave the politicking up to you guys."

Everyone laughed, and as soon as they finished their drinks, they all got up and went to their rooms. Once again, Bart and Cassandra couldn't wait to be alone, and they very quickly wound up back in bed.

Cassandra fell right asleep, but Bart was having trouble sleeping. He kept going over the plan to kill Angler. Had he missed something? Could they do anything better? There wasn't much to do in the hotel room, so he laid in bed next to Cassie and stroked her hair softly. How could he betray a woman so genuine, so beautiful, so honest? He seemed to be lying to her all the time. How could he commit murder and keep it a secret from her? Finally, around 2 a.m., he dozed off.

At 7 a.m., Bart was awakened by his cell phone. It was Donnie. He quietly rolled out of bed, walked into the bathroom, and closed the door softly.

"Hello?" he whispered.

"We need to talk," said Donnie. His voice sounded excited, not like his normal calm self. "And I don't want to do it on this phone."

This was problematic. Bart didn't have a burner phone with him, and he wouldn't be able to purchase one for hours.

"Donnie, are you sure we can't just talk on these phones?"

"No. Absolutely not," Donnie said firmly.

"Well, I won't be able to get a phone for a few hours."

"Okay, turn on the news. Then, when you can, go get a phone and call me back ASAP."

Bart walked into the living room of the suite and turned on the local Albany news. There wasn't much information about New York City, and the information they did report about the city didn't stand out. He watched it on a very low volume for about half an hour before Cassie woke up.

"Who called?" she asked, walking into the living room.

"Donnie. He was telling me about an issue we have with an old case."

She was still half asleep. "He had to call you at seven in the morning for an old case?"

He kissed her cheek. "Go back to sleep for a few minutes. Everything is fine."

Right after Cassandra walked back into the bedroom and collapsed on the bed, a bulletin appeared on the television: "A suspected serial killer was found murdered in Queens early this morning. It is speculated that he was responsible for the murders of ten to twenty women in the Northeast."

Bart couldn't believe what he was seeing. He was in shock. The news report didn't provide a name or a location, so he couldn't be sure who it was. What were the odds it wasn't Angler—especially after the call from Donnie? He quickly got dressed and went downstairs.

"Excuse me, ma'am," he asked the receptionist. "Do you know where I can buy a cell phone?"

"There's a convenience store two blocks away. I believe they sell phones there," she politely responded.

He quickly walked to the store. He paid cash for the cell phone and tried to stay out of view of the cameras. He walked back to the room as quickly as possible. The phone didn't have enough charge for him to call Donnie immediately, so he had to plug it in and wait. He anxiously sat in front of the television, hoping reporters would release a name or information confirming it was the Star Killer. Finally, the phone screen lit up.

By this time, Cassandra was up and ordering breakfast. She once again asked Bart what was going on. He was getting into the habit of lying to her, and it made him extremely uncomfortable and guilt-ridden, so he decided to tell her the truth.

He had never mentioned the Star Killer to her, even when he was helping her with the magazine article. He had never discussed it because it was an ongoing case, and he couldn't disclose any information. But now that he was almost certain Angler was dead, it was time he told her. He told her about the monster terrorizing the Northeast and how he and Donnie had been trying to find him for more than five years. Now, here the sick bastard was, dead according to news reports, with no explanation. She had a million questions, but they both just stared at the TV screen as bulletins popped up about the death of this unnamed serial killer.

Bart took the cell phone off the charger and called Donnie. He immediately answered.

"Have you seen the news?"

"I'm watching it now," said Bart. "Is it who I think it is?"

Bart knew what Donnie was going to say, but how was it possible? He was in Albany, and they hadn't planned on executing their plan for a few more days. Was this some kind of freak accident? Divine intervention? The universe giving the Star Killer what he rightfully deserved?

"You bet," said Donnie.

"What happened? You didn't do anything stupid, did you?"

"Hell, no. From what I've heard, someone broke into his apartment, tortured the son of a bitch, found where he hid all the souvenirs he was keeping from each of his victims, and then threw the bastard off the fourteenth-story balcony."

There was a lull. Bart's mind was racing. If it wasn't Donnie, the only other person it could have been was Anthony. Goddamned Anthony set the whole thing up. He had followed Angler around at Bart's request and then made them believe he was sick so he couldn't go to Albany, all to protect Cassandra. And then he did what Bart should've done.

Bart hung up and answered some of Cassie's questions. He was extremely careful to only provide information that would not associate her with the crime. After she was satisfied with his answers, they crawled back in bed. *It's over. I don't have to worry about losing the woman I love. It's finally over—or is it?*

CHAPTER 47

JUSTICE

Bart, Cassandra, Frank, and Evon met in the hotel lobby with their luggage to wait for the limousine. The ladies wandered into the gift shop while Frank and Bart stayed with the bags.

"I saw the news this morning. That wouldn't happen to be the guy you were telling me about, would it?" Frank asked nonchalantly.

"I don't think we need to have this conversation right now—especially here," Bart said, his eyes fixed on the front entrance.

"Well, if it is, I'm glad the bastard's dead. Justice has been served," Frank replied.

A couple of minutes later, Cassie and Evon returned, and simultaneously, the limo pulled up to the front of the hotel. The bellman put the luggage in the trunk, and they all entered the limo. Just as Bart was getting in, his phone rang. The caller ID read "Capt. Grabowski."

"Sullivan," he answered.

"Everyone wants to know if you'll consult on this serial killer fiasco. I think it's a bad idea. You have investigated this guy, so I'm not sure who else to call," Grabowski responded in his typical callous tone.

Bart wanted to say no, but the truth of the matter was that it made sense for him to stay close to the investigation. If Anthony screwed anything up, even the most minute detail, it could be fatal, and Bart wanted to know about it ahead of time.

"My flight lands at one thirty at Flushing Airport. If you want to send a car to pick me up, I'll be happy to help."

"What do they want you to do?" Cassie asked uneasily.

"They want me to consult on this serial killer case. I won't spend much time on it, but I did work on the case for five years, and I know more about this guy than anyone else in the department, so it makes sense for me to weigh in at least."

She kissed him gently on the lips. "Be careful."

When they landed in Long Island, Anthony was waiting for them in the Escalade. Bart knew it was not the time to ask questions, but as he helped load the luggage, Anthony had a huge smile on his face and said, "It's a beautiful day, isn't it?" Bart didn't respond.

He felt grateful Anthony would take such a huge risk for him and mostly for Cassandra, but he was also bitter. This had been Bart's fight–his mission–for so long–to kill that fucker and make sure he never hurt another woman. He had spent countless hours doing research; he had sacrificed so much, lost a partner—he had risked everything—just for Anthony to take it all away in one night. He felt relieved; there was no doubt about that, but he also felt slightly robbed.

An unmarked car pulled up, and Bart instantly knew it was the one Grabowski had sent for him. He promised Cassie he would get home as soon as possible.

"Where are you going?" Anthony asked, a large smile still occupying his face.

"Just some unfinished business," Bart said gravely.

As Bart got in the car, he could hear Cassie ask Anthony if he heard about the serial killer who was murdered. He slammed the door shut.

"Hey, there," said the detective in the driver's seat.

Bart nodded at him. He wasn't feeling particularly talkative, but that didn't stop the guy.

"You must be the guy who worked on this case for years. You're kind of a legend at the precinct. They assigned Mike Fuller to be the lead detective on the case, but he seems a little overwhelmed by it all, which is probably why they called you in."

Mike Fuller was a squirmy guy who had become a detective through his political ties and not necessarily because he was the brightest bulb on the block. Bart was happy to hear the department needed his help. It felt good to be needed.

When they arrived at Angler's apartment building, police cars were all over the place, and hundreds of reporters were in the streets. Mike Fuller was waiting on the first floor.

"Glad to have your help," Mike said to Bart.

"I don't know how much help I'll be, but I'll do whatever I can," Bart responded.

They walked around to the back of the building, which had been blocked off with yellow tape. The body had been removed, but there was blood all over the concrete where Angler had fallen to his death. A fourteen-floor fall will definitely kill someone and make a hell of a mess.

They walked back inside and took the elevator up to the fourteenth floor. The apartment was full of people; the medical examiner was there along with crime scene investigators and a number of detectives. It was ironic that Bart had seen many similar apartments each time the Star Killer struck—apartments full of people bagging evidence, taking fingerprints, and examining the scene. Now it was Angler's turn. He would never take another life.

"Anything unusual about the body?" Bart asked the medical examiner.

"Other than the fact that he was splattered all over the ground, the only thing I noticed, and this was just a quick examination, was bullet wounds in both knees and a mark on his back that could have been some kind of burn."

Bart noticed a box on the kitchen table full of keys, hair, and ribbons—the Star Killer's trophies. The scene was fairly neat, all things considered. A chair in the kitchen had duct tape on it—obviously the chair Angler had been taped to while he was tortured. Mike told Bart that Angler also had burn marks on his legs and wrists. It made sense. Whoever tortured him wanted to get to all of his souvenirs somehow, but how many people actually knew about them? No more than four or five people could have known, and Bart and Donnie were two of them.

Mike Fuller showed Bart security camera footage on a laptop. It had been taken in the last few hours before Angler met his flying death. The grainy video showed the apartment building's hallways—Angler's hallway specifically—and the front and rear entrances. A normal number of tenants could be seen coming and going.

Finally, Mike showed Bart footage of the back service elevator. They observed an individual get on the elevator wearing what appeared to be a pest control uniform. Bart didn't notice anything unusual; he was wearing black work boots and carried a gallon spray container in his left hand. The individual had on a surgical mask and gloves and walked with what appeared to be a limp. He got off on the twelfth floor and walked toward the end of the hallway, where there were no cameras, and exited through the doorway into the stairwell. At that point, the individual disappeared. Bart couldn't understand how Anthony got into Angler's apartment without showing up on the footage of the fourteenth floor. He carefully examined the video and noticed footage from Angler's floor didn't move forward—it looked frozen, playing the same scene over and over. He said nothing to Mike.

Mike walked Bart out onto the patio and showed him where it appeared Angler had been thrown off the building. Flowerpots were broken, and a chair had been knocked over. It would have taken real strength to pick Angler up and throw him off that balcony. Mike began asking Bart what he knew about Renee Angler.

Bart was caught a bit off guard. His mind began racing; he already knew he was going to deny that he ever met or talked to Renee Angler, but he needed to be sure he had his story straight. He couldn't get caught in a lie.

"I don't know anything about the guy. To the best of my knowledge, he was never even a suspect in the Star Killer case," he said as calmly as possible.

"That seems to be the general consensus. I just wonder how the guy who killed him knew who he was when even our best detectives couldn't figure it out," said Mike.

Bart excused himself and went back inside. The medical examiner had begun documenting the trophies. Bart walked over and looked at them. He noticed two items he recognized immediately—a red, white, and blue hair ribbon and a keychain with a car emblem. He wanted to touch them, to feel close to the victims he had seen and mourned, but touching evidence before it had been processed was out of the question.

Mike and his detectives would have their hands full trying to match the souvenirs to the victims. It would be a tragic and gut-wrenching task to ask people who lost their daughter, sister, or wife to identify the items. No doubt thousands of people with missing children and loved ones would show up to look for them among Angler's victims. It would turn into a circus.

Mike asked Bart for the cases he, Donnie, and Lupo had worked on. Investigators believed they were all linked to the Star Killer's murder spree. Bart agreed to talk to Donnie and pull all the files they had kept on the Star Killer. Bart also mentioned he and Donnie would talk to the families of the victims to try and match them to the items taken from the bodies. He figured he and Donnie could handle things much more delicately than anyone else in the department since they had personally worked on these homicides and had met a lot of the families. Bart also wanted to stay involved to see what Fuller and his team would turn up—any leads they had as to who committed this crime.

Bart stayed for the rest of the day going through the evidence; there was blood around the chair where Angler had been tied down and bone fragments—apparently, he was shot in both knees. Some type of electrical device had been hooked up to his wrists and ankles to torture him.

Donnie showed up a few hours later. He, Bart, and Mike walked through the scene one more time, and Mike explained to Donnie everything he knew about what had happened. They were in the process of canvassing everybody in the building and going through all the video cameras inside and outside when Mike was pulled away by a phone call.

Bart and Donnie were left alone in the stairwell with no one around and no cameras.

"What the hell did you do?" Donnie asked.

Bart smiled. "Nothing. I wish I had thought of this. I would have enjoyed being here to torture and kill that bastard, but it wasn't me."

As they were walking up the stairs to the exit door, Donnie said, "The son of a bitch got what he deserved. You were right. I just wish we would've done it."

Donnie grabbed Bart by the arm, and when he turned around, Donnie looked him in the eye. "Who do you think did this?"

"I don't know," replied Bart, "but they should give the fucker a medal."

NO RESURRECTION

A ngler's apartment had been torn apart from floor to ceiling. A safe hidden in the floorboards under a rug was apparently where Angler stored his box of souvenirs. Whoever tortured Angler did a good job. Mike was told he could view the body at the morgue. He left a few detectives at the scene to continue collecting evidence while he was gone.

Interviewing witnesses and neighbors was chaotic. People came out of the woodwork, saying they saw everything, from a serial killer to a Martian. Bart and Donnie drove down to the morgue and met Mike and his partner. Bart didn't miss the sights and smells of decaying bodies; he had been out of the department for only a few months, but he had experienced more peace in that time than he had since he was a child. Not dealing with death and destruction on a daily basis had entirely changed his outlook on life.

They walked into the viewing area, and there, lying on the metal table, was a body with a sheet over it. Blood was still leaking on the table from immense damage caused by falling fourteen stories—well, actually from being thrown down fourteen stories.

The medical examiner pulled back the sheet and began to explain each marking he had noticed in his initial examination.

Obvious burn marks were on the wrists and ankles. On the right side of his back was a burn mark that differed from the others. The medical examiner thought it might be from a laser. It looked uncannily similar to the burn marks on the last two women Angler had killed.

Bart couldn't help but smile while he thought to himself what happened to Angler was poetic justice—lasers, torture, and then death. Whoever killed that sorry son of a bitch made him feel what it was like for all those women he so brutally murdered.

"You see he was shot in both knees?" Mike said, interrupting Bart's train of thought. "It must've all been part of the torture."

"It was likely a small-caliber gun, probably a .22," stated the medical examiner.

"Did any of the neighbors hear gunshots?" Bart asked Mike.

"No."

"The perp must have used a silencer," said Donnie.

Angler's hair and face were blood-soaked. Bart asked to look at the back of his earlobe. The medical examiner shrugged, barely paying attention. Bart walked closer to the body and saw it—a tiny star. For Bart and Donnie, this was certainly justice, but the other detectives were confused.

The medical examiner walked over and quietly said, "You may want to see this." He rolled the blood-soaked body on its side. Written on his back with a flare pen was the word "ASSHOLE" in large, dark letters.

Bart couldn't help but smile. Anthony sure as hell has a sense of humor.

Once they finished examining Angler's lifeless, defiled body, everyone walked outside. Bart assured Mike that Donnie would pull the files for the Star Killer cases they had worked on.

"Why did you call him the Star Killer?" Mike asked.

"He drew a star on the back of the earlobes of his victims, probably after they were dead," Bart responded.

Now Mike understood the irony of the star on the back of Angler's ear, and it could be a problem. That information had never been released to the media. Only a few detectives and the medical examiner were aware of it.

"What about the word on his back?" Mike asked.

Bart paused for a moment, debating whether to disclose the information. "The Star Killer wrote derogatory words like 'whore' and 'bitch' on his victims' backs."

Bart and Donnie walked together toward the unmarked car. Donnie suggested they stop and get a drink for old times' sake, but Bart wanted to get home. He offered a drink in Frank's office, and Donnie agreed.

During the first few minutes of the drive, very little was said. They were both lost in their thoughts. Donnie wasn't aware Bart knew who killed Angler and wasn't planning on telling him.

They went into Frank's office and poured drinks. The conversation was still scarce. It was a lot of information to process—especially for Donnie, who was completely in the dark. Shortly after they arrived, Anthony walked in, but the conversation remained limited. Donnie stayed for one drink, then said he had to get home.

Bart sat there, staring at Anthony. Neither spoke for quite some time.

"I don't know whether to slap you or kiss you," Bart finally said.

Anthony laughed. "I don't want to be kissed by any guy, not even you."

Bart realized having Anthony tell him that he had killed the Star Killer would prevent him from passing a polygraph test had the department requested one. "Well, how about I tell you how my day went and what we concluded the perp did to Angler, and you can let me know what you think about it all?"

Anthony nodded. "Go ahead." He leaned back on the couch and crossed his arms, his eyes fixed on Bart.

"The only video the department has right now is of someone dressed like a pest control employee, walking with a limp, and entering the service elevator. They got off on the twelfth floor, walked to the end of the hallway, and then disappeared into the stairwell. From what I could tell, the cameras on the fourteenth floor are not working and must be on a loop."

Anthony sat very stoic, still staring at Bart. "Sounds like a hell of a mystery to me."

"At this point, we don't know how they got into Angler's apartment, but whenever they did, apparently, they used a stun gun to immobilize him."

"Huh, quite a story."

"Then, apparently, they sat Angler in a chair and duct-taped his hands and feet to it. At some point, Angler came to, but his mouth had been duct-taped so he couldn't scream. The murderer hooked up an electronic device to Angler's ankles and wrists and electrocuted him over and over again, and to move things along, he also shot Angler in both knees."

Anthony grinned. "That must have hurt."

Bart quietly said, "Yeah, and I guess that was enough torture for Angler to give up his trophies."

"Without those trophies, nobody would have known who the son of a bitch was," Anthony said passively.

"Right, but unfortunately, not many people knew the box existed."

Anthony raised an eyebrow. "You think that's going to be a problem?"

"No, it can be explained away, but I think it's best I stay inside this investigation for a while and make sure I catch any screw ups."

"Why? Do you think the person who killed him screwed up?" Anthony asked.

"I sure as hell hope not, but it's still best I keep an eye on things. Do you think a video of the vehicle the guy used could pop up somewhere?" Bart asked.

"If this guy is as smart as you think, he probably parked far enough away. I would imagine he walked a mile or two to the apartment building."

"Good. I'm still a little concerned about the surveillance footage from the fourteenth floor. If I noticed it that quickly, somebody else is surely going to pick up on it."

Anthony reassured him, "It's probably just running on a loop. Anybody could have set that up. I suspect the equipment that was used was stolen and would be difficult to trace."

"Well, do you think I'm missing anything?"

Anthony paused. Bart could tell there was something he wasn't saying.

"Christ, what is it, Anthony? Did I miss something?"

"No, it isn't that" Anthony said, looking at his shoes.

"Then what?"

"Lupo's death. It wasn't suicide."

Bart was stunned. "Are you sure?"

"I'm positive." Anthony stood up. "I've got to take Evon into town, but we'll talk again."

As he walked toward the door, Bart said, "I don't understand why you didn't wait."

Anthony turned around and smiled. "You know, for a smart guy, sometimes your head is in your ass. I've told you a hundred times Cassandra is like a daughter to me, and over a lifetime, I've seen her struggle, but I've never seen her as happy as she is now. And I didn't want you to fuck it up. So, I said to hell with it and did what needed to be done."

He walked out and closed the door behind him. Bart poured another Irish whiskey and thought about how lucky he was—and how lucky Cassandra was—to have someone willing to do that. It was like the weight of the world was off his shoulders. The Star Killer was finally dead.

Once Bart finished his drink, he left Frank's and started walking toward Cassie's. When he was about halfway to the house, his phone rang. It was Jerry Morris.

"Hey. What's going on, Jerry?"

"Before I say anything, I want you to take this for what it's worth. I'm hearing rumors of a kidnapping in Los Angeles. Some big tech guy's kids. Paid close to $20 million to get them back. Nobody will confirm it, but I wanted to give you a heads-up. I think it's the Albanians."

"Thanks," Bart said. "I appreciate it, and I owe you one."

"You have no idea," Jerry said. The phone went dead.

He opened the front door. Bear darted out and ran toward Frank's house. Cassie was curled up in the living room, reading a book. Bart gently kissed her on the lips. "Hello, Bella. I'm going to go take a shower."

"Did everything go okay?" she asked, looking up at him.

"Perfectly." He kissed her again. As he walked away from the woman he loved, Jerry's warning was unremitting. Fran was paying extra attention to every tiny detail, and nobody had access to Cassie's schedule except for the family. They were taking every precaution possible to ensure an ambush could not occur—or so he thought.

CHAPTER 49

LOYALTY

The next morning, Bart was up before the sun yet again. He had started returning to his old narcoleptic tendencies, and he figured it wasn't a coincidence that they began when he found out Renee Angler had been killed. Between managing the details of the Star Killer's murder case, manipulating the investigative road down which Mike Fuller was headed, and worrying about Cassie, Bart felt he wasn't doing enough. He couldn't do enough.

He got out of bed, gathered his jogging clothes, and snuck out of the bedroom, trying not to wake Cassie. As he was closing the door, he heard her soft, raspy voice.

"Where are you going?" she asked, still half asleep.

"For a run. I didn't mean to wake you," he responded through the cracked door.

"Don't leave. Stay with me," she said, barely conscious.

He walked back to the bed and kissed her on the forehead. "Get some rest. I'll be back soon."

Daylight was just beginning to reveal itself as Bart followed the five-mile route he usually ran around the property. He couldn't believe he was choosing running over lying in bed with Cassie, but he couldn't find any other way to quiet his mind lately.

When they met, he had warned her that if things got serious, it would be difficult for him to keep his hands off her, and he had certainly lived up to that. Things hadn't changed one bit since they began seeing each other. If anything, kissing her and making love had become more frequent. Bart never imagined he would love a woman as much as he loved her; he'd do anything to keep her safe.

Bear was loose in the yard and started barking at Bart until she realized who it was. Bear was becoming quite the little watchdog, and Bart was thrilled. He quietly entered the house and headed to the guest bedroom to take a shower so as not to wake Cassie. When he finished and went into their bedroom, she was awake and lying on the bed completely naked.

"Come back to bed for a few minutes," she said, cheekily smiling at him.

"Try and stop me," he said, moving toward the bed and removing his shirt and shorts.

He never could say no to her, especially when she was lying in bed, looking at him with those eyes, the eyes that were saying, "come back to bed and make love to me until I'm writhing with pleasure." He crawled back into bed, cradled her head in one hand and her body in the other, and kissed her as if he had never kissed her before and would never do so again.

They had made love and were lying in each other's arms when Bart's phone rang. He leaned over Cassie to answer it. Mike Fuller was on the other end.

"Bart, new evidence has come to light. I need you to meet me at the apartment."

He hung up. "Shit," he whispered. Fuller must be referring to the loop on the surveillance cameras, or at least I hope he is. Anything else could mean bad news for Anthony.

"What's wrong?" asked Cassie.

"Nothing. They have new evidence they want me to look at."

* * *

Cassie had a busy day ahead of her. She had a meeting at the Swan Club, followed by another at her office, and then lunch with her father and Evon. Later in the afternoon, she was meeting with the attorneys to discuss the buyers of Frank's main construction business. Half of the sale would close in November and the other half in January—something to do with taxes. The meeting that day was to determine how much money was to be paid out to Frank and Cassandra as major stockholders in the company. Most of Frank's portion would be given to the foundation, and Cassandra would receive close to $200 million for the stock her father had given her over the past twenty-five years.

She was anxious to talk to her father about her and Bart's plan to move out of New York. Bart had asked her to wait until the weekend so they could sit down together and discuss exactly how they would break the news. He had mentioned Jerry's phone call to Cassandra but had glossed over it to avoid worrying her any more than she already was. Besides, he was confident in Fran's abilities to keep Cassie safe.

As Bart drove into Queens to meet with Mike, he called Fran to reiterate Jerry's message regarding the kidnapping on the West Coast. Again, Fran reassured him she had reviewed all the tapes for the past few weeks on a daily basis and saw no indication she or Cassie were being followed. It would be impossible for anyone to access Cassie's schedule. Bart felt a wave of relief wash over him. He thanked Fran and hung up.

Bart followed up his phone call with Fran with another call to Anthony. Although Fran had alleviated his concerns, he still felt it necessary to tell Anthony. Anthony informed Bart he was taking Evon to meet Cassandra at the Swan Club, and then Evon and Frank were going to meet Cassandra for lunch and then they were all going to the attorney's office in Manhattan. They were taking all the precautions possible to ensure the ladies remained safe. Security couldn't have been tighter.

When Bart arrived at Angler's apartment building, he was directed to the basement, where Mike and a couple of guys wearing black shirts with yellow lettering on the back that read "Bruno's Electronics and Surveillance" were staring into a box on the basement wall.

"What's going on?" Bart asked as he stepped off the last step and onto the concrete floor.

"Take a look at this," Mike said. "The cameras on the thirteenth and fourteenth floors were put on a loop, so they just ran the same footage over and over. That's why we never saw the killer come out of the stairwell on Angler's floor."

Bart looked Mike up and down, vexed by what he had found. He's lucky he had some political clout; otherwise, he would've never made detective. If he wasn't so shitty at his job, Mike would have noticed this the day Angler was murdered. Instead, it took him nearly seventy-two hours.

Mike had people from the crime scene unit with him. He directed them to pull the components responsible for the loop from the box and take them to the lab. He wanted to see if they could find fingerprints or trace the serial numbers to determine who purchased them.

"Let's go back up to the apartment," Mike said after examining the metal box for a few more minutes.

They took the elevator up to the apartment, where a uniformed officer was standing at the door. The apartment was still a mess—clothes, newspapers, and the contents of drawers and cabinets were strewn all over the place. Mike looked around as if he was trying to solve a puzzle.

"What I don't understand about this," he finally said, "is how the person who committed this crime knew there was a box full of mementos here."

"I don't know. What do you think?" Bart asked.

Mike turned to him. "I've been hearing rumors that Lupo knew who this guy was and might've told people about him."

"Really?" Bart said, trying to sound surprised. "Well, I don't know what you heard about Lupo, but he had a million theories; some of them were really far out there, and some of them made some sense, but in the year that I worked with him, I never heard this guy's name once."

"Well, I spoke to Captain Grabowski, and he said the only people who worked on the cases involving this guy were you, Lupo, and Donnie."

Bart looked Mike straight in the eye. "That may be true, but I don't know where you're trying to go with this. Whoever found out who this guy was and what he did to all those women is a mystery to all of us, and if Lupo did have a hunch about Angler being the Star Killer, he may have reached out to the victims' families for more information."

Mike looked stunned. Bart couldn't believe such an ass could possibly be a detective.

"That's true," said Mike. "Hell, that could create another hundred suspects."

Bart grinned at successfully having planted this seed in Mike's dimwitted brain. Now he had to let it ferment for a few days. It would undeniably confuse Mike more and hopefully send him poking around elsewhere.

"So, do you have any leads so far? Can I help with anything?" Bart asked as they were walking down the stairwell.

"No, at the moment, we have no idea who the guy from pest control was. The apartment manager didn't hire him, so we think he might be the killer."

"When you get information on him, let me know, and I'll help," Bart said.

As they were walking away from the building, Mike turned to Bart and asked, "How many women do you think Angler killed?"

"I only have an educated guess, but I would say as many as thirty."

"I've only heard numbers around twenty."

Bart looked Mike dead in the eye. "This guy was meticulous. When he killed someone, if he thought he made any kind of mistake, he disposed of the body. The corpses he allowed us to find were perfect crimes—no semen, no DNA, nothing. So, if you're feeling sorry for this guy, you're the only one."

"So you're glad he's dead?"

"I'm glad he'll never kill another woman."

* * *

After Cassandra's meeting at the Swan Club, Fran drove her to meet her parents for lunch so they could make a few more decisions concerning the wedding. Cassandra wanted Bart there with her, but she understood the gravity of the case he had been working on. Although she knew very little about it, she could tell it was weighing very heavily on him. Her mind wandered to making love to him earlier that morning. If she had her way, they would never be apart. After lunch, she headed to her meeting in the Seagram's building.

Fran interrupted her daydreaming. "Do you want me to park out front or in the garage?"

"My father said it's easier to go through the underground garage. It drops you right at the elevator."

Fran turned right on the corner and through the entrance to the underground garage. One second, they were in the daylight of the city, and the next, it was completely dark. In the center of the large parking lot were glass doors with the elevators behind them. Fran slowly drove toward them but noticed an old pickup truck parked in front of the doors with the hood up.

Fran decelerated until the Range Rover came to a complete stop. Two men in coveralls were standing alongside the pickup truck, but instead of looking at the truck, they were staring at her. Fran immediately had a bad feeling. Her stomach was in knots, and her heart rate began to increase. She looked for an exit to the right, but before she could locate it, a large white van pulled up beside her. She looked in the rearview mirror. Another car was behind her. In the driver's seat was a man in a suit and tie who was talking on his phone.

Fran couldn't get a look at the driver of the van. Suddenly, the two men standing near the pickup truck began to walk toward her SUV. Concrete abutments were to the left, the van was on the right, and a car was behind her. They were trapped. Instantaneously, Fran opened the car door to hide behind and pulled her gun out. She pressed the automatic lock button, locking all the other doors so no one could open the rear doors. "Get on the floor and call 911 now."

CHAPTER 50

TRAPPED

"How could this happen?" Fran wondered to herself. The two men were standing in front of her. They both had dark, brown eyes, black hair, and beards. She knew she should've just dropped Cassandra off outside of the building instead of going into the garage, especially with all of the warnings Bart had given and the eerie feeling she had been dismissing for weeks.

Now here she was, trapped between a pickup truck with two suspicious men outside of it and a huge white van with God knows who inside. There was nowhere for her to go, but she had to protect Cassie. She crouched behind the car door. She motioned to the two men, who were now approaching her.

"Stay back!" she shouted, trying to keep her voice loud and steady.

Fran struggled to keep eyes on the men and was still concerned about who might be waiting in the white van.

"Get the fuck back, or I'll shoot!" she yelled again, shaking her gun at the men, who were still walking toward the Range Rover.

She wasn't sure how much time she'd be able to buy, but she suspected it wouldn't be enough for the police to arrive, and that's if

Cassandra was able to get through to 911. As Fran alternated pointing her gun between the two men, she noticed the one to her left reaching near his belt. Suddenly, he pulled a gun from his right pocket.

The sounds of gunfire echoing throughout the concrete parking garage were deafening. It sounded like a cannon had gone off. Everything moved in slow motion. She refocused her gaze in front of her and saw the man who had been reaching for his gun; he was lying on his back, surrounded by a pool of blood, with two gunshot wounds in his chest.

The second man, who was standing on the right, glanced down at him and quickly pulled a sawed-off shotgun from behind his back. He fired directly at the front of the Range Rover, where Cassandra was hiding. Glass and metal were flying everywhere. The vehicle's windshield collapsed, and Fran could hear Cassandra let out a yelp.

The shots momentarily ceased. Fran took a deep breath, stood up from behind the door, and fired in the direction where the shooter had been standing. He went down on the first shot with a bullet hole in the center of his chest. A stream of blood slowly ran down the concrete.

She heard tires screeching. The white van raced out of sight. She hadn't been able to see who was inside of it or where they went, and if they circled the garage and returned to the rear of the SUV, she and Cassandra were sitting ducks. She had already electronically locked all of the doors before closing the driver's door, but the collapsed windshield made Cassandra especially vulnerable in the vehicle. Fran knew that her only option at that point was to make a run for the concrete stanchion. Although it couldn't have been more than four feet wide, it would conceal her while providing visibility to the rear of the SUV.

Fran ran toward the column as quickly as she could. It was only about ten feet away, but after a few steps, she heard a gunshot echo, and she immediately fell to the ground. The gunshots continued. She couldn't tell which direction they were coming from. Suddenly, she felt excruciating pain in her left leg. She grabbed it and noticed her hand was covered in blood. She crawled to the stanchion as fast as she could, leaning on her right side and dragging her wounded leg as best she could. The pain was unbearable, and when she looked to the rear of the SUV, she saw a man walking behind it with an automatic weapon. Cassandra.

Fran fired twice in the man's direction, but her vision was getting blurry, and she was extremely light-headed. "Fran, Fran!" she could hear Cassandra yelling. She felt someone embrace her and support her head in their arms, but she was too weak to open her eyes. "Keep your eyes open," a voice said. Fran heard the faint sound of sirens as she faded out of consciousness.

Unknown to Cassandra and Fran, a second man was in the van. The last two shots Fran had fired wounded the one with the automatic weapon, who was undoubtedly headed for Cassie in the SUV. The second man returned and helped his wounded partner back into the van, and they sped off while Cassie was tending to Fran.

Lying in front of the SUV were the first two men from the pickup truck; the one who had been shot twice wasn't moving, but the other one muttered something, obviously in agony. As Cassandra was observing the two men, she saw something in her peripheral vision. A man with a gun was running toward her. She tried to grab Fran's gun, which was lying about two feet behind her. She reached for it, but Fran's weight on her made it difficult to move. She finally reached the gun, turned to shield Fran's body with hers, and aimed.

"Police! Police!" a deep voice yelled. "I'm a police officer! Don't shoot!" She could see the shield around his neck reflecting the lights of the garage. Within seconds, police cars and ambulances were swarming all over the parking garage. Police with guns drawn searched the SUV. Cassandra was covered in blood; her face was bleeding from glass shards, and her hands and arms were saturated in Fran's blood.

Bart was returning to the house when his phone rang. It was Donnie.

"Where are you?" Donnie asked.

"I'm on my way back to the house. What's going on?"

"I've got some bad news."

"What kind of bad news? What the hell are you talking about?"

"I got a call from a friend of mine in the Midtown precinct. Cassandra and Fran have been ambushed. I don't know anything else at the moment. I'm really sorry, man, but I think you should get down there. I'm heading down there right now myself. I'll let you know as soon as I know more," Donnie said.

Bart tried to recall where Cassie's meeting was that morning, but he couldn't remember what she had told him. "What's the address?"

"It's the Seagram's building."

Bart hung up and hit the gas, heading toward Manhattan. He had a gut-wrenching feeling of responsibility for what had happened. *I didn't do enough to protect her. After all the information—the warnings—why didn't I take them more seriously? Why the hell didn't I do more?* After about ten minutes, his phone rang again.

"Don't go to the Seagram's building," Donnie said. "They took Fran and Cassandra to New York Hospital. As far as I know, they're okay, but I'm just arriving on the scene. Apparently, a van and a truck boxed their SUV in, and the guys in them started shooting. I'll call you back in a minute."

Bart kept racing toward Manhattan, trying to reach the hospital as fast as he could. He felt sick to his stomach, and the words of retribution continued to echo through his mind. How could I have let this happen? I promised I would always protect her—the love of my life and future mother of my children—and I didn't.

He called Anthony, who was with Frank and Evon, to inform them of what had happened. Bart told him the best thing to do was to go to New York Hospital because he didn't have all the details yet. Anthony disregarded the information and fired a series of questions at Bart.

"The only thing I can tell you is they're okay." He could hear Frank in the background yelling something. "Just get to the hospital," Bart said and hung up.

Cassandra was in the ambulance with Fran, sirens blaring and rolling back and forth. Fran had an oxygen mask on, and her leg was exposed. The paramedics had placed a tourniquet on the upper part to stop the bleeding. The ride seemed to take forever. Cassie was still in shock; she had never been so terrified. If it wasn't for Fran, only God knows what would've happened to her. She could only think about where Bart was. She needed him more now than ever before. The tears began rolling down her cheeks, and before she realized it, she was weeping uncontrollably.

About twenty minutes later, Bart finally pulled up in front of the hospital. Two marked police cars and an ambulance were sitting in the emergency drop-off area. He parked his car next to them and ran inside. Uniformed officers standing in the waiting room told him doctors had rushed Fran to surgery.

"Where is Cassandra?" he asked beseechingly.

They motioned toward the emergency room doors, and he ran through them, looking in every room he passed, but he didn't find her. Finally, he passed a doctor, who pointed to a room down the hall. His heart was racing, and his stomach was in knots; he had no idea what to expect. When he entered the room, a nurse was standing in front of Cassandra with her back to Bart. He was breathing heavily and walked slowly toward the bed, where he could only see Cassie's legs under a hospital blanket. The nurse heard him and turned around.

"You need to get out of here," she said to him.

When she turned, he could see Cassie's face covered in cuts and blood, and then he noticed blood on her hands and arms as well. His eyes welled with tears.

"No, no, please," Cassandra pleaded. "He's my husband."

Bart walked over and took her hand. A tear rolled down his right cheek.

"Is she going to be okay?" he asked the nurse.

"She is going to be fine."

"Do you know about the other woman?" he asked.

"You'll have to talk to a doctor. She's in surgery right now," the nurse said and walked out.

As the nurse exited, a man with a suit on entered the room with a doctor behind him. Cassandra seemed to know him. He introduced himself to Bart as the administrator. Apparently, Frank had called and asked him to make sure everything went as well as it possibly could.

Within a half hour, Frank and Evon arrived with Anthony. They were distressed but relieved Cassandra and Fran were alive. Glass from the window had hit Cassandra in the face, but other than that, she escaped with no injuries. The administrator spoke to the emergency room doctors, who reported Fran was also doing well. A bullet had gone through her upper leg, grazing the bone but not shattering it completely. She had lost a lot of blood, but she would make a full recovery.

Donnie appeared. "Are you okay?" he asked Bart.

"I'm fine, but I was wondering if you could try to find Fran's phone so I can notify her husband and daughters about what happened. I don't have their numbers, someone will have to call them."

"No problem," Donnie said and left.

Bart, Frank, and Evon made their way to the small waiting room, thanking God Cassandra and Fran were alive, but Bart still felt sick to his stomach. He had been so preoccupied with Angler's bullshit he had neglected to protect the most important person in his life, but something else was bothering him. They had been extremely careful not to allow anyone access to Cassie's schedule. How was it possible that four men were waiting at the exact location at the exact time of her meeting? Something wasn't adding up, and he was going to get to the bottom of it.

CHAPTER 51

WOUNDED

The detectives finished examining the crime scene in the parking garage. All the empty brass had been picked up, the bodies had been removed, and Cassandra's SUV had been towed to the impound lot. The videos from the cameras in the garage and all surrounding areas were collected, and detectives would sift through them during the following days.

The hospital waiting room had become a hub for the families, doctors, and police officers investigating the attack. Fran was finally out of surgery. The doctor said everything went well in the operating room, but he would know more once she woke up. Cassandra had spoken at length with the detectives about what she saw and heard, but since she had taken cover on the floor of the vehicle, she hadn't seen very much. While they spoke to her, she held Bart's hand, which she had taken hours before and refused to let go.

Bart studied the detectives closely as they questioned Cassie. He didn't want anyone asking her if she knew how the assailants knew where she was going to be and when. She had enough on her mind and was already horrified. If she thought for one moment someone she trusted had betrayed her, it would only make things far worse.

Shortly after Bart asked Donnie to find Fran's phone, he returned with it in hand, and Bart notified her husband about what had happened. He was flying back from Europe, and their daughters, who lived out of state, were both trying to get to the hospital as quickly as possible. Bart could tell they were worried, but he assured them Fran was doing well.

Fran had saved Cassandra's life—there was no question about that. Bart's decision to hire her was a good one, but he still had a nagging sense of guilt. As Bart was wallowing, Cassandra stood up abruptly.

"I'll be right back," she said, letting go of his hand for the first time since she saw him.

She and Evon walked to the ladies' room. Anthony instantly stood up and walked over to sit next to Bart.

"I don't understand how this was possible. Those guys were waiting for her. No one knows her agenda, and no one knows where she goes except the family. How could this have happened?" Anthony asked Bart.

Bart looked around the room and noticed cameras in every corner. Until they knew who was behind the ambush, it was best not to talk in public. He placed his hands in front of his lips and whispered to Anthony.

"This is not the place for us to discuss those details." Bart gestured to the camera above them, and Anthony subtly nodded.

"You're right," Bart said, his hands still covering his mouth. "Something is not right with this entire scenario, but let's talk about it later."

Bart's phone vibrated. It was a text from Jerry. Restroom. First floor.

Bart stood up "I'll just be a few minutes. Tell Cassie I'll be right back."

Anthony stood up, looked him right in the eye, and teased, "I'll tell her, but you realize she's never going to allow you a minute to yourself for the rest of your life after all this." They both laughed.

Bart walked down to the first floor. At the end of the hallway was a men's restroom with an "Out of Order" sign on the door. Jerry was standing in front of the sinks. All of the stall doors were open; Jerry had obviously checked that no one else was there. As they shook hands, Jerry said, "That Fran is one hell of a woman. If I ever get in a gunfight, I want her with me. She put down three out of four of those assholes. Killed one of them and wounded the other two."

"Yeah. We sure were lucky to have her."

"I wanted you to know our informant told me a few hours ago they knew where Cassandra would be because they have somebody on the inside."

"Do you know who it is?" Bart asked intensely.

"No. He said, they knew where she would be so they could ambush her versus having to follow her around."

Bart stared pensively at the hand dryer on the wall in front of him.

"Do you have any idea who it could be?" Jerry inquired.

"I honestly have no idea. Only her family knows her movements; occasionally an attorney or accountant might, but usually it's just the family."

"I'll keep after this guy. Maybe he knows more than he is saying."

"Thank you," said Bart.

"You owe me," Jerry said, smiling as he turned toward the door.

"That's the damn truth." Bart went back upstairs, where he found everyone standing in the middle of the waiting room, listening to the doctor. He quickly walked over to join them.

The surgeon was reiterating that Fran's surgery had gone well. She would have to do physical therapy. He believed she would make a full recovery, though. They were all elated, and it was decided that Anthony, Cassie, Evon, and Frank would return to the house to get some rest while Bart remained at the hospital and waited for Fran's family. She had twenty-four-hour security, but Bart wanted to stay.

Everyone began to walk toward the elevator, but Cassandra balked. She didn't want to leave Bart and made no attempt to hide it. After a few minutes, he convinced her to go home and get some rest. She gave him a long kiss, mustered all of her remaining strength to give him the tightest hug she could manage, and walked over to her father. Before the doors opened, Bart grabbed Anthony's arm and took him aside.

"I just met with a friend. He's telling me this was an inside job. Those guys knew where she was going to be and were waiting for her."

Anthony looked stunned. "Don't worry. I'll make sure everybody makes it home safely, and after Cassandra gets some rest, I'll drive her back to the hospital."

Bart walked them out to the car and asked Anthony to increase the private security around the house. He walked back into the elevator and returned to the waiting room. For the first time in the past twenty hours, he had time to think. Cassie was fine, but he needed to completely restructure her security or figure out another way to keep her safe. Until they could determine how the attack happened, he needed to be with her all the time.

About half an hour later, Bart's phone began ringing. The caller ID said "Frank." Bart assumed Frank was calling to let him know Cassie was home safe.

Frank quietly said, "I didn't want to have this conversation in front of anybody else, but I want you to understand that whatever it takes for Fran to get well and whatever you think we need to do for her, go ahead and do it. She saved my daughter's life. I can't put a price on that."

"I understand," replied Bart. "And I will."

"I never thought this foundation and money had a dark side. I don't know what to do."

"This has nothing to do with you or the money or the foundation, but you're right. We have to make some changes to keep the family safe. It will all work out," Bart reassured him.

"Thank you for hiring Fran and caring so much about my daughter. I can't even begin to think about what would've happened if we hadn't taken those precautions."

Bart could hear Frank's voice wavering with emotion.

"Don't worry. I will make this right, and we will sort everything out."

Bart hung up and noticed a young girl walking toward him. She looked lost and was peering into various rooms and reading signs. Bart thought she resembled Fran, so he got up and introduced himself. It was Fran's youngest daughter. She began crying as soon as

Bart told her that her mother was out of surgery, but they were still waiting for her to wake up.

He motioned toward a seat in the waiting room, and they sat for quite a while, talking about Fran and how fearless she had always been. For the first time, Bart didn't only see her as someone keeping Cassie safe. Fran was a wife, a mother, and a friend, and she'd be profoundly missed if anything happened to her.

CHAPTER 52

JUDAS

Over the course of the following week, everyone took turns visiting Fran, so she was rarely alone. Her wound was healing nicely, and she was scheduled to start physical therapy in the next few weeks. Her family spent as much time as possible with her, and she was in good spirits. Detectives had interviewed her consistently regarding every aspect of the shooting, but they were playing it close to the vest when it came to who they thought set the whole thing up. At Bart's request, Jerry was keeping track of the Albanians so Bart could settle the score when he was ready.

Cassandra still refused to let Bart out of her sight. Being together every second of every day would be a problem for most couples, but for the two of them, it was perfect. Cassie wanted Bart around to protect her, and he wanted to keep her close for the same reason. He was careful not to talk too much about her fears—maybe if he didn't bring them up, she would start to feel safe again and even start sleeping at night without waking up in a cold sweat with tears running down her cheeks.

He had suggested she see a therapist, but she wasn't ready yet. She had undeniably been through a traumatic experience and was suffering from PTSD. Bart also mentioned moving out of New York several times, and since the shooting, Cassie believed it would be the only way they could ever live in peace. They agreed they would have that conversation with Frank once they were certain of where they would relocate.

While they were visiting Fran at the hospital, Bart received a phone call from Vito.

"Hey, Vito. What's the news?" Bart asked.

"I met with the accountants in Florida. I know where the Bandell family is hiding their money."

"I'm listening."

"They have four homes, each worth more than $2 million. They've also purchased some vacant properties, and apparently they have a few million dollars in gold, but I'm not sure where the gold is stashed. They probably have around $15 million in assets that he knew about. The accountants seemed surprised Frank had not seen this theft coming. When I pressed them about how no one noticed it, they said his attorney had kept it hidden from the family. They said if we wanted to know exactly where everything was, it was going to cost."

"How much?" Bart asked.

"The accountants want $250,000 to disclose exactly where everything is hidden."

"I don't mind paying them, but I want you to double-check that all of their information is accurate," Bart quickly replied.

"I'll take care of it," said Vito. "Also, I'm sorry to hear about what happened to Cassandra. If you need me to settle the score, I'm your man."

"Thanks, Vito. I really appreciate that. I'll be in touch."

Bart and Cassandra returned to the compound. Even with everything that had happened, the wedding was still scheduled for December, and Cassie and Evon had an appointment with the planner.

"Are you sure you don't want to postpone the wedding?" Evon constantly asked Cassie, and every time it was the same answer.

"Under no condition."

Bart thought the wedding distractions were good for Cassie. They also gave Bart a chance to sit down with Frank and Anthony and discuss some dire issues. It was the first time since the shooting they actually had a chance to be alone and talk. Bart kissed Cassie and walked over to meet Frank in his office.

"How the hell did this happen?" Frank asked as soon as the door closed. "I don't understand how these guys were waiting for my daughter at a location no one knew."

Frank was irate, but Bart knew Frank's anger wasn't directed toward him. He understood better than anyone how he was feeling. The woman he loved was almost kidnapped, maybe even murdered, and someone was responsible, but they didn't know who yet. The only thing Bart knew for certain was that whoever it was wouldn't make it out alive.

"I've heard from different people that someone was working on the inside," Bart responded.

Anthony appeared abruptly; it was difficult to tell who was most upset about the shooting—Frank, Anthony, or Bart—but Bart was the best at maintaining a level head and looking at the situation methodically. He explained to them Cassie had calmed down exponentially, aside from the night terrors, but she was glued to his side, and he believed it would be that way for a while.

"Well, I'm glad you two are so in love because being together 24/7 would drive any normal person nuts," Anthony joked.

"I think it would drive Rose nuts first," added Frank, and both of them laughed.

Bart went on to explain his theory about what happened. "I have been thinking about this day in and day out, but let me go over a few details before we get into whodunit. I had a conversation with Vito today, and he told me two accountants in Florida know where the Bandells are hiding their money. I realize that doesn't seem important at the moment, but they told Vito they think Bill Wright was in on the cover-up, and that's how they were able to steal so much money over all these years. He let it happen; he knew what was going on and never tried to stop it. Now, with that said, the only person besides us who knew where Cassandra would be the morning of the shooting is Bill Wright, and now that we know he can't be trusted, it doesn't seem like much of a stretch to accuse him of betraying Cassandra."

"Bill doesn't work in any of our family businesses anymore, so how would he know where she was going to be?" Frank interjected.

"I was thinking about that myself. Claire was at the meeting that morning, and you know she keeps her appointment calendar on the company software program. So, I'm going to have my IT people find out if Bill Wright still has access to that calendar and if he accessed Claire's schedule." Bart turned to Frank and asked, "Did Bill ever attend a meeting with you at the Seagram's building? Would he have known where you would park underground?"

Frank thought for a moment and then said, "Son of a bitch. He did attend a few meetings with me at that office, so he would've known where I would park."

"I need time to dig into this, but if I had to bet, Bill Wright is the culprit," said Bart.

"Well, what are we going to do about it?" asked Anthony aggressively.

"At the moment, we aren't going to do anything." Bart again turned to face Frank. "If you don't mind, I need to talk to Anthony alone."

Frank stood up and reluctantly stepped outside. Once the door was closed, Bart began speaking quietly.

"I believe Michael Bandell's daughter has a nine-millimeter gun registered in her name, and she keeps it in her car."

"Okay. Why are you telling me this, Bart?"

"Because I would like to get my hands on that gun without anybody knowing—leave the holster in the car with some type of weight in it so no one notices the gun is missing."

Anthony looked perplexed. "What are you going to do with the gun?"

"Let's just work on getting the gun, and we'll take it from there."

Bart opened the door and motioned Frank back inside. Anthony left to take Cassandra and Evon shopping. Once he had gone, Frank carefully assessed Bart's disposition.

"Don't do anything foolish," said Frank. "We have to be strategic about this."

"I won't do anything stupid, but I learned a long time ago that if you let people steal from you and hurt your family without repercussions, they're going to continue to do it. I'm going to put an end to all this shit and make whoever's responsible pay. Justice is coming."

CHAPTER 53

CAUTION

Bart had come to the realization that Bill Wright and Michael Bandell were going to have to be dealt with, but he knew it would be unwise, to say the least, to draw any more attention to himself or the D'Angelo family. The Star Killer was dead, and Fran had been in a shoot-out with the Albanians. Any more killings that could be traced back to him could be his undoing.

Thanksgiving was around the corner, and a huge, lavish family dinner was just what everyone needed. Cassandra and Evon had been planning a big celebration at Frank's house for the past few weeks that would include all of Cassie's and Bart's family and friends. It was going to be fabulous.

Cassandra had asked Bart if he thought it was finally a good time to discuss with her father their move out of New York. She knew Frank loved Thanksgiving, so he would be in good spirits and possibly more receptive to the idea. Bart agreed they would mention it to him but not go into vast detail. That way he would have time to digest it for a while, and after Thanksgiving, they would get serious about exactly where and when they would move.

Bart and Cassandra had decided to honeymoon in Tuscany since Frank owned a small villa there with a beguiling view. The family rented it out when they weren't using it, but Frank made sure it would be vacant following the wedding. Everything was falling into place, but as usual, business came first. Bart and Anthony had a meeting in Frank's office to discuss their next move.

"Before we talk about Bandell, I have some information regarding Bill," said Bart. "The software people looked into Claire's scheduling program and confirmed Bill looked at her date book every day for the past month."

"That son of a bitch," said Anthony furiously. "I'll fucking kill him."

"I know you're pissed. Trust me, I am too, but I don't want to bring any extra attention to you, me, or the family, so we need to be careful about how we handle this."

Anthony glared at the wet bar adorned with decanters of fine scotch and Irish whiskey.

"I have a plan," continued Bart. "I found out Bill Wright is a big gambler. When he isn't in Vegas, he's at the track betting on horses. So, if something were to happen to him, it wouldn't be too much of a stretch for everyone to think he got into debt with the wrong people."

Anthony continued glaring. "What are you thinking?"

"Once you steal the gun from Bandell's daughter, I want someone to use that gun to kill Bill Wright. Two birds, one stone. But listen to me, Anthony. This must go exactly as I say."

Anthony looked at Bart and nodded.

"Someone puts two bullets into Bill Wright from the daughter's gun. The shooter is to leave one casing behind and take the other one with them. It must look like a robbery. I want it to happen before the wedding, so I have time to meet with Michael Bandell and get the family's money back. When I leave for my honeymoon, I want all of these issues behind us."

"That sounds great and all," said Anthony, "but even with Bill's history of gambling, his death is going to draw attention to the family. He was their attorney for a long time, and they just recently replaced him with Claire."

"I agree, but the only way we're going to get this money back is to act quickly. If we sit on this for too long, they'll sell everything and hide the money."

It was late afternoon by the time Cassandra and Evon had finished most of their planning for Thanksgiving. Frank walked into the kitchen while they were discussing the final details. He grabbed three wine glasses and poured himself and the ladies a glass of merlot.

"I need to have a serious conversation with you," Cassie said.

Frank led Evon and Cassandra into the living room. He and Evon sat down on the couch, and Cassandra sat on the love seat across from them.

"What's on your mind?" Frank asked.

Cassandra took a sip of wine and set the glass on the table adjacent to the love seat.

"You know how much I love you and Evon," she began. "You've been wonderful parents to me and have given me everything I've ever wanted, which is why this is going to be difficult for me to tell you, but please give me a chance to do the best I can."

Evon and Frank both sat there attentively.

"I didn't realize how much everything in my childhood affected me—specifically, my mother's death and, before that, the kidnapping attempt. When we had to talk about increasing the security—by hiring Fran and getting new systems in the homes—things got more intense, and I realized how afraid I was. I don't like being afraid, especially in my own home. I've always viewed myself as a strong woman, but I find myself living in fear all the time. I'm sure you both noticed I never leave Bart's side anymore, and it's because that's the only time I feel safe."

Frank interrupted. "I'm so sorry that everything I worked for—this foundation and everything else—has brought all this unwanted attention to you. If I had known this was going to happen, I never would've done what I did. I never would've started the foundation."

"It isn't your fault. It's none of our fault. We didn't do anything wrong. There's just evil in the world, and we have to protect ourselves from it, which brings me to my next point. I want you both to consider how vulnerable I feel living in New York. I think it's time for us to start looking at other places to live where people aren't trying to hurt us all the time. It also doesn't help that I'm the face of a billion-dollar foundation. Although it does great work and I want to remain a part of it, I don't feel comfortable having that kind of bounty over my head."

Cassandra paused for a moment before saying, "The only way I would move away is if both of you go with me. Otherwise, I won't do it."

Frank looked intrigued—sympathetic even—which surprised Cassie since she and Bart were sure he'd be angry and unreceptive to the notion of leaving New York.

"We can keep the homes here in New York," Cassandra continued. "We will keep the foundation and commute back and forth when necessary, but we will have a new beginning someplace safer."

Frank and Evon were holding hands on the couch, and he turned to look at her. Evon nodded at him, and Frank began speaking.

"I understand exactly what you're saying, and I agree with you. I think we all have to sit down—Anthony included—and decide what's best for the family. I know you and Bart want to have children, and we can't expose my grandchildren to this craziness."

Cassandra had tears in her eyes. "You must both understand that when we have children, I want to be with them all the time. Having lost my mother so young, I want nothing more than for my children to always have me, and I'm afraid that won't happen if we stay here. While I must do what's best for everyone, we have to look at what kind of life our children will have. Am I going to be afraid to let them go to school? Little League? The store? I can't live that way, so we have to figure out a better way for us to live—a safer way."

Frank stood up, walked over to where Cassie was sitting, and gave her a hug. "I know. We will all sit down and figure out something that will work. You and Bart develop a plan that we can discuss in the near future. It will all work out, but for now, I want you to enjoy this time in your life. Your wedding is near and then your honeymoon. After that, we will make a definite plan to get the hell out of here. I promise."

Cassandra left and walked toward her and Bart's house. Bear came running up to greet her. When she entered the house, Bart told her he was going to confession.

"Do you mind if I come along?" she asked.

"Of course not."

She kissed him tenderly on the lips and wrapped her arms around his neck. "What could you possibly have to confess?"

If she only knew—all the secrets, all the lies.

On the way to church, Cassandra told Bart about her conversation with Frank and Evon.

"Sounds like it went well," said Bart. "I guess it's time for us to pick a location. I've been thinking Kentucky or North Carolina would make sense—somewhere I can buy a horse-breeding business."

She agreed, and they sat in silence for a while, contemplating their pasts—all the events that had led them to one another and all the madness that had happened in the short time they had been together.

"Will you teach me how to use a gun?" Cassandra asked Bart.

She had never mentioned owning a gun or using one before, but in light of everything that had happened, it made sense. "Of course I will," he said. "Do you have one?"

"No, not yet."

"Well, I'll take you to the shooting range so you can try out a few different types and see what you like best."

As they got out of the Escalade in front of the church and began to walk inside, Cassie turned to face Bart. "I'm sure I have more sins than you do," she said, almost bashfully. "Having sex with you—I should've waited until we were married."

Bart smiled at her pink cheeks. "Surely you can tell God it's my fault. I just can't keep my hands off you."

They both laughed and continued walking toward the entrance of the church. Once inside, they sat in one of the pews near the back, and Bart kneeled with his hands clasped in front of his face and his eyes closed.

Cassie entered the confessional first, and as Bart expected, she wasn't in there for long. What could she possibly have to confess?

"You're up," she whispered as she sat back down in the pew.

Bart finished his Hail Mary and made the sign of the cross with his right hand. He stood up and walked toward the small room. He pulled the emerald curtain back and stepped inside the booth.

"Forgive me, Father, for I have sinned. I do not know when my last confession was." He paused, searching for the words. "I helped kill someone. I planned it, and I might as well have committed it. I am the reason he is dead, but the worst part is that I don't regret it. He was an evil man—a monster—who killed dozens of women and ruined more families than I can count. I'm glad that the evil one is dead. I have also lied to my friends, my family, and the woman I love. It was for their protection, but they were lies, nonetheless. I'm sorry for these and all my sins."

The priest absolved Bart of his sins and told him God forgave him, but Bart wondered. Could God really forgive someone for killing another human being? Would He forgive Bart for what he was about to do? For the people he was going to kill? When would it end?

CHAPTER 54

THANKSGIVING

Thanksgiving had finally arrived. Cassandra and Evon were elated to be preparing dinner with Jonathan. He had been tutoring Cassandra in the fine art of cooking for the past few months. Her mother had been a great cook, Evon was skilled in making decadent Italian dishes from scratch, and Cassandra discovered she knew more about cooking than she thought, but making a meal for nearly fifty people was no easy feat. However, if there was one thing Cassie was no stranger to, it was large parties.

Bart had asked the ladies if he could assist with anything, but they politely declined. He had suspected he would be more helpful if he was out of the way before he even offered. He decided to go for a run. He walked over to his and Cassie's house to change into his jogging pants, a T-shirt, and tennis shoes, and then returned to Frank's before beginning his run.

"Are you sure you don't need any help?" he asked.

"We're sure!" said Cassie, Evon, and Jonathan simultaneously. They all broke out into boisterous laughter.

Cassandra walked over to Bart, took his hand, and walked him to the patio. As soon as they stepped outside, she closed the door behind them and began to passionately kiss him.

"I'll be over here cooking for a few hours, but when I get back to the house, I'm going to need some alone time with you before the party starts." She planted another kiss on his lips, her tongue delicately alternating between his top and bottom lips.

"Just say when," he responded with a big smile on his face.

Evon knocked on the patio door. "Get a room," she said, laughing. "Or, better yet, we need to get back to work. Hands off my sous chef!"

Bart always found her very charming, even though sometimes he could hardly understand what she was saying through her heavy Italian accent. He laughed and let go of Cassandra.

"I'll be seeing you later—all of you." He gave Cassandra one last quick kiss and walked toward the front door.

As soon as he began running, Bear was immediately at his side. He put the leash on her so she could go along. The last few times Bart had gone on a run, he had felt slightly light-headed, so he decided to take it easy and pick up the pace if he felt up to it. His head injuries sometimes manifested themselves in feelings of light-headedness, dizziness, and sometimes both. The weather was beautiful for November—the perfect temperature for a brisk run—and Bart didn't feel any dizziness on that particular day. He ran nearly four miles before returning home.

When he got inside the gate, he let Bear off the leash. She immediately took off running toward Frank's office. Bart assumed it was because Frank had company, so he walked over to see who it was. Frank was doing paperwork inside.

"Hey, Frank," Bart said, poking his head in the office. "Is everything okay? Bear hauled ass over here, so I thought maybe you had company."

"Just me. I thought I should get out of the house so I'm out of the way. They're cooking up a feast."

Bart walked into the office and sat on the couch.

"Are you doing okay?" Frank asked.

"I am. I just got back from a run. It's beautiful outside, and it's going to be a great day. We have a lot to be thankful for."

"In light of what's happened lately, I think we certainly do have a lot to be thankful for." Frank set his pen down and looked at Bart. "You know, Cassie talked to Evon and I about relocating."

Oh, shit, thought Bart.

"The more I think about it, the more I realize it's not such a bad idea," added Frank.

Bart was surprised. Cassandra had told him the conversation went well, but he never imagined it went that well. She must've made a strong case.

Bart said, "I think Cassie will be a lot happier out of the limelight. She's been through so much this year, and she's almost become paralyzed with fear. Besides that, you know she wants a family, and it's important she's confident her children will be safe."

Frank said, "Well, you know I want grandchildren, and I'm not saying that to rush you but to make the point that obviously I want my daughter, my grandchildren, and my wife to be safe. Have you thought about where you'd like to relocate?"

"We haven't made any absolute decisions yet, but we did establish that we want it to look like a strategic move. We don't want anyone to think we're running away from New York out of fear, so I want it to appear to be a business decision."

"What kind of business?"

"Horses. There's some good horse country in Kentucky and North Carolina, and it will be much safer, but you realize Cassandra won't do this if you and Evon don't come with us?"

"I know that, and I want to go. We can keep these houses for when we're in town working on the foundation." Frank furrowed his brow as if recalling an unpleasant memory. "I know Cassie thinks the Albanians targeted her because she's the face of the foundation. So, I'm going to ask you for one more favor. I want you to know that when you entered Cassie's life, my intention was never to involve you in all of this. But fortunately, or unfortunately for you, if anybody can handle these types of things, it's you. The only time she feels safe is when she's with you."

"Listen, Frank, I know you're probably tired of hearing this, but I don't think you understand me when I say that all I care about is your daughter, and I would do anything for her, especially to keep her safe."

"I need you to become the face of the foundation. Cassie can run things from behind the scenes—it's a finely oiled machine that can be run from a remote location. But I want someone in the family to be the face. It's too important to me, and there are too many people who need help to just give it up."

"Whatever I need to do to make this work, I'll do it."

Bart stood up to leave. Frank shook his hand, gave him a hug, and whispered, "Thank you, son."

Bart walked back to their house to get ready for dinner. As he was opening the front door, his phone rang. It was Mike Fuller. If he thought Bart was going to leave Thanksgiving for another one of his crazy theories, he was sorely mistaken. Bart stepped back outside and closed the door. If Cassie was home, he didn't want to worry her.

"Hello?"

"Hey, Bart. I hate to bother you on Thanksgiving, but I want to pass a little piece of information along."

"I'm listening."

"A friend of mine works for the district attorney's office. He called to let me know they are going to ask you to come in. They have questions they want you to answer."

"Questions concerning what?"

"If I had to guess, I'd say it has something to do with the Star Killer. They're not going to subpoena you or anything. They're just going to ask you to come in and answer a few questions. Beyond that, I don't know much."

"Okay, well, thanks for the heads-up. Happy Thanksgiving, Mike."

"You too, Bart."

The line went dead. Bart wasn't too alarmed. It could be routine questioning, but on the flip side, it could be more than that. He had gone over the details a million times—what the department knew about the Star Killer, what they found in Lupo's apartment, and what they knew about Angler's death. As far as he was concerned, there was nothing to connect him to anything other than the investigations into the Star Killer's victims prior to his death.

When he entered the house, he walked toward the master bathroom. He could hear Cassie in the tub, and he walked over and kissed her softly on the lips.

"I'm going to take a shower," he said.

"Fine, but don't be too long. We don't have much time, and you and I have business to tend to." She winked seductively at him.

As he walked out of the bathroom, he stopped for a moment and admired Cassandra's wet, naked body, which was perfectly covered with bubbles, leaving little to the imagination. For Bart, every day he spent with her was Thanksgiving.

By two o'clock, fifty-five guests had arrived. Everyone was talking, drinking, and laughing. The food was delicious, and everyone ate until they were more stuffed than the thirty-pound turkey in the center of the table. Bart got to spend quality time with his family, and best of all, in a few short weeks, he would be married to the woman of his dreams.

Fran had been at home recuperating, and after dinner, Bart and Cassandra had taken a care package to her house to make sure she and her family had a proper Thanksgiving dinner. She was in good spirits and wanted to get back to work. As they were driving back home, Bart was more quiet than usual and had a distinct frown line running down his forehead.

"What's on your mind?" Cassie leaned over and grabbed Bart's right hand.

"I was thinking. When I hired Fran, I knew she was the right person for the job, and I'm so thankful she was there when you needed her. I don't know how I can ever repay her. I want to give her something for all she has done for us. We can think about options and decide later."

Bart didn't mention to Cassie that he had spoken to Frank about moving, although he should have. Thanksgiving had been such a wonderful day, and he didn't want to stress her out. When she asked him if her father had said anything, he replied with a simple, "not yet." Again, Bart found himself lying to his fiancée. He had hoped once the Star Killer was dead, the lies would die too. Then, when he found out about Bandell stealing money, he said the same thing. Then he discovered Bill Wright had arranged the shooting, and it was the same. Would the lies ever stop? Would there ever be a time when he could just be honest with the woman he loved?

As they walked into the foyer of their house, Cassie stopped and turned to Bart.

"Thanksgiving has always been my favorite holiday, but today I got to be thankful for being with the man I've been looking for all my life. I'm the luckiest woman in the world."

Great. As if he didn't feel guilty enough already.

CHAPTER 55

SUSPICIONS

Thanksgiving had been a welcome reprieve from the chaos of the few weeks prior, but once the holiday was over, it was back to business as usual. The sale of Frank's construction company was originally scheduled for the day of the shooting but was delayed for obvious reasons. While the buyers and the attorneys completely understood the urgency of the situation, it was imperative that it be closed before the wedding, so they agreed it would take place at the Long Island foundation office during the coming week.

As the primary business owner, Frank would attend, and since Cassandra was his business partner and a major stockholder, she would also be present. Bart, Frank, Evon, and Cassandra traveled to the Long Island office. Cassie seemed at ease; as long as she was with Bart, she had no fears, no worries, and no inhibitions.

The wedding was in less than three weeks, and while the closing lasted only about an hour, Cassandra and Evon had one last fitting for her wedding gown and her bridesmaids' dresses. They all met at the bridal shop while Frank and Anthony went home, leaving Bart with the women since Cassie refused to be anywhere without him.

While he was in the waiting room, Bart received a call from one of the assistant district attorneys. They asked him very politely if he would come in for an interview regarding the Star Killer. Bart agreed but told them it would have to be done quickly since his wedding was just around the corner. They planned to meet the following week at the district attorney's office in Manhattan. Bart wondered whether he should take a lawyer with him. After about an hour, the women were done, and he took Evon and Cassandra for a late lunch. Evon and Cassandra's excitement couldn't be contained. They were talking and giggling like two schoolgirls.

When they returned home, Bart explained to Cassandra he had to appear at the district attorney's office. Although she knew very little about the Star Killer, she was still his fiancée and a smart businesswoman with good instincts, so he decided to quickly explain his dilemma to her. She was more understanding than he had anticipated, which made him regret lying to her that much more.

"We've just gone to a closing where we received $200 million. If you want to hire the best lawyers in the world, don't think twice about it. Just do what you need to."

"Thank you for understanding." Bart walked closer to Cassie and kissed her on the forehead, then took a step back. "I have no idea what they want to talk to me about. I think for the first meeting, it may be best to show up alone and ask them if an attorney is necessary."

During that moment, Bart felt reassured about appearing before the district attorney, but he promised himself that if things began to go even slightly sideways, he would hire the best lawyers he possibly could.

While Bart was talking to Cassie, Anthony called and left a voicemail stating he wanted to talk. He had gotten ahold of Cindy

Bandell's gun, and while Bart was a little reluctant to drag Michael Bandell's family into things, it was clear that, as the accountant, she must have played a part in the theft her father and Bill Wright had orchestrated. Now that they had the gun, it was crucial for them to act quickly before someone realized it was gone. Within the next week, Bill Wright would have to be killed, and then Bart would need to meet with Michael Bandell and lay out his demands.

Anthony had known Bill Wright for years, so he knew where he lived and had begun monitoring his comings and goings. Bill was a big drinker and an even bigger gambler; it wouldn't be hard to catch him off guard and do what needed to be done. Anthony had no qualms about it—Bill had set up Cassandra to be kidnapped and possibly killed. Justice would be served.

Bart had a quick conversation about the district attorney with Anthony, who was slightly concerned but also felt it could be normal business. They had to cover all of their bases when interviewing anyone who had knowledge of the crime, and since Bart had worked on all the Star Killer cases, it didn't seem out of the ordinary that they needed to question him.

The next course of action was to meet Michael Bandell. It had to appear to be a simple business meeting—nothing more. If Bandell got spooked and began hiding assets, things could go south quickly. Bart called him and set up a meeting for the following week, telling him he would text him the address before the meeting. The real estate office seemed a logical location. The only issue was that it was their territory, and if they wanted to set up a listening device, it wouldn't be difficult. Of course, Bart would bring along his trusty jamming device to alleviate any privacy concerns, but he was still a little uneasy about the location.

SUSPICIONS

After the meeting with Anthony, Bart received a phone call from the attorneys who had been working on selling Frank's four smaller businesses. They advised him that contracts had been accepted by the employees of all four businesses and that the closing would take place around February. Bart called Vito to tell him the good news and assured him he would receive his money as soon as the businesses officially closed. Vito was elated but seemed more concerned with helping Bart deal with whoever had tried to kidnap Cassandra.

"Thank you. We will get together and talk after the wedding."

Vito was invited to the wedding; his father was a business client of Frank's, so they could get away with having him there without raising any suspicions. Bart was sure the department would videotape the wedding even though Frank had no actual Mafia ties. They wouldn't be able to resist.

Cassandra returned from a workout and decided to take a bath; she asked Bart to sit and talk with her. She was overjoyed about the wedding, and he could tell most of the anxiety from the kidnapping attempt was diverted, at least for the moment. She talked giddily about her dress, the decorations, and the honeymoon plans.

Suddenly, she became less animated, and her expression turned solemn.

"There's something I have to tell you, and I hope you won't be upset." Her voice sounded serious, and Bart anxiously waited for what she could possibly have to tell him.

"I-I stopped my birth control about a month ago. I just want you to know."

He stood up, walked to the edge of the tub, leaned over, and kissed her on the lips. "Why would I be upset? We've discussed children more than once and agreed we want them."

"Yes, but—" She paused. "But if I get pregnant as soon as we get married, it will change things for us. I'm afraid it may hurt our relationship if it happens too quickly."

"I promise nothing can change the way I feel about you. I love you more every single day, and our relationship is only going to get better with time—children or not. So, if you want to have a baby right away, that's fine, and if you want to wait, that's fine also. In a few weeks, you're going to be my wife, and that's all that matters."

He kissed her again, but this time it was longer and more passionate. He could feel his impulses vibrating through his entire body. Cassie had that effect on him. He reached down, scooped her up out of the bath, and carried her to the bed, still soaking wet. She screamed with delight. Bart laid her on the bed and made love to her until she was fast asleep in his arms.

When Cassandra woke up, the sun was setting, radiating a warm golden light throughout the master bedroom. She looked up at Bart and smiled, her eyes still heavy from sleep. "Do you think we could take a quick trip to Lexington and then maybe North Carolina to look at land?"

He was elated and kissed her again. In a few weeks, Bart would be married to the woman he loved, and they'd be headed to Tuscany. After that, he could possibly fulfill his dream of owning a horse ranch and starting a family. Things couldn't get any better. However, living on the edge with Bill Wright, Michael Bandell, and now the district attorney made him skeptical. All he wanted was to be with

Cassie and have a semblance of a normal life. His desire to finally experience some peace hadn't been fulfilled yet. He was beginning to wonder if it ever would.

CHAPTER 56

FAMILY MEETING

Frank had never considered leaving New York. He grew up there, fell in love there, and raised his daughter there, but everything was about to change. The atmosphere was charged with recent travesties, which, most of all, Cassandra couldn't seem to shake. It seemed that there was an inability to escape violence, and it was not only frustrating but seemed to be an endless battle. Cassie and Bart had made up their minds. They refused to raise their future family in an unsafe and noxious environment, but if Frank, Evon, Anthony, and Rose were not all on board, an alternate plan had to be made. Cassie made it clear that she would not move unless they all did.

Everyone met early in the morning at Frank's house. Jonathan had prepared breakfast, and tensions seemed high. As they sat around the table, Cassandra started the conversation. "You know how much I love all of you, and if I thought there was any other way we could deal with this, I would be the first one to do it. But in light of what's happened lately, I don't see an alternative. I think this has to be a decision we all agree on."

"Why don't we go around the table and have everyone give their opinion and see what our options are?" suggested Frank.

Anthony went first. "Rose and I have discussed this at length, and as long as we are going to keep the homes in New York so we can travel back and forth to visit family, we don't find any flaws in moving. If we don't make a dramatic change, we are going to spend 24/7 looking over our shoulders, waiting for the next disaster. We will just have to keep increasing security by hiring more people, and I don't see any end in sight."

Rose nodded. "I agree. Something must be done. I hate feeling this way."

Evon went next. "I want Cassandra to be happy. She's finally found someone she's truly in love with, and they are going to start their own family. That's the way it should be. I want to enjoy any grandchildren we may have, and I don't see how that can happen if we continue living in fear. These two things are not compatible. We have to do something."

She glanced over at Frank, whose expression was somewhere between sorrow and trepidation. "I understand we are here today to decide if we're going to move, but I think it's more than that. The more I think about the situation with the foundation, Cassandra being the face of it seems to be a large part of the problem, and it needs to be dealt with along with the move. I think the two matters are intertwined."

Frank turned his attention to Bart. "You need to disclose to everyone where you think we would move and what a life there would look like."

"As I've told Frank, I think we have to make this look like it's a business decision. I think the perfect cover is for me to go into the horse breeding business. We buy a couple hundred acres, build the homes we want, and do it in a small county. In my mind, it must be a place where it's conducive to running a horse business, and that's considering climate as well as location. There are two locations I think we could look at: Lexington, Kentucky, and Tryon, North Carolina. Lexington is a bigger city than Tryon, but I think if we're looking for the ideal small town, Tryon is the best. The winters are mild, the summer is cool, and the taxes are low, but it is a small town, and I don't know if all of you are ready for such a dramatic change."

Anthony snickered. "You had me at mild winters!" The room broke out in laughter.

"If Cassandra is not the face of the foundation anymore, she can run the foundation from anywhere in the country. That allows us to keep control and continue to do all the good everyone does through the foundation. It's a different world, but I think the upside is that if we keep these homes, everyone can come and go as they please, and if Cassandra and I are blessed with children, they will be safe. Cassandra wants to take a trip within the next few days to see both towns. Everyone's welcome to come along. I think it would be better to wait until after the wedding, but she wants to get this done now."

"We will take the company jet and visit Lexington and Tryon in the next few days," confirmed Cassandra.

"Alright, so what does everyone think?" asked Frank.

It was unanimous. Everyone was on board.

They all stood up to leave. Frank said, "Bart and Cassandra, can you stay for a few more minutes?"

They followed him into his office, and Frank closed the door behind them. Bart and Cassandra sat on the leather sofa, and Frank sat in the large leather chair behind the desk.

"I'm fine with moving. It makes sense—it's something that we have to do, but changing the face of the foundation concerns me. I understand Cassie can run things from behind the scenes, but I want someone in the family to represent the foundation. I think it's a must, and the only one I believe who can do it safely is Bart."

There was silence. Bart and Frank both looked at Cassandra, waiting for her response, but she was deep in thought. Finally, after what seemed like an eternity, she spoke. "If that's what it takes for us to get out of New York, then that is entirely up to Bart."

"If I can just be the face of the foundation and I don't have to do any politicking, I don't mind doing it—whatever keeps my wife safe."

As Bart and Cassie walked hand in hand back to their house, he could only think of all the other issues looming—Bill Wright, Michael Bandell, and the death of the Star Killer. They all needed to be resolved so he could find peace, but it seemed that as soon as he got one problem under control, another two reared their ugly heads. Cassandra was determined to spend the next few days visiting Kentucky and North Carolina; she wanted to settle on something so they could enjoy their honeymoon and begin making plans for their new life. Bart had the woman he loved and the financial ability to go into a business he really loved. For him, it should have been a time of joy, not fear and worry.

CHAPTER 57

MOVING

Before leaving for Lexington, Bart needed to talk to Anthony one last time to confirm how they were going to handle Bill Wright. They met the night before he and Cassie went out of town in the usual place—Frank's secure office in the antique car garage. Anthony wanted to kill Bill himself, but Bart would not hear of it. Bill had put Cassie's life in danger. He was the reason Fran got shot, and he sold out the family. I'll be damned if I'm not the one who gets the satisfaction of making that son of a bitch pay.

Anthony had been watching Bill for the past couple of weeks. He was constantly out playing cards and gambling at some very suspect places and usually stumbled home drunk during the early hours of the morning. After observing his routine night after night, Anthony said the best way to catch him off guard would be to wait for him to get home when he was trashed and not paying attention, then execute him and either leave him to be found or set the house on fire to hide the evidence. Bart said he would think about it while they were out of town, but it needed to be taken care of ASAP. If Michael Bandell found out his daughter's gun had been stolen, he'd report it, and the whole plan to frame her would go up in smoke.

Bart and Cassie were up early the following morning. They wanted to get on the plane by seven. The flight to Lexington took two and a half hours, and since they had only one day to see the city and look at real estate, it was going to be a tight squeeze. The plane took off from Flushing Airport en route to Lexington.

Cassie was in good spirits and was finally beginning to look like herself again. She had been seeing a dermatologist every other day to treat the small cuts on her face. Nothing was going to stop the wedding, and if anyone mentioned postponing it, they got a vicious death stare from Cassie, which was still nicer than most people's resting expression, but she did her best.

Bart was convinced that as much as the trip was about scouting a new place to live, it was also an escape for Cassie—a chance to get out of the city, away from all the craziness, and be alone with him. Whether they were walking, sitting, or driving, she never let go of his hand. He watched her closely; he was concerned she was masking the immense fear that had come over her. She appeared to be doing better, but between the wedding, the move, and the fear of being attacked, she must have been stressed. It was a lot to handle, even for a woman as strong as her.

The jet landed in Lexington. They were met by a real estate agent who gave them a quick tour of the city. It was much different than what Cassie was accustomed to—entirely different from New York City or Long Island. Unknown to Bart, she was ready for a small town with friendly people who knew their names and cared about what happened to them. Most of her decisions would be based on her family after they moved; Frank, Evon, Bart, and any children they may have would be what drove all her sureties from that point on.

They viewed historic sites and bourbon distilleries and had a late lunch at a small but quaint restaurant in the middle of town. The real estate agent gave the impression it was a fairly safe city, but like every other city, some parts of town were dangerous. Compared to what happened in New York, however, Lexington was a sanctuary. The real estate agent showed them two properties: one was four hundred acres, and the other was five hundred. They both had beautiful homes on them and plenty of room to build additional homes for her parents and Anthony and Rose.

The horse business was huge in Lexington, so they would fit in quite well. The initial cost of buying a home and the property would be in the millions, and setting up an operation that would actually be a horse breeding facility would be another few million. Cassie was quick to remind Bart they were about to receive $200 million, not to mention the $250 million she already had. Money shouldn't factor into their decision.

They got back to the room about eight o'clock that evening and ordered room service. Considering all that Cassie had been through, Bart was surprised at how affectionate she still was. They were making love just as much—maybe even more—than before the shooting. Most of the time, she couldn't keep her hands off of him, and Bart loved it. As soon as they finished eating, Cassie moved the plates to the small table near the kitchenette. As she was walking back to the bed, she began removing one article of clothing at a time, looking at Bart seductively but with a playful glimmer in her eyes. By the time she got back to the bed, she was completely naked. Bart looked her up and down, taking in every inch of her beautiful body before pulling her into bed with him and kissing her up and down.

The next day, they were up early and back on the road. The flight to North Carolina seemed to go by quickly. When they landed in Tryon, they were met by someone from the Chamber of Commerce who was also a real estate broker. Tryon was much smaller than Lexington, and Bart wasn't convinced Frank, Evon, Anthony, and Rose could live in such a rural place. For Bart, the smaller, the better. After a few years of living in Oklahoma, he got a feel for what a small town was actually like and preferred it to a larger city. Small towns meant fewer people, and fewer people meant less drama.

Cassandra was enchanted by Tryon. There were 360-degree views of the mountains and miles and miles of white fences—and the people! Everyone held doors open for Bart and Cassie and said hello even though they were complete strangers. Cassie was smitten. She wore dungarees, a purple set of cowboy boots with colorful flowers on them, and a silk blouse. She fit right in and loved talking to everyone. Bart couldn't help but stare at her with adoration; she was beaming with excitement.

The realtor showed them a few large tracts of land—one with a home and the other without one. Both properties were beautiful, with rolling hills and mountain views. After they were done looking at the town, they had dinner at a small restaurant. Bart noticed Cassie wasn't drinking the wine he ordered for the table.

"You don't want any merlot?" he asked.

"No. I'm not feeling very well, and I don't want to push my luck."

Cassandra was exactly where she wanted to be in life. She had found the man she was going to marry, and they were starting over, just the two of them—maybe three—on this new venture. She didn't care whether or not she'd fit in in a small town. It didn't concern her. As a matter of fact, the idea of starting a life that was, for lack of a better term, simple excited her. The only doubt in her mind was whether everyone back home was ready for such a drastic change.

The next morning, they were up early and had a lot to discuss on the flight back to New York. It was a short flight from North Carolina to New York, which would be an easy trip going back and forth if they did decide to move. Cassie fell asleep almost as soon as they got settled in on the plane, but Bart was wide awake thinking about Bill Wright and what had to be done as soon as they returned. He had thoughts about hiring somebody to do it, but he knew deep down inside that was the kiss of death for getting caught, so it had to be him or Anthony.

When they landed in Long Island, Anthony was waiting with the car to take them back to the house. On the way, Cassie enthusiastically told him about how beautiful North Carolina was and how she wanted to show everyone the town after the wedding and honeymoon. Bart knew Anthony would do anything for Cassie and would go to great lengths to punish anyone who hurt her; she was like a daughter to him, and he would do whatever he had to do to keep her happy.

"That sounds great!" Anthony responded with a huge smile.

Bart had to go to Manhattan in a couple of days to meet with the district attorney. Cassie had asked to go along so she could shop—after all, they would be gone on their honeymoon until Christmas Eve. He didn't mind bringing her but disclosed that she would have to wait outside the room while he answered their questions about the Star Killer. Shit. Am I a suspect?

CHAPTER 58

THE DISTRICT ATTORNEY

The building had huge concrete columns that seemed to extend up into the clouds and resembled the US Supreme Court. Manhattan was on the precipice of winter, and the November air was harsh against Bart's face as he exited the SUV.

Bart and Cassandra arrived early for his nine o'clock meeting. They were greeted on the fifth floor by a leggy blonde secretary, who took them into an empty conference room.

"Mr. Thompkins will be right with you," she said with a smile teetering on the edge of flirtatiousness before she closed the door.

Not five minutes later, the district attorney, Vance Thompkins, appeared in the doorway. As they were exchanging pleasantries, the door opened, and three other people entered the room—his assistants.

"I heard about what happened to you," said Vance to Cassandra. "I'm so sorry to hear about that, but I'm happy you're okay. There are some truly awful people in this world."

"Thank you," she said with a subtle smile. "I hope the police will find out who was behind it all."

"In light of what happened, I've been keeping Cassandra close by," said Bart. "I almost lost her once, and I won't let it happen again."

"I have a quiet conference room next door. She is more than welcome to wait in—make phone calls or use the computer. And anything else she needs, she can let the secretary know. We shouldn't be too long with you."

He walked her through the doorway and into an adjacent room that was separated by glass so Bart could see her the entire time. He knew these people played mind games, and he was aware he had to be very cautious about what he said. While he was going to cooperate, he was not going to get pushed around. He sat at the head of the table to establish his dominance. In their world of gamesmanship, something as simple as where one sat was important.

They got right to the point. "Do you know why we asked to meet with you?"

"You said on the phone it had to do with the Star Killer." He had his hands clasped in front of him, and he could feel the moisture increasing between his palms. Did they find new evidence concerning Angler's death?

"Would you mind starting from the beginning?" asked Thompkins. "From the first time you heard the Star Killer's name mentioned."

"No, I don't mind, but keep in mind that some of the information is factual, some of it comes from hearsay, and some of it is just my opinion."

Thompkins nodded. "Go ahead. Tell us everything you can."

They aren't treating me like a suspect. Maybe it is just standard questioning after all. Bart took a deep breath and let it out slowly, thinking back to the first time he ever heard about the infamous Star Killer.

"The first time I had heard the murderer referred to as the Star Killer was five years ago, from my old partner, Bill Lupo."

One of the assistants interrupted. "Why did he call him the Star Killer?"

"To the best of my knowledge, every victim had a little star etched on the back side of their earlobe. It was drawn with a pen and was usually the same style of star, but it wasn't neat by any means."

"How many of those did you see?" asked the other assistant, a plump middle-aged man with glasses.

Bart paused for a moment to recall each victim. He remembered them all. "Physically, I've seen five of them in the past five years."

"So, you think this person killed five people?" asked the man with the glasses.

"No," Bart scoffed. "If I had to guess—and this is only a guess—I'd say it's closer to thirty."

Thompkins looked astounded. "Thirty? We only know of five people in New York City."

"I suspect he's killed all throughout the Northeast. I believe it can be as many as thirty women."

"How do you know? What are you basing this information on?" asked a bald man on the right.

"I'm basing it on speculation. Lupo tracked down a number of women in the Northeast—in Boston, in Massachusetts, and in Vermont—that he believed were victims of the Star Killer. He had no proof; he was just going on their age and how they disappeared."

"So Lupo's theory was any woman of a certain age who disappeared was a victim of the Star Killer?" Thompkins asked condescendingly.

"No, that's not what I said. You have to consider that some of those women were in the age range, but their bodies were found, so that eliminated them as victims. The Star Killer was precise—methodical. And if he didn't want his victims' bodies found, they never were.

"Can you clarify that?" asked the man on the left.

"If the Star Killer wanted the bodies found, they would be, but they were the perfect crime. There was nothing to link the victim to him. You're not dealing with an amateur here. You are dealing with a sick son of a bitch who happened to be very good at what he did and probably never would've been caught."

Thompkins had a puzzled look on his face. "If this guy was as good as you're saying, then how did someone find out who he was, learn where he hid his trophies, and sneak up on him and kill him?"

Bart had to be extremely careful with how he answered that question. He still wasn't sure what Thompkins knew or what new information he may have obtained.

"That's the million-dollar question, and I think it's the question that has stumped everyone involved in this investigation." Bart needed to manipulate the interrogation in his favor. "If I'm correct and there were actually thirty victims, and if any of their family members found out about who this guy was, surely somebody would've avenged their loved one."

"Who would have told them his identity?" interrupted Mr. Glasses. "If he was that smart and secretive, who could possibly know?"

Thompkins quickly interjected. "Do you think Lupo could've told the families?"

This was a bombshell of a question Bart needed to be very delicate in answering. He hated to throw Lupo under the bus, but he was dead, so it wasn't like he could go to jail. Bart, however, was very much alive and could very well spend the rest of his life in an eight-by-six-foot concrete box.

"I don't know what Lupo told people. He worked on this case for years before he became my partner. He was also a full-time alcoholic, a conspiracy nut, and not the most reliable person. I don't know what he told people."

"And he committed suicide?" asked Thompkins.

"That's what the department said."

The third assistant spoke up for the first time since entering the room. He was a tall man and thin; his suit looked like it was two sizes too large on him, making him appear even more underweight. "You don't believe he killed himself?"

Bart stared right into the man's sunken-in brown eyes. "I didn't work on Lupo's case. They wouldn't let me. So, I don't know exactly what happened. If they say it was suicide, then I guess that's what it was."

The man to Thompkins's right was flipping through papers. He removed his glasses and looked up quizzically. "How do you know Maria Passenti?"

"I thought we were here to talk about the Star Killer. Maria has nothing to do with it."

"We'll decide whether she has anything to do with it," said Thompkins.

"If you want to look into my time undercover, go ahead, but I was told I was asked here to discuss my work on the Star Killer case, and that's what I'm here to talk about. I'm here as a courtesy, and I have no problem leaving right now."

"Well, then let's wind this up for the time being, but I have one last question for you."

Bart nodded.

"What do you think the odds are that someone found out the Star Killer's identity and managed to kill him without leaving any clues?" asked Thompkins.

Good. They still don't have any leads.

"Again, I don't know. The law is the law, but knowing what he did to these women before he took their lives, I think whoever killed him should get a medal."

The lanky man spoke up again. "So, you're okay with vigilante justice, Mr. Sullivan?"

Bart smiled haughtily. "You need to go through the files. Look closely at the pictures. Look at what that guy did to those women, and that's only five of them. Think about the other twenty-five. Think about their families. In my experience, justice reveals itself in strange ways sometimes. I'm not condoning what the so-called vigilante did, but if the Star Killer was lying dead in front of me, I would spit on his cold corpse."

They sat in silence for a moment, absorbing what Bart had just said and probably thinking about what they would've done in the same situation.

"I think that's all we need for now," said Thompkins, standing up. "Thank you for your time."

Bart stood up and shook Thompkins's hand before walking out of the room to retrieve Cassandra. He poked his head in the room next door, and she greeted him with a toothy grin.

"All done," he said, reaching his hand out to grasp hers. They walked to the elevator and headed downstairs to leave. Once they got in the SUV, Cassie wouldn't stop asking how things went, but Bart curtailed her questions as much as possible.

"Everything was fine. They were just fishing."

He parked near 49th Street, and they walked over toward 51st Street.

"Before we go shopping, I need to take care of something," said Cassie as she pulled him into a building on Park Avenue.

"Where are we going?" asked Bart.

"I want to stop in and see my doctor."

They stepped into the elevator, and Bart asked her if everything was okay. It was an unplanned visit, and he was worried.

"I'm fine. I just had some lab work done, and I figured while we are in the area, we may as well pick it up."

The elevator doors opened, and they walked into the waiting room of a doctor's office. The marble slab on the wall read "S&M OB/GYN." Bart's heart rate began to increase.

The receptionist greeted Cassie and asked for her name and reason for visiting. Cassie quietly provided the details, and the small brunette woman smiled and immediately escorted them into the doctor's office. There were two leather seats in front of the large chestnut desk. On the desk was a name plate that said "Dr. Meredith Hamilton, M.D." They sat in the two chairs, and Bart looked at Cassie.

"Is everything okay?" he asked again. This time, he looked concerned.

"I'm fine," she said, grabbing his hand.

Within a few moments, the door opened, and a female doctor appeared. Cassandra introduced Bart to her, but his mind was racing. He didn't understand what they were doing there. Is she sick? Can she not have children? He didn't know which thought worried him more.

Dr. Hamilton sat down behind the desk and opened the folder she had in her hand. She put on a pair of reading glasses and looked over the paperwork in front of her.

"The blood work looks good. I'm glad we did it." She removed her glasses and placed them next to the folder on the desk. "Everything appears to be normal, except for one thing—you're pregnant."

Pregnant? Bart was never caught off guard. He was always prepared for anything, which meant he was never shocked or surprised, but for the first time, he was irrefutably and completely stunned. All the color drained from his face, and he had a blank expression.

Cassandra jumped out of the chair and kissed him. "I hope you're happy," she nearly squealed with excitement.

He said nothing. He couldn't process what he had just heard. We're going to have a baby? Finally, after a couple of minutes, a huge smile invaded his face. His color returned, and he stood up, wrapped his arms around Cassie, and kissed her on the lips.

"As long as you're healthy—as long as you're both healthy, I'm perfect."

The rest of the day was fuzzy. Maybe it was due to the intense questioning he had endured that morning; maybe it was from the fear of thinking Cassie may have been sick or worse; or maybe it was because he still had to murder a man and frame another for it. He wasn't sure. There was only one thing that was certain—Bart was going to be a father.

CHAPTER 59

KILL BILL

Bill Wright had committed the ultimate betrayal; he had deceived the people who made him successful. Not only did he turn on them, but he also put Cassandra's life at risk—an unforgivable sin. The day of reckoning was near, but Anthony had reservations. He called Bart for a last-minute meeting to clear up some lingering details. They met in Frank's office, and Anthony explained to Bart his concerns.

"In order for us to do this, you're going to have to be out of the house for three or four hours in the middle of the night." Anthony's words were passionate yet austere. "If Cassandra hears you leaving or wakes up during the night and you're not there, what are you going to tell her?"

"I think I can sneak out without waking her up," Bart said.

"If we're going to do this, there can't be any uncertainty. If things go awry, she's going to get dragged into it, and then she's either going to have to lie and say you were in bed with her all night or know you weren't. Either way, we're making her an accomplice."

"I have to do this, Anthony. What other choice do I have?"

"Hasn't she been through enough? If something happens to you, what do you think is going to happen to her? And another thing. You'll have to get off the property without anyone seeing, which means we'll have to shut off the cameras and hope the security people don't see us coming and going at three in the morning."

Bart got up from the chair and began to pace around the office. He knew where this was going; he knew what Anthony wanted to do. Anthony had already saved his ass with the Star Killer, and now he wanted to do the same thing with Bill Wright.

"So, what do you want to do?" Bart asked, even though he already knew the answer.

"I have a brother who lives in Queens. He is a stone-cold alcoholic, I can stay with him tonight. He won't know whether I'm coming or going because once he goes to sleep, he's out like a light. That gives me a solid alibi in case I ever get questioned." He looked right at Bart. "I don't understand how someone as smart as you doesn't see the writing on the wall here. Frank thinks you're going to be the face of this family—of his foundation—and you're willing to throw it all away and incriminate the woman you love."

"Anthony, I can't have you do every piece of dirty work. It isn't fair to you."

"There are a lot of things you don't know," he snapped. "For the past thirty years, Frank has treated me like family. He's made me rich beyond anything I would have made elsewhere. I owe him everything. And as far as getting even—you don't think I want to get even with that son of a bitch for what he did to Cassandra? I want to protect her, and having you involved in this thing is not protecting her; it's only a juvenile vendetta for you at this point."

Bart was caught off guard. Anthony had never spoken to him so severely, but he understood where he was coming from. Although Cassie was about to be his wife, Anthony was her family. He helped raise her, he helped protect her, and he intended to continue doing so.

"I already have a stolen car," Anthony continued. "I know how Bill Wright operates. I can wait at his home for him, and I can end this thing. There's no need for you to be there. What I need from you is to take care of Cassandra and this family."

Bart walked over to the wet bar and poured himself a neat Irish whiskey. He let out a long sigh. He knew Anthony was right, and it was hard to argue with someone who is a hundred percent right, but for Bart, this was about justice. Maybe he had to come to the realization that he didn't always have to be the one to level the playing field; he just needed to make sure someone did.

While they were talking, they heard the keypad beeping outside. The lock released, and the door opened.

"What are you two up to? Can't be anything good," Frank said and chuckled.

"No, everything is good. We're just talking business," Anthony said seriously.

Frank laughed again. "Don't forget Evon has to go to the florist—last-minute planning or something along those lines."

"I'll be there in a few minutes," Anthony said, his eyes fixed on Bart.

Frank mumbled something to himself and walked out. As soon as they heard the lock re- engage, Bart began speaking.

"I don't want this thing to go badly. You have to be extremely careful—more than usual. Don't assume Bill is drunk and sloppy. He might realize we're onto him and have somebody tagging along."

"I understand, and I'll be careful—the stolen car, the gun, the ammunition—nothing is traceable back to us. I'll be careful."

That was it for the moment. Bart realized his role was no longer that of an enforcer; now he was the person who hired reinforcements to decide what retaliation would be carried out. He shook Anthony's hand and gave him a hug with a pat on the back. They walked out of the office together. Bart walked back toward the house, hoping he had done the right thing.

The next night, Bill Wright was drinking heavily and playing blackjack at a private game in Queens. It was two in the morning when he stumbled into his car drunk and drove home. He was nearly $200,000 in debt, had sold out the people who trusted him, and needed more money than ever before. In his drunken stupor, he was oblivious. He didn't suspect that anyone knew he had betrayed the D'Angelo family in more ways than one. He allowed the Bandell family to steal almost $20 million, he gave the Albanians the information they needed to ambush Cassandra, and now he needed to figure out another way to steal from the family to support his gambling habit. There was a time when he respected Frank for being a successful entrepreneur and an honest man, but now he treated him as someone he could steal from at will.

He arrived home after three in the morning, exited the car, and nearly fell down walking to the front door. When he finally made it to the door, he fumbled around with his keys, trying to unlock it, but he had never locked it when he left, so he kept turning the key back and forth for several minutes. He finally opened the door, staggered inside, and slammed the door behind him. He threw his keys on the table next to the entrance, collapsed on the couch, and was almost instantly snoring.

He was in a deep drunken sleep when he felt a tug on his left wrist. Someone was pulling off his watch, but he was too inebriated to open his eyes. He mumbled gibberish. Then he felt his ring slide off of his left index finger and his wallet being removed from his pants. Anthony pulled the little bit of cash out of the wallet and threw it on the floor. Bill was still trying to wake up but was unable to comprehend exactly what was happening.

Anthony grabbed him by the hair and pulled him up so he was sitting straight. Bill winced in pain. "This is for Cassie, you sorry sack of shit."

One shot between the eyes, and he was dead, but Anthony put another bullet in his chest, just to be sure.

He picked up one of the shell casings and left the other lying on the floor, as Bart told him to. He took a gallon of gasoline, poured it all over the couches and the floor, and soaked the drapes. He took a matchbook from his pocket, plucked out a match, and struck it on the side. As soon as the flame sparked, he threw the gas can in the center of the living room. The house was immediately ablaze, and Anthony ran toward the back door.

He exited the rear of the house and crossed over to the adjacent street behind Bill's, where he had the stolen car parked. He got in and started the engine, slowly driving without turning on any lights, quietly working his way down the street. When he turned onto the side street, he turned on his headlights. In the rearview mirror, he could see the ball of fire that was Bill Wright's house, and he continued slowly driving down the street.

Anthony finally got to the intersection of Main Street and Northern Boulevard and turned left at the light. He could see fire engines coming in the distance. His job was done. No one in the family would have to be involved. Cassie was safe for the moment, and Anthony once again had delivered justice to the family—his family. That was his job, and he was damn proud of it.

CHAPTER 60

RETRIBUTION

Bart drove out of the compound and turned left onto the main road. Although it was a chilly day, the sun was out, and between that, the beautiful terrain, and the view of Long Island Sound, his mind drifted to a future where he could actually enjoy those views and not just see them in passing. He was on his way to meet Michael Bandell, his last piece of business before the wedding. Marrying the woman he loved had been his primary focus since the first time he laid eyes on her, but it seemed the universe had other plans.

There was a slight concern that Bandell was under investigation. It wasn't a stretch considering the lifestyle he lived—stealing money, buying and selling real estate, and hiding gold. Where they met had to be strategic; the real estate office or the foundation office were out of the question. If something went wrong, it would drag the D'Angelo family into this criminal activity. Bart chose a small meeting room in one of the virtual offices.

He had texted the address to Michael that morning and told him to meet him at 10 a.m. As usual, Bart arrived a few minutes early to survey the parking lot in the rear of the building to make sure that there were no vans or cars that looked suspicious. He stepped out of the SUV and walked inside. Michael was already seated in the meeting area. Bart introduced himself, shook his hand, and placed his small jamming device in the middle of the table.

"Is that a recording device?" asked Bandell.

"No, it's a jamming device in case someone tries to listen in on our conversation."

Bandell looked perplexed. Bart had been vague on the phone about why they were meeting, and now he was pulling out jamming devices in case people were trying to tap the room.

"It's nice to meet you," Bart began. "I hope we can amicably resolve any business matters."

"I don't know what business matters you're referring to," Bandell said, cutting Bart off.

Bart took an envelope out of the inside of his jacket and removed several pieces of paper. He pushed them toward Bandell. "This is the documentation of the profits and losses from the real estate company for the past ten years, but there's a problem."

Bandell's eyes widened, and his face went white. He knew what Bart was about to say.

"A significant amount of money is missing. It was cleverly stolen and took a long time for anyone to notice, but we know it's gone, and we know you took it. With that said, I have a proposition for you." Bart leaned in so his face was closer to Bandell's. He stared him right in the eyes. "That money belongs to the D'Angelo family, and it's only right it's returned to them."

"How much money are we talking about?"

"Michael, you've got the books. You know exactly how much money has gone missing. Twenty million."

"That's a bunch of bullshit!" Bandell yelled. "There is no way $20 million is missing."

Bart pointed at the documents and tapped his finger on the table, still looking at Bandell. "These are your profit and loss statements. They came straight from your company's software."

"Where did you get these?" Bandell snatched the papers off the table and looked them over.

"It doesn't matter where I got them. Let's not get distracted from why we're here," Bart said, taking the papers back.

Bandell leaned back in his chair and crossed his arms. "I don't have anywhere close to that kind of money. I guess you'll have to take me to court if you really think we've been stealing."

"I'm not interested in going to court, and if we do, it's not going to be about the money; it's going to be about the fact that you've been stealing from the hands that have been feeding you for nearly two decades."

"Why does it even matter to you? Doesn't the D'Angelo family have enough money? I know you're the golden boy, and when you marry Cassandra, you'll be filthy rich, but you don't scare me."

"I'm not trying to scare you, Michael. I'm trying to work out a deal with you. Trust me, it will be in everyone's best interest. I'll even be reasonable and only make you pay back $15 million, and we'll call it even. Also, once the money's returned, the real estate company will be sold."

Michael sat there blank-faced with his arms still crossed. "I think the best thing for us is to go to court. Aren't you getting married this week? This is what you're spending your time on? I'm sure Cassandra loves that."

"Don't say her name," Bart snapped. "What's right is right. You took the money. Just return it, and we can end this thing once and for all."

"I already told you I'm not afraid of you, golden boy. You can't scare me."

Bart paused for a moment and sat there, looking at Bandell. "You heard what happened to Bill Wright? Tragic, but let's face the facts. He was involved in this theft also, so his death is going to lead back to you."

Michael looked shocked and slightly confused. His brows were furrowed, and his dark brown eyes searched Bart's face for answers to questions he hadn't asked yet.

"What happened to Bill? I've been out of town for a week. What are you talking about?"

"Apparently, there was an accident. He died in a fire in his home. I don't really know the details, but it's tragic."

Bandell was clearly agitated. He stood up, put his hands on his head, and slid them slowly down his face. "If this is a threat, it's not gonna work."

"Michael, you might want to sit down. What I'm about to tell you is going to be hard to digest."

"I don't know where you are going with this shit, but I'm not afraid of you." Bandell's voice was becoming shaky.

"Have a seat." Bart motioned to the chair.

Michael nervously slumped back into his chair.

"Bill died in a fire, but the autopsy will reveal that he had two bullet wounds in his body." Bart reached in his pocket and pulled out a spent cartridge wrapped in a Kleenex. He laid it on the table. "This is one of the casings from the gun that killed Bill Wright."

Bandell looked at it. "I don't give a shit. What does that matter to me?"

Bart moved his chair closer to Michael, whose breathing was erratic. Fear consumed his eyes despite his saying several times he wasn't afraid. Was he trying to convince Bart or himself?

Bart whispered in his ear, "This brass came from your daughter's gun."

His breathing completely stopped. He looked down at the brass casing and then looked back up at Bart. He was unequivocally speechless. Suddenly, he realized what Bart was alluding to. "I don't believe you," he said, tears gathering at the base of his eyes.

"Michael, do I look like the kind of guy who would bluff? The other casing from the second round was found at the scene, and as soon as the police find the weapon and run it, they'll discover it belongs to your daughter."

Michael sat there, still unable to put his thoughts and emotions into words.

"The whole thing makes sense," said Bart. "You, Bill, and your daughter were involved in the theft of $20 million. Bill got greedy, and your daughter killed him."

Michael was sweating profusely, and when he moved his hands to the table, Bart noticed they were shaking. Good. He understands.

"I'll go to the police. I'll tell them what happened. I'll tell them what you told me. I swear to God I will."

Bart smiled and said, "That will not go over well for you— going to the police and telling them Bill Wright was killed by a gun that belongs to your daughter, but she somehow had nothing to do with it. And then there's the fact that you were all involved in the $20 million theft. Come on, Michael, you're smarter than that."

"What do you want? I can't have my daughter go to jail."

"I don't want your daughter to go to jail either. I hate to even see her involved in all of this, but she was the accountant for the company. She's a front-runner in the theft. She's not an innocent bystander here. You and her were in this with Bill."

Bart moved his chair back closer to the table. "This is what we're going to do. You're going to sell off all the real estate you own— all the homes, commercial buildings, vacant land, everything—and you're going to transfer that money back into the real estate company. The gold you have hidden away will be sold, and that money will also be put back into the real estate company. That should be at least $15 million worth of assets. If Frank gets any less than that, the deal is off. Once the money is returned, you'll get the gun back, and your daughter will be exonerated. Are we clear?"

Bandell still just sat at the table, sweaty, pale, and stunned. It took him nearly ten minutes to regain his composure and finally respond. "I don't know if I can get that much money." His voice was barely above a whisper, and his eyes were fixed on the table in front of him.

"You can do it because you have to do it. If you don't, then your daughter goes to jail. But, Michael, let me warn you. If you try to get cute, not only will she go to jail, but I'll kill you, and I won't pay someone to do it. I'll do it myself. You stole from the D'Angelo family, and you're going to fix it. Don't get fucking cute."

Bart stood up and left without saying another word. As he walked outside, he was careful to observe vehicles and people moving around. He didn't think Michael had any intention to try to hurt him—not before the meeting at least—but he couldn't be too careful.

Bart got in the SUV, and he drove the short drive back to the estate. It was just as beautiful outside as when he left earlier that day, but on the way home, Bart pulled the car over near the main gate and stepped out of the vehicle. He looked around at the beautiful property he called home and took a deep breath. He felt a huge weight lifted from his shoulders and finally enjoyed the view.

CHAPTER 61

THE WEDDING

The early morning sun began to leak through the transom over the French doors and into the bedroom. Bart was sitting in the big, oversized chair, watching Cassie sleep. The last few nights, she seemed to be sleeping until morning without being awakened by nightmares, which made him happy. Once the stream of light reached the bed, she began to open her eyes.

"What are you doing sitting over there?" she said in her drowsy morning voice that he loved.

"Just enjoying the view," he replied, still staring right at her and smiling.

"Why don't you come back to bed and enjoy the view from a little closer?" she said, still half asleep.

He walked over to the bed and crawled back under the blankets. Cassie moved closer to him and began kissing him passionately. "I can't wait for you to be my husband," she said in between tasting the coffee on his lips. From underneath the covers, she removed her satin nightgown and helped Bart slip his pajama pants off of his waist. They got stuck on his feet, and Cassie had to crawl under the blankets to help him get untangled. They both laughed until they were crying. At that moment, it was as if nothing bad had ever happened to them—no dead parents, no serial killers, no attempted kidnappings—just pure, unfiltered happiness.

Once she successfully removed his pants, she kissed her way back up his body until her face was aligned with his. Again, she leaned in and kissed him. Instantly, his hands were all over her, exploring every part of her body, paying extra attention to the intimate ones. They made love for more than an hour that morning, the last time they'd ever do so before being husband and wife, although they felt like they'd been married for ages.

They laid in bed and talked for a while; it was a big day—arguably the biggest day of their lives thus far. It was the day Cassie had dreamed of since she was a little girl—her wedding. She spoke to Bart about how she wished her mother could be there to see it and how sad she was that Bart never got to meet her.

"Your mother will be there. She's always with you, Bella, watching over you, and I know she's happy."

"And how do you know that, huh?"

"Because you're happy."

Cassie gave Bart another kiss and got out of bed. She opened the curtains, letting the sunlight touch every inch of the bedroom. "Let's get dressed. We're supposed to meet everyone at my dad's house for breakfast."

It was a beautiful day for December in New York—warmer than usual for the time of year. Cassie was convinced God did it purposely, just for their wedding. They walked over to Frank's house, with Bear trailing behind. When they arrived, Anthony and Rose were already there, sitting in the kitchen with Frank and Evon. As usual, Jonathan made a delicious breakfast—French toast, bacon, eggs, fresh fruit, and coffee. The house smelled heavenly. Cassie and Bart walked into the kitchen to join everyone. While everyone enjoyed the food, they discussed the details for the day. The women were going to get ready at Frank's house and go to church from there, and the men would get dressed at Bart and Cassie's.

She had hired a professional makeup artist to try to cover the last of the remaining marks on her face and arms from the shooting. Of course, she had other scars—those that couldn't be detected with the human eye, but hopefully, they too would fade with time.

Bart could see the joy cascading from Frank and Evon's eyes. Cassandra was their only child, and even though the past few weeks had been chaotic, they couldn't be happier for their daughter's wedding. Frank had an exceptional relationship with Cassie; after her mother died, everything fell on him to try to make her feel secure and loved, and he did the best he could. But that trauma brought them close, and Bart was aware of just how close they were.

After breakfast, Cassie and Bart walked back to their house. She had to be back at Frank's at 11 a.m. to meet the bridesmaids and begin getting ready. The wedding was at 4 p.m., and she hoped they'd have enough time for hair and makeup. Luckily, the church was close by. Anthony had agreed to keep an eye on everything. This would be the first time in Bart's adult life he wouldn't have a gun with him, and the thought of it made him uneasy.

Anthony could tell Bart was uncomfortable about being unarmed and couldn't help but laugh. "Don't worry. Between your friends in the police department and my friends in the family, there will be more than enough guns around to protect us."

Before Cassandra left, she held Bart tightly. "The next few hours are going to be pure insanity, but I just want you to know how happy I am that this day has finally come." She had tears in her eyes. "I can't tell you how glad I am. I want to thank you for making me feel like the most beautiful and special woman in the world."

They held hands and walked over to Frank's house. Evon chased all the men out, and he watched Cassie disappear up the stairs.

Around 3:30 p.m., the black limousine carrying the men arrived at the church—the same church where Bart met Cassie's family for the first time. Between her family, his family, and all their friends, there wasn't an empty seat in the house. The bishop was going to officiate the wedding, and the church looked stunning. There were arrangements of white calla lilies, red roses, and bells of Ireland at the end of every pew. The arrangements led to the front of the church, where an elaborate arch donning the same flowers and greenery was situated in front of the altar. As it was the Christmas season, there were lights throughout the church that sparkled against the gold accents and created an enchantingly romantic ambiance. It was magical.

Bart walked through the back door. He didn't expect to be nervous; there was no doubt in his mind Cassandra was the love of his life, but he still couldn't believe she felt the same. The bishop walked out and stood at the altar, and Bart followed, accompanied by Donnie, Bill, and Charlie. He could feel sweat forming under his Calvin Klein tuxedo as he stood at the front of the church, and he patted his forehead to make sure it was still dry. A few moments later, the organ began to play. Cassie's three best friends walked in from the narthex. They wore silk emerald dresses and carried bouquets of red roses. Once they were situated at the front of the church, the organ player began playing Wagner's "Bridal Chorus," and all the guests stood up.

Frank and Cassandra appeared at the back of the church. Bart's heart was beating in his throat, and he suddenly forgot how to breathe. He had never seen such a beautiful sight in all of his life. Cassie was literally breathtaking. Her dress had been custom-made by Vera Wang. Cassandra had seen one of her gowns a few years earlier in Manhattan and had fallen in love with the design. It was silk with lace embellishments on the bodice. The long sleeves were also lace but sat off her shoulders to display her feminine neck and collarbones. It had a cathedral train that made her look like she was an angel floating down the aisle and a veil that was the same length. Her bouquet was made entirely of calla lilies, perfectly completing her ensemble. She was a vision in white.

As Frank escorted her down the aisle, he couldn't have looked prouder. He had raised a warm, beautiful, and intelligent woman, and the realization moved him to tears.

Bart couldn't take his eyes off Cassie or stop smiling. His vision became blurry, and he realized it was because his eyes were filled with tears. Why shouldn't they be? It was the happiest day of his life.

When they made their way to the end of the aisle, Frank kissed Cassie on the cheek and left her with Bart, sneaking a wink at him before he found his seat. Bart lifted her veil and couldn't believe his eyes. She looked even more beautiful, which he didn't think was possible. The marks on her face were no longer visible. He took her hand, and they walked up the stairs to the altar. The mass took about an hour, and the bishop officially pronounced them husband and wife. Bart kissed his bride like she was the first, last, and only woman he had ever loved.

They worked their way to the back of the church. Everyone was laughing, smiling, and cheering. As they waited to get in the limousine to head to the Swan Club, everyone was throwing rice and applauding. They finally got in the limousine and closed the door. Cassie looked at Bart and smiled. "Well, that's it, buddy. I got you for life. You had better get used to it." He kissed her the entire way to the reception.

The drive to the Swan Club only took a few minutes, and when they arrived, the sun was still warm and shining. The facility was located on seven acres and had several waterfalls, fountains, gazebos, and lush gardens. They had a suite so the women could touch up their makeup and have a few drinks before the guests arrived.

As soon as they touched up their makeup, the photographer knocked on the door of the suite and brought the ladies outside, where the men were already waiting. The next half hour was a whirlwind of pictures—the bride and groom, groomsmen, bridesmaids, family, and group pictures. Bart was happy when it was over. He never liked taking pictures, but it was a special occasion.

They entered the banquet hall, and the following few hours were filled with toasts, dancing, and speaking to friends and family. Bart's mother was still using her oxygen tank, but Cassandra had bought a small purse-like device she could carry around that wasn't very noticeable. She had also made an appointment to take his mother to a specialist at Johns Hopkins once they returned from the honeymoon. Cassie truly was an angel.

Vito and Jerry both attended. Bart made a mental note to himself that when he returned from his honeymoon, he had to do something special for Jerry. If not for him and his persistent warnings, they never would have been prepared for the kidnapping, and things could have ended so much worse. He really did owe him.

Anthony and Rose were like proud parents. Anthony had spent nearly twenty-five years of his life protecting Cassandra, and since they had no children of their own, she was like a daughter to him. When they weren't in business settings, she always called them Uncle Anthony and Aunt Rose.

Donnie was the best man, so he gave a heartfelt toast and said he had almost given up on Bart finding the love of his life until he met Cassandra. He said he believed the two of them had been looking for each other for years but kept missing one another. Finally, thanks to Donnie, they met. Of course, he had to take credit for their marriage. Everyone got a good belly laugh out of that. The hours flew by. Family members Bart very rarely saw—aunts, uncles, and cousins who lived out of state—attended. They didn't have a second to themselves the entire evening, but Cassandra never let go of Bart's hand.

Several Italian family traditions were carried out, specifically the bonbonniere, which were five almonds in a little gift box that were given to all the guests. It signified health, wealth, happiness, longevity, and fertility. Bart couldn't help but laugh—only he and Cassandra knew the fertility aspect had already been fulfilled. After all, the wedding wasn't just between the two of them; it was the three of them.

During the toast, Cassandra drank ginger ale, which the waiters had been instructed to pour out of a wine bottle so no one would notice. They danced the tarantella, and the hours flew by. When it was time for them to leave, they said goodbye to everyone, which seemed to take a lifetime, but they finally made their great escape.

Anthony drove Cassie and Bart back to their house, where they spent the night before catching an early morning flight to Italy.

It was the most beautiful day of Cassie's life, just as she had always imagined. Now she was going to start her new life with the man she loved, a baby on the way, and a new location. But for now, it was time to wind down and pack for the honeymoon.

CHAPTER 62

THE HONEYMOON

The large blue commercial jet sat on the runway at JFK, poised for takeoff. It was a nonstop flight to Rome, and Bart and Cassandra were in the first row of first class. Since she still had a lingering fear of flying, Cassie held Bart's hand and squeezed it tightly as the engines kicked on and the train began to move down the runway. As long as she could hold her husband's hand, her fears were alleviated. She knew he would never let anything happen to her.

As the plane lifted off the runway and into the air, Cassie pressed her head back into the cushion, closed her eyes, and squeezed Bart's hand even tighter, although he didn't think that was possible. "Everything is okay," he whispered in her ear and kissed her on the cheek. She kept her eyes closed but smiled at the gesture.

When the aircraft was finally in the air and at cruising altitude, they settled in for the nine-hour flight. Cassie was exhausted; all of the excitement from the wedding, Thanksgiving, the attempted kidnapping, the shoot-out, pregnancy, and everything else they had dealt with in the past few months seemed to all catch up with her as soon as they were in the air and far, far away from Long Island.

After Cassandra fell asleep, Bart thought about what the next few months would be like, especially for her. He wondered how her pregnancy would be. Would she be tired all the time? Would she experience debilitating nausea and morning sickness? Or would she have a wonderful pregnancy where she was beaming all the time and picking out tiny little clothes and colors for the nursery? He smiled at the last thought.

While she slept, she never let go of his hand. He looked at her—so beautiful, even when sleeping—and he couldn't believe there was a time when she wasn't in his life. He thought to himself, If I had known I was going to meet her when I did, would I have taken all those chances? The risks that got me shot, hit by a car, and trapped in an exploding building. Would I still have done all of that crazy shit?

Everyone thought Bart took too many chances, but he never imagined there was another option. He had taken an oath to serve and protect, and that's exactly what he always did.

The flight to Italy was long and loud. Cassie slept for the first two hours, and when she woke up, it was difficult to have any kind of conversation over the noise of the jet engines. So, they just sat there and read or rested.

They arrived in Rome. Frank had arranged a tour and a licensed security guard to accompany them since Bart couldn't legally carry a gun in Italy.

After their arrival in Rome on Sunday they were going to go to Tuscany on Wednesday. Then they'd return to Rome to meet the pope. Frank's generous donations to a number of charities gave him the ability to arrange a private meeting.

They took the four-hour trip to Tuscany. It was magnificent. The hills seemed to extend to the ends of the earth. It looked like a Monet painting that used every shade of yellow and orange. The hills seamlessly extended into the sky, adorned with soft white clouds that seemed to exist only for their viewing pleasure.

Frank and Evon had arranged for them to take several sight-seeing trips around the country while they were there, but Bart and Cassandra decided they just wanted some alone time, so they had told the security guard that they would stay at the villa until Tuesday night, return to Rome to see the pope, and then return to Tuscany. They were both excited to have some alone time—no drama, no problems, no one around except for the two of them. They had a lot to discuss since they would begin the moving process when he returned to New York. Frank and Anthony still wanted to see both locations before deciding which one would be better for all of them.

Moving Cassandra from the front of the foundation to behind the scenes would also take a great deal of planning. She was concerned about their personal finances. Bart would have to be added to all of her bank accounts—checking, savings, and investment accounts—and credit cards and everything else. While he was not concerned about money, she wanted him to have access to their finances.

Wednesday rolled around quickly. They had arrived the night before in Rome and stayed at a hotel. They were both excited to meet the pope and had been given specific instructions as to what to do and what not to do. Frank advised Cassandra to introduce herself to the pope so he would know who she was.

On Wednesday morning, they went to the Paul VI Audience Hall. The doors opened, revealing the exquisite auditorium. The massive room was concave so no matter where you stood in it, you could see the pope standing on the papal throne. On either side of his throne was a double parabolic vault that made the one in the center appear to be floating in thin air. As Bart and Cassie walked in, they could see the pope walking down a long hallway, the same one they were standing in before he met the crowd.

He approached them and smiled. "Good morning." His voice was soft but deep.

"Good morning, Holy Father, my name is Cassandra D'Angelo, and this is my husband, Bart Sullivan."

A big smile appeared on his face. "You just got married a few days ago?"

"Yes," said Bart and Cassandra simultaneously.

"Let me give you and your holy matrimony a blessing." He took one of each of their hands in his. "May God bless your marriage, keep you healthy, and keep you happy."

A gentleman standing alongside him motioned for him to go out and meet the crowd. He smiled softly at them and said, "Goodbye."

They both stood there motionless, realizing they had just met the pope and that he had blessed their marriage and had unknowingly also blessed their baby. Afterward, they returned to Tuscany and spent the next few days visiting the town, meeting some of Evon's family, and eating some of the most wonderful food either of them had ever had before, prepared by a staff that Frank had hired.

There were two days left when Bart's phone rang early one morning. He had been leaving it at the house or villa since they began their honeymoon—he wanted uninterrupted time with his new bride—but when he heard it that morning and noticed it was Anthony, he picked it up.

"Hey there, Bart. I'm sorry to call while you're on your honeymoon, and if this was anything else, I would've waited, but it's Frank."

Bart's heart sank into his stomach. Frank? God, no. Don't say it, Anthony. "Is he okay? What happened?" he reluctantly asked.

"Well, there isn't any easy way to say this, but here goes. He had a heart attack earlier today. He's stable right now, but other than that, they haven't told us much. He's got the best doctors, and they think it was pretty mild, but they are keeping him sedated."

Bart exhaled a sigh of relief. He's alive. Frank's alive. "We'll get the first flight back. Please keep me updated. I'll text you as soon as we know our flight information and when we'll arrive. I'll go tell her now."

"Alright, bud. Good luck," said Anthony, and the line went dead.

Bart walked out onto the patio, where Cassie was lying in the warm morning sun. He never wanted to have to deliver this kind of news to her. She was so close to her father. For so long, he was all she had in the world, and he knew she was going to be devastated.

He sat down in a chair alongside her, and she opened her eyes and looked over at Bart with a sleepy smile. "I guess I must've dozed off."

"You've only been asleep for a few minutes." He tried to force a smile but could only manage a sympathetic look.

"I heard your phone ringing. Is everything okay?"

"Yes, but I need to tell you something."

She sat up in her lounge chair and spun her legs around, so she was sitting up and facing him. "What is it?"

He took a deep breath to prepare himself for what he was about to say—as if there was any way to prepare for telling someone their last living parent may not be alive for much longer. He exhaled. "Your father had a mild heart attack. He's doing well right now, but he's at the hospital. That was Anthony on the phone." Bart had his phone in his hand and handed it to her. "Call Anthony, and while you are doing that, I'll arrange the first flight out of here."

She looked down at the phone and then back up at Bart. Her green eyes were wide with concern, but her pallid face was masked in resolve. She grabbed the phone and began dialing as quickly as her fingers would allow. She walked back inside, but he could faintly hear her asking Anthony a million questions—questions he probably didn't have the answers to. When did it happen? Where was he? Who was with him? What are the doctors saying? Is he awake? How long will he be in the hospital?

While she was on the phone, Bart called their travel agent, Nadine. She made all the travel arrangements for the foundation, and he knew she'd be able to get them home as quickly as possible. He asked her to arrange the first flight available out of Rome and back to New York, no matter the cost.

He hung up the phone and walked downstairs to inform their security guard that they would need to return to Rome immediately. "There has been a family emergency."

When he returned to the villa, Cassie set the phone on the table next to the couch. She drew in a large breath of air and closed her eyes before opening them and saying vacantly, "I guess we'd better start packing."

The foundation arranged for a private jet to meet them in Rome, and within six hours, they were in the air. Everything had happened so quickly that it almost seemed like a bad dream. Earlier that morning, they were in marital bliss, relaxing and enjoying their honeymoon in paradise, and now they were on a plane headed to see Frank, who had suffered a heart attack.

All of the stress from worrying about her father couldn't have been healthy for Cassie's pregnancy, but she wasn't ready to tell anybody about it yet, so Bart just tried to keep her as calm as possible at all times. Anthony must have done a damn good job reassuring her Frank would be perfectly fine because she hadn't shed a tear since receiving the news.

The flight back to New York lasted an eternity, and when they landed in Long Island, Anthony was there to pick them up. He took them straight to the hospital, and when they walked into the room, Frank was sedated. As soon as Cassie saw her father hooked up to machines and unconscious, she began weeping. She ran over to his bed and took his hand in hers. She put her forehead on his chest while her body pulsed with every tear that fell.

Evon walked over to her and placed her hand on Cassie's shoulder. "The doctors are confident he's going to make a full recovery," she reassured her, but Cassie was smart. She knew how serious a heart attack was—even smaller ones. Frank wasn't out of the woods yet.

Cassandra and Evon stayed for the next few hours. Bart told them to go home and get some sleep; he would stay overnight at the hospital with Frank. They reluctantly left and told him they'd try to get some sleep but would be back first thing in the morning.

Bart sat in Frank's room, just the two of them and the beeping of the monitors. He looked at the man who had built a billion-dollar empire. Frank had always seemed so powerful, so strong, but as he lay in the hospital bed, he looked smaller. He looked frail. For a moment, Bart prayed to God that nothing would happen to Frank. It was a selfish prayer; he wasn't ready to fill the shoes of a man like Frank. He couldn't. Someone would have to guide the family and protect them. Somebody would have to deal with the Albanians, Michael Bandell, and any investigation the district attorney might be thinking about beginning.

It was silent in the room except for the faint drone of the machines keeping Frank alive and the rhythmic beeping of the others that were monitoring his pulse and heart rate. Bart rarely felt fearful, but in that moment, it seemed like it was the only sensation he had ever known.